T0305013

THE
GODS
BELOW

BY ANDREA STEWART

The Drowning Empire

The Bone Shard Daughter
The Bone Shard Emperor
The Bone Shard War

The Hollow Covenant

The Gods Below

THE
GODS
BELOW

ANDREA
STEWART

orbit-books.co.uk

ORBIT

First published in Great Britain in 2024 by Orbit

Map by Rebecka Champion (Lampblack Art)

A CIP catalogue record for this book
is available from the British Library.

HB ISBN 978-0-356-52067-4
C format 978-0-356-52068-1

Typeset in Fournier by M Rules
Printed and bound in Great Britain by
Clays Ltd, Elcograf S.p.A.

Papers used by Orbit are from well-managed forests
and other responsible sources.

MIX
Paper | Supporting
responsible forestry
FSC® C104740

Orbit
An imprint of
Little, Brown Book Group
Carmelite House
50 Victoria Embankment
London EC4Y 0DZ

An Hachette UK Company
www.hachette.co.uk

www.littlebrown.co.uk

For my parents, who have always been a shining
example of deep and enduring love

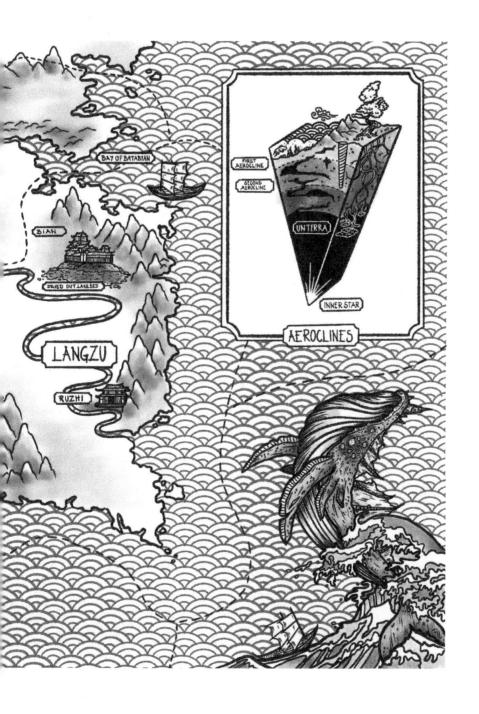

BAY OF BATABIAN

BIAN

DRIED OUT LAKE BED

LANGZU

RUZHI

FIRST AEROCLINE

SECOND AEROCLINE

UNTERRA

INNER STAR

AEROCLINES

I

Hakara

561 years after the Shattering

Kashan - the Bay of Batabyan

The mortals broke the world. They took the living wood of the Numinars, feeding it to their machines to capture and use their magic. Once, the great branches reached into the sky, each tree an ecosystem for countless lives. By the time the Numinars were almost gone, the world was changed. The mortals tried, but they could not repair the damage they'd caused. As the skies filled with ash and the air grew hot, the mortal Tolemne made his way down into the depths of the world to ask a boon of the gods.

And the gods, ensconced in their hollow, in the inner sanctum of the earth, told Tolemne that the scorched land above was not their problem. The gods ignored his pleas.

All except one.

Maman lied when she told me there were ghosts in the ocean. Cold water pressed at my ears, the breath in my lungs warm and taut as a paper lantern. Shapes appeared in the murk below, towers rising out of the darkness. Strands of kelp swayed back and forth between broken stone and rotting wood with the ceaseless rhythm of breathing. There were no ghosts down here – just the pitted, pockmarked bones of a long-dead world. I forced myself to calm, to make my breath last longer.

A shark swam above, between me and the surface, its shadow passing over my face. I hovered next to a tower wall, not even letting a bubble free from my lips, my elbow hooked over the stone lip of a window. An abalone lay in my left hand, the snail curling into itself, the rocky shell of it rough against my palm. My blunt knife lay in my right. A shimmering school of small fish circled next to me, light catching their silver scales like so many scattered coins. I willed them to swim away. There was nothing interesting here. Nothing to see. Nothing to eat.

Somewhere beyond the shore, Rasha curled in our tent, silent and waiting.

The first time I went to the sea, my sister had begged me not to go. I'd held her face between my palms, wiped her tears away with my thumbs and then pressed her cheeks together until her mouth opened like a fish's. "Glug glug," I'd said. I'd laughed and then she'd laughed, and then I'd whisked myself to the tent flap before she could protest any further. "That's all that's down there. Things that are good to eat and to sell. I'll come back. I promise."

Always told her I'd come back, just in case she forgot.

I imagined Rasha in our tent, getting the fire going, sorting through our stash of dried and salted goods to throw together some semblance of a meal. The fishing hadn't been good lately and now I had a snail in hand, as big as my face. I could begin to make things right if I could make it home.

If I died here, Rasha would die too. She'd have no one to

defend her, to care for her. I counted the passing seconds, my heartbeat thudding in my ears, hoping the shark would swim away. My throat tightened, my chest aching. I was running out of time. I could hold my breath longer than most, but I had limits.

There was a stone ledge far beneath me – the remnants of a crumbled balcony. I had two things in hand – my abalone knife and the abalone. I *needed* that abalone and they were so hard to find these days. Each one would buy several days' worth of meals. But it wasn't worth my life. Nothing else for it. I dropped the snail and moved, slowly as I could manage, around the tower.

Its shell cracked against the ledge and the shark darted toward the sound.

I swam upward, the tautness of my chest threatening to shatter, to let the water come rushing in. The bright shimmer of the world above seemed at once close and too far. I kicked, hoping the shark was occupied with the abalone. My breath came out in short bursts when I broke the surface.

I swam for the closest rock, doing my best not to splash. Any moment, I imagined, the beast from below would shear off a leg with its bite. The water that had welcomed me only moments before now felt like a vast, unknowable thing. And then my hands were on the rock and I was hauling myself out of the water, my fingers scrabbling against slick algae and barnacles, doing my best not to shake. A close call, but not the first I'd ever had. Another diver was setting up on shore. "Shark in the ruins!" I called to him. "Best wait until it's cleared off."

He waved me away. "Sure. Children always think they see sharks when they're scared."

Did he think just because I was young that my eyes didn't work right? Went the other way around, didn't it? "Go on, then." I waved at the water. "Be a big brave adult and get yourself eaten."

He made a rude gesture at me before fastening his bag to his belt and dropping from the rocks into the water. Not the wisest decision, but he was probably just as desperate as the rest of us. I could smell the shoreline from my rock – sea life rotting under the heat of the sun, crisped seaweed, thick white bird droppings.

I wrapped my arms around my knees and watched him submerge as I breathed into my belly, calming my too-fast heartbeat. Waves lapped against the shore behind me. Early-morning light shone piss-yellow through the haze, the air smelling faintly like a campfire. Not the most auspicious start to the day, but most mornings in Kashan weren't. My smallclothes clung to me, trickles of water tickling my skin. I'd head out again once I thought the shark had moved on. Or once it had taken a bite out of the other diver and had a nice meal. Either way, I'd slide into the water again, no matter the dangers.

I think Maman told me about ghosts in a misguided attempt to scare me. Like I was supposed to look at her, round-eyed, and avoid the ocean ever after instead of eagerly asking her if underwater ghosts ate sharks or people's souls. Had to admit I was a bit disappointed not to find spirits lurking around the ruined city when I'd finally hauled my hungry carcass to the shore and plunged my face beneath the water. Would have had a lot of questions to ask my ancestors.

Maman wasn't here to warn me away, and our Mimi had rid herself of that responsibility when she'd sighed out her last breath a year ago. We had no parents left. Besides, who was Maman to warn me against danger when she'd walked into the barrier between Kashan and Cressima? At least our Mimi had died through no fault of her own.

Sometimes I could hear Maman's voice in the back of my head as I swam down, down, so far that I started free-falling into the depths.

Don't go too far. Don't push yourself too hard. Stay safe.

And each time that voice in my head spoke up, I stayed down a little longer, until my chest burned, until I felt I would die if I didn't gasp in a breath. I couldn't listen to Maman's voice. Not with Rasha counting on me. Mimi had told me to take care of my sister. She'd not needed to say it, but I felt the weight of her last words like the press of a palm against my back.

This time of year, when the afternoon sun bore down on the water like a fire on a tea kettle, the abalone I fished for retreated deeper. They clung to the sides of the ruins, smaller ones hiding in crevices, their shells blending in with the surrounding rocks. Hints of metal and machinery lay deeper down, artifacts of the time before. All broken into unrecognizable pieces, or I'd have gone after them instead. There was always some sucker with money fascinated by our pre-Shattering civilization.

Rasha and I could eat fish, but abalone we could sell – the shells and their meat both – and children always needed things. It seemed I could get by on less and less the older I got, my fifteen-year-old frame gaunt and dry as a withered tree trunk. But Rasha was nine and I knew she needed toys, warm clothes, books, vegetables and fruits – all those little comforts she used to have when both Maman and Mimi had been alive. Every year got a little harder. More heat, more floods, more fires. Kluehnn's devoted followers prayed for restoration to take Kashan, to remake its people and its landscape, the way it had realm after realm. It was our turn, they said.

Couldn't say I relished the thought of being remade. I'd run if it ever came to that. I'd make for the border with Rasha and I wouldn't look back. Kluehnn's followers said that was a coward's choice. I was perfectly fine with being a coward if it meant I kept my bodily self unchanged and all in one piece.

I frowned as I glanced back at the shore, rocks fading into yellowed grasses and wilting trees. There should have been more divers out by now. I might have always been first, but others usually followed quickly, jostling for the best fishing spots.

It was deserted enough that I managed to find three more abalone once I got back into the water; only one other diver made her way into the ruins. My mind picked over all the possible reasons. A fire come too close? Rasha knew what to do in case of fire. A sickness passing through camp? It had happened before. I cut my diving short and walked back to our tent barefoot, the well-worn path soft beneath my feet, the scattered remains of dried seagrass forming a cushiony surface.

Ours was not the only tent pitched near Batabyan Bay. Together with the others we formed a loose settlement. This morning, though, three flattened areas of grass lay where tents had once been pitched. They'd been there when I'd left for the ocean.

Rasha had started a fire in the pit, the musty scent of burning dung drifting toward me. A covered cast-iron pot hung over it, the lid cracked to let out steam. She ran toward me, nearly bowling me over with a hug.

I squeezed her back until she wheezed. Maybe got a bit carried away, but she didn't complain. Her long black hair had some indefinable scent I only knew as home. Something of Maman and Mimi clung to the thick walls of our tent, permeating our clothes and our skin. I waved away the pungent smoke as I let her go, gesturing toward the empty campsites. "What happened over there?"

She shrugged. "They left just as I woke up. All three. Packed up their belongings and just hauled them out."

I smoothed the hair from her forehead. It was quick as instinct, the way I moved to soothe away her worries. Worrying was for me, not her. "Did they leave anything behind?"

She gave me a tentative smile before holding up a comb and

a horsehair doll. I held my hand out for the comb. That one had been left by mistake. Tortoiseshell, carved with the face of Lithuas, one of the dead elder gods. Her hair flowed out to the tines of the comb, which had been left smooth. I should have been excited by the find; instead, uneasiness rose like a high tide. Most people would have scoured their campsite. Most people would have taken the time to find what they'd lost. The people here weren't rich, and the comb was a luxury, one that had passed hands from one generation to the next. No one carved the elder gods into combs anymore.

I lifted the abalone in my mesh sack. "I got something too."

Rasha's eyes sparkled, and her expression was a bulwark against anxiety. "Is it enough?"

I gave her a mock-startled look. "For what? What do you mean?"

She laughed before grabbing a pole to take the pot off the fire. "You know what."

"Pretty sure you called me stupid the other day, and stupid people have terrible memories."

"I was *joking*."

"Yes, being called stupid is a very funny joke."

"I said 'don't *be* stupid. You can't go to the mines.'"

I mussed her hair. "Please. Same difference. Besides, if the ocean stops giving us what we need, I might be able to find work at the sinkholes. I have to consider it."

She spooned out the porridge with the air of someone who'd come to the realization that this shitty gruel was her last meal. "No, you don't."

Ah, I'd ruined the mood in one fell swoop, hadn't I? Count on me to crush delicate hopes with the clumsiness of a toddler wandering into a seabird's nest. "We have enough, and I can dive deeper than most. Let's not think about it. Not when we have this, eh?" I brandished the comb. "I'll sell it at market with the abalone. And then yes, I'll see about the garden you want."

Wished she would answer me with a sly "So you *do* remember", but she'd never been as able as I was to recover a good mood. It was a big ask. We both knew it. I could buy the seeds and we had water, but the weather was unpredictable. Crops had to grow quickly to be harvested before heat or flooding ruined them. Only thing that would make them grow more quickly was god gems, and I wasn't going to risk the black market.

Magic wasn't for the likes of us.

Maybe a few herbs, though. Some small greens we could carry in pots. I could do that. I dug into the porridge she'd made, putting on a show of how incredible it tasted until she smiled again. I'd once gotten drunk on fermented mare's milk when a passing traveler had left a skin of it out after he'd gone to sleep. It felt like that, getting Rasha to smile, to laugh. But better. No pounding headache the morning after, only a soft satisfaction that for one more day, I'd mattered.

But both were fleeting feelings. When we made our way to the market, it was nearly empty. Two stalls remained.

I'd never been as attuned to the community as perhaps I should have been. Rasha and I were a unit, and I couldn't afford to let anyone too close in case I'd misjudged them. We were young, and though my sister didn't understand our vulnerability, I did. All it would take was two armed, halfway-skilled grown men or women, and our stash of food would be ransacked. Maybe they'd kill us both for good measure. The law didn't mean much when you lived on the fringes. We had one another and that was enough. Or I'd thought it was enough.

I took the abalone to one of the two remaining stalls, where a woman clasped her hands together, her face rapturous. Rasha clung to the end of my shirt. I could feel the tension in her fingers, in every errant tug. It unsettled me more than it should have.

"Hey, Grandma – where's everyone?" I plunked the abalone on her counter, though I had no idea if she wanted to buy it.

She didn't even seem to notice. "It's Kluehnn," she breathed, her eyes bright.

The back of my neck prickled. I *knew* right then what was happening, though I still searched for a gap, for some other explanation. Restoration had been coming to realms quicker and quicker these days, but it was too soon after Cressima. I wasn't ready. Rasha was too young, we were too small. "What, the one true god popped up out of the ground and gave everyone a holiday?"

She smiled and shook her head, wisps of white hair floating around her face like spiderwebs. "No. People have seen the black wall. It's moving over Kashan and it's on its way here. Everyone is setting their affairs in order. Restoration. It's our turn."

My heart pounded faster than it had with the shark overhead. I grabbed the abalone and Rasha's hand. I ran.

2

Hakara

561 years after the Shattering

Kashan - the Langzuan border

Everyone agrees that the Numinars were burned for their magic. That the magic was captured and used to create a lifestyle for mortals beyond our current knowledge. There are pre-Shattering relics we don't understand — fractured items made of strange materials, paintings of cities with buildings that defy imagination, old engravings that describe magical weapons used to fight in the wars between realms.

We only had one pair of shoes as we fled the shadow wall, so I'd given them to Rasha. Dried grass and gravel crunched beneath my throbbing feet. All around us people screamed, they shouted, they lifted their voices in prayer. Rasha's wide brown eyes looked up at mine, her nostrils flaring.

I bent and pressed my lips to her hair, knowing she couldn't hear my whispers. "Breathe. This will all be over soon. Just breathe." I took my own advice, the damp, smoky smell of the shadow wall filling my nostrils. The lullaby our Mimi always sang hummed in my throat, and I held Rasha's cheek to my chest, hoping she could at least feel it. The surrounding crowd jostled, sweat beaded on brows and upper lips, the whites of eyes punctuating the sea of people – bright stars against a darkening sky. They moved like water, every so often a wave breaking against us. My body curled around Rasha's, protecting her even as I tried to give her space for air. I risked a glance back down the hill.

A billowing black wall swept over the landscape, swallowing everything in its path. People ran ahead of it, clutching children, loved ones, belongings. One by one, they fell, they grew tired, they stopped and gave up – and restoration took them. I would not be them. I would not let Rasha be them.

Our tent was gone, the settlement we'd lived in, gone. I didn't know what else would be gone when the restoration was complete; perhaps the entire ocean would disappear, the animals within irrevocably changed. That was what a restoration did. It made things green and lush again, but that took magic and matter. Half of the population of Kashan would be altered to suit the new landscape. Half of us would disappear, our matter used to remake our realm. The pact with Kluehnn was a two-handed bargain – one giving and one taking away.

I'd never personally agreed to it.

Stones dug into my knee as I knelt and tapped Rasha's feet. I was the one who had to do the talking at the border, and I wouldn't be convincing without shoes. She kicked them off. Swiftly, I pulled out the padding at the toes and strapped the shoes onto my bruised and swollen feet. Each tightening of the laces sent a jolt of pain up my legs.

I stood and pushed toward the Langzuan tents set up by the border, using my elbows and knees when the crowd didn't give way. My sister and I were both small enough to slip through most gaps. Ahead of us, the churning, dust-filled barrier between our realms rose toward the sky, the remaining population of Kashan crushed between two insubstantial walls. The closer we drew to the tents, the more my hands shook. I didn't have money to pay for a guide through the barrier. I wasn't a doctor, I wasn't a skilled artisan or anyone of note. All I had were forged papers and the desperation of a rat in a swiftly closing trap. We might still make it through to the other side, though I wasn't sure what came next. It was easier, most days, to think only of survival. A breath held, the air aching in my lungs, the water pressing against my back as I wedged my knife beneath the abalone that I sold to keep food in my sister's belly. All moments, all things that passed, all things that didn't matter.

What mattered was Rasha.

A horse by the tents stamped and tossed its head. If I closed my eyes and ears, I might think it any other morning. A morning where I'd throw off my blankets, shove my feet into my shoes and rush to the shoreline before the boats disturbed the water.

There I would breathe, hearing the rasp of air in and out of my lungs as I filled my chest to its limits. And then I would slip into the chilly water, tasting salt against my lips and feeling icy wetness permeating my hair.

But I didn't know if I'd ever swim again. We'd had to sell most of our belongings to buy forged papers, had packed the rest into small bags. The shadow wall had crept forward slowly enough that we'd been able to catch a few hours' sleep every day. But each time we awoke it was there again, threatening to bear down on us.

"We don't have a guide," Rasha gasped out.

I took her by the hand, laced my fingers in hers and squeezed. "Look – we made it this far. What's a few steps more?"

The smile she gave me was weak, but it was there, and it firmed up my heart. I wouldn't be like Maman, whom I'd always seen as giving up. She'd walked into the barrier of her own volition, certain she could find her family in Cressima. She'd left us. Sometimes I wasn't sure which was stronger: my grief or my anger.

There was no order here. There was not enough time for order. Ahead of us was the line for most of the refugees. To our right, a row of guards, weapons in hand, separating the riff-raff from those who'd had enough money to pay privately for escorts and guides.

Someone swathed in gray pushed past us, his voice raised. A large embroidered white eye stared at me from the back of his robe as he made his way toward the wealthy citizens. "Fleeing restoration is a weakness! Become altered or let your matter join in the effort of restoration. This is the pact we willingly made with Kluehnn. Our mortal flesh is weak! All realms will one day be altered. Will you keep running, or will you accept the blessing of the one true god?"

Someone spat at him and he ignored them. I caught a glimpse between the guards of palanquins, of bright handkerchiefs being tied over mouths. Little good some scraps of cloth would do those people when it came to the aether in the barrier, but I couldn't blame them for trying. I *could* blame them for using all that money to save themselves in comfort. One of those richly carved palanquins could have bought me enough shoes for a lifetime.

And then we were close enough to the opening of the tent, a bureaucrat from Langzu hunched over the desk they'd set up there. Armed guards stood on either side of him, scale armor gleaming dully, swords drawn in a clear message: *Stay back*.

"I have papers!" I shouted in Langzuan, drawing them from my vest pocket. "We are legally allowed to cross!"

The bureaucrat looked at us over metal-framed glasses, his

beard pinched by the press of his lips. He lifted his chin and waved us forward. A few people near us muttered curses, but I couldn't care about anything except getting to Langzu, where nothing had yet been restored.

I slapped the papers into his hand as soon as we reached the front, Rasha's fingers still twined in mine. She did her best to hide her bare feet. The bureaucrat looked us up and down with a skeptical gaze, and I knew what he saw. Our birth father was from Cressima, our Mimi from Kashan. Someone from Kashan might pass for Langzuan, but we never would. My heart pounded in my throat, a headache building at my temples as I forced myself to stand still, to stand taller, to look like the woman the papers had been written for.

"You are a scholar?" he said in Kashani.

Heat crept up the back of my neck. It was clear my Langzuan was not passable. "Yes," I replied in Langzuan. "I have studied both here and in Langzu. My sister is not a scholar, but she has assisted me and also speaks both languages." I clenched my teeth, hoping he wouldn't test that lie. Hoping that he saw the approaching wall and knew he had to be quick.

He gave a short nod and wrote something in his ledger. "Then you'll have the passage price."

I felt the dry crack of my lips as I opened them, knowing this was the tipping point. We'd gotten this far. This was the last test. "I do not. We were robbed as we made our way to the border. We are both young, sir, and the people here are desperate." As though I was not one of them. As though I hadn't practiced these exact Langzuan phrases over and over the past few days. "But you'll never meet anyone as willing to work as me and my sister. I can pay what I owe when we get to Langzu."

The man sighed as though he'd heard this tale one too many times. I could feel that door closing, the opportunity slipping.

"*Please*," I tried. Someone jostled me from behind and I stumbled a little to the side. Too late I realized I'd spoken in Kashani and not Langzuan. Ah, my mother tongue, betraying me at the last.

His face closed like a book. "No passage price, no passage. Next!"

I opened my mouth to protest, but the guard nearest to me took a half-step forward. I held out a hand for my forged papers, but the man only tucked them beneath his ledger. "Next!" he called again. I was floating, watching myself from some distant part of my mind, my heart a clenched claw.

"Hakara . . . " Rasha's voice sounded quiet in my ears.

My feet returned to the earth as I breathed through the panic. I had to acknowledge that this way was closed to me. If I threw myself at the guards, I'd accomplish nothing except my death. I led Rasha away from the most crushing part of the crowd.

"You did your best," she was saying, her voice smaller than even her size would suggest. "Just . . . hold my hand when restoration comes? I don't want to be alone."

"No."

"No?" Her voice was on the edge of tears. She was trying to be strong. My sweet Rasha, who tried to mend the broken wings of birds and who'd wept when I'd slaughtered our old camel for food.

I searched the churning border wall as though I could find a gap. The aether inside whipped dust and sand into a frenzy; I could not see through to the other side. Each realm was separated from the others by these barriers, so that Kluehnn could gather enough magic to change the world in pieces. "There has to be another way. We won't be caught here, Rasha. What if one of us doesn't make it through restoration? What if one of us disappears?" I could live with being altered, with both of us being altered. I wasn't sure which I dreaded more: Rasha disappearing or myself. Both sent a spike of fear through my heart.

Kluehnn's priests told us restoration was necessary, that it was glorious. Half of us would be remade to better survive in the new landscape, in forms that held none of our mortal weaknesses. I'd heard stories of Cressima after restoration, and the landscape had gone from cold and barren to lush.

But the cost felt too dear to me and to all the other refugees gathered at the border.

Why couldn't things just remain the *same*?

There wasn't time to dwell on that. The shadow wall was moving closer, its progress inexorable. Think. I had to think. I'd failed at getting us past through the official channels. There would be other groups at the border, not just the fabulously wealthy ones. Ones who'd spent most of their money to hire their own guides, who already had something waiting for them on the other side. They'd be going through on their own. I was strong, I was quick – there had to be *something* I could offer.

"Come on." I tugged at Rasha's hand and we left the tents of Langzu behind. People still crowded the border beyond the tents. I watched as a few took in a breath and decided to chance the swirling, dust-filled barrier, their backs fading into the space between. No one bothered to stop them. They wouldn't make it. Most would fall victim to the toxic air within the barrier. Some would slip into the cracks that opened up into the earth below. You needed a guide – someone who knew the way, who could hold their breath long enough to make headway and who had a strong natural resistance to the aether.

That was what I needed to find if Rasha and I were to make it before restoration hit us. We weaved in and out of weeping mothers, terror-stricken children, between those who had at the last moment turned faithful and dropped to their knees to pray.

We dodged a few who had changed their minds, who ran toward restoration with open arms.

I was an arrow, drawn and loosed with only one purpose.

None of the groups I spotted by the wall looked suitable. The mercenaries – they wouldn't take me on. The horse breeders with mounts much finer than the stubby ponies that habited the Kashani coastline – I had nothing to offer them. And then, just when I'd begun to grit my teeth against despair, I saw a group of sinkhole miners.

Their clothing was rough, fingers blackened from working the mines. Their faces were lean and hard, muscles like corded ropes. I counted eleven, plus one foreman who was negotiating with a guide. An odd number, which meant they'd lost someone. Sinkhole miners always worked in pairs.

Which meant there was an opening.

There were other stragglers near to them, pressing at the group, begging the miners to take them with them. To take their children or their wives. They pushed these people back, sometimes with a flat hand, sometimes with a fist or a foot. I turned to Rasha as I unslung my pack. "Stay here. Stay right here and I'll be back."

Her eyes, a softer brown than mine, brimmed with tears. "Hakara. Don't go. Don't leave me here. I can't—"

"Hush." I ran a hand over her dark hair. "I wouldn't leave you. But miners are rough people. I want you to be safe, and we still have a little time. I'll be back, I promise. Would I break that promise? Have I ever broken that promise?"

A tremulous smile touched her lips. "No."

I gave her one last pat on the shoulder before I turned to the mining crew and picked my way across the rocks. Sinkhole mining was hard, dangerous work. The sinkholes opened up and just as quickly collapsed, often taking miners with them.

It meant crossing the first aerocline into the aether below – the same toxic air that filled the barriers. If you couldn't hold your breath for long enough while you dug the gems from the side of the sinkhole, you'd succumb. Diving into the ocean was less dangerous.

If I became a miner, I couldn't always promise Rasha I'd come home. But we'd be in Langzu. We'd both be alive.

Panic described the foreman to me in flashes. A roughly stubbled chin, black dust settling into the cracks of his wide face. A bald pate, and arms as thick as his legs. He might not have heard my approach; the din surrounding us drowned out my footsteps. Still, he did not turn even as I addressed him.

"You're short a crew member."

"I'll pay you the rest when we're on the other side." He slipped some coins to the guide, a hulking woman with a rope wound over one shoulder.

"Hey! Did you hear me? You're short a crew member."

He shot me only the barest glance, dark eyes like caves beneath the crags of his brows. For a moment I thought he might strike me, but then he gestured to the miners to fall into line as the guide unrolled the rope at her shoulder. I was too young, too small to be a threat.

I'd counted on that.

I dogged his steps, glancing back every so often at the rock where Rasha waited, where I could still catch glimpses of the black top of her head. "I know I look young, but I work as a diver. I take up abalone, sea slugs, pearls – anything that can be found on the ocean floor. I'm lighter than most of your crew, so I wouldn't be too much weight on the line."

"Quickly, now! We don't have much time," the foreman called to his miners. They each took a handful of rope, wrapping it around their wrists, taking care to put some distance between themselves and the next in line. In case any of them breathed too much aether and became violent while inside the barrier.

"I'm giving you an opportunity, one you shouldn't pass up. I can hold my breath longer than any of them," I went on, my heart pressing at my ribs, pushing me forward, because I had to *try*.

Now he turned to me, and I knew: I had him. "Is that so?" He glanced at the approaching shadow wall. And then he knelt and clapped a hand over my mouth and nose.

I hadn't had the time to prepare, to stretch my lungs and keep sipping in breath until I could hold no more. I caught the faint whiff of ash before my air was cut off completely, the skin of his palm rough against my cheeks. I wanted to claw his filthy hand away, to flee, crying, back to Rasha.

He watched my startled expression with satisfaction. "This ends when you give up."

I would *not* give up. Panic shifted inside of me, turning from liquid to a sharp, resilient hardness. I thought of the cold water closing over my head, the quiet of the morning, the lap of waves against the rocky shore. My heartbeat slowed.

This was it: the last chance I had to get Rasha and me safely into Langzu.

The satisfaction on his face melted gradually into stony silence, and then into slight concern. "Just tap my arm when you've had enough."

I lifted my eyes to his, wishing I could burn a hole into his head with my gaze. I placed my hand over his wrist slowly, deliberately. And I did not tap.

I let it rest there, his pulse beneath my palm – his speeding up as mine slowed, as I quelled the desperate feeling that I *needed* to breathe, that told me I would die if I didn't tap his wrist right now. I'd been past this point before. I knew there was another side to it.

There it was.

An easing of that desperation, the feeling of blood leaving my fingers and toes, retreating into my core.

And still I did not tap.

"You'll black out," he said, his voice almost pleading.

I did not. I kept his gaze until I knew I'd passed the point he'd expected me to last, until I passed the point he was sure I would not last. For Rasha.

My stomach spasmed. Spots formed in front of my eyes. Then and only then did I tap his wrist.

He withdrew and I breathed. Air had never tasted so sweet, even filled as it was with the scent of sweat and smoke.

"Impressive," he said. He scratched his chin, and I could see the calculations he was running, how much money I might be able to make him. "I suppose we could use you. Do you have papers?"

"I lost them," I said, gasping. I couldn't get enough air. My tongue felt fuzzy; my vision only able to take in the foreman's face. I pressed past the admission. "I'll go with you, but only if I can bring my sister. I need to bring her."

He shrugged. "Fine."

I whirled, looking for the rock where I'd left her, where I'd told her to wait. We would make it. We'd get to Langzu and escape restoration. Together.

Just as I located the top of her hair again, something struck the back of my head, and the spots swallowed my vision.

3

Rasha

561 years after the Shattering

Kashan - the Langzuan border

Numinars were burned in machines that separated the magic from the smoke, capturing the magic for later use. Though scholars have pored over pre-Shattering relics, no one has been able to discover how these machines worked. Some scholars believe the gods wiped the knowledge clean, though how they might have done so, no one knows.

The wall of black approached, the panic rising to a roar around me. Some people cowered. A few found some inner defiance and stayed standing, legs trembling. Even fewer still rushed toward the wall, though whether they were deciding to get it over with or they'd had a change of heart, I wasn't sure. I clutched the rock, my innards smooth and brittle as glass. *Hakara will come. Hakara will come.*

The last of the bureaucrats had packed up, retreating into the barrier, their guards backing into the swirling dust, blades drawn to keep the refugees from following.

And the wall of black approached. Even as I shrank against that rock as though it would provide me shelter, I thought: *She will come back.*

Closer and closer. Wind rippled before the wall, flattening the dried grass by the border. I caught the white-rimmed eyes of a middle-aged woman close to me, her mouth open in silent terror before restoration swept over her. She disappeared into the black.

At that, the fear broke free, pounding up my throat. No one was holding my hand. Hakara was not here. Hakara was not here and the wall was. It towered above me. I couldn't see over or through it. It blocked the sun and the clouds. A soft breeze touched my cheeks. And then the shadows, insubstantial though they were, hit me with force. I took in a breath. Pain.

I was on fire. I was being torn. I could not feel my hands or my feet or my arms or my legs, only the ripping and the hot-cold sensation of everything gone wrong.

I think I screamed. There was no sound in the black. For a moment, everything went dark. Even my lonely, terrified thoughts.

And then, some time later, I could feel again. My hands. My feet. My face. My lungs.

Breathe in. Breathe out. Again. Sunlight shone red through my eyelids. I existed again. I was still here.

I opened my eyes to a green so intense it hurt to look at it. It was true what they said about restoration. It changed the world. The rock I'd ducked behind – once barren and black – was now covered with moss, plants springing from its cracks. A tiny insect I didn't recognize crept along the top of its dew-covered surface, prismatic wings fluttering.

The skies, high above, were not hazy yellow. They were a blue I'd rarely seen. Where there had once been flat, dry land, there was now a dense forest. Was this what the world had been like before mortals had broken it?

Around me, I heard cries of wonder and dismay. Far fewer cries than I'd heard before the shadow wall had overtaken me. Some had disappeared, their matter absorbed and remade.

Hakara is here. Hakara will still come for me.

I lifted a hand and then realized with a start that it was no longer my hand. It did as I told it to and turned front to back before my eyes. But my fingers were longer, the tips blackened and tapering into claws. The heartbeat in my chest didn't feel like my own. Perhaps it wasn't. I swiped my tongue across my lips and felt sharp teeth. Every movement made me aware that I was different. My limbs were more sinewy, my clothes now tight across a body that was longer than it had been before.

There were . . . horns on top of my head. My questing fingers found the rough spot where they met my skull, just above my hairline, and followed them as they curved up and around.

My first panicked thought was that Hakara might not recognize me. How could she return to take me with her if she did not know who I was?

"Hakara!" I shouted. My voice joined other voices in the trees, other voices shouting other names. I stumbled to my feet and began to search. I swept past figures in the underbrush as we skirted the barrier between our realm and Langzu's. Each of us recoiled as we spotted one another. I saw people with wings sprouting from their backs, with antlers curving up from their foreheads, with fur covering their bodies or scales dotting their cheeks and arms.

Something rustled in the brush when I passed a woman with red skin and a long, winding tail. Our eyes met for only a moment before a brown, shaggy creature as big as my old tent sprang from the trees, jaws closing around her body.

I turned and ran, unheeding of her screams. Everyone had been screaming lately; this was only one more horror added to the rest.

"Hakara!" I tried again, louder. "Hakara!" And then *I* was the one screaming, my voice rising into the trees until it grew hoarse.

At some point I stopped, though I heard others continuing their searches. I sank to the mossy ground near the border, my knees drawn to my chest, my arms wrapped around myself. I didn't know where the rock was anymore – and somehow that seemed like the most important thing in the world. If I couldn't find it, and Hakara couldn't recognize me, then how would she find me? It was like standing on the beach and having the sand sucked out from beneath my feet – all at once, too quickly.

I'd stayed by the tent when she went to the ocean to dive. She'd said I was too young to learn. But I'd learned to clean and gut the food she brought home, how to cook it, how to sort and save the money. We'd found a way to live with both our Mimi and Maman gone. I needed her.

Night fell, a blur of damp earth, shivering, and the sounds of strange animals. Sleep came in fitful starts. Each time I closed my eyes, I longed for the scent of smoke on the wind, the rocky shoreline, the crackle of dung fires and the huff of disgruntled camels. Each time I opened my eyes, I was returned to reality. I didn't know this world. I didn't know myself.

Sometimes a heart breaks all at once. Sometimes it is chipped away in pieces until you wake up and notice it is no longer the same.

At some point morning came, and with it came hunger. I searched the bushes for fruit, finding some berries I didn't recognize but eating them anyways. They settled uneasily into my belly but they did not kill me. It wasn't until the second day that I started eating the bugs I found gathered on the bark of nearby trees. And on the third day, in desperation, I snatched at a passing bird. To my surprise, I caught it.

I cooked it over a fire of dried twigs – a luxury in Kashan before the restoration – and with my hunger gone my mind wandered. Where was Hakara? Had she been caught by restoration and changed as I was? Or had she disappeared when the shadow wall had hit? Was she now gone forever?

No. She had told me to wait. She had said she would come back. So I waited, and I didn't track the days.

As mornings blended into nights, I heard fewer voices in the trees calling out for loved ones. I watched some of them leave, faces downcast, eyes not meeting mine as they trudged away from the barrier. Once, on a sunny afternoon, I stood as close as I dared, staring into the churning dust, wondering how many steps it would take to get to the other side. To where Hakara might be.

Some must have made it through. Perhaps I could do it if I really tried. Hakara would have fixed her jaw, taken a breath and plunged into the barrier without a second thought – the way she plunged into the ocean each morning.

When she'd bade me wait, had she meant to come back for me before she crossed, or had she meant that she would cross and then come back to me? If I left, she would have no way of finding me. Maman had once told us she would come back, too.

"I wouldn't, if I were you. No one without training walks into the wall and walks back out," a voice said from behind me.

I whirled, my claws lifted, my teeth bared.

A woman with red scales on her cheeks stood beneath the trees, dressed in gray robes that hung loose over her body. Several white eyes were embroidered across her chest, looking like nothing so much as a cluster of grapes made flesh. Her hair was brown, the shape of her yellow eyes and her fair features still faintly Cressiman.

One of Kluehnn's priestesses. Hakara and I had always steered clear of them. I was so startled by her appearance that it took me a moment to realize that she was holding a basket over one arm and was proffering a twine-wrapped bundle. "Are you hungry? Or would you prefer to walk into the wall?"

"What does it cost?" My voice was still small, though there was a metallic vibration in it that hadn't been there before restoration had caught me.

"Nothing. I'm only here to do the work of the many-limbed god. He pities the ones who have been left behind. He wishes to show them mercy." Her voice was soft and even, as though coaxing a lamb.

My stomach growled as the scent of freshly baked goods reached me. Hesitantly, I approached. I took the bundle from her, expecting at any moment to be chased off.

She only smiled, her lips stretching wider than any mortal's would have. "I am Millani."

My eyes still on her, I untied the twine. A quick glance told me there was flatbread inside, and cheese in waxed cloth, and round, sweet-smelling fruits I didn't recognize. My mouth watered.

At her encouraging nod, I lifted the bread and bit into it. There is no spice that can match hunger; I had never tasted anything so fragrant in my life. The sides of my throat ached as the food passed over my tongue. I fell upon the rest of it without a second thought.

"I was once like you," Millani said as she watched me eat. "I tried to escape restoration at the borders of Cressima. But Kashan wasn't letting many through. Not as many as Langzu did. I thought I would die, and I closed my eyes expecting the end. But I did not. I changed. And a priest from Kluehnn fed me as I waited by the border for my family to return to life. They did not."

Her shadow fell upon my face and I realized she'd stepped closer. I gathered the bundle of food to my chest and stepped back, closer to the barrier.

She stopped, her head cocked to the side, considering. "You're very young, aren't you? You've been altered to be larger and taller, but your face . . . "

I ducked my gaze, suddenly wary and ashamed. "I'm nine."

"You could come with me, back to the den. We could find a place for you. There would be food, shelter, a safe place to sleep. A job." She gestured to the surrounding forest. "It's not safe here." One more step and she knelt, so that her face was below mine. Something in me eased.

"What's your name?"

"Rasha," I said.

"Rasha," she repeated. "The creatures that once roamed Kashan before the Shattering have been restored and altered too, and many are dangerous. We can protect you."

I thought of what Hakara might say in this situation, and drew myself up. "I can be dangerous too."

Again that appraising look. "I'm sure you can be."

"I don't need your help. My sister is coming back for me. She promised to." My voice broke.

Millani only waited until I'd gathered myself. "Little one, people break their promises. I've learned that many times over. Only the one true god does not. Kluehnn does not."

The breath rose hot in my throat. "You don't know her! Don't talk to me like you know her." I lifted my clawed hands.

She rose. "My apologies. Think on what I've said." And then she was gone, vanished into the underbrush with her basket.

The rest of the food she'd given me was salty with my tears.

I hated that I was so *weak*, that I wasn't facing this with the stoic determination that Hakara always had. I curled up in the damp roots of a tree, my belly full but my heart hollow.

Over the next days, I watched two people walk into the barrier, their faces blank. Neither returned, and I thought only of them drowning in the toxic air when they ran out of breath. I lost my taste for it after that.

Millani came by the next day. And the next. Each time there was less food in her basket, fewer altered to feed. Still Hakara did not appear.

"Rasha," Millani said gently when she found me the fourth time, my clothes now tatters, "you cannot wait forever. You have a life to be lived beyond waiting."

I thought of all the mornings Hakara and I had spent after her dives – my sister drying her hair by the fire while I gutted her catch. The way she always made sure my blankets were tucked around me before she left – even when she thought I was asleep and did not notice. How she gave me the choicest bits of food, how she'd held me after Maman was gone and it was just the two of us.

"She's not coming back, is she?" I couldn't look Millani in the eye.

"You are the last, little one. Everyone else has left." She unfurled a hand toward me.

Hakara would have waited for me. She would have waited until the end of time because that was who she was. But she was not here. I was. And much as I didn't want to face it, she'd either died or she'd broken her promise. I wasn't sure which would hurt me more. And I was not Hakara.

Millani's palm was still outstretched, waiting for me. "Come with me, Rasha. Come home."

I put my hand in hers.

4

Hakara

10 years after the restoration of Kashan
and 571 years after the Shattering

Langzu - the Northern Sinkhole Flats

*Just when Tolemne despaired of ever fixing the world above,
Kluehnn appeared to him. "I will heal the world above,"
he told him. "Though it will take time, and it will cost."*
　　"I will pay any price," Tolemne answered.
　　*So they made a pact. Aether churned from below, push-
ing violently into the cracks between the realms, rising ever
upward. And the world above was shattered.*

My lungs burned as I pried a bright green gemstone
from the surrounding black rock. I was used to the
feeling. Half of being a good diver was learning to sit with the
sense that you were drowning, and sinkhole mining was no different. The air past the first aerocline felt thicker than that on the
surface; a few of my stray hairs floated in it as though caught in
the slightest breeze.

A tiny tremor worked its way through the thin soles of my boots. It was a warning. I tugged on the rope attached to my harness so my partner above would know we were close to done.

You only ever had so much time once a sinkhole opened.

I risked a glance up, the opening marked only by spots of lantern light, far above. There were two more gems above me I might be able to grab on the way back up. Behind me, another miner gave a final tug on his line and then started hauling himself upward. I was always the last one down the hole.

Below, a myriad of gems glowed. They tempted me, just a length too far, just a length too deep. A gentle shimmer shone in the sinkhole, a line delineating the division between the first and second aeroclines. Miners were forbidden from passing the second aerocline. It was too dangerous, too much risk. Get a lungful of air from past the first and you'd feel dizzy and itchy. You'd get to feeling like there was nothing wrong with the world. And that was part of the danger. Plenty of people who sucked in the aether ended up thinking they had more time than they did before the sinkhole collapsed. Some fools dove, laughing, for the bottom. Even those who got out safe were itchy and nauseated for days afterward.

Get a lungful of air past the second aerocline, you might live if someone pulled you up, but you were likely to mutilate yourself or murder a teammate. Gods and altered could use the aether, but it was toxic to mortals. Made a person right sick – mind and body.

Too many horror stories made the profession unappealing for most, and Kluehnn needed his tithe of gems. So we were the dregs, most of us refugees from other realms. And wasn't I, an illegal refugee and half-Cressiman to boot, the dreggiest of dregs?

Another tremor. I tugged at the line again and started back up. My pouch was full and Guarin, the supervisor, would give me my pittance for it. Keeping one arm on the line, I dug a couple gems out and slipped them into the secret pocket between my breasts. Kept my feet moving.

My partner hauled as I climbed and I made good time to the rim. I caught a glimpse of her face – her clenched teeth, her thick arms straining. The ground rumbled again as soon as I tumbled over the edge, my head light. My breath came fast as I tried to make up for all the time spent holding it. The other miners had already packed up and moved a safe distance from the perimeter.

"Hakara . . . " Altani gasped out.

A few gems fell loose from my pouch. I crouched to grab them.

"Leave them!" she said, already ahead of me, the stakes secured haphazardly at her belt, her rope only partly coiled over her shoulder, the rest trailing behind.

But it was too late. I was already scooping them into my hand, half running, half stumbling away from the rim. I heard the sinkhole collapsing behind me, the crack of stone and the roar of so much moving dirt.

I would make it. I always did.

Something gave way beneath my feet, and I leapt. The air was dusty when I rolled over. Where the shaft of the sinkhole had been was now a wide depression in the land. I coughed as I pushed myself up from a crouch.

"You cut things too close." Altani's voice shook. "We're partners but you don't listen to me. You've never listened to me. Someday I'll have to leave you. Someday you'll get caught by the collapse and you'll fall."

"But today wasn't that day."

"Not yet," she said grudgingly. I reached for her hand and she pulled away. "But it will happen soon, Hakara. You keep pushing your limits further and further and someday you'll hit a wall. You'll curse me for it and you won't understand that I have needs and wants too. And most of those involve not dying."

I didn't try for her hand again. We'd been close, once, two lonely sinkhole miners trying to fill a void left by others. I think we both understood the other was just a resting spot, a place to pause before we each continued on our way.

Or maybe that was just how I'd seen Altani. I couldn't speak for her. Having my setter mad at me wasn't great for my health or my lifespan. I tried a little wheedling, a charming smile. "Come on, Altani. I'm not dead. You're not dead. I know how to judge these things. Been doing this job for ten years, and that's twice as long as you. You really gonna cut me loose someday?"

She sighed, her big shoulders hunching. "I still care, Hakara. I just can't care too much." She turned from me to join the others.

I understood the sentiment. My fingers were dry, black and cracked. I could feel the dirt and dust caking my cheeks with every twitch of my expression. But my gem pouch was full and I had a couple in my secret pocket. And that meant I was that much closer to finding Rasha.

The thought of her threatened to send me into another spiral of panic.

Ten years since I'd lost her. So long. *Too* long. I'd woken up on the other side of the barrier on a pallet, my head still swimming with the aether I'd breathed while unconscious. They'd given me a sleeping draft until the worst had passed, so I wouldn't start tearing at my skin or biting at others.

Which meant by the time I'd awoken, it was too late. Restoration had taken both Kashan and my sister. The closer I came to actually finding a way back through to Kashan, to Rasha, the more my feelings mirrored that early state. The clawing, hollow-bellied desperation, the need for the truth to not be true, the wild hope that somehow I could break all rules and return to the moment in time when I'd left my sister at that rock because anything else was unbearable.

I'd tried to go back to the barrier, sick and dizzy, demanding to know who'd knocked me out. The mining crew had stopped me. It was a death wish, they said. Wasn't it better to be alive? While I'd screamed and cried, Guarin told me I was supposed to be grateful. He'd saved me, he said, just as I'd asked him to. And then he put me to work.

I didn't know whether Rasha was alive or gone, and living with any fullness felt impossible without that knowing. But I'd thrown myself into the work, letting resentment keep me alive, and slowly I'd learned to live in that impossible space. To become a person who could push that question aside.

But the closer I came to finally knowing, the closer I came back to myself.

I squinted up at the sky, trying to catch a glimpse of the stars beyond the haze, turning my focus back to the present. The miners shuffled toward camp, forming into a loose line as we handed our haul in to our supervisors and the Sovereign's enforcers gave us each a cursory pat-down.

The gems were not for the people of Langzu. They were for Kluehnn – the one true god. The only one we were permitted to worship by the terms of the god-pact. Or that was what we were told, anyways. Over and over. Enough times to make even those with young ears feel deaf. The only ones who didn't live by those rules were the Unanointed – and few were keen to join a group of ragtag rebels fighting a god – and the rich. Money and madness: the two prerequisites for tossing all rules aside. Pick one or do as you're told.

I veered off from the group once we reached camp, sliding along the perimeter. It was a dusty, stinking place, the latrine ditch somehow constantly in need of maintenance, lamps flickering out, smoke lingering in the air – because you might as well indulge when you weren't expected to live long. The faint sounds of fists meeting flesh, and then loud cheers and jeers as betting money exchanged hands. Five mining teams, killing time as they waited for the next sinkhole to open up. We all migrated as the sinkholes did, when one area became a pitted landscape and another began to sink.

My contact lingered in the dark space between two tents, his gaze on the sky, his locked chest of god gems tucked beneath one arm. One of the very same liaisons chosen by the Sovereign and then confirmed by Kluehnn's dens. The liaisons took those god gems and allegedly whisked them straight away to Kluehnn, no stops along the way. It was all a very neat and tidy process, if one looked at it from a good distance. Get too close, though, and there was always mess to be had.

I waited until someone passed by before fishing out the two gems from between my breasts. They were bright in my hand, shading my palm in blues and reds.

He shrugged, as though what I was showing him was unimpressive.

I snorted, my whisper a hiss in the wind. "These are bigger than your pinprick of a brain if you think they aren't a good size."

"I saw one sold to the Otangu clan recently. Big as the end of my thumb and multiple colors. These don't look so impressive compared to that."

"Sure you did. And I saw a godkiller taking a piss out back. Said he was done with godkilling and wanted to try mining. Do you want them or not?"

He barely glanced at me as we transacted – quick, efficient, a small hiccup as we flashed our fingers, shook our heads and debated price on the larger gem – but then it was done and there was extra coin in my purse. I'd heard rumors of what these gems could do. They could heal wounds, increase virility, make plants grow more quickly. The penalty for trading them was death, of course, but threaten a tired populace with death often enough and it just starts to sound like a nice nap.

I fingered the coin, doing the math in my head as I ducked out into the general bustle of the camp, making my way toward my tent. My heart clenched. I finally had enough to get a good forgery of official documents, to hire a guide and to purchase supplies for my foray into Kashan.

Ten long years ... I didn't know what Rasha would look like now that she was altered, how much she'd grown, what she might have had to do to survive. All I knew was I needed to make everything right and I finally had the means.

Guarin stepped into my path.

Ten years hadn't changed him much. His arms were thinner now, the stubble on his chin peppered with gray. But he had the same bald pate, the same deep crease between his eyebrows, the same square set to his jaw. His clothes were as rough as mine, dust and dirt settled into the folds, his fingers cracked. I made as though to move around him – I always did my best to ignore him – until I saw what rested between his dry hands.

My entire stash of savings, everything I'd been working toward. My box of hidden coins.

5

Hakara

10 years after the restoration of Kashan
and 571 years after the Shattering

Langzu – the Northern Sinkhole Flats

*Despite his greatness, Kluehnn could not restore all the
world at once. But he could manage it one realm at a
time, until the whole world was restored and the land could
finally be healed. In exchange for this service, Kluehnn
asked only for two things: a yearly quota of god gems from
each of the unrestored realms and the promise that the
mortals would seek no god other than him.*

"You went into my tent." It was a stupid thing to say.
Obviously he'd gone into my tent or he wouldn't have
found my stash, and it was his right as supervisor. I hated Guarin.
Hated him. Yet I couldn't stop the cold trickle of betrayal that
settled at the back of my throat. He'd never ransacked my tent
before. He would have had to in order to find the box. Maybe he'd
just been waiting for the right opportunity.

My emotions flickered between the chill of fear and the heat of anger, never quite settling long enough on anger. "That's mine."

He only watched me, and had the temerity to look disappointed. As though he were a father to me. As though he hadn't stolen me away through the barrier like a thief. "I didn't want to do this," he said, his voice gruff, "but I wasn't left with much choice."

His voice was like a tap, draining away my shock. This was happening. Ten years of scraping, clawing together every bit of coin, of risk and of heartache. He stood there with my life in my hands – or at least, the only bit that mattered. "Give it back."

He held it out to me.

I moved to snatch it, but as soon as I touched it, I knew. Its heft was not nearly what it should have been. No heavy slide of coin to the side; just a pathetic rattle.

"Someone saw you trading gems, Hakara."

"Who saw me?"

"Doesn't matter. You were going to get caught someday. I had to keep 'em quiet and I didn't have the funds myself. Knew you had them somewhere."

Anger exploded, hot and fiery. "Of course it matters! I've got to know whose face will be meeting my fist. You had no right, Guarin. That money was *mine*!"

And Guarin, because he was Guarin, responded in kind, his thick brows joining together. There'd hardly been a day since we'd met that we hadn't fought. "You wanted me to let them just come and arrest you and take your damn head off? Better to live and be short some coin."

It felt like being kicked back to that moment outside the sandy barrier, my throat hoarse and raw, like being shoved into the skin of that fifteen-year-old kid, unable to claw my way back to the present. "You know it means more to me than that. Someone knocked me on the head when I was about to go get my sister. It was you. I know it was. You brought me here. You kept me here."

Frustration and pity washed over his face in competing waves. "And you're determined to think that's what happened?"

"That's what I *know* happened." I stared into his face, fixing my mind on that moment when I'd woken up on the other side of the barrier, not letting it waver to other memories.

He shook his head. "Don't go chasing shadows, Hakara. She's gone. And if she's alive, she's not the sister you remember."

I lifted a finger, wishing it was a dagger, wishing I could stab it straight into Guarin's eye. If he were any of the other miners, I would have beat him bloody. But he knew my status here in Langzu wasn't legal, and he knew he was the only avenue I had to make a living. "Rasha is my sister. She will always be my sister." Nausea swam up my throat; the edges of the box beneath my arm felt too sharp. I blinked against a sudden gust of wind, stirring up dust. How long would it take to earn the money back? Another ten years?

A slight tremor shook the ground beneath my feet, a rumble sounding in the distance. A horn sounded from the makeshift watchtower.

Another sinkhole in the same night. Rare, but it happened. The camp exploded into action. I shoved the box back at Guarin. "You hold it. And don't you dare touch another coin."

I found Altani and the others already at the edge of camp, gear strapped to their backs. I was stepping into my harness before anyone else, fastening the buckles and ducking out into the night. Altani joined me soon after, her stakes at her belt and rope coiled over one arm. A lamp swung wildly from the other.

Night-time sinkholes were dangerous, a second one in the same night even more so. Crews got tired too. But the more dangerous the sinkhole, the more potential profit was to be had. Less competition.

The horn sounded again. Short short long short long short. The valley had been divided into a mutually agreed-upon grid, the horn giving the coordinates of the latest sinkhole. The way there was treacherous, the ground uneven. It was far. We'd need to take the carts. This was no mad rush, though we all felt the urgency. We needed to keep the horses whole and hale.

Our crew was quick and ruthlessly efficient. Only a short time later, we were bundled onto two lantern-lined carts, the horses in front stomping and snorting with impatience. "Move out!" Guarin called.

I heard other carts behind us, creaking over the landscape. Only a few more had decided to risk it. The hour was late and it was a new moon. Halfway to the sinkhole, it started to rain.

The miners in my cart groaned. Needed this last spot of rain before the endless heat of summer, but rain was never good for mining.

"The trifecta of poor conditions," Altani muttered next to me. "Guarin!" she called. "We still doing this?"

He peered into the darkness, and I knew he was watching the other carts. "Two quitters," he said. "Only two other carts still moving, from the same team. We'll have less competition and can afford to be careful." His gaze flashed over us. "What, have you all grown soft with success? We make this a good run and we'll spend a few nights in town. We've the money for it."

No one cheered, but backs straightened, heads nodded. My heartbeat quickened as I anticipated the work ahead. If I smuggled away a big enough gem, I could make back the difference. My contact could have been lying about that multicolored gem, but maybe he hadn't been. Maybe I could find one just like it. I had to. I couldn't wait another ten years, and neither could Rasha.

I imagined Guarin's face when I made back that money, when I finally left this stinking mess of a mining camp. Would serve him right to wake up one morning, sinkhole horn blaring, only to find his best diver had disappeared.

Fuck. I could *do* this.

The wagon wheels rattled as we picked our way around a collapsed sinkhole. The rain pattered down harder, filling the air with the smell of damp wood and petrichor. My hands were cold but the rest of me was warm, limber, ready to dive.

The wagon rolled to a stop, another two carts nearly at the rim to our left. We were the first ones here and would be the first to stake our claim. Guarin was already on the ground, looking into the darkness of the sinkhole, picking out the dully glowing pinpricks that told him where the god gems were. A supervisor had to have good eyes.

He pointed out spots for the four other teams. "Hakara and Altani, here." He pointed right at his feet. "Go."

We surged for the edge. I attached the rope to my harness as Altani drove her spikes into the earth ten paces from the edge. Then I forced myself to calmness, focusing on my breathing. My ribcage expanded. I reached my limit, stopped, and then sipped in a few last bits of air.

I dropped into the pit.

My eyes were not as sharp as Guarin's, but they didn't need to be. The air shimmered below me like the surface of a pond at night, and I rushed toward it, kicking off the wall and feeling Altani loose more and more rope. I passed the first aerocline. The air thickened, becoming slightly warmer. The glow of the gems that had been dim when viewed from above suddenly brightened.

Rain still fell, cold droplets against the back of my neck. I bypassed a smaller gem and went for a larger one lower down.

The scraping of feet against stone sounded as others descended into the sinkhole with me.

I kept a prying knife and a small pickaxe at my belt, and I quickly went to work. Black veins ran through the sides of the sinkhole, and this was where the gems were most concentrated. I didn't take note of the colors. Some were rarer than others, but our payment was calculated by weight and nothing else.

I fell into the rhythm of it, tucking gems away into my pouch. I came up past the aerocline for air once, twice. No rumblings yet, no indications of the sinkhole collapsing. Sometimes I didn't get to come up for air at all. This one was more stable than most.

Which meant I'd have to start going deeper if I wanted to keep collecting. I noticed a couple of divers calling it quits, tugging at their lines and climbing back to the edge. They'd got enough. I felt the weight of my pouch. It was substantial and it would make a dent, but I hadn't found anything that would be worth fencing. I hovered at the edge of the aerocline, my face above and the rest of me below. I took in a deep breath. This close, I could smell the air beneath.

It smelled like the ocean – both inviting and forbidding. I fell back and went down, down. I wondered what Altani was thinking up there, watching the rope continue to spool out. She'd think me foolish, but it wasn't her job to worry. It was her job to bring me back. I pried loose a few more gems, checked the weight again. My fingers were sore, but I still had air left in my lungs.

And then I saw it, a little ways beneath me. The bright red gem jutted from the sinkhole wall, as big as my thumbnail. This was no pinprick; it glowed with an inner fire. But the air between me and the gem shimmered.

I was deep enough already. That telltale shimmer told me how far I'd gone. Past that was the second aerocline. The air there would be even thicker, even more toxic. Nearly all the supervisors, Guarin included, forbade the divers from going past the second aerocline. Too much risk, not enough to gain. Every so often, someone made the attempt. Once they breached that aerocline, they typically stayed down, forcing their setter to either cut the line or pull up a corpse. I'd heard a story of a man who'd gone past the second aerocline and had returned so crazed that he killed his setter and two others on his team before they put him down.

Yet the gem was *right there*.

Rasha's face flashed in my mind, her black brows drawn together in concern, eyes wet with unshed tears. *Don't leave me here.*

I dove.

The air here seemed to seep past my collar, filling my ears, making me feel lighter than I was on the surface. Altani would *kill* me. So would Guarin, for that matter. But I had to go back to Kashan. If Rasha was dead, I had to know it for myself. And if she was not, she was still my sister, no matter what form she'd taken.

I touched the gem. It was warm beneath my fingertips. I pulled my pickaxe free and chipped at the surrounding stone until I could feel a seam between gem and rock. The surrounding air pressed at my nose and mouth, begging to be let in. I risked a glance up and caught a quick glimpse of lanterns above before a drop of rain fell into my eye, blurring my vision.

I blinked it away and reached for my prying knife.

The sinkhole wall trembled. *Shit.* I knew instinctively that the smart thing to do would be to climb right now. Past the second aerocline and past the first and back to solid ground. But I needed this god gem. I was close. Pressure built in my chest as I wedged the knife into the seam and pried. It was the largest gem I'd ever worked and I had to put all the strength of my arms into it. My muscles burned, screaming for air.

The wall shook again. Dust filtered down from above, drifting slowly as it hit the second aerocline. The rain was undeterred, falling harder, slicking the gem and my hands.

Altani would never forgive me. But I'd never forgive myself if I left it.

I gave one last wrench of my arm and the gem popped free. I caught it before it could fall and fumbled with my pouch. It wouldn't fit securely inside; I'd collected too many gems already. I didn't have time to fiddle with my hidden pocket. Quickly, I popped it between my teeth, resisting the urge to breathe as soon as I opened my mouth.

I pushed past the panic, forcing myself to relax as I climbed toward the shimmering barrier between the first and second aeroclines. Somewhere above me, Altani began to pull.

The sinkhole shook again. Rocks tumbled loose.

I caught only a glimpse of something blacking out the sky above before the rock struck me. It hit my face first, tumbling to catch my shoulder. In that brief, surprised moment of impact, the gem slipped from between my teeth and past my throat.

I swallowed it. And for all my training, all my discipline, pushing myself over and over again past the limits of most mortal endurance, I did what I knew I must never do.

I breathed.

The air this deep down tasted of the ocean too, briny and filled with the scents of so many sea creatures. I didn't take just a sip; I breathed in deep, unable to stop myself once I'd started. But I held that breath, my teeth gritted. How much of the poison air could I take in before I felt the effects? Was that odd fizzing in my belly the beginnings of toxicity? The only thing I really knew was that I wasn't ready to give up yet. If I died climbing to the surface, I would at least die on my way back to Rasha.

A fresh burst of strength flooded my arms. The world around

me rumbled as if in response. The sinkhole was collapsing. I climbed as quickly as my legs would allow, running up that length of rope like my life depended on it.

Through the clamor I heard shouted words, though I couldn't make out what they were. Altani and Guarin, arguing.

Dread formed a knot in my belly.

I seized the rocks in front of me just in time, just as the line went slack. I'd pushed myself to the limit, but I'd finally managed to push Altani past hers. She'd left me in order to save herself. I'd taken a lungful of poisoned air. My rope was slack. I was dead in the water as a boat without sails or oars. I closed my eyes briefly against the rain, feeling the rock beneath my hands shake. Maybe I'd see Maman and Mimi again. Maybe I'd even see Rasha.

No. I wasn't sure if I'd spoken the word or just thought it, but my eyes snapped open again. I reached. It was impossible. I couldn't make it without my setter. There wasn't enough time.

My shoulders burned and itched. Something tore.

For a moment, I thought it was an effect of the aether. And then something in my awareness *shifted*. My arms felt different — larger, stronger.

But there was a sinkhole collapsing around me and I'd never sat still long enough to consider the wider mysteries of the world. If the world gave me a stronger pair of arms, I was going to use them. I pulled at handhold after handhold, the wall a blur as I passed. My arms did most of the work, my feet only following after, steadying my passage.

Another rock fell, a big one, missing me by a hand's breadth.

My face broke the first aerocline. A little farther and I was grabbing the edge, the dirt and rocks crumbling beneath my hand. But then I was launching myself up and out. I unhitched the rope from my harness and I was running, running, running.

My shoulders tingled as I finally remembered to breathe, something like smoke dissipating into the night air.

The lamps of my crew swung wildly somewhere in front of me. I couldn't hear my footsteps or my own thoughts over the roar of the collapse behind me. Fear drove me forward, not just fear of death but fear of that brief moment in which I'd given up. I needed to put as much distance between now and then as possible.

I almost ran past my crew, but Altani caught my shoulder, her eyes wide. Her gaze raked me up and down. "Hakara? You're alive?"

I gasped out a high-pitched laugh. The rumble died down as the last rocks tumbled into the hole. "Don't I look it?"

"You shouldn't be alive."

"And aren't you happy I am?" I remembered the dread as the rope had gone slack. "You *left* me, Altani."

She looked at me with a mixture of disbelief and disgust. It would have stung had my head not been swimming with shock. "What did you expect me to do? To die with you? Hakara, I went to the edge. I saw what happened. *You went past the second aerocline.*" I heard the hush as others stopped what they were doing, as conversations halted. Gazes fixed on me. "You shouldn't have been able to get out. You were too far down, you were out of breath and you had a slack line. You shouldn't be standing here."

"There was a gem . . . " I trailed off, touched my mouth. "I had to risk it." I brushed her big hand from my shoulder. My body still felt strange, humming with energy.

Altani shook her hand out. "Aye? And where is that gem now?"

"I . . . " The whole reason I'd risked myself was gone. For a little while, at least. I'd pass it in the next day or two, and then I could find another contact to sell it to and be away with the full amount before any of the Sovereign's enforcers could catch me. I could still make it to Kashan. "I lost it."

Altani let out a huff. "You listen to me. Next time, I cut loose sooner. I'm not dying for you. We're not lovers anymore and now? Now we're not even friends." She stalked to the cart and sat in her spot, looking like an extremely disgruntled statue.

The other miners eyed me warily, as though unsure whether I'd take out my pickaxe and fall upon the lot of them. I was tempted, just to give them a fright. Just to get them to stop staring.

Someone from another group lingered on the edge of our crew. I caught a glimpse of lank black hair and a trim beard before he turned away and faded into the darkness. Had I caused *that* much of a stir?

I flexed my fingers and noticed they were no longer cold. Some people died from merely taking a breath in the first aerocline. Guides built up their tolerance to the air in small increments.

Yet I'd taken in a deep breath from the second aerocline, where toxicity was even more concentrated. And somehow, by some miracle I did not understand, I was still alive.

6

Rasha

10 years after the restoration of Kashan
and 571 years after the Shattering

Kashan - Kluehnn's den

The mortals broke the world, but the gods did not try to fix it. Instead, they took advantage of the turmoil the world above was experiencing.

Instead, they took their armies and they invaded.

Aether always smelled like a dung fire to me. It wisped up from the stone floor of the ravine, a snatch of scent and shimmering air before the collared man in front of me sucked it into his mouth. The gem he held between his teeth glowed brightly for a moment and then he spat it into the basket next to him. I waited until he had another gem between his teeth. With a flick of my wrist, I drew more aether up from below. I shifted on my cushion, unfolding and refolding my legs.

It was a tedious job, but it was a job.

The call of birds mingled with the click of gemstones and the creak of cart wheels as workers brought gems into the ravine and then carried them away into the depths of the caves. I never asked why we did this. I never asked where the gems went or what they were for. No one did. In exchange, our bellies were kept full, our fires lit, our bedrolls clean. I wondered briefly if Hakara would have taken this job too, or if she'd have insisted we brave the wilderness together.

"Rasha."

I twisted to find Millani behind me, red scales scattered in patches across her face, glittering in the dappled light. A tail lashed behind her, her face long with slitted eyes. A red crest peeked out from beneath her brown hair. The altered often resembled the old gods.

She touched one of my horns, letting her fingers trail into my hair. The gesture felt both motherly and possessive. "Walk with me a while. You've been ahead of quota. You can spare the time."

I rose to my feet, my mouth suddenly dry. I'd once followed her away from the dusty barrier between Kashan and Langzu, though back then I'd been a lost little child, salt tracks staining my cheeks. My sister wriggled back into my mind, the wounds she'd left in my heart cracking open. She'd told me to wait by the rock, that she would be back. So I'd waited, my faith in her never wavering, not even as the black wall of restoration had swept over me, as my skin and bones had begun to burn. Each moment I thought I'd find her hand in mine again.

Hakara. You always kept your promises. Mimi died, Maman left us, but you – you were a mountain. Unwavering.

My gaze focused on the knife strapped to Millani's side, a shimmering violet god gem embedded in the hilt. Back when I'd met her, she'd been merely a priestess. At Kluehnn's direction, she'd set immediately to the task of converting those who'd been left. And now she was a godkiller. Just as I wanted to be.

Infusing the god gems with aether was a job, but what I wanted was a calling.

One yellow eye focused on my face as Millani turned her head. "You're humming that song again."

The lullaby our Mimi used to sing to us. The one Hakara had taken up after she'd died – singing it to me each night before we fell asleep, curled into an exhausted pile in our tent. Heat rose up the back of my neck and I bit the inside of my cheek. "I'm sorry."

"Don't apologize. You just don't seem to know when you're doing it." She cleared her throat. "The den elders have heard your request." Her words set my heart to racing, though I kept my lips firmly closed. We picked our way down the ravine toward the den entrance. On either side of us were teams of altered, with mortal men and women chained to the ravine wall. The scent of dung fire lingered in the air as baskets of gems were filled, emptied and then refilled. I rubbed my nose.

"Most godkillers are from legacy families. You are not."

I couldn't feel the ground beneath my feet. Was this a denial? I knew most godkillers came from families who'd been devout even before restoration, who had trained their children for such a possibility. For my family, Kluehnn had been not a comfort, but something inevitable to be dealt with – just as a passing storm or a wolf hunting one's sheep. I'd come to conversion in a roundabout way. Through charity, not choice.

But I was choosing now, and I hoped that would be enough.

"Most converts who wish to become godkillers die during the trials. Some live but are forever scarred. Even those are cast aside. Only a very few make it to the end." Millani whirled then, her movements unnaturally swift. She caught my face in one clawed hand, her forked tongue tasting the air between us. "Are you sure this is the path you wish to take?"

I felt the lullaby bubble up in my throat and shoved it back down, trying to replace it with the litany I whispered each day in worship. *Kluehnn is the one true god, the all-father, the savior. As he has favored me, I will favor him.* It steadied me enough so I could meet her yellow-eyed gaze with my black ones. "Yes. I am willing to die for this."

One claw scratched my cheek as her hand fell. "Your request has been approved, little one. Your training begins today."

Something in my heart twinged. It was what Millani had called me when she'd found me by the barrier, ready to step inside.

I had lived through that. I would live through this.

We stepped through the cave entrance and into Kluehnn's den. This was the closest den to the Langzuan border, though Kashan was dotted with them. Places of worship and industry and charity. In the aftermath of restoration, Kashan had lost one Queen and had hurriedly selected another, but officials were dead and scattered. A few had escaped to Langzu and had promptly been disavowed by the government as cowards. Not many saw her as their rightful Queen. The dens had survived restoration and the dens had held the country together.

The air in the cave was cooler, the ceiling above punctuated every so often with a tunnel that let in verdant light from above. Rainwater trickled down the walls.

Millani's tail swayed behind her. "Trainees are assigned a burrow. You will eat with your fellow trainees, you will spar with them, and eventually you may die with them. Only three from each burrow will become godkillers."

I wanted to ask how many converts there were to a burrow, but I held my tongue. I would find out soon enough.

"This is my burrow. You've been assigned to me." She opened a door and we stepped into a long and low cavern, cots lining the walls. Tables and chairs sat in a corner, along with several basins of water. An opening in the center of the room let in light, a large grate beneath it redirecting any rain. This was also, apparently, the spot where the trainees sparred. Metal clanged as feet danced over the grate, as bodies were slammed into it, the cross-hatch pattern pressing indelibly into flesh. Twenty, at least, though dizzy anticipation made it hard to count.

Millani called to the converts. "Line up!"

They fell into a line facing us. All five kinds of altered were represented by this group – the winged ones, the scaled ones, the horned ones, the wood-rock ones and the furred ones. There had always been altered in Kashan, though only a few who'd found some way through the barrier from Cressima or other realms.

They stood with the sort of confidence and competence I'd always admired in my older sister. Muscled limbs shone with sweat, wooden knives held tightly. I could feel myself shrinking, falling behind Millani as though I could hide.

"This is Rasha. She is the last convert to join this burrow. Your cohort is now complete." Millani strode down the line, leaving me exposed to so many curious gazes. "These are the altered you will fight against. These are the altered you will fight with." She studied them, looking each of them in the eye. "Kluehnn will meet with you now." Her gaze flicked to a wood-rock altered and she nodded. The girl's skin was rough as tree bark, her eyes like two polished pebbles.

They left the room together, leaving me with the rest of the converts, all of them sizing me up. I avoided their gazes, finding an undisturbed bed near the door. I had nothing to bring with me except the clothes I already wore, so I sat and patted the hard pillow as though that might improve the situation. This was what I'd chosen, I reminded myself. This was my *choice*.

"The new one's bait." The voice echoed off the stone walls.

My gaze flicked up to meet the sharp hazel eyes of a winged altered. It was hard to tell once you were altered, but he looked like he had Cressiman blood in him, just as I did. Angry words tangled in my throat, getting mixed up somewhere and feeling frighteningly like tears.

He waited for a moment for a response, and when I said nothing, he went on. "Bait means you're just here to test our fighting instincts. To get the rest of us used to killing. You're not here to win."

I know what it means. My mouth opened, but the words wouldn't come. Instead, horrifyingly, I felt the lullaby rise, the only thing that had given me comfort in those early days when Mimi had died and then Maman had left us.

"What's that, are you *singing?*"

I swallowed the tune and pushed off from the bed. "I'm not bait. I'm here just the same as you. To become a godkiller."

He snorted, stalking closer, his black wings tucked close to his back. He tossed me the wooden knife in his hands. To my relief, I caught it.

"Prove it." He opened his arms wide. His chest was bare, his shoulders flecked with tiny feathers. His fingers ended in claws.

Millani hadn't given me any direction on what I was to do once I was in the burrow. I'd joined in the sparring classes in the den in my spare time, and while the instructors there had always praised my efforts, I'd not had a devout family. I'd not had private tutors.

The man before me might have been wearing only pants, but even those looked soft, the seams neat, the stitches small. I wondered where his money had come from. Had his family bred the prized Kashani horses? Had they owned herds of black camels, or had they owned mines?

"Come on . . ." his lip curled in a sneer, "bait."

I lunged forward, striking for his chest. In the next moment my cheek was pressed to the cold stone floor, his foot scraping against my scalp. My arm ached and so did my knee. I couldn't remember how he'd struck me, he'd moved so quickly. The wooden knife that had been in my hand was now underneath one of the beds, still wobbling.

The ringing in my ears faded, replaced by the sound of laughter.

I'd make him pay for this. If I survived, I'd make him pay. I swallowed the tears at the back of my throat and waited for his foot to lift. I was not Hakara. I knew when I'd been bested.

"Rasha."

The boy's foot moved away and I pushed myself into a crouch. Millani stood in the doorway, the rock-wood altered girl slipping past her and into the burrow. "Kluehnn will see you now."

No admonishment of the winged boy; no comforting words for me. She only turned away, expecting me to follow. I'd thought there was nothing left in me to crush, yet I felt my heart compress anyways, buried into the dark spaces between tree roots. I'd learned across the years that it didn't matter what was going on inside of me. What mattered was what I made of this opportunity. Hakara might be strong through and through, but I could make a shell for myself; I could hide the hurts in a place no one could see. I lifted my chin, striding after Millani and into the deeper tunnels of the den.

I'd seen a god before, in Kashan, while I'd waited for Hakara to return from the sea. I'd heard shouts and had lifted the tent flap to see a great horned man thundering through our encampment, a lithe little godkiller on his heels. I'd watched the air shimmer around him as he drew aether from below, the dust lifting at his feet. Two golden swords had formed in his hands and he'd turned to face his pursuer. It was over quicker than I'd expected, the godkiller's knife lodged in the god's throat, his blood spreading like an oil slick over the ground.

But Kluehnn was the one true god; he was no petty god

wandering the earth without followers. A part of me wished to flee, but as Millani had said, there was no turning back now. I let my feet lead me forward, my mind in an adrenaline-fueled haze.

"Here." She stopped at a small, nondescript door. "He has risen to greet you." I waited, but she only gestured me forward. "You go in alone."

The doorknob was cold to the touch. The cave beyond had no skylights. A single lamp adorned the wall to my right and a pit lay open a few paces ahead of me. I waited by the door, not daring to venture closer; my instincts told me that the pit sank into the very bowels of the earth.

The door clicked softly shut behind me and I was left alone with my terror, my own breath loud in my ears. A scraping sound filled the air, soft at first, and then louder. A hand gripped the edge of the pit. And then another, and another still.

A monster rose from the depths. His skin fluctuated between smoothness and the rough texture of wood and rock. One face stared at me, the eyes black and rimmed with gold, the mouth a discontented slash. Horns graced the top of his head, so many that they looked like the points of a crown. Other eyes and mouths dotted his shoulders and his body. Sharp teeth glinted in the lantern light as multiple pairs of limbs pushed him free of the hole.

"Rasha." His voice was a rasp and it lifted the hairs of my neck. "Millani has told me about you."

I fell to the floor, touching my forehead to the ground. "Kluehnn." He needed no honorific; his name itself was an honorific. One foot landed to the right of my face, and I studied it out of the corner of my eye. I thought I could see the pump of blood through his veins. I thought I could even see the telltale shimmer that revealed him as a god. I opened my mouth to ask what Millani had said about me, but found my tongue dry.

I crouched there for what seemed like forever.

"Rise," he said finally.

I dared not stand, but I unfolded myself, my forehead still cold, my cheek still burning. "Kluehnn, thank you for accepting me as a trainee."

The three-armed, four-legged man before me rose to his full height, his head nearly scraping the ceiling. "You think I make these decisions?" A short, harsh laugh. "Do you think that even this is my true appearance? I am but an aspect of Kluehnn, sent from his body in the homeland of the gods."

I bowed my head again. "Forgive me."

"So pliant," he said. A finger touched the top of my head. "No wonder Millani likes you. But you'll have to move beyond that if you want to survive. If you want to become one of my godkillers. Can you do that, Rasha?"

"Yes." I answered without hesitation.

He sighed, the sound echoing against the walls. "You have no idea what that means, yet you answer. How foolish. How *disappointing*. If I'm to take an interest in you, you must do better than that. Tell me your thoughts."

I flinched, struggling to keep my shell from breaking, to cram the shameful parts of myself away. I'd found a place for myself here, I'd been judged worthy enough to compete. But all I could think about was my time by the border, the ways I'd failed to live up to my imagined self. Small, pitiful, *weak*. Was this what he meant by pliant? I'd followed Hakara everywhere, and now I'd begun to follow Millani. "The others . . . " I stopped, licked my lips, thinking of the altered in my burrow, the way they moved with confidence and held weapons as though they were born to them. "The others are stronger than I am. They said I am bait."

"So this is what you have for me." His lips peeled back, revealing row after row of needle-sharp teeth. "Excuses. Pathetic.

Yes, they'll eat you alive like this, and I will watch and wonder why you wanted to become a godkiller at all. You think this is a place where you'll be coddled and held and told how wonderful you are? You are *nothing*."

Tears stung my eyes and I longed for the warmth of Hakara at my back in the winter mornings. The way she would stroke my hair and we'd share dreams of buying another camel, or even a horse. A bigger, warmer tent. A small library of books for me and fresh greens every day. I'd been so alone since she'd left me by that rock. I was just a body to everyone here, someone at the periphery of their vision – a paper puppet that existed in space but not in anyone's heart or mind. Sometimes I felt that way even to myself.

Hakara would have stood shouting at this god, not caring at all that he was Kluehnn, that she was so much smaller and weaker than he was. She had a will as stony and hard as a mountain, only breaking open to spew hot ash.

The finger at the top of my head moved across my scalp, through the path of tears on my cheeks and down to my chin. He lifted my gaze to his and there was no softness there. "Millani told me of your sister. Was she as weak as you are?"

"Hakara was never weak!" I protested, and then bowed my head again.

The god laughed. "So there *is* some liveliness beneath the meekness. Rasha, you do not have to be nothing. *I* do not believe you have to be."

Something in me fluttered awake. I did not shout at Kluehnn, but I was not Hakara. She was gone, and our dreams of a simple life on the shoreline were gone. I had to make new dreams for myself. "None of the others in my burrow had to survive as I did. None of the others have been alone like I have."

And the god, who had so much more power than I did, gave an

approving nod. A surge of warmth filled me. He let my chin go. "Millani said you were the last one waiting at the border. Saplings are always pliant before their roots dig deep, and the strongest trees grow in the harshest conditions. It has always been so."

I rose to my feet and realized with surprise that this aspect of Kluehnn wasn't that much taller than I was. "I am not a sapling anymore."

"Then show me," he said simply, his tongue settling behind his teeth.

I set my jaw, new purpose flowing through me. My dream couldn't be of camels and tents. But it could be of a knife in my hand. "I will."

He drew back. "I cannot favor you, Rasha, but I hope you are one of the last three standing."

7

Hakara

10 years after the restoration of Kashan and 571 years after the Shattering

Langzu

Kluehnn promises a return to a pre-Shattering world, once the realms are all restored and their inhabitants altered. The aether will stop churning, the barriers will fall. And the way between will once more be open.

I did not pass the gem. It shouldn't have taken more than a day, and yet there I was, staring at an absolutely fruitless pile of shit. Could have made back nearly enough with just that gem alone. I gave the shit one last poke with a stick before giving up. The gem had been one of the largest I'd seen. It wasn't there.

I walked away from the latrine ditch, feeling more than a little unsettled. I didn't feel unwell, but was the gem trapped somewhere in my innards? I pressed at my belly, wondering if there'd be a lump. Nothing.

Altani passed me, studiously avoiding my gaze.

"You can't still be mad, can you?" I called after her. Only her stiff back and a stony silence answered me. "Fine. See you at the next sinkhole then."

I cast another of my crew a can-you-believe-her look, only to have his gaze slide away from mine too. Ever since I'd barely escaped that sinkhole, people had begun to treat me differently. Even Guarin frowned when he looked at me, like I was a problem he didn't know how to solve.

Suppose I should have died then, just to make it all easier to understand. My mind flashed back to that night, the rain cold against my neck, the itching at my shoulders, my arms unreasonably strong as I'd hauled myself bodily out of the hole without any help from Altani. People did strange things when they were desperate – couldn't that be explanation enough?

But sinkhole mining was dangerous and sinkhole miners were a superstitious lot.

We were in a lull. After our last haul Guarin was content to wait for bigger sinkholes instead of chasing the smaller ones. He'd been in charge of this crew for over a decade; he knew that when people burned out, they were far more likely to make mistakes. In these mines, mistakes could cost lives.

I prodded at my belly again, and again felt nothing. Idleness wasn't my strong suit. So it was I found myself in the mess tent, sliding onto a cushion next to Yen, our liaison to Bian, the capital. He was nursing a cup of herbal tea that smelled strongly of grass, his legs crossed as he stared blankly into the middle distance. With his slender neck and knob-kneed legs, he reminded me of a crane that had come to roost. His bodyguard stood by the tent flap, gaze sliding between his charge and the bustle of camp.

The whole tent stank of overcooked amaranth greens. Had to overcook 'em to get the woody stems to be palatable.

"Yen," I said, and then tried again, my voice more friendly. "Yennn."

His gaze slid to mine. "What."

I supposed I deserved that lack of enthusiasm. I'd tried on more than one occasion to persuade him to make an exception to the set rates Langzu paid for the god gems, only to be met with exasperation. That wasn't his *job*, he'd told me over and over.

"What are the god gems for?"

"Why are you asking." He always managed to make questions sound like statements. "The gems are for Kluehnn."

"I know that." I picked at a loose piece of thread in the rug at my feet. "But everyone knows there's a black market and some gems get sold to the clans. No one's ever followed you and tried to take the whole chest of them?"

"They would be executed. The gems are for Kluehnn."

"So? What does *he* do with them?"

Yen shrugged his narrow shoulders. "He's a god. It's not really my business."

"But you've never wondered? This is your whole livelihood and you've never thought to yourself: but *why* am I doing this? What is the purpose?"

He fixed his gaze on mine. "The purpose is to pay the tithe and to ensure that Langzu will be restored. That's all I need to know. That's all *you* need to know."

Maybe someone else would have stopped there, but I never knew when to quit. I patted the rug to get his attention and then drew an imaginary line across it. "So you collect the gems and give them to Kluehnn's priests, and Kluehnn promises to restore our land." I circled a spot on that imaginary line. "But what happens *here*? Why does Kluehnn need or want so many god gems? Is he making an enormous necklace to encircle the world?"

He took a sip of tea and then gazed irritably at the cup, as though blaming it for not staying hot through my relentless questioning. "Do you want my advice."

"No."

"Leave it alone. Do your job. You don't want to fall afoul of Kluehnn's converts or priests, his neophytes or his acolytes. Or even worse, his godkillers."

He rose to his feet, his chest of gems under one arm, taking himself and his clay mug to the other side of the tent.

I followed. "So you just give the god gems to the dens and that's all?"

He whirled, the tea threatening to jump from the mug. "Let me be even more clear, since that's apparently what you require. Stop asking questions, Hakara. Stop. Asking. Questions." He dumped the rest of his tea into the pit by the fire, dunked the mug into the wash bucket and stalked from the tent.

Should have known I wouldn't get any answers out of Yen. The man had the personality of a stick. But there were other places I could ask, and now the thought was rattling in my head, I couldn't get it out. Had the gem gotten stuck in my innards or had it just . . . disappeared? I was in trouble if it had. If I didn't pass it, that meant I couldn't get paid for it, which meant I'd never get to Kashan. To Rasha.

It was morning, but the air outside was already hot, burning off the moisture of the rain. Either way, my shirt was always upsettingly damp, the hair sticking to the back of my neck. Seemed we'd gone straight from winter into summer, and summer in Langzu had a habit of lasting for most of the year. There was no way of telling if a sinkhole would appear anytime soon, but the town was just over the river and there were folk there who might answer my questions. I slid through camp on silent feet. If they were all going to avoid looking at me, might as well take advantage of it. Guarin would kill me if a sinkhole opened up and

I wasn't there, but on the other hand, his promised trip to town hadn't yet materialized.

Could always say I was making good on that.

The river was a churning brown, sediment stirred up from the rain we'd just had; the bridge was a ramshackle thing of wood and rope, the washed-out remains of the previous bridge still littering the banks. I ducked my head as the dirt road turned to gravel. Someone had put a god on a pike on the outskirts of town and I didn't like to stare. This one was tall, or he had been, before he'd been cut in half. His entire lower half was missing, as were his eyes. Long, golden hair was slick with shimmering blood and his skin was as sallow as his hair. His hands grasped at the pike below his ribs, fingers clenching, too weak to remove himself from it. The corded muscles of his arms suggested that he'd been able to fight, though the fact that mortals had defeated him suggested that perhaps he could not. Or maybe he was a pacifist.

It wasn't my business. Sooner or later, one of Kluehnn's dens would send a godkiller to end him and to take what was left back to Kluehnn.

"Please." The god spoke in Kashani. It was uncanny how they knew – the gods always knew.

I rushed past before I could find out what he was pleading for. Before I could feel any pity. I'd heard a storyteller say, once, that all the gods that had lived in Unterra were now dead. The gods we saw were only their offspring, raised in a world that was not their own.

Miners moved in and out of the town, taking some time off or collecting supplies for their camp at the market. They moved in groups – Kashani sticking with other Kashani, the Cressimans easy to pick out by their rosy, pale skin and features as sharp as the mountains they used to live in. Didn't belong in either of those groups. Some of those I thought were Cressimans were probably Albanoran – I didn't really have the best eye for telling them apart – but I could always spot the divers by their cracked and blackened fingertips, the setters by their broad shoulders and abraded palms.

The single salon in town was an older building, one of the few with a tile roof instead of thatch, the copper-colored eave ends molded with the faces of the seven elder gods in repeating rows. Mud clung to the soles of my boots as I trudged up the stairs. Streets here were paved but rarely cleaned, and the rain had made the whole place into a stinking pit. Sweet-smelling hay had been strewn into the gutters, though it didn't mask the faint animal smell left by passing horses and oxen.

The salon was fairly empty this time of day – but that just meant the people inside now were of the more disreputable variety. I couldn't pay for information, but I was pretty good at annoying it out of people. I spotted my target as soon as I entered, neatly stepping over a haphazard patch job on the floorboards. Another liaison from the camps, this one sunk into her cups, her bored, bleary eyes scanning the other patrons. None of the Sovereign's enforcers around her, though her bodyguard sat at the bar, keeping a loose watch. The liaison was middle-aged, soft in body but with a sharp set to her jaw. I let her gaze land on me before I flashed her a smile and approached.

She didn't seem pleased at my company, nor did she seem upset at it, so I let the silence sit for a while as I took my time settling onto the cushion opposite her at the table. It was thin enough I could feel the wood beneath grinding against my bones.

"You're a diver," she said, nodding at my fingers.

"And you're a liaison." I gave a corresponding nod to the chest she held in her lap, the cuff that linked her wrist to it.

"Good to meet you, diver." She lifted her cup in my direction before taking another sip. I could smell it clear across the table – a pungent liquor distilled from local grains. "Are you as bored as I am?"

"It might be time to move to another field. There are fewer sinkholes here these days."

"I've heard another promising area may be starting to the south, near Ruzhi."

I gave a non-committal shrug, trying to think of a way to ease our conversation into the track I wanted. Deciding a moment later I didn't care. If another sinkhole opened and I wasn't back at the camps, Guarin might even follow through with his threat to turn me in. "I was wondering, do you know what Kluehnn does with all the gems he collects from us? The clans want 'em – I've heard they can do all sorts of things with them. But a god? Why?"

She raised an eyebrow. "Quite the conversation-opener."

"Just curious. Why does he want them?"

"People say different things. They say he needs them to restore our lands. They say he uses them to grant the godkillers their power. They say he consumes them. Maybe he does all of that. Maybe he does more."

"Consumes them?" I thought of the bright red gem slipping past my teeth and sliding down my throat, the fizzing sensation of it in my belly.

"Yes. Surely you don't think gods eat the same things as you or me. Can you imagine? A god sitting down to a human feast and biting into a piece of bread?"

I actually *could* imagine that, quite easily, but I held my tongue.

"Ah." She lifted her cup again. "But it's all just gossip. No one knows, except perhaps his highest acolytes or his godkillers."

Another patron spoke up from the table behind her. "You shouldn't talk of such things. Kluehnn is the one true god and the savior of humanity. You want to sit in this rotting hot hole of a realm until the end of time? Or do you want it all fixed and the barriers to come down?"

The door swung open. The breeze that entered with the air turned my blood frigid. I'd known from the god on a pike that a godkiller would soon follow. It seemed that the godkiller had followed *now*. But usually they just tended to their business and then went on their way. What was she doing in the salon?

She had a narrow face, her ears higher and larger than they should have been. Two curling horns adorned the crown of her head. Her golden eyes were as luminous as god gems. They were always altered – the godkillers. One of her clawed hands gripped a staff. The other rested on the jeweled hilt of her knife. The godkilling knife.

I knew, even before her gaze landed on me, that she was here for me. Call it instinct, call it intuition, but that whisper of dread climbing the back of my neck hadn't served me wrong yet. Yen, that bony old shit! Was it him? Had he warned me off questions and then gone straight to the nearest Kluehnn devotee he could find? Another part of me registered, distantly, that he couldn't have done so that quickly. And I couldn't imagine Yen speaking to a godkiller.

I scrambled out of my seat, ducking my head before she looked at me, hoping she didn't recognize me as her target. I was close to the back, in the shadows.

"I'm looking for a diver," the woman said, her voice as cold and smooth as a blade.

I kept my head down and hurried toward the kitchens.

There was always a back way out in the kitchens, and this establishment proved no exception. The cook began to berate me, but I waved him off; I'd be out of his way soon enough. I dodged a crate of cabbages before shoving through the back door and into the morning.

The warm, dry air was no comfort to my lungs. My feet kept carrying me forward though I wasn't sure where I was going. She might not be looking for me. She was looking for a diver. Not me specifically. But I was still feeling the unease from my narrow escape and I couldn't convince myself. I needed to get out of here. I needed to lie low until whatever godly attention I'd unwittingly attracted had passed.

There was money in my hidden stash still. I hurried toward the road to the mining camps, doing my best to lose myself among the others traversing this small town. There were other miners here, other divers. If all the godkiller had to go off was that the object of her search was a diver, then I had time. My heartbeat slowed as I considered my options.

The godkiller stepped into my path.

Her ears flicked back and forward again, her golden eyes narrowing as they fixed on me. I made quick study of the buildings on either side of us. Both were private residences, their doors shut. Well, damn.

"Come with me and you won't be hurt." Her voice cut through the murmur of the people around us, all of whom decided suddenly they had better places to be.

I wasn't here legally, I'd accidentally swallowed one of Kluehnn's precious gems the other night, and I somehow, briefly, had a stronger set of arms. Whatever Kluehnn and the godkillers wanted with me, I couldn't imagine it was to sit me down somewhere with a cup of tea for a nice chat.

Besides, going with her meant giving up, and I just wasn't very good at that. There was always a slim chance I could make it out. I took it.

I feinted to the left and then sprinted for the building on the right.

A fair bit of luck graced me, as the door wasn't locked. I burst into the small living space, a startled face looking up from his sewing. There might not be a back entrance, but there was an overhang on the second story and I could jump off from there. I made for the stairs.

A clawed hand grasped my upper arm.

I'd known godkillers were quick, but wasn't I quick too? Not quick enough, apparently. I twisted my arm and her grip held firm. "Come quietly." Her voice sounded next to my ear. Too damn close. Oh, I'd give her quietly. I screamed, I kicked, I flailed. I even tried to bite the hand that held me, but she just whipped it away and then replaced it before I could run.

And still she dragged me back out of the house and into the street, like a fish caught on a line, my struggles slowly diminishing as my strength ran out.

She swung me about until my back was facing her, pulled my arms, and before I could turn, I felt a rope tightening around my wrists. A few people watched, their gazes flitting away and then back. One person met my eyes. Altani. She'd risked going to town too. Her big shoulders were hunched. She stood by a street stall, her recent purchase of roasted carrots still steaming.

All I needed was a distraction.

I tried to keep her gaze as the godkiller secured her hold on me, as she drew the knots closed. If Altani shouted, if she threw her carrots, if she did something, *anything*, I could break free. I knew it. Altani must have known it too. Hadn't we had some good times together, made some memories? She'd left me in the pit, but she'd had to. Surely she wouldn't leave me to this fate too, not when she had a second chance.

Yet she bowed her head and turned those big shoulders deliberately away.

I was too breathless to scream anymore. The godkiller marched me down the street and to the edge of town.

An oxcart stood by the pike that had once held the god. His body was now splayed across the bed of it, blood seeping into wooden boards that looked as though they'd already been stained, and more than once. Rust bloomed across the surface in deepening shades.

She didn't ask me to climb into the back; she lifted me bodily inside as though I were a prize, then, when I tried to hop back out again, jerked on the rope. I fell, my shoulder soaking in the sticky, glittering blood of the god, my face staring into his sightless one. I barely heard the hiss of rope as she tied my wrists to the metal bar mounted on the side of the wagon.

I knew godkillers didn't just take gods' corpses. They took people too sometimes, though no one spoke much of it. They were stories you told to someone to scare them at night, not anything anyone thought might actually happen to them.

"I thought you weren't going to hurt me!" I called to the godkiller as she climbed behind the ox. She settled into her seat as the animal grunted and tossed its head, the multiple eyes sewn onto the back of her robe staring at me unblinking.

Her shoulders heaved as she sighed. "What do you have, a bruise?"

I pushed myself into a sitting position, the blood on my shoulder dripping down my bicep. "You could have broken my arm."

A hand appeared at the side of the cart, a knife held tight between the fingers. The blade began to saw away at the rope. I looked to the godkiller – who hadn't noticed – and then back at that hand.

"I could have. If I'd wanted to."

Someone was here to get me out. I didn't know who – Altani? – but I knew all I had to do was to keep the godkiller talking for a little bit. Slow her down. She picked up the whip.

I cleared my throat. "What does Kluehnn want with a mortal like me anyways? I'm not a god."

She didn't turn. "Clearly you are not."

"Does Kluehnn pay you? Do you get a decent salary?"

This time she whirled in her seat, her golden eyes narrow. "What?"

The hand retreated just in time, but I could see, out of the corner of my eye, that the rope was cut. Sweat beaded in the small of my back, itching. I needed her to not notice. Just a moment more. "If you're taking me to a den, I want to know my job prospects."

She snorted and turned her attention back to the ox. I crouched low in the cart, sliding my feet along the blood-slicked floor, and dropped off the back as she drove away.

It wasn't Altani. It was that same man I'd seen by the sinkhole the night I'd popped out like my legs had been on springs. The one who'd lingered at the edge of our group, listening as I'd tried to explain away what had happened. Black eyes, goatee, crooked nose, long dark hair swept into a ponytail.

His hand clamped around my arm, pulling me toward him. "She'll notice you're gone soon. But I can get you away if you come with me." He lifted a bag and gestured to my head.

Well, *shit*. Should have known there'd be a catch. I made a split-second decision. "Fine."

The bag dropped over my head, shrouding the world in darkness.

8

Mullayne

10 years after the restoration of Kashan
and 571 years after the Shattering

Langzu – a cave system west of Ruzhi

Are there gods still in Unterra, waiting for their feckless brethren to return? No one has been to Unterra since Tolemne's time. We don't know what's down there — if the palaces and the inner star and the sea still exist, or if they're all gone.

The only way to know is to find Tolemne's Path. To walk it all the way to the center.

Mullayne had always believed himself capable. If someone else had managed to accomplish something, he should be able to do it too, as long as he put his mind to it. In his forty-three years, this had nearly always proved true. He'd experimented and extrapolated and, using his filters, could safely descend into the earth past the first aerocline. More importantly, he could stay there.

He adjusted the mask over his nose and mouth, the sealant on the sides more than a little itchy with sweat. What was more questionable was whether Tolemne had also utilized filters when he'd made his way to the center of the earth. Was this how that journey had been accomplished? The records were more stories than actual records, the details vague. Mull held his breath and scratched at his stubble. He wasn't sure what was making him sweat more — the exertion of the descent or the fact that Pont, his muscle and his right-hand man, would not stop shouting.

"It's a waste of time," he was saying. "Another dead end, Mull. I don't care what your sources or your books have said. This isn't Tolemne's Path. It can't be. How many times have you come to us, insistent that *this* time you'd found the right tunnels?" Even muffled through the filter, Pont was *loud*. "And how many times did it turn out you were wrong?"

"Seven," Mull answered briskly.

Pont drew back. "By all the elder gods, has it been *that* many times?"

Mull let out an impatient huff of breath, tracing a finger down the map he'd laid in front of him. The lamp next to it threw everything into sharp relief. Pont was putting on a show because that was who he was. He'd done this each of the seven times they'd tried to find the entrance to Tolemne's Path. Granted, he had been right each of those times, and Mull had been wrong.

But this time, Mull was right. There were only so many places the entrance could be. Someone had come along with a stone tablet from Kashan before it had been restored, and he'd bought it — for a pricier sum than he perhaps should have. But what was important was that it had contained more details about where Tolemne had started and had even had a rudimentary map of the cave system. All his research had led here, to Langzu — which was fortunate, since this realm was Mull's home. At the confluence of two rivers, it had said. Two days west of Ruzhi. Taking into account the means of travel back in those days, and the fact that one of those rivers was now a dried-up riverbed, Mull had been able to pinpoint a cave system that looked promising.

"The only reason I came was because you promised this would be the last time. You said that the last time."

"So who is the fool then, you or me?" Mull said lightly.

Imeah, next to him, touched his arm in warning. That sobered him. She was his whole reason for this venture. The degenerative illness she was suffering had thus far resisted every single treatment the doctors had tried, and even obscure ones Mull had researched from realms they'd long since lost contact with. This was his last chance to see her cured.

"The map is old. Caves shift and change." He spoke quickly, trying to erase the harshness of his prior words. Imeah might have been his oldest friend, but Pont was his second oldest. When Mull had expressed interest in learning the Cressiman language, his parents had found him a full-blooded Cressiman as a tutor. Sure, Pont had been a wrestler and not a teacher, but Mull had always been good at prying information out of sources.

Pont was only five years older than Mull and they'd become fast friends. More like brothers. Which meant they fought like brothers too. Even so, Mullayne had never once pulled rank on him. Pont had once asked him why, and Mull had only blinked, startled. He'd never really thought of it as an option – not out of any idealism, but because rank was a thing he'd simply forgotten.

He'd always been single-minded.

There were two tunnels branching in front of them where the map indicated three. He was vaguely aware of the rest of his team shifting uncomfortably behind him, unsettled by Pont's words. Imeah turned from him, her cane tapping against the cave floor as she went to reassure the others. "Give him just a moment, he'll figure this out. He always does."

One of the tunnels had caved in, but the entire cavern was rocky and he couldn't tell whether one pile of rocks was the result of a more recent collapse or just a thing that had been there since the beginning. They were meant to take the center tunnel. Given how far apart the two remaining tunnels were, he'd wager that it wasn't the center tunnel that had collapsed – though he also knew he couldn't trust an ancient map to be to scale.

So was it the right tunnel or the left one?

Oh, to the aether with it all. "It's that one," he said, pointing to the left. "The positioning of the rocks on the opposite side indicates a recent collapse. You can see the angle of the pile and the fact that the largest rocks are situated on top. Plus the composition of the stone here shows . . ."

He knew no such things, but he watched Pont's eyes glaze over as he droned on about fractures and sediment.

"Fine," Pont said. "If you're sure."

He brushed past Mull and into the left tunnel. It was the taller one and looked more inviting besides. Might as well give it a try. The last of his crew unspooled a length of string so that they could easily find their way back. Mullayne went to Imeah and offered her his arm, though she waved it off.

"So much bother for one person," she said, her voice light.

"Not just any one person," he said. "You."

"I'm blushing," she said dryly.

"Say you wouldn't do the same for me," Mull pressed as they passed into the tunnel. The air behind his filter was thin and sweet, but he could feel the thickness of the aether between his fingers.

"I wouldn't." She let out a sigh. A few strands of black hair stuck to her forehead, dark veins against her pale skin; the rest of her hair was pulled back into a plaited tail. Mull couldn't see her mouth, but he knew as surely as he knew his own expression that she'd pressed her lips together. "I don't want to argue with you again. I'm here. That should be enough."

His heart constricted. "I don't want ... I don't want you to *resent* me for it." He waited a moment as Imeah navigated an uneven spot of ground.

She was smiling now beneath the filter. He could see it in her eyes. "I don't. I couldn't. But this is tiring, friend."

He turned his gaze back to Pont's broad back at the front, unable to meet Imeah's gaze any longer. Every time he did, he remembered her screaming at him that she was done being prodded at by strange doctors. She was *done* watching him search fruitlessly for cures that did not exist. She wanted to enjoy whatever life she had left, to move on.

He'd begged. He wasn't proud of it. But there was too much shared history for him to let her go so easily. His older brother, the heir to his clan's leadership, had always been given the best of everything. Pont had been directed to teach him Cressiman too. But Mull's friendship with Imeah had always been a bright spot in his life, a thing all his own. They'd met at a festival as children and had promptly decided to run away together, even if they were from different clans. Their parents had given them both Cressiman names – it had been the fashion that year – and they'd felt so alienated by it that they'd bonded quite intensely.

They hadn't gotten far, both of them losing their nerve, but that didn't matter. Their parents had tolerated and even encouraged their friendship, perhaps seeing some political gain to be had down the road. Mull didn't give a shit about politics, though, so whatever hopes they'd nurtured had withered.

If this didn't work, if they didn't find the way Tolemne had taken to the home of the gods, he'd let it go. He'd let *her* go. He couldn't let this become all about himself and what he needed. Only he was certain that Imeah needed this too. She just . . . she was just giving up too easily.

"You should make your peace with Pont," she said, nudging his shoulder with hers. "If this is truly Tolemne's Path and we go all the way to the center, you'll need him. The tales say the tunnels aren't empty."

"They're tales."

"Tales you believe have a grain of truth in them."

Mull touched her arm in acknowledgment, then brushed past the others to join Pont at the front. "This is the right path. And I need you with me," he said.

Pont didn't look at him, broad shoulders slightly hunched, lamp held in front of him. His jaw was as sharp as the surrounding rock, the lamplight turning his brown hair into gold. "How long have we known each other, Mull?"

"Twenty-six years and eighteen and a half days."

Pont closed his eyes briefly, touching a hand to his forehead as though soothing away an ache. "Fine, yes. I trust your count better than mine." He shook his head. "Don't you think I'd know by now when you're lying? You might be able to convince everyone else, but they've only known you for the span of a decade at most. We've both done enough spelunking in our lives to know that caves are dangerous, even with the filters. It's not safe to go traipsing down unmarked tunnels."

"They're marked." Mull's hand went to the map he'd lifted from the stone tablet.

"You and I both know you're not sure which tunnel we've actually taken."

Mull said nothing.

"Fine. You don't owe me anything. Maybe you don't even owe the rest of them anything; they've each got their own reasons for following you on this fool's errand. But Imeah deserves better than this."

"Better than a cure?" He could hear the brittleness in his own voice, on the edge of snapping.

"We should turn back. I know it. You know it too."

"It's only been a day and a half."

"And it'll only be a day and a half back again."

They both fell to silence as the tunnel widened into a cavern. The group fanned out. There had been a cavern on the map Mull had copied. That could mean they were on the right track. He couldn't know for sure. So much of this was conjecture, and he'd dragged Imeah along based purely on that. Perhaps Pont was right. He could always trust Imeah with his deepest fears and he could always trust Pont to tell him the truth, no matter how unsavory it was.

"Mull!" Jeeoon beckoned from the left side of the cavern with one wiry arm. "You need to see this." She sounded excited. Jeeoon rarely sounded excited. Even during their last expedition, when they'd encountered a narrow ten-span drop absolutely lousy with spiders as big as Mull's head, she'd only lifted the coil from her shoulder and said, "Not enough rope."

His breath hitched in his throat and he rushed toward her, his lantern swinging so wildly that the flame nearly extinguished. He opened his mouth to ask what she'd found and let the words die in his throat.

The scorched remains of an ancient cookfire marred the floor. Stones still ringed the area; a few discarded bones off to the side. Someone had been here. Someone had slept here. And then his gaze lifted to the wall where Jeeoon stood.

Something was carved into the wall there, in Old Albanoran. His gaze passed over the words, barely reading them. This had to be a message from Tolemne himself.

They'd taken the correct branch in the tunnels. They were walking in the footsteps of a legend – the very man who'd bargained with Kluehnn before the Shattering, who had brought restoration to the world.

"Well?" Pont came up behind him. "What does it say?"

"It'll take me time to translate, but I think this is Tolemne's writing carved into the wall."

Excited murmurs filled the cavern.

"You sure you want to stay down here? You don't even know what that says yet, and you'll be away from your workshop for longer," Pont said in Mull's ear. "I know it brings in a good deal of revenue for your clan. You sure you don't want to go back, get more supplies and *then* return?"

"We have enough," Mull said. He didn't know how quickly Imeah's condition would deteriorate. She had good days and bad, but even on her good days he could tell she still had balance issues and numbness in her legs. It had to be now. "Besides, I left the workshop in good hands. She'll make sure everything is kept in order. At least, I hope she will." Yes, she was a bit erratic, and he never quite knew what she was playing at on any given day, but she'd been the only one he could think of at the time.

Pont put a heavy hand on his shoulder. "*She?* Who is 'she'? Wait, who *exactly* did you leave it with?"

"My cousin," Mull said, with more lightness than he felt. "Sheuan Sim."

9

Sheuan

10 years after the restoration of Kashan
and 571 years after the Shattering

Langzu - inner Bian

*In the inner sanctum of Unterra, a god was only born when
another died. On the surface, beneath the vast and open
skies, in lands that stretched as far as the eye could see, the
gods could multiply beyond their original numbers.*
   And so they sought to take these lands for their own.

Sheuan Sim watched the young man, trying to ascertain
exactly who he wanted her to be. Her tutor had drilled into
her this simple fact: a person would fall all over themselves to
help someone they felt a rapport with, and rapport could be
manufactured.

So she tested him as she led him around the workshop, edging
into different personae, seeing which one he responded to the
most. It wasn't merely a matter of experimentation. There were
only so many facets you could show before your subject started

to feel you were erratic rather than charming. So she watched him, studied his gestures, his replies.

"What does this one do?" Nimao touched a wooden contraption, flicking at the metal gears. He was a little older than she was, though he acted younger. Sheltered – a plant cultured and cultivated with gentle fingers. His jaw was sharp, his lips generous, his black hair half bound up into a bun.

Oh, if Mull were here, he would give the man a scathing look and tell him to keep his hands to himself. He'd scowl, muttering that Nimao wouldn't understand if he told him.

And that was why Mull didn't make nearly as large a profit as he could.

"That one?" Sheuan ran her hand along the wood, noting the way his eyes followed her fingers. She made her touch into a caress and saw his pupils dilate. Ah, so *that* would be the play here. Dull. Simple. Disappointing. But effective. She preferred the targets that could be charmed by skill, by words, by games. But he was nearly as young as she was, and she'd do whatever she had to. Her family was counting on her. "You have a setter and a diver for the sinkhole mines. One to set the rope and haul, and the other to dive. This takes the place of a setter."

"Does it now?" He raised a brow.

She pulled the lever, ratcheted it back until it clicked into place. Then she released it. Two metal stakes drove hard into the tabletop. Mull would bemoan the damage, but Sheuan knew: sometimes a flashy display was the clincher in a deal, and Nimao seemed the sort of man who appreciated a flashy display. So she flashed him a smile, too. Then she maneuvered another lever, which worked a clamp. "That grabs the rope. You still need someone to work the crank, but they don't need to be as big or as strong as a setter. Your workforce won't need to be as specialized. Which means cheaper labor."

"Remarkable," Nimao said. He touched the machine again and Sheuan removed her hand, though not before "accidentally" brushing the tops of his fingers. Inwardly, she grimaced. She was so much more than just a pretty face. Not that she had compunctions about using said prettiness. He cleared his throat. "But what about when the sinkhole collapses? How do you move this contraption out of the way in time?"

She showed him. "It removes the spikes faster than a setter can. And it's on wheels. Keep the axle greased and it moves better than any carriage or wagon."

"How much?"

"Fifteen parcels." Mull didn't want to sell it yet – he'd told her as he'd rambled on about each of his contraptions that he wanted to find a way to automate the crank. Once he figured that out, he wanted to sell it for ten parcels. But her cousin was somewhere near Ruzhi, traipsing after rumors again, certain this time he had found the entrance to Tolemne's Path. Always chasing legends and stories, that one. He'd given her vague answers when she'd probed for when he'd be back and asked that she keep his true whereabouts from his parents. They thought he'd gone off to court some other noble. Sheuan wasn't one to complain – not when he'd given her free rein over the precious asset of another clan. Mull wasn't supposed to associate so closely with the Sim clan, and propriety dictated that he should have put someone from his own clan in charge, but when had Mull ever cared about the delicacies of politics? Every time they met, he greeted her like a brother – a kiss to the forehead and a friendly embrace – even though he should have ignored her as a pariah. That was one connection she knew would only fray due to her own machinations. He couldn't get angry over an early sale, though, could he? The point of the workshop was to make money.

Besides, if she sold the contraption for fifteen, she could tell him she'd sold it for eleven and skim off the top. Four parcels would be a nice addition to the money he'd paid her to watch over his workshop, and he'd be netting more than he'd thought he would.

"Ten parcels," Nimao countered.

She gave him another winning smile. "Fifteen. It'll revolutionize sinkhole mining. Don't you want to be the first one?"

He raised his hands. "Ah, you've outdone me. Fine."

He'd given in easier than she'd expected, and she knew in that moment that he *liked* to be outdone. Dominated. Something unexpected sparked within her, warming to him. His hands were still slightly lifted, his lips a soft invitation. One step closer and she could slide her fingers around his wrist. She imagined his startled, half-hearted retreat, his back meeting the wall, his quickening pulse beneath her palm. Her heart beat faster in response. Oh, she *wanted* it. There was no one else in the workshop; she could take this small pleasure. But then what would she do afterward?

She swallowed, focusing on the wood and dust and debris, forcing herself to flick through the possibilities. There was no future in which this sort of tryst proved more than a pointless distraction. She'd let herself be distracted before and it had only ever wasted time. The moment passed; she filed the information away. It could be useful if she ever needed anything else from Nimao, or it could be information she sold to someone else. Her mind was a catalog of traits and flaws and rumors, each tucked away neatly, ready to be brought into the light when it was most needed.

She was the last weapon her clan had against downfall, and she would hone herself to a cutting edge. It was the only way she would survive. It was the only way *they* would survive. If it was known exactly how tight their coffers were, the Sim clan would fall. After the Sovereign had united the clans, he'd forbidden open warfare, but there were hidden ways to cut at an enemy. And one couldn't simply wave away decades of enmity. The Sims clan had already been whittled away by defectors, by marriages like the one Mull's father had entered into, by the natural attrition of aging and death. If they lost the protection of their royal status, the vultures would quickly clean their bones.

It had begun with her father's fall from grace. Langzu's Sovereign had executed him before he could pick up the pieces himself. Bitterness clung to the back of Sheuan's tongue, and she wasn't sure if it was the lingering sawdust or her memories that made it so.

Embezzlement. A trumped-up charge, she was sure of it. Her father had been a loyal trade minister. Back then, her family hadn't needed the money. But whatever back-channel bargains and betrayals he'd orchestrated had finally run afoul of the wrong parties. She'd searched and researched and had found no trace of the manufactured evidence among any of the other clans.

Which meant her father had been framed by the Sovereign himself.

She tapped a nail against one of the tabletops, trying to center herself. "I'll have the workers package it up for you and deliver it to your house."

He wouldn't chase her, not overmuch, but he licked his lips and tried again. "Are there any other wonders left in this workshop?"

"Plenty." She touched his shoulder to guide him, but the tension had fizzled out, a mist evaporating into the afternoon sun. Perhaps there were other plays she could make here. The four parcels' profit was nice, but connections were richer and more profitable in the end. "Why, Liyana Juitsi was in here the other day, and she bought two of the spice grinders for her kitchens."

"Liyana?" If Nimao were a dog, his ears would have pricked. Liyana was pretty and young and *rich*, and that last bit mattered a half more than the other two. A union between the Risho clan and the Juitsi clan would be fortunate for both. "You know her? Could you introduce us?"

Sheuan knew her in the sense that they'd bumped into one another at a party once, and she'd whispered a soft and modest apology to Liyana's indignant face, though the girl had been the one to step on *her* toes first. "Of course I know her. I'd be happy to arrange an introduction."

More scrambling, more maneuvering. She'd have to find a way into Liyana's circle to fulfill this promise. It would be difficult, especially with her family's reputation, but it could be done, and she'd net herself a solid ally if she pulled this off. Her gaze fell to Nimao's wrist as she briefly wondered if Liyana could truly make him happy, or if he'd always seek to meet his needs elsewhere.

"What about that box? What's in there?"

Mullayne's desk lay in the corner of the workshop, beneath a large window that she'd often caught him gazing out of. She had teased him that all he did all day was dream about being outside, which he'd stiffly countered with the explanation that watching passers-by helped him concentrate. He'd still laughed when she'd done a fair impression of him at his table, his chin in his hand, dolefully glaring at the street outside.

When she was with Mull, she only rarely felt the need to be someone else. He simply didn't care about politics, and she was steeped in them by necessity. Yet there were still places in her mind and heart she closed off.

Nimao pointed and Sheuan's gaze followed. There was a box wedged between the chair and the wall, two handspans tall and twice as wide. She passed him, putting herself between him and the desk. "You have a sharp eye. That's Mull's desk. It's where the creator himself works on his secret projects. All before he's ready to let anyone else see."

"Must be something interesting in there." He gave her a mischievous sidelong look. "Shall we?"

She really was only supposed to sell the items Mull had approved of. He was going to *murder* her when he got back. With his eyes. Which somehow felt a worse fate than being murdered by his hands. She shrugged off the feeling. "A look can't hurt."

If she couldn't swing an introduction to Liyana, Nimao might at least remember her fondly for this small bit of companionable trespassing. So she obliged, striding to the desk and crouching to pull out the box.

A note was tacked to the top of it, Mull's handwriting stating clearly: *DO NOT TOUCH*. There was another sheet beneath it, so she peeled the top one back. *SHEUAN I REALLY MEAN IT.*

The lid slid easily to the side. If he'd not wanted her to snoop, he should have made it a little more difficult to open. Really made her take the time so that guilt could seep between the cracks. Granted, she didn't have many cracks.

A sheaf of paper lay inside, bound on one side with twine. Sketches and notes covered every page, calculations she couldn't quite understand. She pushed the paper to one side and found several oddly shaped lumps beneath, ribbon attached to them. They were somewhat round, gray, one side forming a peak. The light from the window came in at an angle, not quite illuminating the bottom of the box.

Nimao peered over her shoulder as she reached out.

A touch was all it took. They were not lumps. They were cloth – layers of it, with something rubbery at the edges. The outer layer felt soft and expensive. Silk.

Masks. Meant to be worn over the nose and mouth.

She slid the box shut with a snap, her heartbeat pounding faster than it had with Nimao.

"What are they?" His voice sounded at her ear.

Was she truly playing him, or had he played her? Sometimes she became too confident in her skill, too comfortable with her ability to slide in and out of social circles, to get people to like the persona she'd assumed.

"I don't know. I'm not sure." Oh, but she did know. Mull had always wondered how Tolemne had made it to the realm of the gods. How had he traipsed through one layer of aether and then past the second aerocline without going completely mad? Without the toxic air filling his blood and killing him? Theologians often preached that the people back then were hardier, stronger, that the changed landscape had weakened each subsequent generation, made their lungs more vulnerable to aether.

But Mull had found another way. And he'd gone to test it.

Imeah hadn't accompanied him for some fresh air. She'd gone because they intended not just to discover Tolemne's Path, but to follow it into the depths of the earth. To find any gods left in their homeland, in the seat of the gods' power. To ask them for a boon.

Mull, by all the gods, what are you doing?

The water clock by the door chimed to mark the half-hour. Sheuan startled. Had she missed the hour mark?

Nimao groaned. Apparently he had too. "Ah, shit. I'll be late." He brushed sawdust from the front of his tunic. "Are you going?" He caught himself, too late.

The Sovereign's naming-day party. The Sovereign wouldn't have invited her, a youthful member of a disintegrating royal clan, one whose family member had embezzled funds from his coffers. One whose father he'd executed.

"Ah." Nimao lifted a finger, trying to move past the blunder. "I'll see you later, then? Send a letter. I'd still love that introduction to Liyana."

And then he was rushing out of the workshop, the setting sun briefly illuminating the doorstep.

Sheuan hurried to lock the door behind him, finding the bag she'd stowed behind a bench. She had her own preparations to make. The dress inside was dark, simple, high-collared, but sleeveless to accommodate the heat of an early summer. Both sides were split to mid-thigh to allow for movement while still having the appearance of formality. Blooming cherry branches wound around the bodice, the embroidery a nod to the Sovereign's seal.

Everyone important would be at the naming-day party, and the Sovereign would be occupied by the crush of his admirers. His guards would be mostly in the great hall, ensuring no one got too close or too familiar. The rest of the castle would be nearly empty. Including the Sovereign's study.

Nimao was correct. She had not been invited.

Which didn't mean, of course, that she wasn't going to go.

10

Nioanen

52 years before the Shattering

Albanore - the Vast Plains

Just as there are three layers to the world — the sky, the ground and the hollow within — there are three peoples. There are the mortals, with their quick lives. There are the gods, who once lived at the core of this world and whose lives are timeless. And then there are those between. The ones reshaped by Kluehnn's will.

The altered.

Nioanen fled across an alien landscape, a cat curled in his arms. The moon seemed too bright, the air too thin, the sky a thing he might fall into if he dared to open his wings to it. But more than that, flying into the skies would mean he was not taking a momentary pause from the battle. It would mean he was retreating. Farther from home, farther from the tunnels and the vast caverns and the welcome of the warm earth. The thought burrowed into his heart and hollowed it from the inside out.

The cat stretched his neck and sniffed. "They're behind us and gaining. You should take flight."

"We were meant to push Kluehnn back. We were meant to go *home*. This was supposed to be our last stand."

Needle-sharp teeth nipped at his arm. "And it still will be if you don't get us out of here. Quickly. I'll distract them."

Nioanen felt the shift in the air, the *thickness* of it, as his companion summoned aether from deep within the earth. He caught the metallic whiff of magic before the cat inhaled it, his fur standing on end. Once, magic had smelled to him of baking bread and dewy moss. Now the scent always reminded him of blood and steel.

Irael scrambled to his shoulder. "*Now*, Nioanen."

He snapped out his wings and leapt into the skies just as the cat shifted into a bird that shot out spiny feathers from its tail. A blazing arrow grazed his left shoulder, but then they were up and away, soaring toward the smoke-laden clouds.

It always smelled like burning here.

He hit the clouds and every breath was sharp and aching. The world beneath was half obscured, but Nioanen knew what he would see: ash and gray and the stunted remains of vegetation. The cities of the mortals, all metal and stone, towers rising like fingers toward the skies. Gray and black vehicles hovering above the earth, mounted with magical weapons. Vast machines eating magic and pumping out everything the mortals felt was necessary for a comfortable life. Once, the surface had been lush, a kaleidoscope of green, punctuated with the reds, blacks and golds of loam and rock. The anger he felt was muted.

It was not his fault. It was not the fault of any of the gods. But perhaps Kluehnn was right and they'd let this happen. They'd let the mortals above pillage and burn, using the vast above-ground branches of the Numinar trees to fuel their magical machines and opulent lifestyles. It had never bothered him until the roots and the trees below had started to wither. Until it had started to affect *him*. Perhaps it should have.

Treasonous thoughts. Kluehnn had chased the gods to the surface in the first place. According to him, both the gods and the mortals were to blame for the current environment. The gods had done nothing to repair the damage and needed to be punished. The mortals needed to be changed so that their weakness and greed would never harm the world again.

Kluehnn had told the mortals that the gods were invading them, but where else were the gods supposed to go with Kluehnn forcing them out of their home? Not that all of Nioanen's brethren had comported themselves honorably on the surface. Some of them had killed indiscriminately, insisting that this broken world was solely the fault of the people above. The mortals had reason for fear and hate. It ... wasn't simple, this war they'd found themselves in. Whatever his complicated feelings about the man, Kluehnn was right: the land above was nigh uninhabitable, a result of cascading ecological reactions that cracked the earth and made the air hot. That sent rain and floods and rising oceans.

But it was not the role of the gods to impose limits.

"You're spiraling again, aren't you?" The bird shifted back into a cat. "One bad thought leading to another."

And why wouldn't he be? They'd lost. They'd *lost*. Nioanen clenched his teeth, clutching the creature tighter to his sternum as he rose higher. "It would be easier if Kluehnn were fighting alone, or even just alongside mortals, if other gods had not joined him. I don't know why they have; in the end he will just consume them."

"We left many dead comrades on the ground," the cat said

after a long pause. "And their side suffered fewer losses. Some people are not made for fighting. Some people want to fight as little as they can."

"And you, Irael?"

The cat's huff of breath warmed a small patch of Nioanen's skin before the night air banished it. "I will fight until my last breath, until I can no longer draw upon the aether. Until every last one of the Numinars is dead and we can no longer sup of the sap that leaches from their roots."

"Then so will I."

"Good."

And then Irael, who had always been better at closing himself off to the thoughts he did not want, curled his tail around Nioanen's arm and went to sleep.

It was nearly morning by the time they landed in Sanctuary. Nioanen wasn't sure which had exhausted him more – the battle or the morbid thoughts that had chased him through the sky. The ground gave beneath his clawed feet, the surrounding vegetation closing in around him, his heartbeat slowing and the tight coil of his muscles unwinding. The forest was dense, broad-leafed trees mixed in with pines, the sharp scent of sap a bright note above the richness of freshly turned leaves underfoot.

They were not safe – not here, not anywhere – but at least this was an oasis in a desert of scorched landscape.

Irael uncurled himself from Nioanen's arms and shifted as soon as they landed. There was still something feline about him in his young man form – a sharpness about the eyes, a narrow chin, and a nose that seemed liable to twitch with every shift in the winds. His soft, short hair was ticked at the very ends with black, his eyes golden and flashing.

Other gods emerged from the underbrush – some large and some small. Not many, just those who'd had to stay behind because they were children, or with child, or too frail to engage in a fight. They'd put everything they'd had into this battle. Nioanen sized up their numbers and felt his throat constrict. They could still fight, given time to heal and to regroup. It would be hard. Even harder than before.

"Are you all that's left?" A woman with scaly, shimmering skin stepped into the dappled light.

Irael went to her, taking her hands in his. He leaned back to take in her swollen belly. "Are you well? Is your child well?"

Nioanen faded into the branches, tightening his wings to his sides, letting Irael do his work without hindrance. Irael coaxed and comforted with aplomb, hands and voice soft. All Nioanen could think about was how the gods were more fertile on the vastness of the surface world, which only meant more for Kluehnn to kill and to consume. No one needed him looming, his morose thoughts wafting off him like a stench.

A boy approached, horns sprouting from his forehead, a pitcher in his hands. "From the local villages. There is still some sap left and you need your strength."

Nioanen took the pitcher between clawed fingers and downed the lot. It was sweet and pungent and settled heavily into his belly, waiting to be combined with aether so he could create miracles. For now, they still had some worshipers. They still had some Numinars left.

But without access to Unterra, to the inner star, they were each frozen in time, unable to advance in power as they were meant to. Eventually, as they created more and more miracles, the divine magic in their flesh would run out. This place wasn't meant for them.

Everyone was tired, their limbs dragging through this thin air as though it were syrup. But they were making do. They could hold the borders of Sanctuary if they tried, taking a defensive position instead of trying to dig their way back beneath the earth. Back to where the aether was stronger.

Already Nioanen was strategizing, and hating himself for it. He should be grieving the fallen. He should be out there with Irael, offering kind words to those who had lost loved ones. They'd all been much more solitary before they'd been forced to the surface. This closeness felt unnatural, though necessary. Up here they'd have to live like mortals or they'd have to die like them. Nioanen would have said Irael was his closest friend when they'd lived in the hollow center, and even then he'd only seen him perhaps once a year. Now they fought together, ate together and slept together.

He made his way to another clearing before taking to the sky again. There was a Numinar in Sanctuary, the trunk half the width of a mountain. The ground where its roots met the earth glowed; a subtle bright pulse beneath its bark. Those roots went all the way down to Unterra, sprouting into whole forests back home. He'd made a nest near the base of this Numinar and he flew there now, the twinge at his shoulder the only reminder of the lost battle.

He was sitting at the edge of his nest, scowling at the delineation between the green below and the blackened surrounding landscape, when Irael leapt inside in cat form.

"You should have stayed," Irael said, striped tail whipping back and forth. "You're strong; they take comfort from you. You used to live for the attentions of others. You used to spread those dusky gold wings and those who feared you would fall back and those who loved you would fall into them."

"We've all changed," Nioanen said gruffly, though he couldn't put any bite into the words.

Irael sat next to him on the edge of the nest. "Tell me what troubles you."

"The same things that should be troubling you."

"Who says they aren't?" Irael said lightly, his tail curling around his feet. They lapsed into silence, the wind teasing at both hair and feathers. It was silent here in the branches of the tree, far above the ground below.

Nioanen reached out, pressing a palm to the smooth bark. A slight glow emanated beneath his touch. He felt like this Numinar sometimes, holding in not magic but so many unspoken words. He let some slip. "We can sustain this for a time, but Kluehnn is relentless. Will you and I someday get tired? Will we all someday get tired? What happens to the world then? It's changed too much. We cannot go back to the way things were. It would take too much sacrifice. It would take too much time. And even then . . . "

He broke off. That was what filled him with the most despair. No matter how hard they tried, no matter what they did, they could not *fix* the world. The Numinars were dead and dying. The mortals had broken the world, and maybe the gods had too. All they could do was survive. He wasn't sure that was enough.

A soft head nudged his hand and unconsciously he lifted it, scratching Irael between the ears. "Lie down," the cat said.

Nioanen, who was loved and feared by the other gods, did as he was told, folding his wings around himself until the edges of his brown feathers brushed his cheeks. The cold pads of Irael's feet touched his chest and then his shoulder, claws pricking a little as paws kneaded his collarbone. Irael settled into the crook of his arm.

"I cannot tell you the future. I cannot tell you what will happen to the world or to us. But I can tell you to sleep, Nioanen. If you worry about being tired, then you should rest."

He did.

11

Rasha

10 years after the restoration of Kashan
and 571 years after the Shattering

Kashan - Kluehnn's den

*We know the realms warred before the Shattering, before
the burning of the Numinars changed the landscape.
Cressima once conquered Albanore. Aqqil was once an
empire. Langʒu once traded heavily with the southern
continent, importing weapons to sell to others.*

Shattering should have been a relief. It wasn't.

I had never pushed myself as hard as I did when training with
the other converts. Kluehnn was right – they were stronger
than I was, they were faster, they were more prepared. But none
of them had known the hardness I had. So when they grew tired
or hungry or reached the ends of their limits, I pushed on.

There was combat training, for which I was given a small
dagger, but there was also training in summoning aether. This
came easily to me after long years of practice.

"Use your hands," Millani said as she paced through our burrow. "You won't be physically pulling the aether up with them, but you can use them to focus your thoughts. Only the altered can draw magic from below, a gift given to us by Kluehnn so that we may infuse the gems before we give them to him. We are his caretakers and he needs us."

He *needs* us. Something stirred within me at those words – pride and a sense of purpose. Hakara hadn't ever needed me. She'd needed to *protect* me. I'd only been a burden to her in the end. One she was finally free of, one way or another. But I felt the strength of Kluehnn's love and regard suffusing me each time I dared to question my path.

He'd given me gifts to survive in this restored landscape, gifts that would allow me to serve him.

"Rasha. Are you paying attention?"

I snapped to the present, meeting Millani's yellow eyes. "Yes."

The hands clasped behind her back tightened, scales rasping against one another. "What are the symptoms of aether intoxication?"

"First there is a slight itching, and then a general sense of euphoria and detachment. Logic becomes muddled. Dizziness can ensue, and then, as intoxication increases, reason begins to fade completely. Paranoia kicks in, after which the victim may senselessly attack others."

She stared at me, waiting, and then I remembered.

"The final symptom is death."

She turned the intensity of her yellow-eyed gaze elsewhere and I relaxed a little. She had beaten us more than once when we'd not answered correctly. She did it out of love, she told us. If she did not beat us, we would feel no consequence for failure, and the beating would help us remember so that next time we would not forget. Failure during the trials often meant death, and the pain of the beatings was small in comparison.

We'd all felt the sting of the whip at her belt, though I'd felt it more often than the others. If suffering made us strong, then I would be stronger than all of them.

I would make it to the end.

"The first trial begins today," Millani said.

Everyone in the line straightened. The girl next to me, Khatuya, a small altered with skin like tree bark, trembled a little. She'd suffered almost as many beatings at Millani's hands as I had. I only knew her name because of how often Millani shouted it. "Today? When?"

"Now."

Murmurs broke out, and I couldn't tell if the tone of them was frightened or eager. Both, perhaps. Panic swelled at the back of my throat. I wasn't prepared, I'd not had enough practice. There were things I should do beforehand, more things I should know. I touched the hilt of the slim, curved blade at my belt. It was the one I'd chosen my second day in the burrow, though I still felt unsteady in its use.

But none of us voiced any protest. We followed Millani meekly from the burrow and into the deeper caves. She led us to a heavy iron door and then through it. My gaze lingered on the tiny glass window fixed into the door. Thickest piece of glass I'd ever seen, the light wavering through it, the view beyond distorted.

The room was small, interrupted with half a dozen pillars, lamps lining the walls. Someone had already lit them. There was no opening to the sky here, no green filtering through the leaves above. We all fit inside with space to move about, but there was no place to hide and no way out except through the iron door.

Millani stood blocking the entrance. "The aether past the first aerocline is poisonous to mortals and affects us a little more mildly. The aether past the second aerocline is extremely poisonous to both mortals and altered. We can exist in it for only a little while before we begin to show symptoms.

"You've summoned aether from past the first aerocline. This is your task for this trial: summon aether from past the second aerocline. You will each be tested on this before you can go back to your burrow. If you are unable to demonstrate proficiency, the penalty is death."

She turned to leave.

"Millani." Khatuya spoke up. Her black hair hung lank over her rough brown cheeks, swinging as she tilted her head. "We summoned aether from beyond the first aerocline while we were outside, under your supervision. It had space to dissipate. Here, underground, it won't have many places to go."

"That's true," Millani said. And then she strode back through the doorway and shut the metal door with a *clang*. We all listened in silence as she barred it.

"She can't be serious," said a young man with tusks and spotted fur. An axe hung from his belt, and he touched the top of it with nervous fingers. He glanced between the others and the door, where Millani watched us, her face just on the other side of the glass. "If we all just stay here and stay calm, she'll let us out."

"Yes, but how will we summon aether from beyond the second aerocline if we've not practiced?" someone else said. "You heard her – she said we either prove we can do that before we return to the burrow, or our lives are forfeit."

"She can't kill all of us," the tusked man said.

"Can't she?" My voice sounded quiet, even to myself, but everyone turned to look at me. "She beats us regularly. She says that most of us will not survive to become godkillers. Why would all of us survive to become neophytes?"

I felt the stirring of panic in the air, a drifting thing touching us all, like the first scent of smoke. I glanced round at them and saw one winged young woman, her face still with concentration, her feathers twitching. "Look at her. She's already trying."

Everyone moved away from the woman, eyes wide.

"It doesn't matter," another of the converts cried out. "The aether will spread through the room. We'll all breathe it."

But those closest to her would get the strongest whiff. Aether, like air, was finite. I moved toward a corner, my hand on the dagger at my belt.

"We should wait Millani out."

"We'll run out of air in here eventually, and before that we'll get hungry and thirsty. Better to get this over with."

They were all going to do it. They were all going to reach past the second aerocline, draw its air into this chamber and intoxicate us. I found an unoccupied spot behind a pillar, took a deep breath and turned my hands palm up.

I would do it too.

There wasn't any way I would let myself be caught unable to draw the aether from past the second aerocline. If I made it through this part of the trial, I would make sure I made it through the next.

I only managed to summon aether from past the first aerocline on my first few tries. I could feel it shimmering around me, smelling like a dung fire. Pungent but reminding me of the days spent by the tent with Hakara, watching the smoke curl up toward the sky.

The muttering of the other converts echoed from the chamber's walls, their feet scuffing the floor as they too tried to reach past the second aerocline.

On my fourth try, I slowed down, thought about what I was feeling when I drew air from past the first aerocline. It felt like throwing my mind beyond the stone below and into the depths of a vast and great sea. But there was another sea below that one. I just had to find the bottom.

I tried to calm the fast beating of my heart. I could smell the aether around me, as I was sure the others could too. The more we saturated this cavern, the faster we would fall to the effects of the magic. Was that an itching I felt on my forearms? I couldn't think about it. I had to focus.

With an effort, I breathed in, then out, and cast my mind down, down into the depths of the first aerocline.

It felt like it took forever to reach the bottom. Was this what diving felt like to Hakara? A sinking into the depths, doing her best not to be aware of how far above the surface was? And then I felt it – a shimmering skin where the concentration of aether suddenly shifted.

I dipped my hands low and lifted. The air that filtered through the stone was thicker than the air I'd brought up before. I could feel it sifting through my fingers. It smelled like the blankets Hakara and I had slept in, musty but warm. I wanted to breathe that scent in deep and I barely stopped myself.

The aether always smelled comforting to a person, always tempting them to take in more of it. I waved away what I'd drawn up, doing my best to force it somewhere else in the cavern, trying to find a spot of clean air. I'd done it, at least. Now, if I made it out of here, I could prove to Millani I was capable.

Claws scraped across my forearm. I looked down and found myself scratching a spot near my wrist. It started with the itching.

I stilled my hands, drawing them tight to my sides. I clenched my teeth, running my tongue over all their sharp points. Next would come the euphoria, the sense that everything was well with the world, even when it was very, very not.

When I scanned the room, I saw a few faces that were brighter than they should have been. Others scratched absent-mindedly at their necks or arms. Twenty of us, all crammed into this space. I saw the shape of the trial's intentions with a cold clarity. Even though my forearms kept itching, I did not move to scratch them.

There were other symptoms of aether poisoning before death. Disorientation. Violence.

If we did not kill the ones who reached that final stage, they would kill us. If I did not hide my symptoms, the others would kill me.

I moved through the room, trying to put as much distance as possible between myself and the other altered, trying to find some space where I could breathe. The scent of dung fires and blankets was thick in my nostrils, no matter where I went.

Panicking quickened the breath. More panic meant a faster progression through the symptoms. I thought of Hakara doing her breathing exercises in the mornings before she dove. I imitated those patterns now, keeping my breath long and deep.

The fast thud of my heartbeat slowed. There were only two ways out of this room – death or outlasting my competitors.

I'd gone days without food before. I'd helped Hakara pack up our tent and move it to better locations as the weather and winds changed. She might have been my older sister and my protector, but she could not protect me from everything. Especially not after we'd lost both our Mimi and Maman. We'd had a hard life. I'd only thought myself soft in comparison to her. She was stronger than me, but that didn't mean I was also not strong. I could live through this.

No one said anything, everyone moving. One young man had gone to the door, heedless of Millani's staring face, and pried at the handle and the hinges. There was a desperation to the silence, everyone wondering when the first of us would die.

An arm bumped against mine.

I whirled and caught the wide eyes of a young man with brown scales spattered across his forehead. Naatar – that was his name. He staggered a little as our gazes met, and I wasn't sure if it was from the impact or the intoxication. He scratched at his neck and I grabbed his forearm, pulling his hand away. I bent my head close to his. "The longer you stay calm, the less the aether will affect you." I wasn't sure why I was telling him this. Depending on how things worked out, I might have to kill him. But his frightened nod made me feel a little less alone.

A scream sounded from the opposite side of the room. A winged altered was bearing down on a boy with scales, her sword drawn. Before anyone could say or do anything, she hacked into the other convert's side. Blood sprayed as the scaled boy gurgled.

Whatever silent truce that had existed before now broke. Weapons came free of belts and sheaths. Everyone tried to find a wall or a pillar to put their backs to. Two of the other converts fell on the winged altered. She snarled as they attacked.

As soon as she was dead, I heard one of the converts cry out, "That one! He's dizzy; he'll try to kill us next."

"No! There was a rock. I was just—"

I watched three converts converge on the young man. He only managed to block one of the blows before the rest made their way through his guard, hacking an arm off at the shoulder, stabbing into his guts. He screamed as his arm thudded to the ground, and the metallic smell of blood mingled with the scent of dung fires.

I turned my horrified gaze away, my shoulders tense, my gaze searching the others for some sign they would turn on me. Meat – we were all just meat in the end. I put my back to a corner as what had once been a quiet panic descended into a melee.

Screams and the clash of metal against metal echoed in the small cavern.

I kept my breathing slow and steady, trying to push back the fear, because I knew at some point someone would notice me here. I could not hide forever.

When we'd been children, and both our Mimi and Maman had died, we'd had to kill our remaining camel for food. Hakara had done it, her back straight, the knife held in confident hands. She'd told me to wait in the tent, but I'd watched through the flap as she'd approached the tied beast, knelt and pulled the blade across his throat.

If she'd cried, she hadn't let me see.

I shut my eyes tight for a moment. I couldn't think. I had to be just moving arms and hands. I had to find that part of myself that only wanted to *live*. The world tilted around me, my arms and neck awash with a prickling itch it took all my will not to scratch. The air was thickening, my hair beginning to drift as though a breeze wended its way through the cave.

I had done this before – the waiting.

I opened my eyes and my mouth, screaming out my rage and fear. Millani had done this to us; she'd forced us into this position. I could barely hear my own voice above the cacophony around me, but the scream filled my throat with a hollow ache. I would not hide here, waiting to die. I'd waited before, hoping for an outcome that was impossible. This time, I would fight.

My claws ripped into the back of an altered who'd been focused on someone else. Her wail joined the voices of others, her blood slick on the cavern floor. I pivoted to face another opponent, gray wings nearly buffeting me off my feet. I seized one of those wings and felt the bones crack beneath my hands. Before the man could even react to the pain, I had him by the throat. I ripped my hand away and felt the blood pour across my wrist.

There was some small part of me that felt horrified by this violence. I locked it up tight. There was power in my movements. I'd always felt like a stranger in my new body, my limbs too long, my height a clumsy, awkward thing. During trainings all my movements seemed stilted, the connection between my mind and my hands tenuous. Fear banished that discomfort; I could not afford it.

Was this the aether working its way through my blood? This satisfaction in letting loose and using my power to its fullest? Kluehnn had truly blessed me when I'd been altered. My face might still have held the echo of my old countenance, but everything else had changed.

I seized the wrist of another convert and yanked the knife from her hand before plunging it into her eye. A woman approached from the side, her gaze wild, and without thinking, I reached down into the earth and pulled a heavy handful of aether from below the second aerocline, focusing it at her face.

I whirled away before I could breathe any of it in, and saw her fall to the ground, gasping in the final throes of aether poisoning. Another altered put his dagger into her back.

The floor was a coppery-scented mess of blood and entrails, the screaming dying down to the echoing, ragged breaths of the other survivors. I cast my gaze over them, making sure a pillar was at my back. I could do this.

I could kill them all.

The metal door opened. I felt the aether rushing from the room, dissipating into the caverns, the air around me growing colder and thinner. It took me a moment to orient myself, my head still swimming, my hands sticky with blood. My belly lurched as I looked around at the entrails and limbs that littered the ground. The bodies hacked into unrecognizable pieces. The few converts who were miraculously still alive, blades lodged between ribs or stuck into limbs, their bodies too broken to scream.

Fewer than half of us were still on our feet.

Millani entered the room, her tail waving behind her as though to fan away the remaining aether. "Those of you still standing must prove your ability with the second aerocline. Then you may return to your burrow, where food and baths await. Kluehnn will see you after."

I was the third to be tested, and I pulled a small amount of aether up from past the second aerocline with little effort. What was this test compared to what I'd just endured?

Millani nodded and I was dismissed.

In the burrow, we ate and bathed in silence. The tubs were set up in a row, the water still steaming. I shucked off my robe and stepped inside. When I was younger, I might have balked at bathing in the company of strangers. Now – in this strange body, in this strange realm, in this strange place – it seemed such a trivial thing.

Cuts I hadn't known I had stung as I sank into the wooden tub. Water sloshed over the sides. Fresh water had been a luxury in unrestored Kashan. I'd bathed in the ocean and had counted myself lucky that I had access to such a large body of water, no matter that the salt dried, flaky, on my skin afterward. The water of the tub grew pink with the blood I scrubbed from beneath my claws. I let the warmth of it close over my head, my hair floating, wishing I could stay beneath in the silence and never have to face the world again.

I did not taste the food. I could have been eating dust. None of us met the others' eyes as we sat on our cots and waited. There were so many empty cots now, their occupants dead and gone. I wondered exactly how many of them I'd killed.

Millani came for me first. "Come." She beckoned to me.

She shut me in the chamber where I'd first seen Kluehnn, and this time I was not startled by his appearance as he crept over the edge of the hole. His horns nearly scraped the ceiling when he stood.

"Ah," he said when he saw me. Another mouth on his shoulder moved soundlessly as he spoke. "You made it past the first trial. I am glad."

The words tugged at me unexpectedly, making me feel *something* for the first time since I'd walked out the metal door of the trial cavern. The horror I'd been staving off came rushing back in, a flooding river, rife with painful debris. "You made us kill each other." My eyes burned even as I tried to swallow back the tears.

"Oh Rasha. Sweet Rasha." A hand came up and cradled my chin. "Don't worry yourself over the fallen. It was for the best. You may think the Kashan you lived in once was harsh, and yes, restored Kashan is gentler in some ways. But it is wild, too, and no one has tamed this land yet. I need the strongest."

"We could have proved ourselves another way." I couldn't stop the tears that fell from my eyes this time. I wanted to be held. I wanted to seek solace in the arms of someone larger than me, stronger than me, wiser than me.

Another of his hands found its way to my cheek. Thumbs wiped the tears and then dug into my jaw. "So fierce and yet so soft." His voice was low and mocking.

I pulled away and felt one of his nails leave a scratch. It burned as I dashed away the rest of my tears. "No." My voice trembled and I took in a shuddering breath. "No." This time it was steadier. Mimi had let me creep into her blankets at night. Maman had always given me the fattiest bits of meat. Even Hakara had carried on that legacy, giving me her shoes when we'd fled restoration. Doing her best to shelter me, to let the tender tendrils of my heart take root. If my body could be made anew, then so could my soul. "I made it through your first trial. I am not soft." Everyone had thought me sweet and delicate. They'd never given me the chance to be anything else.

Kluehnn gave an approving nod, and warmth flooded my chest. "No, child, perhaps you are not. Kneel." I did as he asked. He touched the top of my head, his claws lightly scratching against my scalp.

"Rise, neophyte."

12

Hakara

10 years after the restoration of Kashan and 571 years after the Shattering

Langzu - ??

How to detect a god:
They look similar to an altered, though not completely alike
They coerce mortals into following them
They have no legal papers
They invoke an emotional reaction with their appearance —
*   their aura*
They lie when cornered
Their blood is red, with an underlying shimmer
They will not die, no matter how many times they are cut

The hood my rescuer had placed over my head was dark, but the lighting wasn't much better by the time he took it off. The click of a lock sounded before I could orient myself, and then the creak of wood under pressure. I was in a cage in a cellar, surrounded by stone, dirt and crates and barrels. There were no windows, only a lamp sitting atop one of the crates. The light provided a dim silhouette of a man sitting in a chair, broad shoulders hunched. In the dark, the outline of my jailer looked even more familiar. I'd escaped whatever the godkiller had wanted with me, but who was this? One of the Sovereign's enforcers? If it was, he was out of uniform.

I scrambled to my feet and tapped on the bars to get his attention. "You were there the night I went into the sinkhole. I saw you hanging around when I came out."

He said nothing.

He'd crept away and now he was here. Had he been observing me? Had he spoken to Guarin, and the man had decided I wasn't worth the trouble I might bring upon his head? Illegal status and selling god gems to boot. It wasn't exactly a mark in my favor.

"Can I ask why you're holding me here?"

Nothing.

I tapped the bars again, just in case the man was asleep. The metallic sound rang through the cellar. "Is it something I did? I mean, something you think I did? I haven't done anything wrong." If I listened carefully, I could hear his breathing echoing from the stone. So he was alive at least. "Is it my status? Do you need to see papers?" I wasn't going to bring up fencing the god gems. They never punished the clans; they only punished the miners and the go-betweens. Better to assume he didn't know rather than give myself up for execution.

I waited again, though I might as well have been talking to the walls themselves. "I may not be a legal resident of Langzu, but that wasn't my fault. And I've been here long enough – I mean, it's been ten years – that under the Sovereign's new edicts I could become legal if I had the funds for it. But I'm a sinkhole miner; I don't get to keep much of what I earn. Especially since I'm not legal. My supervisor takes most of it." No need to mention the parcels I'd been saving for my expedition. "And that brings me back to my first point. The crossing wasn't even my fault. Guarin, my supervisor, he knew I could hold my breath a good long time. He knocked me out and brought me with him. I didn't have a choice in the matter. If you want to imprison someone for a crime, it should be him, not me." I thought for a moment. "Well, I can see why you'd want me too, but if you'd give me a chance to earn the money, I'd—"

"Quiet."

The word reverberated through the cellar. I thought I could hear it knocking against those empty barrels like a fist. Took closer note of the walls this time as the sound echoed off them. Faint chipped paint. A carved alcove. Images of gods – the seven elder ones. Weren't supposed to talk about them, but everyone had a story, and stories spread, keeping some semblance of them alive. I caught a glimpse of golden wings, of silver hair. Nioanen. Lithuas. Their epithets were carved beneath their images. Nioanen, Defender of the Helpless. Lithuas, Bringer of Change. I let out a soft snort. Guess it was a good thing they were dead, because I couldn't imagine they'd be much help in a world like this. Maybe not a cellar then. The ruins of a church?

I waited for the echo to fade before I started in again. "I've heard illegal refugees are sometimes thrown into the barrier between Langzu and Kashan. Just tied up and tossed in. Is that what's going to happen to me? Seems like a waste. I'm a good diver, or so I've been told."

The man sighed like the bellows at a forge fire. "I don't give a damn about your status, woman."

I blinked. "Well what *do* you care about then?" I was starting to think maybe it would have been better to go with the godkiller. Criminals did sometimes throw themselves at the mercy of the dens, asking to serve Kluehnn as a way of escaping execution. It was a harder life than mining, but it was a life.

For a while, I thought he wouldn't answer. I ran a finger up and down one cold bar of my cage, eyeing the lock. Could he see me better than I could see him? The lock only looked like a dark square in my vision, but the cage smelled of rust. I wondered if I could kick it free.

"It won't budge," the man said. "And it's what you did with the god gem that we're interested in. Same thing as Kluehnn's interested in."

We. So at least now I knew for sure he wasn't a convert, and he was part of another faction.

"What I did with the god gem? I don't know what you're talking about. Are you from one of the clans? The Sovereign?"

Another creak of wood as he shifted in the chair. "Don't try to pretend you don't know what I'm talking about. The sinkhole collapsed. You went past the second aerocline. You lived when you shouldn't have and there are damned few people who can do that. Kluehnn's godkillers take most of those gifted people back to their dens. The clans get some. We need your help."

My help? I ran my gaze along the top of the cage. "Fine way to ask for it."

"We need to break the god pact with Kluehnn. We need to stop restoration."

So this was who I'd run afoul of. I let out a huff of disbelieving breath. I'd gone from a dinghy at sea into the sea itself. The Unanointed. The only idiots in the world who thought there was a future in fighting a god. I leaned my head against the bars. "I've fallen in with fools."

"Fools who saved you from a life of servitude."

I gave the door an experimental rattle. "Let me out."

"Where will you go?" The man spread his hands wide. "Every realm in this world has Kluehnn's fingerprints on it. Every realm is filled with his dens. His godkillers will find you again."

Wasn't about to be backed into a corner even if I was literally sitting in one. "Well, I'll dive into the sea and find a remote island, just big enough for one. What do you care? Let me out. Or are you just like Kluehnn and his converts? Going to force me into servitude too?"

I couldn't see his expression, but I could read the straightening of his shoulders, the hand tightening around the armrest. If he rose from his chair, if he came a little bit closer, I could grab him by the collar, take the keys clinking at his belt.

"We don't—"

"That's enough, Buzhi. You're not here to chat with her." A light flared at the top of the stairs, illuminating the small cellar. A woman appeared, iron-gray hair pulled back into a tail. Her footsteps were light, her posture confident.

She held the lantern high as she approached the cage, a fisherman inspecting the night's catch. I squinted against the light, my arm lifted to shade my face, hating that she had that advantage over me, that I couldn't study her the same way. Evidently she'd decided I wasn't to be thrown back, because she lowered the lantern and shuttered half of it. The light dimmed enough to soothe my stinging eyes.

"Didn't know the Unanointed were into kidnapping people," I said.

I couldn't tell exactly how old she was; her face remained unlined in spite of the gray hair. She looked Langzuan, with wide-set black eyes and a flat nose that nearly spanned the width of her small, full-lipped mouth. Buzhi had settled back into the chair, and something about this woman and the way she carried herself made me wary of attacking her. I was scrappy, sure, but I wasn't tutor-trained like some of those clan brats.

She met my gaze and neither of us looked away. What was this, some sort of dominance play? Oh, I could stare like the best of them. If she thought she was going to intimidate me, she definitely didn't—

"We can find out what happened to your sister."

Her words hit harder than any fist. Now I was wishing I'd looked away, so she couldn't see the desperation in my eyes, the want, the *need*. She'd laid me out on the table and gutted me in one stroke. I cleared my throat. "Never said I had a sister."

"As soon as we knew what you could do, Buzhi poked around. It wasn't difficult to find out."

Suppose it wouldn't have been, not with the way I'd knocked the teeth out of the last miner who'd told me she was dead.

"We have resources," she continued, her voice firm and smooth. "Our network doesn't span only one realm, even if the majority of us are here in Langzu at the moment. We have two vultures that can fly high enough, that can get past the barrier with messages. I can send word to others in Kashan. It will take time, and it's expensive, but it's not impossible."

She had me pinned. I couldn't even find it in me to wriggle. My hands loosed from the bars. "What do you want?" *I'll do anything. Be anyone you want. Just tell me.* I left those words unspoken, but I knew she absorbed them anyways.

"There is always a black market for god gems. Do you know why?"

I shrugged. "They're pretty. They're magical. People pay money for them. Didn't need to know more."

Her lips pursed briefly as though she were my Maman. As though she were disappointed in me. I didn't give two shits what she thought of me; all I wanted was for her to hurry through this explanation and get to the only part that mattered. "The dens and sometimes the clans take people like you because you have the ability to infuse the god gems with aether. And once infused with aether, they become much, much more than just pretty rocks.

When placed in the ground, they can enhance the fertility of the soil, speed up plant growth. You wonder why the clans seem to prosper in this volatile landscape? This is how. The Sovereign knows. They're all in on it. Deciding who to persecute with his enforcers is partially how he keeps order."

I waved a hand in a "hurry it up" motion. "I already knew the stones did magic things. Most people know that they can help grow crops. And this has what to do with me?"

"I told you she wouldn't care, Mitoran," Buzhi said.

Mitoran didn't even cast him a glance. "Sometimes mining crews find corestones – gems that are larger, more luminous than others. Multi-colored. We believe if we can collect three of them, and infuse them with enough magical air, we can permanently enhance Langzu's soil. Not all of it, but enough to grow the crops we need. We won't need restoration. We won't need Kluehnn. The rest of our plan involves stealing god gems. Currently they're all funneled into the dens, where they're infused and tucked away somewhere past the first aerocline. The only reason Kluehnn would need so many infused stones is to enact restoration. We raid one of the dens, we stop restoration. After that, we can convince the Sovereign and the clans to stop sending the gems to Kluehnn.

"But we need a linchpin. Someone to infuse the corestones. That person could be you."

I wished she'd just tell me exactly what to do, so I could be pointed in a direction and merely told "go". But because I was currently sitting in a metal cage, I obliged her obvious attempts to get me to work it out myself.

I'd breathed in air past the second aerocline and I was still alive. I'd swallowed a gem and a stronger set of arms had sheathed my floppy mortal ones. *Infuse*, she'd said. Was that what I'd done? "Aether past the second aerocline is more toxic.

It's more concentrated. Not everyone can use it, can they? Not even these people Kluehnn takes."

She gave a prim nod.

I watched her face. "And there may be some things you're not aware that god gems can do."

This time, when her lips pressed together, it wasn't with disappointment but with consideration. Should she tell me?

I gestured to the cage. "If it doesn't work out, you can always kill me. Tell me what you want me to do. And then send a message to your people in Kashan. Ask them to find my sister."

The woman gestured to Buzhi, and he handed over the keys. "There is no guarantee she's still alive," she said as she unlocked the door.

I gritted my teeth and stepped down onto the dusty floor. "She's alive." She had to be.

I followed Mitoran up the stairs, rubbing my shoulder where I'd struck it on the bed of the godkiller's cart. At least she hadn't told me I wouldn't want my sister after she'd been altered. So that was a point in her favor. A small one.

The first thing that struck me when she opened the door was that there was an altered in the room. A furred one. Some altered had wandered into Langzu from Kashan or Albanore, their natural resistance to aether making the way a little less dangerous. Still, they weren't a common sight. I wondered sometimes what kind Rasha would be. For some reason I always imagined her as the winged type – all soft feathers and two steps from the sky.

And then I turned and saw that Buzhi had a pair of wings at his back, each as small as my hand, peeking out from a square hole in the back of his shirt. He must have hidden them when he'd been at the mining camp. Two altered.

I suddenly felt a little bit dizzy.

"This is one of our safe houses," Mitoran was saying. "It's in the outskirts of Bian. Built on the ruins of an old, pre-Shattering church. Close enough so we can blend in, but far enough out that we don't attract too much notice. This is where you'll train."

I blinked. "Where I'll what?"

But she was already leading the furred man toward me. White-spotted brown fuzz covered his cheeks. He was big, with broad shoulders that were stooped in a way that told me he was used to hunching to get through doorways. She pointed at him. "This is Utricht. He'll be your arbor and also your bonded partner." Only the name told me that he had once been Cressiman.

"Just throwing her into it, aren't you?" said a woman from the corner. Something about her reminded me of a fox, her curly russet hair tied back, her cheekbones high, her black eyes glittering. A smattering of dark freckles covered the tawny skin of her face. She crossed her arms, which were as lithe as the rest of her. She spoke with an Albanoran accent, but didn't look Albanoran — a reminder that a long time ago, borders had been open and people traveled freely between realms.

I must have looked confused, though no one stopped to give me a primer. I was a fish being asked to suddenly comprehend land. Well, I didn't need to comprehend it, did I? I just needed to survive here long enough to get what I wanted.

Mitoran ignored her. "The bond works both ways. Once you're bonded, you'll be able to sense where Utricht is and he'll be able to sense where you are. It can be broken by mutual agreement, so you needn't worry about being trapped together."

My mind reeled. Just a day ago, a godkiller had captured me. Now I was being thrust into some underground cult and asked to form a magical bond with an altered. Magic was the province of the gods; it wasn't meant for us. Or at least that was what I'd been told as a child. Neither Maman nor Mimi was devout, but when you were surrounded by religion, it had a way of seeping into your conscious thought. It wasn't as though I thought restoration was great or anything, but I didn't exactly agree with the Unanointed either. It was like not wanting a tiger to eat your chickens but at the same time knowing that going out to fight that tiger with a knife probably wasn't the best idea. And how could I even know the Unanointed would hold up their end of the bargain? I studied Mitoran's face, smooth and inscrutable as a muddy puddle. Couldn't trust a woman like that, no matter how long I knew her. At the same time, how could I not at least try? I didn't have any better options for finding Rasha at the moment, even if magic was involved.

"Mortal use of magic is illegal," I pointed out. "So is altered use of it."

"Yes, we're trying to stop a god and reshape a realm, all while keeping within the confines of the law," the freckled woman said. Her arms were still crossed. "She has no idea what she's bought into. Everyone here has lost someone to restoration. What has *she* lost?"

I'd lost everything. I'd lost myself.

This time Mitoran looked to her. "We found the location of a corestone. We don't have time to coddle her or ease her into anything. We're short a bruiser and we've got ten days before the Sovereign pays the next tithe of gems."

"It's too many new people all at once." The woman's eyes slid to the man next to her. Where she was lithe, he was both solid and slim. A goatee surrounded a slightly downturned mouth; his hair was black and fell just past his ears, his skin a bronze shade that spoke of sunbaked earth. I could spot a Cressiman fifty paces away, and could tell someone was Kashani at a glance. Albanoran I got confused sometimes with Cressiman, but this man – I wasn't sure what realm he hailed from. A curved sword was strapped to his side, the hilt covered with white enamel flowers. His gaze met hers and he gave her an affirming nod.

They both looked back to me.

"If I'm to be your bruiser," I said slowly, "then what's everyone else supposed to be? What's an arbor?"

"You pulled yourself out of that pit. Buzhi saw you spring out of the ground with a slack rope. He saw the smoke dissipating from your arms." Mitoran stood a little too close to me, though I resisted the urge to step back. "You swallowed a god gem, you took in a breath of aether, and those combined to grow a pair of god arms. You hold your breath – the arms stay. You let it out, you lose them and your unnatural strength."

I stared down at my hands as though it were the first time seeing them. "What, so I grew a pair of arms like I'm a damned plant?"

Mitoran strode between the three people in front of me, ignoring my question. "The Unanointed fight in teams of four, and each person has their function. You'll be the bruiser – you're the one who goes in and uses your magic to overpower our enemies. But you'll need protection. When you have to take a breath, or if you black out, you'll be vulnerable. The arbor sticks with you and you stick with them. The vine weaves in and out, plugging the gaps, making sure you're kept in the shade. And the pest, well . . . they do exactly as you might think."

The unaltered man with the curved sword shook his head and leaned against the wall. "Too much risk." Only one who didn't seem to mind that I was part of their team now was Utricht.

I bristled. As though I weren't taking on any risk here. The Sovereign might have cracked down on the poor more than he ever would the clans, but he liked to make particular examples of the Unanointed. Everyone had different ideas of what sort of torture he put them through before execution, but they marched to their deaths limp, mysteriously free of wounds, and empty-eyed. It was enough to make me believe in the ghosts Maman kept harping on.

"Hold up. I'm not who you want. I don't want to be one of the Unanointed. I'm not your linchpin."

"You told her about that?" the sharp-faced woman said.

I was focused on Mitoran. "We make the terms of this arrangement clear now."

Buzhi grunted from behind me. "You're hardly in a position to negotiate."

That hadn't ever stopped me before. "I'll help you get that corestone. But that's all I'll do. You send a message to Kashan now."

Mitoran shook her head. "Both birds are in Kashan at the moment. I can't send a message until at least one is back. If that's all you're willing to do, I'll send the message after the corestone is safely in my hands, not before."

This could be a terrible mistake. Could end up getting caught, tortured and executed – all before I ever found out Rasha's fate. Or it could be the way I found her and brought her home. I weighed these two outcomes in my mind, though the dire one felt as fuzzy as a landscape through steamed glass. Rasha's face, however, I could imagine in detail – older, changed, perhaps, but there down to the small, soft hairs at her forehead. I clenched my fingers at the remembered touch of my hands against her cheeks. "Fine." My gaze slid to Utricht, his eyes a blend of green and brown, his pupils ringed in gold. "Tell me how the magic works."

13

Sheuan

10 years after the restoration of Kashan
and 571 years after the Shattering

Langzu – inner Bian

*Any mortal who accurately reports the location of a god
to one of Kluehnn's dens will be paid one parcel. Any
duplicate reporting will be paid a half-parcel. Any reports
thereafter will not be paid.*

*If a mortal is able to secure a god for execution, they
shall be paid the amount of twenty parcels.*

Sheuan pressed a handkerchief to her forehead, dabbing at the
sweat that had formed there as she waited and watched from
a tea house across the street. The rain they'd had a few days ago
would likely be the last of it for a while, the moisture burning off
into an oppressive heat. This tea house used to serve three grainy
wafers with a pot of tea; now only one graced Sheuan's plate. It
was small and a little bitter, but she ate it anyways as she studied
the faces of the arriving guests. No gaps yet.

The Sovereign's castle had been built to withstand a siege, rising above the surrounding city, the base of it three stories' worth of sheer rock. Sloping tiled rooftops delineated the layers of the building, stacked one on top of the other like the layers of a cake. There was really only one reasonable way in and out, and the royal and noble clan members funneled up the ramp and through the single gate, their clothing bright against the dull sky and dusty landscape. The surrounding city was slightly less grand, though it wasn't as desolate as the outskirts. No vagrants here, as the Sovereign's enforcers quickly arrested any straying into inner Bian. This part of the city was a world unto itself, top-ranking clan members able to forget the starving poor just outside its gates.

Sheuan was in the strange position of being a part of one of the four royal clans, but fallen far enough from grace that she didn't warrant an invitation to the Sovereign's party. Yet in pursuit of her mentor's goals, she'd become well known and well liked amongst the younger royals and nobles. With them, her status as the daughter of an executed official made her less of a pariah and more of a venomous snake – no one would be clasping her close, but they'd put her in a glass case to gawk at.

Once drinks were had, inhibitions lessened, and she'd always found a way to wriggle out of that case and into conversations containing the information she'd been told to seek.

This mission, however, had not been sanctioned by her tutor.

Her father might not have been an honest man, but he'd been a loyal one. His execution had occurred two years after the restoration of Kashan, and Sheuan had not attended. She'd waited in her bedroom, clutching her pillow, her teeth clenched so hard her jaw ached. Not knowing in that moment whether her father was still alive or if the blade had fallen. Her neck itched as she wondered whether his cheek was even then pressed to the cold stone, if he

begged or wept or thought of her at all. There was no point in
going to the execution. She wanted to do something, to make it all
stop, but everything had so much momentum that it would have
been akin to throwing herself in the path of a galloping horse.

The horse would keep galloping no matter what happened
to her.

When the servant had come to inform her that the deed had
been done, she'd screamed into the pillow, feeling not human
at all.

Sheuan swallowed and lifted the teacup to her lips, taking a
tiny sip. The chamomile-and-mint-scented steam cleared the
tears from her eyes; she breathed it in and let it hiss out her
mouth. The warmth of it made her dress stick to her back, but
she, like most Langzuan residents, drank it hot year-round.

Finally, a gap appeared in the line and she did not recognize
the people approaching the ramp. She rose to her feet, tossed a
coin onto the table and hurried toward the palace. Forgery was
not her strong suit. She'd had better luck using guile, charm and
wit. Her tutor had always told her to rely on the mental arts first.
The physical arts – forgery, fighting, seduction, trespassing –
were blunt tools that often left some sort of evidence. She could
imagine the twist to the old woman's mouth if she'd witnessed the
steps Sheuan had taken to get here. The seduction of Reilun Ito,
the trespassing into his mother's bedroom to find the invitation,
to study it, her eventual forgery of it. The only physical art she'd
not used was fighting.

Sloppy, unreliable, stupid.

Well, it had gotten her this far. If the Sovereign was the only
one left who could have framed her father, then she'd find the evidence of it. She'd clear his name and clear her clan's name. There
was no taking back that single stroke of the blade. There would
be no more dinners in the garden while her father entertained

guests, his boisterous laughter seeming to shake the paper lanterns strung above the table. She would never again bury her face in his robes, taking in that scent of ink and star anise as he patted her back.

But her mother could be proud of her again. Her family home could be saved. The reparations they owed the Sovereign could cease and they might be able to grow again, to retain their status as royals, instead of parceling off land and businesses and cousins to other clans.

She kept her footfalls slow and even, leaving enough distance between her and the people before her, just in case her memory had failed her and someone in that group knew who she was. A quick glance to the side told her that someone was climbing the ramp behind her. With a flick of her wrist, she pulled out her fan and took a surreptitious peek over the top of it.

Nimao.

Of all the misfortunes! He *knew* she wouldn't have been invited. Sheuan sped up. She'd take her chances with the group ahead of her. She handed her invitation to the guard at the gate without looking at it. He checked the seal, the name, the Sovereign's signature.

He checked them again.

The tea sloshed in her belly, threatening to make its way up her throat. She kept her fan between her and the approaching Nimao, fluttering it, hoping she appeared unconcerned and unhurried. At least any flush in her cheeks could be mistaken for the result of the heat.

The guard finally handed back her invitation and she turned to enter the gates.

A hand seized her wrist. "Sheuan?"

She reacted half on instinct, a bird caught by the wing. One step toward her assailant. A twist of her arm, a pivot, a partially raised knee. She stood face-to-face with Nimao, his wrist now in *her* grasp, her knee slipped between his legs, her invitation whispering at his neck. The warmth of his chest heaved against hers. He was still taller than she was, but she held him like one might a kitten by the nape of its neck.

And now she'd used fighting too. What a mess.

But some half-conscious part of her mind had judged correctly, had slipped free the information she'd needed in the moment.

"I didn't expect to see you here," he murmured. He smelled woody and musky, a perfume – an affectation. He'd dressed un-selfconsciously in a white linen shirt, no embroidery on it save a vine of flowers around the high collar. This close, she could see his pupils expand, large and black. While another man might have angrily pulled away, he was caught in this moment, the gears of his mind gone still.

And now she remembered: back in the workshop, he hadn't given her the chance to respond. He'd simply assumed she hadn't been invited. A correct assumption, but one she could twist to her advantage. She let his wrist go, though he didn't take a step back. "The Sims are still one of the royal clans. It's been a long time since my father's transgression," she said.

She turned to go, knowing this would both cut the conversation where she wanted to cut it, and leave him intrigued and wanting more. Not an admission of anything. Not a confirmation. Just something that would allow him to come to his own conclusion. The one he *wanted* to come to.

"Find me inside," he called after her. "We should speak more."

Her heartbeat drummed in her ears as she passed into the cool stone walls of the castle. She might not be executed if she was caught, but her humiliation would be paraded for all to see, word spreading faster than dust in a storm. All the hard work her tutor had put toward her ascension in the ranks would be swept away.

And Sheuan was still beholden to her. For as long as she had breath, she owed Mitoran. It was the bargain she'd made. Act as an informant for the Unanointed, and be given the tools to save her family from ruin.

She slipped behind pillars, avoiding the crush of people in the center of the room. Strange animals hung on the walls, preserved, their eyes glassy, posed as though they were still living. Here was one small, otter-like creature, with branching horns. There was another, big as a wolf, leaves covering its body like feathers. Altered animals, brought over as curiosities, bought with the Sovereign's ample purse. The light streaming in through the windows was sparse, but even so, potted plants had been placed around the perimeter, drinking what little sunlight they could find.

Plants were wealth in Langzu. Good soil was hard to find, as was a long enough stretch of good weather. The land went through periods of extreme heat and fire, as well as bouts of flooding rain that turned fields into lakes and mud. Once, the stories said, Langzu had been a place of soaring green mountains, of plants growing even in the cracks between stones. The rain had been cool and sweet, the seasons gentle.

Restoration would make it so again. And once Kluehnn had restored the entire world, the barriers between realms would fall.

The process would disappear half the population too, and turn the rest into monsters. By Kluehnn's reckoning, mortals could not continue as they were, lest they repeat the mistakes of the past. But the longer they all lived like this, scraping by on stunted vegetables, wilting in the sun, animals dead and stinking in the streets, the more appealing Kluehnn's solution sounded to everyone. Even to the royal and noble clans.

She circled the perimeter, noting side rooms and balconies from the corner of her eye, her gaze lingering on the chair on a dais at the center of the room, the wood so dark it was nearly black. Gods were carved into the legs and back of it, twining like vines over its surface. From what Sheuan had heard, the chair was a relic from before the Shattering, passed from clan to clan as they fought over it. Servants carried trays of food, passing her as she walked, filling the air with a rich, oily aroma – spiced chicken feet, pork spare ribs, steamed pea shoots with garlic.

She wrenched herself away. She'd been to the castle before, when she'd been younger, but those memories, formed at a time when her cares had been fewer, were hardly infallible. Still, the servants' stairs to the next floor were where she remembered them. Guarded, of course, though by only one woman rather than the five guards set at the main stairs. Getting past her was almost too easy. A cut, a bump, and a paper lantern fell onto a potted plant, the paper lighting up.

The guard rushed to put out the flame and Sheuan slipped past her and up the servants' stairs. The stairway was narrow and dark. The steps were too high, but her dress was made for easy maneuvering. She kept her head down, hoping that any servant she might pass would also be in a rush – too busy to consider the appearance of anyone else in this enclosed space. Not that there was much light to make out her appearance by.

The door creaked a little as she pushed out into an empty hallway.

This upper floor was made of wood, the beams above a reminder of the Sovereign's wealth. Some of them were old, pre-dating a world of heat and dust, but some were newer replacements, shipped in from realms that had been restored. Even those were hard to come by, as restored realms tended to cut off trade and communication about a decade afterwards.

What could a withering place like Langzu offer the lush, restored landscape of somewhere like Kashan?

She took a moment to get her bearings. She'd been to the Sovereign's study as a child, nearly stepping on her father's formal red robes as she followed close behind, trying to absorb his words but failing completely, too taken in by the details surrounding her. The smell of the wood, the tapestries on the walls, the soft rug beneath her feet, the drumming of rain against the roof.

She retraced those steps from her memory, feeling as though she walked through a dream. From below, the murmur of the crowd sounded like the wind through branches, rising and falling, punctuated at times by one loud voice, or a laugh that rose like a bell. Her footfalls and her breath mingled with those sounds. She kept close to the wall, as though she could somehow sink into it should someone appear around the corner.

The door to the study was locked. Her tutor hadn't thought lock-picking a useful enough skill to teach, and had said as much, but when Sheuan had harried her, she'd handed over a slim, flexible piece of wood with a sigh. "Wriggle it between the door and the frame," she'd said. "Catch the latch at the right angle and you won't need to unlock the door at all."

Sheuan did as Mitoran had bade her, and though sweat trickled down her back, the door gave way with a *click*.

The Sovereign's study was just as she remembered it, though it seemed so much smaller than it had when she'd been a child. Bookshelves lined the walls, a green silk rug beneath the desk. The light streaming in through the windows was a dusky pink. An empty tea set sat at the edge of the desk, a corner of the tray hanging off, pushed to the side by stacks of papers. She approached and knelt next to it. It smelled woody and sharp – real tea, not the herbal tincture most places served these days. The heat and weather made real tea difficult to grow. Her gaze fell upon the golden enamel. That one teapot would erase nearly a month's worth of debt from her clan's ledger.

But that wasn't what she was here for. She wasn't a thief.

She went to the bookshelf, to the section where the Sovereign kept his ledgers. Her father hadn't made any extravagant purchases in the time he was meant to have been embezzling money. And she'd never found any secret stash. If the Sovereign had framed him, where had that money actually gone?

Her fingers walked over the leather-bound spines, finally finding the ones that covered the years before and after her father had been executed. There would be a discrepancy, and she would find it. She pulled the volumes from the shelf.

The door to the study creaked open.

She slid the ledgers back, but that was all there was time for. She couldn't even hide behind a curtain. She stood there, frozen, for once all her training abandoning her, leaving her limned in the light of the setting sun, clearly in a place she should not have been.

Wit and guile and charm would have to save her now.

The Sovereign stepped into the room.

14

Sheuan

10 years after the restoration of Kashan
and 571 years after the Shattering

Langzu - inner Bian, the Sovereign's castle

*There is always a price. The mortals killed the Numinars
to take their magic. To build power. To grow comfortable.
To live in extravagance. They incurred a debt that would
one day have to be repaid.*

*They would not live to repay it. But their descendants
would.*

All thought, all strategy fled Sheuan's mind. In that moment,
she couldn't even recall her own name. "You're supposed
to be downstairs," she blurted out. *So much for guile.*

The Sovereign was older than her father had been, though
taller and broader at the shoulders, his white hair pulled into a tail.
Only a few errant strands of black remained, framing a face that
had as many layers as his castle. Even at his age, there was something pleasantly aristocratic about him, classically handsome.

The brows were sloping and gentle, the nose slightly curved and hook-like, the mouth firm but supple. The wrinkles at the corners of his eyes were faint, the soft press of a shorebird's feet against sand. The line bisecting his forehead dug a trench into his skin. Each feature told a different story of the man before her.

"I'm not always fond of parties." His voice was soft, plush; it echoed from the walls and sank into the rug at Sheuan's feet. "I try to spend only as much time in them as will allow people to believe I was always there." He gave a small self-deprecating shrug. It did nothing to put Sheuan at ease.

He strode toward her, and Sheuan was reminded suddenly of herself at all those parties, sliding free of her glass case, making her way closer to the people who had let down their guard. She took a step away and found her back to the bookcase. All he had to do was call his guards and she'd be laying her cheek against the very same stone her father once had.

She wouldn't cry.

He stopped a body's length away from her, eyes narrowed against the light. She stood there stupidly, trying not to glance at the ledgers that she hadn't quite shoved back in all the way.

His gaze found them anyway, and then he looked at her a little more closely. "Ah," he said finally. "You have your father's chin. His brows as well. Sheuan Sim." That supple mouth pursed. "You were not invited."

She didn't deny or confirm what he'd said. All her excuses sounded ridiculous. There was no good way to spin this. Not to the Sovereign himself.

"You made it all the way into my study without an invitation." He glanced about. "Alone?"

She nodded, and then finally found her tongue. If she was caught, then she was all the way caught. All she'd ever wanted was answers. "I went to rival clans; I searched their records.

There was no evidence they'd framed my father. The only one left with opportunity and motive was you." It felt dangerous to speak this suspicion aloud, but she'd already been backed into a corner. "Did my father actually embezzle those funds?"

The Sovereign's eyes were dark, the slightest smudge of bronze around his pupils. "You're a smart young woman. You made it this far. Does it actually matter whether or not he did?"

She wanted to say yes. Of course it mattered! But doubt suddenly seized her by the throat.

He went on, as though he hadn't expected her to answer. "Your father is dead. There's no changing that. Even if you happened to somehow find proof that he did not embezzle funds and that I framed him, what do you think would happen?"

"Our name would be restored." Sheuan's lip trembled and she bit her cheek.

The Sovereign gestured to the ledgers she'd carelessly shoved back onto the shelf. "Let me explain something to you, Sheuan of the Sim clan. Information, even proof, is malleable. It is like the flash of lightning across the sky – we all see it, it is impressive for a moment, but it is also easily forgettable in the next. Say you uncovered such proof and brought it forth. First, everyone would be shocked. They would whisper amongst themselves – 'Can you believe it?' – but then they would move on. Do you understand why?"

She finally allowed herself to follow this scenario to its end, applying all the training Mitoran had given her, the hours of lecturing and reading. Her heart, buoyed by hope only moments before, dropped into her feet. People were comfortable. People were complacent. The commoners might suffer and struggle, but the promise of restoration lingered. It was a greater chance at survival than they might face in a bloody revolution. "No one would actually want to challenge your rule."

He nodded, his expression fatherly. "If you tried to keep this information in the public attention, if you tried to keep that lightning in the sky, they would all simply see you as a troublemaker. They do not want to see it."

"But I wouldn't have been the one who did anything wrong." She felt like a child again, complaining to her father about the unfairness of the weather.

He shrugged. "That's not the point, though, is it?" He tilted his head to the side, watching her. "What do you think your father would do if he were still alive?"

If her father were still alive, he would be the one who would be training her, not Mitoran. He would still be there at dinner in the evenings, dressed in his official robes, the deep folds smelling of ink and star anise. He would still be steering their household, instead of her mother, his presence steady, confident, wholly unmoved by all the small eddies and currents.

Her mind clicked into gear again. But this wasn't what the Sovereign cared about. He hadn't called his guards on her yet. She'd impressed him with this little bit of subterfuge, and he wanted to know if there was more to her.

For a moment she agonized over what should have been. All she'd wanted was to prove, once and for all, that her father was innocent. She'd wanted to clear his name and reverse the fortunes of her clan.

But now, standing here, faced with the reality, she understood what a ridiculous notion that had been. She would never, *never* save her family by proving her father's innocence. There was no future in which that revelation led to her clan's prosperity. Not if the Sovereign were the guilty party.

She buried that hope – quickly, without ceremony. He was waiting for a response, and Sheuan knew this moment held both an opportunity and a pitfall. She'd heard her father talk often about Kashan's restoration and how Kashan would likely, inevitably, cut off contact with Langzu. She also knew his questions bordered on blasphemy. What did that matter when restoration was coming? How devout a man was the Sovereign?

She supposed she was about to find out. She met the Sovereign's gaze and didn't waver. "He always wanted to know why realms cut off contact ten or so years on from restoration. He wasn't satisfied with surface explanations. You want to know what he'd be doing? He'd be searching for more answers, making inquiries, maybe even visiting Kashan himself. My father knew that once Kashan cut Langzu off, the situation in Langzu would reach a breaking point. Everyone would yearn for restoration as starvation set into the populace. We don't trade enough with the southern continent. The deep water makes the logistics of sending goods through the barrier too difficult. It puts us all into a desperate situation."

He didn't move closer, yet she somehow felt that he loomed over her, the light catching the silver cranes woven into his black robes. "Ah yes, desperation. Desperation is a spice that can bring out the fullness of a dish or ruin it. Langzu will survive, one way or another, though many of its people may not. The Sim clan is failing. Everyone knows it. But what sort of dish are you?"

There was nothing disapproving in his eyes, so she decided to press back, her tone tart. "Am I a food to be consumed, then? Is that how you see your subjects?"

A breathless little laugh escaped the Sovereign's lips. "Aren't we all here to be consumed? To be looked at, to be judged as savory or sweet, to be licked and swallowed and converted into fuel for others' ambitions?" He turned each word over in his mouth as though tasting it. His eyelashes, golden in the setting sun, fluttered. The gaze he cast over her was the same one a satiated tiger gave a deer. His chin dipped. "Yes, even me. I had to understand this before I could unite the clans."

He *was* looming, his shoulders spread to emphasize his height. If she'd been a less experienced woman, she might have blushed at his insinuations. She wanted him to feel she was clever, but there was danger in being perceived as *too* clever. Briefly, she wondered if that had proved her father's downfall. He'd always dug into his work, never content with simple answers.

So she let her gaze trail away and hoped he mistook the flush of excitement in her cheeks for embarrassment. He wanted to feel that power? Fine. She could grant him that.

She felt his presence diminish as his stance shifted, and he let the silence sit for a moment. "I don't currently have a trade minister," he said. "The last one died of age and illness half a year ago. The position is open. Would you like to redeem your family's name?"

Her spine stiffened; she couldn't help the hitch in her breath. "You're offering me the trade minister position?"

"No." Amusement tinged his voice. "No, I never said that. I'm offering you a chance at it. If you're half as clever as your father was, you'll earn it. Find out why the restored realms cut off trade and communication. Better yet, stop Kashan from doing so. Do that, and the position is yours."

There might never come another opportunity to speak so freely to the Sovereign. And part of her still desperately wanted to *know*. "Why should I trust you? You executed my father for something I'm not even sure he actually did." She let some of the real hurt and anger seep into her voice. A small outburst from someone young and naïve could be dismissed, forgiven, answered carelessly.

A corner of the Sovereign's mouth twitched upward. Oh, he knew he was being baited. She both hated and admired him for it. "My dear, it doesn't matter whether you trust me. And I'm afraid you'll have to live with the knowledge that you may never know what happened with your father. If you ever reach my age, you'll understand that some questions will just float in your mind forever."

He reached out to touch her collarbone, his trailing finger as impersonal as if he were admiring a statue, his gaze fixed at the base of her throat. "If you fail at this task, I will divide up your family and split its assets among the other clans. But," he shrugged, "if you do not take this opportunity, your clan will eventually fail and the same thing will happen." His finger flicked at her shoulder. She flinched involuntarily. "Now go."

She made for the door, but his voice stopped her. "Ah, wait. Take this."

He was at her side, pressing his seal into her palm – the cherry blossom on a budded branch. And then she was being ushered out the door, hearing it click behind her as she once more stood in the empty hallway. It took a moment for her head to stop spinning, for her feet to feel fully beneath her. She'd thought her mind was working clearly before, but now she recognized the intoxicating effect of his presence, the way he had let her focus on nothing else. The gravity of the task finally settled into her gut. She was one woman, from a declining clan, with very little money to her name. And he'd not asked her to settle a clan dispute, or to uncover new ways to use Langzu's goods.

He'd asked her to change the world. She glanced down at the seal, heavy in her palm, her teeth setting into place.

It was the only goddamned resource he'd given her.

15

Hakara

10 years after the restoration of Kashan and 571 years after the Shattering

Langzu - the outskirts of Bian

The altered who appear in unaltered lands are wanderers, unmoored from the places they belong. They are sad creatures, living nostalgically in the past instead of moving into the glorious future Kluehnn has planned for them.

I'd wanted answers, and I got more answers than I could stuff my head with. I'd always known that the Unanointed dealt heavily in the forbidden arts of magic. But in my imagination it had involved chanting and the waving of arms. Maybe smoke. Lots of gibbering and bodily disintegration, eventually, as the aether took its toll.

"That's not how it works at all," Utricht said flatly. I'd finished my lengthy, gory explanation of what I thought happened to people who used magic. It had involved lots of blood streaming from nostrils and eyes. He'd laid out several god gems on a table in front of me. Behind him, the other two Unanointed in my team enjoyed a breakfast of mashed and boiled millet. The freckled, fox-like one, I'd learned, was Alifra. The one with the curved sword was Dashu. They were engaged in a quiet conversation I couldn't quite make out, as two stray cats weaved beneath the table, hoping for scraps. Both cats looked the worse for wear, one with a swollen eye and another missing half an ear, but weren't we all a little rough-looking these days? Buzhi was somewhere else, probably down in the ruins, maybe worshiping some old god who demanded all their followers act like colossal assholes. Seemed like something he might do.

I tried not to stare at the spotted fur covering Utricht's cheeks, the tusks at the corners of his mouth. "The gems absorb the aether, not the body, so you're free of its effects." He lifted one tiny gem between thumb and forefinger. It had a faint rosy glow. "I like to think of them as god seeds. They react with the aether and allow us to use magic in a way that doesn't damage our bodies. The aether is what allows these seeds to grow. As long as you can hold your breath, they'll enhance you." He set it back down and picked up the next gem down the line. This one gave off a faint green glow.

"So you ... what? Grow the arms and legs of gods? Become gods for a little bit?" I said it as a joke, but he gave me a dead-pan look.

Couldn't read this guy at all.

"You experienced it when you were mining. You tell me."

Damn. He was going to make me work for this. They seemed to enjoy doing that here. I leaned back on my cushion far enough that I almost tipped off, but clasped my hands and settled back into place. I pointed to the gem with the rosy glow. "I put one of those between my teeth. Accidentally swallowed it when the sinkhole started to collapse. Something happened to my arms. They got bigger. Stronger."

He nodded. "There are different types of seeds and they allow us to do different things. Some are rarer than others. Those rosy ones, they enhance your arms. The green ones, legs. These are the most common. Less common are the violet ones, which can give you a moment's invulnerability."

My eyebrows lifted in spite of myself. I'd done a fair number of stupid things in my life – imagine if I could have gotten away with them without any scrapes or bruised bones. I cast my gaze down the line of gems. "Blue?"

He tapped his forehead with one gnarled finger. "God eyes. They allow you to perceive the truth, at least among the mortals and the altered. Not uncommon, but hard to get a hold of. No matter what Kluehnn's devoted say about magic use, they overlook it in the noble and royal clans. Many of the blue ones go to the Sovereign, we suspect to be used by a special subset of his enforcers. But none of us have encountered them and lived, so we don't know for sure."

I picked up the gem at the very end – the smallest one. It cast a golden light on the table's surface. "I've never seen this kind."

"We don't get many of them in. This one – they change your fingers. They allow you to manipulate time."

"They ... what now?" I set it down as though it might explode.

"We don't know much about them – as I said, we don't get that many in, and they're small enough that we don't get much use out of the ones we do have. But I've seen one used once. Took away a killing wound as though it had never been there."

"How does it work?"

Utricht shrugged, huffing out a breath through his lips. "I don't know. Never used one myself, and the Unanointed I saw use that one was killed shortly after. We hold them in reserve for only the most dangerous missions. That one is the only one we have right now."

Five gems. Five uses. "Are there others?"

"If there are, we've not found them yet."

"Does she understand enough?" Mitoran's voice sounded from behind me. My heartbeat jumped, and I nearly jumped up with it.

"Only the basics," Utricht responded.

"That's all we have time for. They're moving the corestone from the warehouse to one of the dens in three days."

His lips pursed, the gray skin around them puckering. "That's not enough time."

"It'll have to be." She swept toward the table where the others ate their breakfast.

I walked my fingers back toward the rosy-colored gemstone, remembering what it was like to be stronger, the way I'd had to quickly adjust my mind to that new reality. I opened my mouth to ask about the bonding process when the door banged open.

A man ducked through the entrance – one of the largest altered I'd ever seen. His head might not have grazed the ceiling, but the black wings at his back nearly did. Each step he took shook the floorboards. I'd not encountered that many altered in my time in Langzu. They were often looked at askance, but only because they resembled the old gods. Mostly people liked to pretend they didn't exist – they were a pointed reminder of the fate we all would face at some point: disappear or be altered. This altered had none of the elegance or glow of an old god; he was a hulking brute of a creature, his dark hair falling nearly over his eyes, his heavy jaw hiding what I could only assume were rows of sharpened teeth. He held a sack over one shoulder, and there was something about his hands that made me believe he could easily crush a man's skull with them. Alifra and Dashu were evidently unimpressed by his presence.

I supposed you could get used to anything.

"More for you, Utricht." His voice was low and deep,

reminding me of rocks tumbling loose as a sinkhole collapsed. He set a sack on the table. A gem slid out, joining the four already there. Utricht snatched up the ones he'd been using for our training, returning them to the box.

That was when I realized – that entire *sack* was filled with god gems. I could pay for a guide three times over with that sort of haul. And he'd just casually walked through the streets of Bian with it. What if someone had tried to jump him?

I blinked. Wait, what was I thinking? Who would have the courage and lack of brains to try? Hm. I mean, *I* would have.

The man hadn't even had the decency yet to acknowledge my presence. His sole focus was Utricht, as though I didn't even exist in this space, at this very table, a finger's poke away. I cleared my throat.

His black-eyed gaze flicked to me, studied me for a moment and then flicked back to Utricht. "Taking new people out on your next job, I see."

I noted his use of *your*. Utricht sighed. "Mind your own business, Thassir. Keep out of mine and I'll keep out of yours."

Well that was interesting. "You're not one of the Unanointed either?" I asked.

That earned me a longer look.

A yowl sounded from the other table. Buzhi had arrived and had kicked one of the cats out of his way. "Damned flea-ridden beasts always underfoot," he muttered. Dashu and Alifra watched him the way they might if he'd walked into a tiger's enclosure wearing nothing but a loincloth and a healthy splash of sheep's blood.

I caught only the flash of white teeth before Thassir had him on the floor, his wings spread over him, one clawed hand wrapped around Buzhi's throat and the other clenched around his wrist, bending his arm at a painful angle.

If his voice had sounded like loose stones to me before, now it sounded like those selfsame stones grinding together. "Apparently you have forgotten. Mitoran and I have an agreement. *No one* hurts the cats."

"They're ... cats," Buzhi gasped out. "I didn't even hurt it. They're not people."

"How kind of you to inform me of that. Clearly I was not aware."

I was the only one in the entire room who let out a little snort-laugh. Thassir did not look up, the whole of his attention focused on this one man. He gave his wrist a tug and Buzhi groaned. "You do not kick the cats, you do not push the cats, you do not even give them an annoyed look."

Mitoran uncrossed her arms as though she'd finally seen enough. "Thassir ... "

Thassir bent low to whisper into Buzhi's ear, though his voice was loud enough that I could hear. "If I catch you harassing them again, I won't just break your arm. I'll take it clean off."

He let Buzhi go, lifting his hands and turning to Mitoran as though to show her he had not – this time – removed any body parts from one of her Unanointed.

The sack was still on the table, the one loose gem wobbling with every move Thassir made. It just didn't make much sense to me. "Where'd you get those?" The words were spilling out of my mouth before I could stop them. "The gems."

Thassir turned his black gaze from Mitoran to me. "Were we having a conversation?"

"No, but I work as a diver at the sinkhole mines – or I used to. We give the gems to the liaison right after the sinkhole closes up. They lock them in a box until it's time to deliver them to the Sovereign. Liaisons are under guard. If you're clever, you can sneak one or two away, but that's it. So how did you get your hands on so many?"

I didn't think a scowl could get any darker, but somehow he managed it. He turned to go, his wings trailing against the wooden floorboards.

I followed him. Mitoran shot me a warning look, but I'd never been keen on warnings. If I had, I'd never have started diving for abalone. Never would have kept my sister and me alive. "It's impossible, really. You look like a big, strong … man? Can I call you a man? Not exactly sure how to refer to altered people. Anyways, you look strong, but how did you get past the guards? You couldn't fight *all* of them. Not by yourself."

A tabby cat leapt onto Thassir's back from the table, nudging his cheek before running to his other shoulder and launching itself off. He paused. "What a happy accident that I found you, so I know what I can and cannot do."

"That doesn't work on me."

"What?"

"Sarcasm. Hints."

One black wing twitched. "Then please tell me what will make you go away."

"Answers."

I watched his back heave with a sigh. "I do not know you, but I do not like you."

"I'm nice to cats," I added helpfully. "In case you were thinking about pulling my arm off too."

"I was thinking about crushing your throat, just enough so you can no longer speak."

I hesitated for only a moment, but that was enough time for him to get to the door. He opened it and ducked through.

"Are you working with them? The Unanointed?"

He ruffled his feathers. The building was in the outskirts of Bian, a row of houses opposite us visible over a flat, cracked road with wagon tracks marking the dirt. "Mitoran and I have an arrangement. That's all you need to know." He crouched, his wings spread, and he hopped to the rooftop. I heard his heavy footsteps against the tiles.

Well that was one way to get out of answering my questions. They swirled in my chest with no outlet. Every time I thought over the process of the mining and the tithes, I couldn't imagine how that altered could have stolen such a large quantity at once.

"Leave him be." Mitoran touched my arm.

I shut the door. Thassir was not as uncaring as he made himself out to be – I'd seen the glint of curiosity in his earlier glance. Still, I let Mitoran guide me back toward Utricht. "We should bond the two of you, let you practice. We don't have much time."

16

Sheuan

10 years after the restoration of Kashan
and 571 years after the Shattering

Langzu - inner Bian

*The pattern is thus: weather becomes more unpredictable.
Water dries up or the land receives too much of it. The air
is hot. The animals die. The crops die.*

The people — they begin to die too.

*Restoration comes and saves half their number, alters
them. This restored realm doesn't need the unrestored ones.
Eventually, they stop communicating. They stop trading.*

And the unrestored world becomes ever smaller.

By the time Sheuan returned home, the cherry blossom was
branded into her palm. Each turn she'd taken through the
darkened streets of Bian had only served to deepen her despair.
She was clever, she had training — but what she didn't have was
money, and no amount of cleverness and training could make up
for the lack of it.

The Sim family home still looked grand, vines curving around the arched entrance in the wall. But if one peered a little closer, they would see that the vines no longer flowered, that several tiles on the rooftop were chipped and broken, that the wooden doors were in desperate need of fresh paint.

She unlocked the doors and stepped into the outer courtyard. With each step she felt pieces of the day loosen and peel away. Her time in Mull's workshop, directing his workers with firmness and more confidence than she felt. The flirting she'd done with Nimao. The desperate scramble to make it to the Sovereign's study. And her encounter with the Sovereign himself. That last bit clung to her, settling into her shoulders, never quite falling away.

The one remaining servant greeted her when she stepped inside her family home, bowing and asking if she could get her anything to eat, any tea?

Even the entrance of the home, usually a place that bustled with activity, felt empty. Tapestries had been sold, rugs taken to new homes when family members had married into other clans. These days, the couples inevitably chose to take on the other clan's name, even if they were noble and not royal. No one wanted to become a Sim, not anymore.

But there were still people who relied on the family name. A few younger cousins, businesses that had tithed to the Sims for years, the elders of the family who, often enough, had once fought against other clans. Clans held grudges even if open conflict between them was now outlawed. The only thing that protected the elders was the Sim family name. If the clan was unable to pay their next tithes to the Sovereign, he would dissolve them. Every remaining Sim would be forced onto the streets, clanless and penniless. Her mother among them.

Already their position was tenuous. They'd not held a ministerial post since her father had been executed, their money was running out and their numbers were vastly reduced. There were so many hungry noble clans eager to be promoted to royal status.

Yet none of them had framed her father.

Sheuan pushed the thought down as she waved away the servant and went to the inner courtyard. Her mother liked to spend her evenings there. The courtyard was small but well appointed, one of the few areas of the house that had been kept up. Raised garden beds filled most of the space, a removable canopy spread out over them to help protect them on days when the sun was too strong.

Her mother was holding court outside, going through the ledgers at the same time, her brush quick and precise. Clan members milled about the table beneath the awning. All faces Sheuan recognized, though most had grown gaunt in recent years. Oh, the Sim clan could still feed itself with its lands and holdings. They'd not needed to resort to ration tickets. But fear and stress could hollow a person out.

Her uncle was arguing with one of the aunties. "Rain has been scarce and this year's crop is stunted. We need to make some illegal purchases if we're to stay afloat."

"With what money?" She waved her hands about, as though taking in the shabby condition of their Bian estate.

"If we don't, we won't have enough to sell. We'll be short our tithe to the Sovereign. We won't even have enough for noble tier. He'll dissolve us, sell our assets to make up the difference."

"And do you think we'd get a rap on the knuckles if we were caught with god gems? Maybe if we were the Otangu clan or the Juitsi clan. But we're not. The Sovereign would probably lop off the head of whichever clan member was left holding the empty bag."

Sheuan's uncle clutched at his chest as though her words were a spear. He looked like he was made of only skin and sinew. "You *know* what will happen to me if our clan is dissolved. I assassinated one of the Otangu clan sons."

"That was thirty years ago."

"You think that matters to *them*?"

Her mother didn't even look up from her work. She put down her brush and made a note on the wax tablet next to her. "I'll give you the funds for three gems, brother. Bargain hard. Ask one of our family members in another clan for use of their infuser. Use the gems wisely. Be discreet. Return any leftover coin." She went back to the ledger.

"That won't make up the difference," Sheuan's uncle said.

"It will close the gap. We have four months before tithes are due. We have a little time to see about bridging that final distance."

But the clan members weren't done. A roof needed mending — her mother told them to patch it themselves. An unexpected late winter heatwave had killed nearly an entire flock of chickens — they could buy extra eggs and put them beneath broody hens but they could not purchase grown birds. It went on and on like this, a tirade of problems, most of which could be solved with money. If they had any.

Sheuan hung back, not sure when or if she should disturb her mother.

"These are temporary fixes," her uncle lamented.

Her mother's eyes finally flicked to the side, spotting Sheuan. She set her brush down again, blew on the pages to dry the ink, and closed the ledger with a *snap*. "We can continue this another time. You should all be attending to your estates outside the city, not bothering me in mine. You come here groveling for money that we *do not have*. We need everyone focused on *making* money, not spending it, if we're to get out of this unscathed."

Uncle's gaze found Sheuan. "Yet you'll spend it freely on your only daughter."

"Because she could be our permanent fix. Now get out."

This house might belong to every clan member, in a manner of speaking, but Sheuan's mother had taken over as the head of the clan when her husband had been executed. Her word was to be obeyed quickly and without question.

As soon as the others had left the courtyard, her mother pushed the ledger to the side and packed up her brush and ink. "Where were you and what were you doing?" Her words were as clipped as her movements.

Sheuan approached. "I went to the Sovereign's naming-day party."

Sharp black eyes caught hers. "The Sim clan was not invited. And your tutor did not approve of your going. She would have wanted a say."

When Mitoran had approached Sheuan and her mother, it had been in a moment of desperation. It had been years since her father had been executed, yet the Sim clan had not been assigned a new ministerial position. Desperation had clearly made them a more appealing dish to the Unanointed, at least.

A small influx of cash, specialized tutoring, and in return, Sheuan would spy for them. A risky proposition, but one they could not turn away. And the Sims had never exactly been devout, though they practiced at appearing so. Why not align themselves?

"I was looking for evidence of Father's innocence." Might as well tell her the truth.

Her mother's mouth twisted. "At the Sovereign's naming-day party? You're looking in too-high places, Sheuan. Leave that be. Your father is dead and our clan cannot eat honor."

"I was looking in the Sovereign's study."

The ink stick dropped from her mother's fingers. The lantern she'd set at the edge of the table made her face ghoulish. Her mouth moved but nothing came out.

"I was caught. The Sovereign caught me and he made me an offer."

Color returned to her mother's face in measures as Sheuan explained the bargain he'd offered her. Her jaw set, and Sheuan recognized herself in her mother's expression. She'd made up her mind. "You must take the Sovereign's offer. You must go to Kashan."

It was the same conclusion Sheuan had come to, though for reasons she couldn't explain, it felt different coming from her mother. "There's no way past the barrier without a guide. Mother, our funds have run thin enough that paying for a guide would be too large an expense with the tithes and the reparations we still have to pay."

"He did not give us a stay from those?"

"No."

A huff of breath. "Did I raise a daughter who only makes excuses? Every time Mitoran comes here to train you, we feed and house her and spend coin we do not have. We buy you clothes so you can fit in among your peers, so you can rise, so you can be noticed. So the Sovereign will decide you are too valuable to be discarded. So he will assign you a post. You are the only chance we have to keep this clan intact. You are young, beautiful, smart – you have everything you need. What have you spent all those hours studying for if not for this? Look at everything I am already dealing with. You want me to fix this for you?" She waved a hand. "Figure it out."

Something swelled within Sheuan, some long-forgotten feeling. It choked her breath, threatening to drown her. Once, her mother had looked at her with sparkling eyes, her hand securely tucked in her husband's arm. Sheuan wondered if the life before was only an imagined thing, embellished in her memories to be something it was not.

Regardless, *this* was her life now, no matter what it had been before. She owed it to her clan, to her mother, to *try*.

There had to be a way; her mother was right – she'd simply not thought this through. She'd come to her mother with a problem and hadn't even bothered trying to think of a solution first. It was thoughtless and beneath her.

"Yes." She bowed her head. "I will find a way. I will go to Kashan and find out why the restored realms stop trade and communication."

Her mother didn't acknowledge her response, but by the tightening of her lips, Sheuan knew she'd heard her.

She retreated to her room and found a tray of tea laid out on the bed, along with the seated figure of a woman she still knew very little of.

"I asked for the tea," Mitoran said. "In case you were wondering." She lifted a cup to her lips and blew, the steam briefly obscuring her face. She tilted her head in the direction of the window, the shutter slightly ajar. "I heard your conversation with your mother."

Sheuan found herself edging along the wall, as though this wasn't her room. She took a deliberate few steps toward the bed and then picked up the other cup of tea. Might as well, if it was brewed. "You didn't come here to eavesdrop on me."

"I could have sent a letter, but I was in the area. I wanted to know if you'd heard any more rumors of corestones being found during mining."

In truth, she'd been distracted searching out evidence of her father's innocence, but she wasn't about to tell the Unanointed that. "No. Nothing else. I would have sent word."

Mitoran's hand tightened around her cup. "And now you won't be able to. Not from Kashan." She took another sip and then set the cup down. "If you meant to ask me for help getting through the barrier, you should know that I won't give it. The bargain we made was for training and the one sum of coin. Nothing more."

"I didn't expect your help." Mitoran might have spent years with Sheuan – teaching her to fight, teaching her the subtleties of politics, teaching her how to write elegantly and how to do complicated sums – but they'd never truly grown close. Mitoran never gave any personal details of herself. Never told Sheuan how she'd come by all this knowledge – whether she'd had her own tutor or whether she'd just collected it piecemeal over the long span of her life. So Sheuan had never divulged anything of herself.

Not that she'd needed to. Mitoran had a way of digging information out of her, the way her mother had taken a needle to Sheuan's fingers whenever she'd gotten a splinter.

"You don't have to go to Kashan, no matter what the Sovereign or your mother might say. There are still other ways to help your clan out of this hole they're in. You think he hasn't worked at this problem before? He's asking you to do something no one else has been able to accomplish."

Sheuan heard the slight emphasis on "you" and it stung her more than she'd thought it would. Most times she believed herself impassive, emotions experienced on a surface level as part of whatever persona she'd assumed for the task at hand. "You trained me. You know what I'm capable of." Or perhaps Mitoran didn't. She'd never been out among the people of Bian with Sheuan; she'd never actually seen her at work. Sheuan knew, without conceit, that she was exceptional in many ways. It was why Mitoran had approached her in the first place. "You want to protect your investment. And I want to protect mine. We both know the reason we made this bargain was so I would have the tools to save the clan. The Sovereign has given me that chance and I have to take it."

Mitoran waved a hand. "You could work for the Unanointed. Forget the ties of your clan. We have the means to arrange a marriage for you that would . . . lift you out of this situation."

Sheuan imagined her mother cast from the only home she'd known, the house she'd grown up in given to some other clan, the legacy of her father divided into pieces. The path forward was narrow, but it was still there. "I want to save my family. I still can."

Mitoran let out a sharp huff of breath. "And what of yourself?" She gestured to the peeling walls. "Others have left. You may be the only daughter, but that doesn't mean you have to stay here."

"I *am* my family."

Her tutor shook her head in disgust. "If that's your attitude, I won't dissuade you." She rose to her feet, her skirts swirling. "If you're going there anyways, keep an ear out for mention of the corestones I've asked you about. And remember two things, Sheuan." She set her teacup down and approached, reaching out to straighten Sheuan's collar. It was a way to get close, to manufacture a sense of familiarity. Touch could be powerful, if used in the right ways.

There was always a reason to everything Mitoran did. Sheuan waited, determined not to waver.

"Don't turn back in the barrier. Never try to turn back. Do your best not to breathe the aether. And remember Kluehnn's precepts. You may seek to meet with the Queen, but Kashan is different now that it's restored."

Her hands fell, her gaze holding Sheuan's only a moment longer. Sheuan gave her tutor a firm nod. With one last shake of her head, Mitoran left.

Do your best not to breathe the aether. The words triggered a memory, flipping Sheuan's mood from abject dejection to a wild, spiraling hope.

The box she'd found beneath Mull's desk with the prototype filters. If they protected against the aether as he descended into the earth, they might also protect against it within the barrier. The way would still be fraught – filled with wind and stinging sand and the crack between realms – but this eliminated the greatest danger.

If the filters actually worked.

17

Hakara

10 years after the restoration of Kashan
and 571 years after the Shattering

Langzu - the outskirts of Bian

*Kluehnn killed all seven of the elder gods: Lithuas, Irael,
Nioanen, Velenor, Ayaz, Rumenesca and Barexi.
And then he began to hunt down the rest.*

The bonding process was both stranger than I'd expected
and not as strange as I'd expected. Mitoran oversaw us,
holding our hands pressed to one another, our palms opened
and bloodied, as one of the altered summoned aether from below
and let it suffuse the air around us. I could smell the magic in it,
thick and pungent as seawater. The fur on the back of Utricht's
hand prickled at my fingertips. When my palm began to tingle,
I studied Utricht's face.

"You feel that too?"

Mitoran glanced at me, her gaze sharp.

I sighed. "If I was supposed to be quiet during this, you should have mentioned it at the beginning." Alifra and Dashu had cleared away the tables and cushions and were sparring. No use of god gems. I supposed they needed to be saved for actual combat.

Mitoran lifted her hands away from ours. "Breaking the bond requires the same process, which means that just as you both must agree to be bonded, you both must agree that the bond should be broken."

"What if one of us dies?"

Mitoran wasn't the only one who cast me a sharp glance this time. "Yes, that will break the bond as well."

Utricht raised a brow at me. "Are you planning on committing a murder?"

"Just want to know all the aspects of what we're getting into. I'm doing this willingly, aren't I?" I gave the altered man an encouraging pat on the shoulder.

Utricht cast a long, pleading look in Mitoran's direction that said, quite plainly, "So this is who I'm to be saddled with." All of them were so committed to the cause. Going up against a god. Was I the only recruit who didn't really believe in all this?

Mitoran gave Utricht a nod. He wheeled about and marched into the next room, closing the door behind him. As soon as he'd disappeared, she held out a strip of black cloth between her hands.

"Seriously?"

"We always test the bond." She held it up.

I turned around and let her tie it around my eyes. I wished I could say my other senses sharpened, or that I felt the magic suddenly stirring in my blood, but all I felt was darkness and annoyance. "When will I grow a stronger pair of arms again?"

"Focus, Hakara." Mitoran's voice had the crisp quality of a tutor's, and my spine involuntarily straightened. I did what she asked without thinking.

It was like standing, eyes closed, facing a wall and knowing it was right there through the subtle cues of breath and sound. I knew that Utricht was in this building. The hairs on my right arm pricked. Somewhere to my right.

"Point."

I lifted a hand and pointed, feeling like a human lodestone.

Mitoran brushed past me, her passage smelling faintly citrusy. "Utricht?"

"Here!" he called.

The blindfold came off. "The bond is solid." Mitoran reached into the pouch at her side and pulled out several god gems of varying shades. Each was the size of a grain of rice. They lit her palm with a soft glow. "You'll need to practice with these. Get used to the order of things – swallow a gem, take in the aether that Utricht will draw up for you. Notice how long it takes for your god limbs to grow. Let the feel of them become second nature to you, so that you can use them like your own. Hold weapons in them, get used to their strength." She nodded to the two other Unanointed – the ones she'd said would be part of my team. "They will help you."

Two more days, and then I'd be tossed into the field.

I lifted one of the red gems, studying it. "Do I have to swallow it to infuse it? What if we did it the other way around, so you didn't have to know where I was? We just infuse all the gems now and then I swallow them later?"

"We've tried that before." Alifra leaned against a chair. "The aether seeps out after a while. Something about air densities. Someone in Xiazen was studying the mechanics of it."

Utricht lifted a hand, wiggling his fingers. "It also needs to be inside the body when the aether hits for the magic to work properly. It's like growing a plant in water instead of planting it in dirt. It works in a sense, but not as well as dirt."

I shuddered. "Love to think of myself as a plot of dirt waiting for a plant to grow in it. Maybe stop using the seed analogies? They're a bit creepy." I caught Alifra hiding a grin behind her hand before I swallowed one of the red gems. A quick gesture from Utricht, and the air around me smelled of seaweed. I breathed it in and held it. Felt odd to do it deliberately, but that was the point of practicing, wasn't it?

The itching at my shoulders felt familiar now. The growth of my arms didn't surprise me. But both Buzhi and Alifra attacking me at once did.

I ducked a swinging punch from Buzhi. A lot of unreleased aggression, that one. I tossed one of the green-tinted gems into my mouth and seized Alifra's foot before she could kick me. I pushed her back and found my strength greater than I'd expected. She flew into the table that had been moved to the corner. The wood cracked but didn't break.

I let out my breath and felt the god arms dissolve, smoke drifting from my hands. More aether surrounded me and I breathed it in. My hips began to itch.

My legs grew at least another couple inches. It felt odd, being in a body that didn't quite belong to me. A blow landed on my ribs. A kick hit me square in the jaw, even as I pulled away to try and avoid it. My vision swam with black and red.

"Don't overthink it," Utricht called to me.

I towered over the four Unanointed, and quickly realized that these feet were much quicker than my own. Power surged in my veins, intoxicating and sweet.

What would Rasha think of me now? Would she be frightened that I'd used magic, or would she simply look at me with all the trust and awe she'd granted me when I'd first come back from diving for abalone? I laid about with my fists, using my god legs to duck and dart. I got one good hit on Buzhi's shoulder, and then I had to breathe. My god limbs began to dissolve, tendrils of black smoke rising and disappearing into the air, taking with them the scent of the ocean.

"Not a bad start," Utricht said, his hands still out, ready to summon more aether. "We can't spare too many gems, but we'll try again tomorrow. And pull your punches a little. We'll need everyone's help." Dashu was tending to Alifra, offering a hand up and an arm to lean on.

I nodded at him. "Why didn't you fight me too?"

His beard twitched as he cast me a quick smile. "I don't fight hand-to-hand. And we don't want to kill you just yet."

Bold. I liked that. Hopefully he wasn't just words. I glanced upward. "If we need everyone's help, what about Thassir? If he can manage to bring in that many god gems—"

Utricht held up a forestalling hand. "He won't come with us."

"Has Mitoran ever asked?"

He frowned and opened his mouth to respond.

"He is not one of the Unanointed," Mitoran interrupted. "Get her some food," she told Utricht. "Practice more, without the gems. Her technique is sloppy. She's like an alley cat trying to fight off the rain. Two more days is not enough."

He ran me through my paces as the other Unanointed sparred and offered suggestions. "Hold your arms up, cover your face." "Keep your feet moving." "Hit with your whole upper body, not just your arms." Halfway through the day, Utricht tossed me a wooden blade and every bit of advice suddenly changed.

By the time night fell, I was as tired as though I'd mined three sinkholes, one after another. Dinner was a silent, sullen affair, Buzhi nursing his drink and still rubbing at his shoulder, casting glares at everyone who dared speak.

Utricht led me upstairs to a small room after dinner, pointing at a bedroll in the corner. "That one's yours." He pointed to another across the room. "This one's mine. I wake up early, but I'm quiet. They'll come to get you soon after anyways."

I tried lying down on the bedroll, focusing on the ceiling above. Was Thassir still up there? "Utricht?"

"Hm?" He'd pulled a blanket over his shoulders and was facing the wall.

"Who did you lose?"

He grunted and didn't answer for a while. Finally, he sighed. "My wife. Twenty-three years ago. Cressima. I was altered. She wasn't. I took work in Kashan, and I fled through the barrier to Langzu before restoration could take me for a second time. Didn't want to disappear or become even more monstrous. I made it, but it was a reminder, so I went straight to looking for the Unanointed." His voice grew soft. "And you? Have you lost anyone?"

I hadn't lost Rasha, not really. She was only out of my reach. Someday soon I'd make my way back to her. "No."

Something clicked above. Two tiles, pressing together.

I sat up. "I'm going up there."

"The roof?"

Before he could say anything else, I'd thrown off my blanket and was at the window, the glass shuddering as I forced it open and climbed out.

"Hakara . . . "

The wind took the rest of his words. Up on the roof I could see all of Bian – the center of the city with its clan houses, the castle rising above the rest. The walls encircling it, the gates. It was quieter here on the outskirts, but lamps still lit the inner city, the bustle a rattling hum.

Thassir sat on the edge of the roof, staring out at the cracked plains, toward the mountains. The sinkhole mines lay between here and there, though I couldn't see them.

"I'm not really one of them," I said into the night. "I'm here because they have resources I might be able to use, and I lost my sister in Kashan. She's not dead. Restoration." I hadn't admitted it to Utricht, but the words fell easily from my lips now and I wasn't sure why.

He registered no surprise. Only his back met me, the velvet of his black wings seeming to absorb my voice.

"She's all that I have left of my family, and I can't reach her." Still nothing.

He'd stolen an entire *sack* of god gems. I'd watched him take down a grown man as though he were nothing but a child. I knew how tightly liaisons guarded their gems. If someone had found a corestone, it would be well protected. I needed someone like Thassir on my side if I wanted to see Rasha again. Even if he was grumpy, mean and completely mad.

Didn't mean I had to like him.

So I tried a different tactic. "Your cats could use some medical care."

This time he turned. "Are you a doctor?"

I spread my hands wide. "No. But surely Mitoran knows one. And if the Unanointed have the resources to get through the barrier, they have the resources to pay for a doctor." I hadn't run this by Mitoran, but she'd have to see the wisdom in having Thassir along.

He considered a moment. "The doctor could not come here. I would have to bring the cats to the doctor. I would need help."

If he hadn't been watching me, I would have closed my eyes, taking a moment to wonder what in all the aether I'd gotten myself into. The cats might have liked Thassir well enough, but I also knew that tossing a cat into a bag meant carrying around a breathing, yowling, *moving* cactus. Might as well go hug a sea urchin. But instead I plunged ahead. "Help me get word to my sister and I'll help you take them there."

"Fine."

"What? Really?" It had been a gamble, but I hadn't completely expected it to pay off, especially with all his posturing about not being one of the Unanointed.

"I'll help you find your sister. You help me take care of the cats."

"Do you promise?"

It was like I'd stuck a lance straight through his spine. He went so stiff and so still, I started to get the odd feeling I should apologize to him. Like I'd stepped on his foot without meaning to, only his foot was broken and now might never be right again.

His lips finally unsealed. "I promise." He turned back to gaze into the distance again, the feathers at the end of his wings rustling with the wind.

And I, for some reason, felt I'd made a bargain even more dangerous than the one I'd made with the Unanointed.

18

Mullayne

10 years after the restoration of Kashan and 571 years after the Shattering

Langzu - west of Ruzhi, deep in an unexplored cave

There are so many unknown variables. Is this how Tolemne made his way to Unterra? If not this, how did he make it down so far? Was the use of magic forbidden back then? Did they have some reserve of Numinar wood to power a machine?

The books are rotted. The world has changed.

All we have are the stories we tell each other, and half of those are wholesale fabrications.

Mull watched the shimmer of the second aerocline as he ate. He'd perfected the technique for eating before they'd undertaken this trek, and had made all his crew members practice it before they'd even begun their descent. Take a breath, lift the filter to bite, lower the filter, blow out to clear the air inside, chew and swallow. Repeat.

No one talked while they ate. It was too easy to forget and to skip a step in the sequence, to expose yourself to the toxic air past the aerocline. He'd done it once during his experiments and he could still remember the swimming in his head, the sense of euphoria that told him he was perfectly fine even though some deeper part of him knew he was not. But popping back above the first aerocline and into fresh air to clear his head had been an easy matter. A night's rest and he'd been ready to go again the next morning.

There was no room for error this deep down. It would take more than a day to get back to the surface. Mull wasn't sure if an affected person would keep their filter on, or for how long.

"You're delaying," Jeeoon said as she settled onto the rocks beside him. She'd long since finished eating. Her shaggy black hair hung into her eyes, streaks of gray catching the light. "Delaying won't change how the filters react to the second aerocline."

He swallowed his last bite and readjusted his filter. "It's just that I never had much chance to experiment with the second aerocline." He'd tried to pay a supervisor at the sinkhole mines to let him dive with the miners, but the woman had only given him an incredulous look and told him that he'd likely get one of them killed and he couldn't pay her any amount of money to let some half-trained ranking clan member drop himself into the hole. She valued her life, you see. Unlike him.

"Theoretically," he continued, tapping the seal of his mask, "the filters should work just as well in the second aerocline as in the first. According to my research, what we think of as toxins are actually just particles of magic. Density changes between the aeroclines. There's a very clear delineation between the two layers, and the second layer is much thicker. More magical particles. This is part of what the gods draw upon to work their miracles. But humans – we can't contain it. It's poison to us. And—"

Jeeoon was making loud snoring noises. "Sorry, Mull, but you get really boring when you're nervous. You've tried to give me this lecture before, remember? I don't care what it is about the air here that kills us. I just want to see how deep we can go and live to tell the tale."

Mull's gaze slid to Pont, who'd taken a rock and was nudging at the second aerocline with it. The surface rippled at the rock's touch, a barely noticeable distortion of the cave floor beneath it.

Jeeoon leaned in. "He's over your argument if you are."

That was Pont, kicking at a wasps' nest and then walking away, confused at why the wasps were still angry. But Mull knew he was a wasp who kept trying to sting long after any harm had passed. He had trouble letting things go; he was old enough to know his own faults.

"Go talk to him before we make the descent. I know you, Mull, and it'll bother you if you don't. You need your head in this if you really want to go all the way." *If you want to save her life.* She left that last part unspoken, but she looked to Imeah, who was speaking to one of the crew Mull had hired to join them. She laughed through her filter and the man smiled. Everyone was always telling him to make peace with Pont. Why wasn't Pont ever the one making peace with *him?*

Mull sighed before wiping his hands clean and going to the dip in the tunnel where the second aerocline lay. He crouched next to Pont. "We might find more camps down there. More signs of Tolemne's passage."

His words were a prod that released whatever pressure had built up behind Pont's chest. He deflated, letting out a long breath. "Look, I'm sorry, Mull." At least he always apologized quickly. "We're friends. I should have backed you up instead of arguing."

"Well, so many of the other times you've argued with me,

I've been wrong." Mull scratched the back of his neck. "Can we forget about it? Wait, no, give me a hug. Imeah and Jeeoon are watching. They won't believe we've made up otherwise."

Pont grinned and gave him a quick embrace. "Onwards together, right?"

Dammit if both Imeah and Jeeoon weren't right. If only he could make his peace with Imeah so easily. Technically, they weren't fighting. So why did it feel like they were still at odds? He shook his head and beckoned to the rest of the crew. "Form up when you're ready."

They gathered behind him as he lifted his lantern over the dip into the second aerocline. "We'll be ankle-wading for a bit, then knee-deep, then waist, and then we'll submerge. No need to take in a deep breath beforehand or do anything different. But everyone pick a friend and check each other's filters. Past this point we cannot afford any mistakes. A breath of air from the first aerocline will put you out for a day – more if you don't catch it in time and keep breathing it. The concentration of particles in the second aerocline is over one hundred times the amount in the first aerocline. One breath is about the equivalent of seven minutes of breathing first-aerocline air. That'll kill you. It's done that and worse to sinkhole miners. So pay attention!"

He waited until he saw a nod from each of them. "Let's go."

He stepped into the second aerocline. It was a subtle sensation. For some reason he always expected it to feel like he'd stepped into water; instead, it was like a warm breeze had brushed his ankles. Imeah, next to him, picked her way down, leaning on her cane. He knew from experience not to help her unless she asked for it. "I'm weak, not fragile," she always said.

Despite what he'd told the others, it was a struggle not to take a deep breath as the second aerocline reached his neck, the heavier, warmer air seeping past the cloth buttons of his shirt. Lead by example, right? This should be routine, simple.

If only he'd had the chance to test the filters in the second aerocline. Jeeoon thought him too cautious. Pont thought him not cautious enough. And Imeah didn't want him doing this at all. But they were close to their goals. After so many years, they were close.

The second aerocline closed over his head and he felt his hair lift a little, lighter in the thick air. It was warmer down here. He lifted a hand, experimentally, trailing it through the space in front of him. If he concentrated, he thought he could feel the aether against his palm.

Breathing was normal, the filter was working. He searched his mind for the telltale lightheadedness and felt nothing. "We're in," he said. His crew murmured excitedly behind him. He'd paid them, yes, but anyone who was willing to go deep into a cave system had other things driving them. He knew from the whispers that some of them were worshipers of the old gods. What better pilgrimage than a journey to Unterra, where the old gods once lived?

He wondered what his parents would think of him now, following in Tolemne's footsteps. They thought his research foolish, though they tolerated it for the sake of his workshop, which was a profitable venture for the Reisun clan. He was the younger son, to be indulged but not believed. He had seen them roll their eyes more than once when he started talking about possible locations for the cave system Tolemne had taken to Unterra. What if his research and his inventions saved Imeah? That would be something. But he didn't care that much whether they respected him. As long as they gave him his allowance and left him alone, that was enough.

He did feel guilty for the soft lie he'd told them, that he was visiting the summer home of the Temiki clan in the mountains near Ruzhi. They were so pleased – the Temiki clan was noble, and had a daughter ten years younger than him they considered a good prospect. He was forty-three, and his parents longed to see him settled; what better way than with a spouse and children? He shrugged off the uncomfortable thought. Marriage was not for him. He'd never been interested in anyone in that way. The longing looks, the hesitant flirtations, the way others spoke of pounding hearts and quickened breath – well it all sounded so distracting. How did a person *live* with that humming in the background of their mind? If his mind was a cave, he hadn't shut out that particular tune; it had just never entered.

They descended deeper into the cave system, Mull stopping every so often to check his map and sketch out some unmarked passages. They needed a more accurate view of this place if anyone ever wanted to come back. The crew member at the back continued to spool out the string.

That was something he hadn't thought ahead to. If they made it all the way to the realm of the gods, if there was anyone there other than Kluehnn left to grant a boon, then others might also wish to follow. They'd need filters. He'd have to expand his workshop to meet demand, and the proprietary weave took some rather rare fibers, so he'd have to—

"Mull! Mullayne Reisun!"

He stopped as Pont called his name and realized he'd been about to step into an underground lake. He backed away from the edge.

"Mull." Pont caught up to him and ruffled his hair like an affectionate older brother. "What would you do if I wasn't here to stop you walking off into the sea?"

"It's hardly a sea."

"You'd still drown in it."

Pont was right about that; Mull couldn't swim if his life depended on it. "Yes, well thank you for stopping me."

The big man only grunted through his filter and turned to join the others. They were heading to the far end of the cave, away from the lake. Mull swung his lantern over the water, curious to see if anything was living down here.

He spotted only small white-scaled fish, and they didn't seem to notice the light at all. And then he saw something else.

He thought he saw the impression of something in the silt below the school of fish. Wide as a dinner plate, with four prongs at the top. *A footprint?* It could have just been the light, or the way the dirt had settled.

He pivoted away, the hairs at the back of his neck prickling. He felt the impression of phantom teeth against his back, from some giant-jawed creature that had followed them into the darkness.

Foolishness. He shook out the fear and hurried after everyone else. Didn't Pont always say he had a wild imagination?

Better not to mention it.

19

Rasha

10 years after the restoration of Kashan
and 571 years after the Shattering

Kashan - Kluehnn's den

*The old gods are usurpers. They want to take your land,
your homes. They want to push you to the side until you
are the ones who are forgotten and hunted.*

*Look at their strange bodies, their animalistic counte-
nances. They will bleed when you cut them but they will
not die. How could they ever know what it is to be mortal?*

Millani met me outside the door. "He spent a long time
with you," she said. I could still feel the sensation of
his claw on my cheek. When I didn't respond, she huffed a little
and turned. "Kluehnn always has his favorites."

I touched my face, my own claws smaller. Was she *jealous?*
She'd gone through the trials a long time ago. It seemed Kluehnn
didn't bestow the same favor on everyone, no matter whether
they made it to the end.

A bell rang, the faint sound bouncing off the cavern walls. It was time for worship.

Millani halted, her tail whipping behind her. She had ten more converts to bring before Kluehnn. If she hurried, she could make it before the session concluded. No one wanted to miss a full session of worship. I understood why – they always left me with a sense of euphoria, a feeling of renewed purpose.

I studied the walls. We were in the deeper parts of the den, places I'd never been allowed into before.

Millani took my arm, pulling me forward. "You can find your way to the nave yourself, can't you? Follow this tunnel to the first fork, take a right, and at the first room, take the second tunnel on the left. Can you do that?"

I'd barely nodded before she had swept away, leaving me there alone, a lamp flickering on the wall ten steps ahead. Just enough light to keep a person from tripping over their own feet. I stood there a moment, feeling the weight of the earth around me, the way the warm, moist walls almost seemed to breathe. If I closed my eyes and stretched out my inner awareness, I could feel the aether beneath my feet, an ocean of it, waiting to be called upon. Part of me still felt suffused with Kluehnn's regard, his touch, the rumble of his voice in my ears.

The bell rang again.

I started down the tunnel, taking the right at the first fork as she'd told me to. But when I found the small room, interspersed with pillars, I couldn't recall which tunnel on the left she'd told me to take. My mouth was dry; my mind littered with cobwebs that stuck each time I tried to clear my head. After-effects of aether poisoning.

Footsteps shuffled toward the room from the opposite end, accompanied by a low scraping sound.

Not knowing exactly why, I ducked behind a pillar. I wasn't

doing anything wrong. I was in the deeper parts of the den, forbidden even to neophytes, but Millani had escorted me here and
left me. It wasn't my fault that I was here alone.

But I didn't know how much that would matter to godkillers.

I ventured a glance from behind the pillar. A rock-wood altered strode across the room. He was tall and broad, the sinews
of his shoulders visible between the gaps of his armor, covered in
a layer of pebbled skin. A sword graced one hip, the godkilling
knife the other. The scraping sound emanated from the corpse
he was dragging across the floor.

A god's corpse. The blood pooled on its chest still shimmered a
little in the lamplight. It was a small horned god, its limbs slender,
its face narrow. A child. Female.

It was strange for me to imagine the gods having *children*,
though that was the only way I could think to describe them.
Offspring? Regardless, all the elder gods were dead; only their
descendants lived on in the world above. And it was the godkillers' job to destroy them. They were false, they were liars,
they cared nothing about the people on the surface; they cared
only about power and their own lives. And they were so much
stronger than mortals. We needed to protect people from them.

The corpse blinked.

I caught my breath and held it. A trick of the light? Or was the
god somehow still alive?

The godkiller dragged the god down a tunnel to the right.
He hadn't spotted me. Maybe the aether was still affecting me
more than I'd thought. A feather-soft sensation worked its way
over my skin, a reminder of the itching I'd experienced when
Millani had shut us in that room. My feet weren't as steady as
they usually were. I'd heard about the after-effects of aether
intoxication, though experiencing them was a different thing
entirely.

I'd ducked out from behind the pillar when footsteps sounded again. In a flash, I had my back to the stone once more, my breathing ragged. I'd lingered too long in my thoughts. The godkiller had already finished his business. He stepped into the room, and this time, I did not hear the telltale scrape behind him.

He'd brought the god to its destination.

I debated, for a brief moment, telling him what I'd seen. But then he was gone, and I was alone.

And there might very well be a living god in the depths of the den. I did not have a godkilling blade, but I had a knife strapped to my side. What would Millani want me to do? She would tell me to mind my own business, to make my way to the nave to worship.

Kluehnn?

He'd called me soft.

My fingers wrapped around the hilt of the blade. I was *not* soft. I crept out from behind the pillar, steeling myself before starting toward the tunnel the godkiller had left from. I could be determined, I could be cold. I could be brave. I'd survived the first trial, and it hadn't been through luck. I'd killed. I'd lived. I'd proved myself.

If there were a living god inside the den, someone would have to raise the alarm. Someone would have to do something. I'd heard the stories of what gods could do – drawing aether into their lungs, using their own bodies as conduits for magic. They could move mountains, alter reality.

No sounds met my ears except my own breathing and my footsteps.

This hallway was even darker than the last; I crept ahead one careful foot at a time. Slowly I drew the knife from my belt. An archway appeared ahead to my left, a dim square of light shining onto the stone floor.

When I finally peered into the room, it took me a moment to comprehend what I was seeing.

Bodies and body parts hung from various hooks in the walls and ceiling. The room smelled slightly sweet; gods didn't decay the way mortal or altered bodies did. I spotted horned heads, scaly skin, vast feathered wings.

The small god hung from a hook in front of me. Her head lolled to one side, arms and legs limp. Thick black horns spiraled up from her forehead. The hook pierced one shoulder, shimmering blood coating the end of it. My gaze flicked over the rest of her, my palm slick on the hilt of my knife. Her clothes were ragged and looked as though they'd never seen a fine day.

For a moment, all I could think was how sad she seemed, how frail. She looked no older than I'd been when Kashan had been restored. The god I'd seen crawling up from the hole in the ground had been impressive, frightening, strong. This didn't look like a thing Kluehnn should be afraid of.

I took another step closer, reaching a hand out to make sure she was in fact dead.

Her fingers seized mine.

They were cold, slippery with her blood. I heard a clatter and realized, dimly, that I'd dropped my knife. Hadn't even lifted it.

"Please." Her eyes were green, dappled as the sunshine through fresh spring leaves. "Help me."

I could only stare, fresh new horror tightening my throat. "A god speaks only lies." I finally forced the words past my lips. "There can be only one true god, and he is Kluehnn. Do not worship false gods. Do not speak to them." My whispers seemed to slide around the hanging bodies like an errant wind.

"My parents . . . " She coughed, blood splattering her lip. "Get me down, please. I don't want to die."

The bodies on either side of her seemed to sway – a god with trailing wings and a beakish nose, and another who looked part tree.

If I wanted to be a godkiller, I would have to kill gods like this one. But I couldn't seem to pull my hand away, or to reach for my knife on the ground. Her fingers were so cold, her grasp so delicate and so desperate.

Her palm slowly warmed beneath mine. "Do you think he does this for you? He does it for himself. Just take me off the hook. Just . . . get me down." A little mewling sound left her lips. "It *hurts*."

I was moving before I'd even considered the consequences, my hands beneath her arms.

And then she went stiff. For a moment, I thought she'd died, the cut from the godkiller's blade finally proving too much for her. But her chest heaved and her gaze focused somewhere over my shoulder.

I went still, my heartbeat pounding in my ears. I heard it too – a low scraping, as *something* climbed into the room behind me. I'd been so focused on the small god that I hadn't taken the time to thoroughly look around.

I knew that sound. I'd heard it only a little while earlier, when Millani had taken me to commune with Kluehnn. I dropped my hands, ducking behind the winged god. I caught a glimpse of Kluehnn from between the bodies: the horned head, the multiple eyes and mouths, the spines along his back. He went straight to the first body hanging from the wall and began to eat.

My mouth went dry; I breathed, but the air didn't seem to fill my lungs. My head was filled with the fizzing foam atop the waves.

I watched him from behind a screen of feathers, the way his

jaw unhinged, the way his rows of sharpened teeth tore at the god's flesh, the way he chewed and sucked and swallowed, the sounds echoing from the cavern walls.

The little god in front of me did not scream or whimper; she only trembled.

My knife was still on the ground in front of her.

I willed Kluehnn not to see. He'd only just finished telling me he hoped I'd be one of the converts standing at the end, one of the ones who would become a godkiller. I wasn't supposed to be here. I could tell him that little god was still alive. But something stopped me from doing it.

I wasn't sure how long I stood there watching him, growing lightheaded for fear of breathing too loudly. He'd consumed an entire arm and half a torso, crunching through bones as though they were raw vegetables.

His jaw closed. He wiped the shimmering blood around his mouth with the back of one clawed hand.

In a moment, he would retreat down the hole. I would leave this place. I would not look back. I would tell Millani I had seen a godkiller carrying a blinking god to this cavern and then I would leave it all to others.

I was not built for this.

But Kluehnn's gaze trailed across the floor. It found my knife. He sank to the ground, limbs splayed out like the legs of a spider. His head cocked, two eyes on one cheek blinking.

It was not a godkilling knife. It was not supposed to be there.

Do you think he does this for you? The god's voice bounced inside my skull. Had she done some magic on me while we'd stood, hands clasped?

Kluehnn crept across the floor, retrieved the knife and peered up at the little god.

"You," he said.

For a moment I thought he was speaking to me. But the little god let out a breathless sob. "I am not so easy to kill."

"It doesn't matter. My godkiller brought you from your forest to my cave. To me. I have eaten both your parents. I will also eat you."

"I was helping the people there. You say restored realms are better, yet you leave the ones you've altered to struggle."

"There is always a place for them in the dens."

"I may not have ever lived in Unterra, but I know you're not offering this without a cost. When does it all end?"

Kluehnn crept closer. "When the world is restored. When I am the only one left." He lunged forward, teeth sinking into the little god's neck.

She kicked once, a spatter of blood landing on the knife. And then she hung silent, swaying from side to side, her feet bare and limp.

I found myself backing away, the horror of everything that had happened threatening to overwhelm me. I couldn't stop the rapid pace of my breath, my heart beating so quickly I thought it would burst. All I could think about were those horrible moments when my blade had entered the flesh of the other converts, the dizzying scent of aether, the crunch of bones between Kluehnn's teeth. My next breath wheezed past a tightening throat, my chest aching. The world spun. I couldn't hum Hakara's lullaby, but I heard the notes in my head, trying to find some way out. Trying to find some way to soothe me.

The wings of the god in front of me parted. "Rasha." Kluehnn's voice filled the small space between the hanging gods. "You are not supposed to be here. You were not supposed to see or hear that."

I fell. Above me, a body I'd bumped into swayed, arms hanging loosely from its sides. This was it. All Kluehnn had to do was dart forward and he could sink his teeth into my neck. I couldn't run. I had nowhere else to go. And I wasn't even a god. I did not have the strength to fight him.

But he did not bite me. He kicked the knife forward with one of his feet, catching it with one of his hands as it skittered across the stone. With a fatherly patience, he tucked the knife back into my belt. His hand moved to my face. Without even knowing why, I shrank away.

"Let's try this . . . again."

Warm fingers touched my forehead. There was something odd in that touch, something that crept along my skin, enveloping the whole of me.

I was in the room of pillars, studying the tunnels to my left. Which one had Millani told me to go down to get to the nave? I could still hear the second bell for worship ringing in my ears.

A shuffling sound came from a tunnel opposite me. Someone was coming, and I was in the deep parts of the den, a part neophytes weren't allowed in. I wasn't doing anything wrong, but still my heart kicked at my ribs. Millani had sent me off into the tunnels alone; this wasn't my fault.

I moved to hide behind a pillar, and stopped.

Something wasn't right. My stomach swam with unease. Somehow I knew that if I moved to hide behind that pillar, something bad would happen. It was as certain as seeing clouds on the horizon and knowing they meant rain.

I darted toward the tunnels on the left, picking the second one at the last moment. I had to get away from that place. The unease in my belly churned, spurring me forward. The hallway climbed upward, the slope breaking at points for stairs. Whoever had been heading toward the room with the pillars didn't call after me. I'd escaped without being seen.

My pulse finally began to slow. The sound of chanting

hummed through this tunnel, light filtering in again from sky-lights above. I was close to the nave.

Why couldn't I seem to shake the sick feeling that had draped over me? It was like trying to wipe away grease with my hand; it wouldn't come off, no matter how far I'd run.

The chanting filled the whole of the hallway, and I slipped past the open door and into the nave. I knelt on the floor quickly, joining a group of converts I didn't recognize. There were often converts I didn't recognize, brought into the fold by wandering faithful – as Millani had once been. Given food and drink and shelter.

My voice joined the others, though I could barely focus on the words. My gaze had fallen upon the knife at my belt – the knife I'd thoroughly cleaned after the melee Millani had forced us into.

A spattering of blood marked the hilt.

20

Hakara

10 years after the restoration of Kashan and 571 years after the Shattering

Langzu - the outskirts of Bian, waiting

The refugees who flee restoration suffer from a soul-deep weakness. Their matter could be transformed, used to help build a new landscape. Or they could become altered. Both are honorable, blessed fates.

Instead, they flee, putting off the inevitable. All realms will be restored, in the end.

They deny the will of Kluehnn.

The closer we got to our mission, the thicker the tension became. "This is the beginning of the end," I heard Utricht say to Mitoran as they conferred by the window of the old salon.

She pulled the curtain aside for a moment, searching the street. "Don't be so confident."

"I have to hope."

"Do you?"

I sipped from my tea, doing my best to appear occupied in my breakfast. Behind me, Alifra practiced picking a lock while Dashu stood over her and offered unhelpful suggestions. She said something in a low, mocking tone before they both laughed.

Utricht's voice went softer, so low I had to strain to hear. "Are you waiting for someone? Your informant among the clans?"

Mitoran let the curtain fall. "I'd hoped she wouldn't be so stupid, but she's gone. The Sovereign offered her a fool's bargain, and she took it. She went to Kashan to find out if they will follow the rest of the realms and cut us off."

Utricht scratched at his beard. "But her family doesn't have much money. How does she expect to get through to Kashan?"

If I were a cat, my ears would have pricked. This was the same predicament I'd found myself in – no money and a need to pass the barrier.

The leader of the Unanointed shrugged. "She wouldn't tell me. And I wasn't in a position to push her. I have to believe she's found a way, and she's not going to just toss herself into the barrier to appease her family."

"Clan is everything here."

"It's the only reason so many in Langzu have survived for so long. That sense of unity, purpose and sacrifice."

"And the Sovereign."

"Yes, a unique situation."

I tuned out their conversation, downing the rest of the millet. Not enough food, never enough, but I was used to feeling hungry. Most people in Langzu were.

Thassir joined us just as the sun was setting, stooping to fit through the door. He had the carcass of a wild pig thrown over his shoulder. My mouth watered as I thought about that beast carved up, its meat crisping over a fire. But he only took it behind the counter and began to butcher it, feeding the pieces to his cats.

They mewed at him, as if to complain that he wasn't going quickly enough. Little bastards didn't care that the rest of us had to have ration tickets, woody vegetables and stewed millet. Those kittens probably never knew a hard day in their lives once he had taken them under his broad wing. Oh, to be one of Thassir's cats.

"Hakara." Mitoran's voice cut through my thoughts. "Are you listening?"

I wrenched my gaze back to her.

"We've been lucky enough to have an informant among the liaisons. The corestone is being kept in a warehouse at the edge of Bian, on the other side of the city. They're transporting it with another batch to a den northwest of here. The wagon they'll be taking to the inner city will be guarded, though not heavily; they don't want to attract too much attention. It unfortunately can't be a simple and quick smash-and-grab. Our informant has told us the safe is much too heavy to move. So we have to pick the lock. That's Alifra's job."

The slender woman gave a fleeting two-finger salute, her other hand working a toothpick at the corner of her mouth. "Got it." She wore a white linen shirt today, the brightness of it making her freckles pop against her brown skin. Her russet hair was loose, a cloud of curls atop her head as though her face were the peak of a mountain. Her feet were crossed in front of her; she slouched in her chair like she'd eaten enough to make her drowsy. But I'd fought her the other day and I knew that lackadaisical pose was deceptive.

"It has to be quick or we'll attract the attention of the Sovereign's enforcers. Dashu, focus on the wagon driver. Make sure no one takes the reins while Alifra is working. Make sure to block their path."

He patted the hilt of his curved sword. Mitoran turned to me. I could feel Utricht's presence at my shoulder. "Hakara and

Utricht – take out the guards. Don't let anyone back into the wagon. Cover for Alifra when she's finished. Alifra will hand the corestone off to Utricht. He's got the best chance of withstanding an attack. Then you all split up. I've detailed your retreats on the map. Everyone gets there by a different route; everyone returns here by a different route."

I raised my hand.

"Yes, what is it, Hakara?" The barest hint of annoyance crept into her voice.

"How big is the safe?"

Her eyes narrowed. "What does that matter?"

"How big is it?" I said it more slowly this time, as though she merely hadn't understood me.

Her black-eyed gaze never wavered. Could have been staring into the blankness of a well. "It's small," she said. "But thick-walled. You won't be able to move it unless your arms are enhanced, and you can't hold your breath for that long. We have to risk picking the lock."

I pointed to Thassir. "I saw that man almost break a bone with a twist of his wrist. He's huge. Let's not bother with the lock. We all go in. We all distract the guards. And then Thassir here flies in, takes the roof off the wagon, and flies out with the safe. Done." I wiped my hands together as if cleaning them of dust.

Mitoran and Thassir exchanged startled glances.

"I'm not—" Thassir began.

Mitoran let out a soft huff of breath. "He and I have an agreement. He—"

I spoke over both of them. "He and I have an agreement too. He said he'd help me find my sister. And in this case, that means getting the corestone. Because that's what Mitoran offered me in exchange for bringing one back. A message sent to her people in Kashan to track my sister down."

It was with no small amount of satisfaction that I watched her
flounder for a response. I'd met her type before. She was no different from the ration ticket sellers in the mining camps, thinking
they could take two tickets from one hand, give one ticket to
another, and keep one for themselves — and no one would notice
what was happening.

"That *would* work." Alifra sat up, leaning over to put her
elbows on her knees. I wondered if she sat that way not because
she was tired but to conserve energy for those quick bursts I'd
seen while sparring. She scratched at the back of her neck. "And
you've got to admit it, Mitoran. It would be a fair bit simpler. If
Thassir said he'd help, I'd be happy to have him along."

"As would I." Dashu ran his thumb and forefinger down his
goatee.

"Unless there's a reason he shouldn't?" Utricht said, his voice
light.

And I felt it then, the team Mitoran had described. The bruiser,
the pest, the vine and the arbor, just like so. It *was* an effective
formation, just as she'd said.

Mitoran's gaze was locked on Thassir, who steadfastly refused
to look back at her. Whatever had passed between them, he was
done. He'd shut her out. Her lips pressed together, the fingers of
her right hand compressing briefly before relaxing. "It *is* simpler." Her expression melted into one of ease, so quickly that I
could almost believe her discomfort hadn't occurred at all. "So
we move ahead with the new plan. Thank you, Hakara. And
Thassir, I'm grateful you've decided to lend your strength to
our cause."

Alifra, Dashu and Utricht left at intervals, making their way
through the city by different routes. I went to the door after
Utricht had gone, but Mitoran caught my wrist. "No. Not you.
You go with Thassir."

Change of plan. Again. I didn't exactly narrow my eyes at her, but I gave her a longer look than necessary. Did she think I was going to run off into the city?

"The godkiller who captured you saw your face. There may be people out there still looking for you, Hakara. If Thassir is going, he can fly you in and fly you out. It exposes you to fewer people."

Thassir beckoned me upstairs. "We'll leave from the roof." As soon as we were out of earshot, he spoke from the corner of his mouth. "I thought you were just here to use the Unanointed's resources. You conveniently left out the fact that you'd already made a bargain with Mitoran to find your sister. Whatever you've agreed to do for her, the price will be too high."

I ignored his implied question. "What's this understanding between you and Mitoran anyways? You'd think she'd be happy for you to get roped into her cause. I mean, look at you."

"We have a complicated relationship." He didn't elaborate any further.

"Do you have some terrible weakness that could jeopardize a mission? Or are you, deep down, actually a Kluehnn devotee? Or maybe you've taken a sacred vow against killing." I could imagine it. He seemed solemn enough. Didn't think his mouth was capable of smiling.

He'd resumed climbing the creaking stairs, but I caught the flash of clenching jaw. Finally, when we reached the end of the hall, he spoke. "I prefer not to get involved. The cause is hopeless." And then he was out the window before I could say another word.

I climbed out after him onto the rooftop. A warm wind whipped at my hair as I followed him, the tiles somehow feeling less steady than the first time I'd been out here. I could feel every tiny shift, hear them click against one another.

Wordlessly, he held his arms out to me. He was dressed in a

tight dark blue tunic, the back open to allow his wings to move. Several blades of different shapes and sizes adorned his belt. His fingers were tipped with claws.

I knew he was tall, but stepping in close made me all the more aware of exactly how much he towered over me. His wings curved slightly around his body, trapping the heat in that space, making it feel almost as though I were stepping into an alcove of feathers. I lifted my hands and then hesitated, unsure of exactly where to put them.

He seemed to be having the same issue. His fingers grazed my waist before pulling away. His claws missed the light leather vest I wore and caught a little on my shirt. One wrong movement and he could tear my skin from bone.

I squeezed my eyes tightly shut. This was not *me*. I was here for one reason and one reason alone: to find out what had happened to Rasha. To find *her*. I'd fallen into pits higher than this building. I'd held my breath as I'd pried gems loose, as the ground shook beneath my feet.

No altered man, no matter how frightening, was going to stop me from retrieving that corestone. I cleared my throat. "You've never carried a person while flying, have you?"

"I have ... carried cats." His voice this close was the low rumble of distant thunder.

Elder gods preserve me. Perhaps a little more aggressively than was necessary, I flung my hands about his neck, clasped them, and jumped up.

He caught me at the last moment, nearly dropping me from the edge of the roof. One arm wrapped under my ribs, the other beneath my knees. My short sword swung at my belt. His lips parted slightly as he caught his breath, then pressed together as he readjusted his feet. This close, his dark, heavy brows looked less angry and more ... sad? The warmth of his hand seeped through my loose linen pants. I felt the thump of his heartbeat against my side and was pleased to note he was as anxious about this mission as I was.

"Does this work well enough? Can you still fly?"

The brows lowered. Well, perhaps they *did* look angry. "You're heavy."

"What everyone wants to hear," I said dryly.

He snorted. "You want me to say you are as light as a cat?" He didn't wait for my answer, lifting his wings. The black of them blocked the stars.

"I have no problem taking up space. But are you strong enough? Because I could still walk if—"

He lunged into the air. I think I dug trenches into the muscles of his neck as a warm wind caught his wings, lifting us farther and farther away from the earth.

Diving deep into the ocean? Sure. Falling into a sinkhole? I could do that without a second thought. The other direction proved problematic.

The city below was a speckle of lights, the people like shadowy figurines. I was dizzy with the distance. And now, so close to finally finding out what had happened to my sister, I found I did actually care about living.

He said nothing to me and I returned the favor, feeling only his hands around me and the heat of his breath against my hair. This was one of those moments my ancestors would have prayed to the old gods, I was sure of it.

He dropped me at the edge of the old coastline. Bian had been built on the shore of a lake, though it had long since shrunk to near nothing, heat and dust overtaking it. The coastline was rocky, filled with boulders, the footing treacherous. A road had been carved out just above the rocks, the warehouse situated a little ways from where I stood.

"Utricht and the others will be here soon. Hide and wait," he said. I unlocked my hands from his shoulders, still a little breathless, and stepped away. He sprang back into the air. I found my gaze trailing after him, the place where he'd gripped my legs suddenly cold.

Dashu arrived first, giving me a companionable nod. I felt Utricht's presence before he found us in the rocks below the road. And then Alifra joined us.

We waited.

A whistle pierced the air. Thassir, above us, circled lower.

Utricht shooed us toward cover. "Everyone into the rocks. The wagon is on its way."

My heartbeat quickened. I had the sword they'd given me on my person, but I really didn't know how to fight beyond a couple brawls I'd gotten into with other miners. But Utricht had the steady, warm presence of a draft horse. I fell into his shadow as we waited in the rocks for the wagon carrying the corestone.

"You keep close to me," he said, his voice a low rumble. "I am your arbor. I am your safety." He touched the haft of the enormous double-headed ax strapped to his back.

I snorted. "What, do you think I need to be reminded?"

"You *did* chase after Thassir to ask him questions. From where I'm standing, it looks like you're severely lacking in any sense of self-preservation."

"Fair." I knew my role. Or at least I thought I did. Be the bruiser. Hold my breath, get in and get out before I lost my grip on the magic. All my muscles seemed to cramp as we waited behind that rock. I studied the crevices in its surface. I studied the wavy brown hair on the back of Utricht's head, the same color as the fur on his cheeks. I wondered idly if Guarin and Altani and my other fellow miners ever speculated about what had happened to me, or if they only sighed in relief that I was no longer there.

The creak of wagon wheels sounded as it approached. I could see the top of the wagon over the rocks, and though I heard voices, I wasn't able to catch a glimpse of the guards from our hiding spot.

And then Thassir was swooping down from the sky, growling at the horses as he seized the roof of the wagon. The horses whinnied and bolted down the road toward our hiding spot, eyes rolling, as he casually tore the roof clean off. I felt something like fear gather in the pit of my stomach as I realized exactly how close I'd come to mortal peril by harassing him.

He landed on top of the wagon, and all I could see was the black spread of his wings.

"Go. We go now." Utricht stepped back, giving me space to move. I shoved a hand into the pouch with the red gems, another into the pouch with the green ones. I swallowed one of each as I crested the slope.

The horses stopped when the four of us clambered into the road. Five guards chasing the wagon, the unarmed driver gathering the reins in his hands. Thassir's head and wings were visible inside it, twitching with effort. He shouted something I couldn't distinguish, though it sounded urgent. Someone needed to buy him time.

I sensed Utricht on my heels and caught a glimpse of Dashu and Alifra to my right.

Utricht lifted a hand and the air ahead of me shimmered. One step and I breathed in, the scent of seawater filling my nostrils, the thickness of the aether coating my lungs. My shoulders and hips itched. I pulled the short sword free from my belt, lifting it as though it weighed nothing.

The guards got to the wagon first, setting their feet before we slammed into them. I gritted my teeth, bracing for the impact.

That was when I spotted the godkillers.

21

Nioanen

40 years before the Shattering

Albanore - Sanctuary

Defender of the Helpless, they called Nioanen. The God of Many Chances, they called Irael. Lithuas they worshiped as the Bringer of Change. Barexi was known as the One Who Seeks Knowledge or often simply as the Stag. They named golden-eyed Velenor the Glittering One. Ayaz, the Cutter, they feared and loved.

And Rumenesca was simply known as the Mother, though she had no children herself.

There are many others, though in every culture, in every realm, these seven appear over and over.

Nioanen awoke in his nest with a body pressed at his back, one arm draped over his shoulder. Irael still curled up at his side as a cat at night, but had stopped creeping away before morning a couple years ago. Neither of them had remarked on this change; Nioanen wasn't sure if it was because it wasn't important amongst everything else or because it felt so natural that it didn't feel like a change at all.

Irael's breath gusted at his ear, his arm tightening briefly before slackening. "You're awake, aren't you? It's early."

Dew gathered on Nioanen's eyelashes and on the tips of his feathers. He could feel Irael pillowed on one wing, the other falling over him like a blanket. The sky was streaked with pink and orange. He missed the constant glow of the star at the center of the world, but he could appreciate a sunrise. "I'm awake."

Irael drew away, and the cold gust of air at Nioanen's back made him wish for the return of his friend's body. He opened his mouth, about to ask if Irael could stay a moment longer. How selfish of him. They didn't have enough time. Kluehnn's followers would be gathering, preparing themselves to attack Sanctuary.

Time had run out, and though Nioanen had always expected this, he hadn't expected it to happen so soon. He now understood that he never could have been prepared, no matter how long or how short the time had been.

When he rose, he found Irael standing at the edge of the nest in the form of a young man, red hair the same shade as the tabby cat's orange coat, ticked at the ends with black. The rising sun gilded it like a crown and kissed the edges of his slender figure. "There aren't enough of them to surround us, even though our borders have shrunk."

Nioanen shook out his wings and joined the other god at the edge of the nest. An army was gathered on the scrub brush plains outside Sanctuary, their ranks filled with both people and gods. "They'll take heavy casualties if they attack."

"And we will take worse," Irael said. "It has been that way for years. They don't need to kill us all at once. Only a few at a time, until we are no longer sitting at the same table. Until we are the vermin beneath the table, a nuisance and nothing more. Kluehnn will have his way."

There were fewer worshipers now making the trek to Sanctuary and bringing them food and gifts. Even fewer now that the army was gathered at their doorstep. The gods could sustain themselves from the Numinar; the nectar from the branches was nearly as potent as the nectar from the roots. They'd been collecting it, storing it in urns and containers and secreting it away to other parts of the surface world. They knew that Kluehnn might not cut down this last Numinar, but he did not have complete control over the people of this world, and that much magical power was too tempting. Even so, their backup plan felt like an admission of failure. Even so, some of the gods within Sanctuary had stopped drinking the nectar.

Irael's hand slipped into Nioanen's as they gazed over the army. Nioanen felt a strange startlement at the gesture. He shouldn't have. They'd slept night after night with their bodies back to chest, Irael's arm often finding its way across Nioanen's ribs. Yet this simple twining of fingers within his left him somehow breathless. There was Irael, and then Nioanen, and then Irael again, layered between and over, palms pressed as though they could dissolve into one another if they only spoke the right words.

Irael cleared his throat. "Olimeara refused to drink the nectar again. Without the nectar and without the ability to return to our homeland, she is fading away into a ghost; I can see through her. She says that there is no use, there is no hope, and she would choose the manner of her passing."

Nioanen said nothing, grief clenching a fist around his heart. He didn't have the right to ask for a promise, not when gods could not break promises without dying, but he couldn't stop himself. "Don't go that way. Please promise me you won't. I couldn't bear it."

The warm hand in his gave a reassuring squeeze. "I promise I won't. I have been called the God of Many Chances. It's not my way."

The army at their borders shifted. Nioanen thought he could hear a voice on the winds. It crept into his ears like a spider. He knew it was Kluehnn, though he could not say how he knew. "We should prepare."

It felt like they moved through the haze of a dream as they gathered with the other gods at the edge of Sanctuary and readied their defenses. When he saw Irael again, he was still in his young man's form, clad in golden armor, a spear in one hand.

"A mortal weapon," Nioanen remarked, flexing his claws and clenching his heavy jaw. He put his hand to the side and summoned Zayyel, his blade.

"Against mortal opponents." Irael hefted the spear and watched the opposing forces. Some of the mortals rode on their floating machines, gathered on them like sailors on a ship. Others lifted metallic tubes on their shoulders, ones that Nioanen knew from experience shot blue and green fire. Irael pointed at a spot in the army. "There's Kluehnn. We'll need all we've got if we want to defeat him."

Something crawled toward the front lines as Nioanen watched – a mass of limbs and eyes, of horns and thorny edges, roiling and nauseating. He could not look away. This was it. He'd thought before they'd fled to Sanctuary that that battle had been their last stand. But they'd been able to regroup, to retreat. This was something he wasn't sure he could survive. He could make his peace with his own death. As long as Irael made it through to the other side.

He nodded toward the space next to Kluehnn. "And Lithuas too." She stood next to the monster, her silver hair catching the sun and reflecting it as brightly as though the strands were metal.

Other gods had joined Kluehnn, but she was one of the elder seven. That betrayal had hurt. Bringer of Change, the mortals called her. How true that had proven. He remembered the look on her face as she'd stood before him, flicking between the shape of an old woman and that of a young one. She'd settled into the young woman's form. "I won't sacrifice myself to bring the old world back. The mortals would burn it all to ashes again – and then what would my sacrifice be for?" She'd lifted her sword, ready to fight, not with him but against him. Her gaze seemed to pin his down, her searching eyes finding the very core of him. "You won't sacrifice yourself either."

She was right. He couldn't see a way through. All Nioanen knew was that joining Kluehnn was not the answer Lithuas thought it was.

He could sense the gods around them readying themselves, straightening their spines, doing their best to find some courage. He flexed his wings, drew in a breath, pulling aether from below, feeling its magic suffuse him.

"Nioanen." Irael's voice was small, but it cut through the murmurs of the other gods around them. "I promised you I would not waste away like Olimeara. Now promise *me* something." He touched Nioanen's arm, and Nioanen felt each warm finger against his skin like a brand. He bent to hear Irael's next words, afraid they might be the last he'd hear, afraid he might miss them.

"I will promise you anything."

Irael's fingers moved upward, trailing past Nioanen's shoulder, grazing his cheek, his touch light, hesitant. Nioanen caught the flash of golden iris from beneath Irael's red brows and felt all the magic in his blood go still. And then Irael's hand was in his hair, tightening, his voice fierce and louder than the roar of Kluehnn's army. "Live."

He pressed his lips to Nioanen's, and Nioanen thought he

knew briefly what it felt like to die, because he couldn't possibly move on from this moment. He lost himself in the softness of Irael's mouth, the press of his body, the delicate dip of spine beneath his fingertips as he pulled Irael closer. He knew Irael — had known him for years and years — yet this kiss made him anew in Nioanen's mind.

Irael finally pulled away, eyelashes fluttering, gaze downcast. In the next moment they would have to focus on the approaching army. They would have to fight. But Nioanen brushed the hair from Irael's forehead as though they had all the time in the world. "I didn't know . . . "

"Did you really think we were only friends?" Irael let out a soft little laugh, then took Nioanen's hand and kissed the palm of it. "You are frighteningly obtuse." His expression sobered. "We both need to live through this. We have to."

They turned to face the army together.

22

Hakara

10 years after the restoration of Kashan
and 571 years after the Shattering

Langzu - the outskirts of Bian,
under dicey circumstances

*What kind of person sends their children away? What kind
of person lets their child go through the barrier alone, into
a realm they do not know? All to escape restoration.*

There's a saying in Kashan: "Up the side of a mountain
without a tent." Different localities have slightly different
variations – "Up the side of a mountain, naked, without a tent"
or "Up the side of a mountain with no shoes." Maman was fond
of "Up the side of a mountain with your tits to the wind", though
I think she was the only one who used that one. The point is,
you've gotten yourself into a precarious situation with little to
no preparation.

I was without a tent, naked, no shoes, with my tits fully to
the wind. I was a diver and a sinkhole miner. I was not, by

any stretch of the imagination, a warrior ready to take on a godkiller.

Much less six of them.

They emerged from the rocks further down the road, behind the wagon, one after another, their altered features a blur of feathers, horns, and textured skin. All in gray robes and leather breastplates, stamped in the center with an eye. Someone had ratted us out. Whether it was Mitoran's informant or someone else, the end result was the same. We were fucked.

I parsed what Thassir had been shouting. *Ambush*. Didn't know if anyone else had caught it, but I couldn't even shout a word of warning. My breath was held, my heart hammering against my ribs like it was protesting the fact that it had been tied to *my* body, of all things. All five guards funneled toward us on the left side of the wagon. I slammed my blade into the two guards nearest me, throwing one back and knocking the other one clean over. Dashu was there in the next moment, his curved sword drawn, slicing the throat of the guard on the ground. *The vine plugs the gaps.*

The other one I'd hit came at me while Utricht defended my left side, keeping anyone from circling me. Four guards left, but six godkillers on their way.

Alifra must have spotted the godkillers too, because her spine stiffened. She dashed to the other side of the wagon to get a clear line of sight, her hands working at her belt and vest. From somewhere, she pulled out a tiny crossbow. The *click* of loading and release echoed from the rocks. She couldn't fend them off for long. I still remembered being chased down by a godkiller and handled like I was an errant pup. They were quick, strong and ruthless. I could only claim stubborn.

Spots formed in front of my eyes as I blocked a blow from the guard in front of me. I caught a glimpse of his face, his teeth clenched. I pushed back hard and he flew into the wagon, setting it rocking. He fell to the ground and stayed there. Two more guards filled the gap. Another slipped past me, engaging with Dashu to my right. I could feel Utricht's presence at my side – solid, waiting for a signal from me.

I took one last swipe at the guards, missed, and then stepped behind his shoulder, gasping for breath at last.

The strength dissipated from my arms; my legs felt slow, sluggish. I caught a glimpse of a faint, wispy smoke around my limbs before it disappeared, leaving me weak and feeling hopelessly mortal. Utricht's muscles bunched and then he was in front of me, swinging his ax as though he were felling trees. Both guards retreated out of his reach. One of them gasped, a dagger stuck deep into the back of his arm. Utricht's gaze went to our right.

Alifra.

She slid around the Dashu to join us, nearly as out of breath as I was. "They're coming. I slowed them down as well as I could."

Utricht lodged his ax into one guard just as Dashu appeared seemingly out of nowhere, his sword burying deep into the ribs of the other. The guard who'd slipped past me to fight Dashu was on the ground, his throat slit. He'd lost that duel so quickly I hadn't even registered it. Utricht braced a foot against the woman's chest, shoving her back and pulling his ax free. She stayed down. A terrible, brief silence ensued, the sort that exists in the eye of the storm, just before the rest of it comes bellowing in.

Utricht barely seemed to be winded, though the fur at his forehead was damp. He licked his tusks. "Well, you always wondered how a team of us would fare against a cohort of six godkillers. Guess we're about to find out."

Dashu tilted his head to the side, his sword lifted. "It will make a good story to pass down to my children, and they to theirs."

Alifra tucked her crossbow away and pulled out her daggers, clicking her tongue. "If you live to have children."

Four guards were dead and one was missing – regrouping, hiding or fled. I eyed the six approaching godkillers. They were closer now, details coming into focus. The embossed eye at the center of each breastplate was wide open, surrounded by rays as though it was lit from within, and though I couldn't see them, I knew there would be a multitude of eyes sewn into the backs of each gray robe. All the illustrations and statues depicted Kluehnn as being covered in eyes and limbs, a hulking monstrosity of too many parts fitted together in strange ways.

Downright creepy when you thought about it. Guess we'd all gotten used to the idea. Kluehnn of the many limbs. Kluehnn the all-seeing. Kluehnn the—

Dashu elbowed my ribs.

Right.

We backed away from the wagon so they couldn't take us unawares from either side. Then I took a few short, shallow breaths and swallowed another couple gems.

Utricht summoned the aether and I took in that last breath before the godkiller formation spread out three to each side and then came together again. I tapped the toes of my boots against the ground, feeling the speed of my movements. My arms thickened.

In unison, they drew their godkilling knives.

I charged straight at the two in front of me, my short sword tight in my grip, and felt Utricht following close behind. Dashu moved to the right; Alifra to the left, her curly hair bobbing.

My first blow caught the dagger of one of the godkillers and then moved past it, cutting deep into her side. I pulled my blade free from her bark-like skin and danced toward the other as she fell. This one already had his gem-hilted dagger lifted – slower than me but not by enough.

It skittered off my bracer and scored the skin of my upper arm. Pain, bright and hot, lanced through me. Shimmering blood leaked from the wound, slick and reflective as oil. Somehow I hadn't expected pain – or maybe I hadn't considered that gods could feel pain at all. But I kept my breath held.

Feint to the right and then a hard swing at his legs. This god-killer leapt out of the way – smarter than his comrade. But I swept the sword up, cutting through the leather armor on his chest and into the flesh beneath before he could defend himself. He leaned back, the cut shallower than I'd intended.

I pushed past that moment, that feeling that I had to breathe at all costs. My throat involuntarily swallowed.

I followed through with another blow. He bared sharp teeth, the green scales on his cheeks covered in a thin layer of brown dust as he blocked with his dagger. I shoved him back, he stumbled, and then Dashu lashed out, taking advantage of his uneven footing. My vine was fending off two godkillers now, but I couldn't help him.

My stomach convulsed and I gave in, taking a breath. My legs nearly gave way.

Utricht was there in an instant, a solid wall for me to lean against, his ax discouraging a horned godkiller who had two of Alifra's knives stuck into his torso.

"Any moment now!" I shouted at the wagon.

Thassir grunted from inside. "It's welded to the frame."

I could barely hear him above the din of battle and the ringing in my ears. We hadn't counted on having to act as a distraction for this long. We hadn't counted on six godkillers. The one I'd pushed down had forced Dashu to retreat. Another godkiller pushed toward Dashu. He needed help. We'd managed to kill only one, and only during that initial rush.

Didn't know if I was doing well by my team, or poorly. I

hastily downed another couple gems and elbowed Utricht's back. Barely had the time to catch my breath, but the aether was hitting me and I was breathing it in and holding it, my pulse and my head pounding.

The green-scaled godkiller turned from Dashu to come at me again, his tail whipping behind him, the eye on his leather breastplate gashed and bleeding. I whirled out of the way and lifted my sword to block the second dagger he'd drawn. It caught on my sword's hilt. My arm strained beneath the full weight of his effort.

And then I felt strength infusing my limbs as the gems absorbed the aether in my blood.

A measure of confidence flowed back into my veins. I was not the best fighter. I was not the best magicker, either, by the looks of things. But I could refuse to quit and I was damned good at that. I pushed the godkiller back again, as hard as I could. He stumbled over a stone.

I rushed forward, bearing down on him with my sword. Dimly I was aware of Utricht's presence several paces away as another godkiller came abreast of the one he'd been fighting. They paced around him, searching for openings. Dashu kissed the flower hilt of his blade and then attacked the two godkillers that were pursuing him, his movements flowing and beautiful. Wasn't sure how long he could keep that up. I didn't know where Alifra was. Somewhere behind me, close to Utricht, catching a moment's rest. The godkiller I was fighting grimaced, a drop of sweat sliding down the side of his nose. It slicked his black hair to the sides of his face.

I gave one last shove and punched my sword at her chest with all my strength. It pierced the gash in his leather armor, sliding between his ribs, finding the organs beneath. He dropped his sword, his mouth going slack. Blood spilled onto my fist.

There's something a little horrible about killing someone.

There's something even more horrible about killing someone so easily. His armor had been like paper beneath my blade.

I had no time to dwell on this victory – one of Dashu's godkillers fell upon me, gray fur covering her ears and her long, pointed ears. I put my back to Utricht, trying to keep her from passing me. I caught the gasp of someone behind me and hoped that was another godkiller meeting their end on Utricht's ax. I could sense his presence, so he was still alive.

With my enhanced limbs, I was quicker and stronger than the godkillers. But these enhancements were fleeting, and their blades could still hurt me. I slashed and darted, hacked and lunged.

A godkiller I hadn't seen before emerged from the rocks, making his way toward the road. Small, speckled wings sprouted from his shoulders. That meant there were others on their way – everyone knew they moved in packs of three. We were outnumbered. Utricht might have been stronger than your average mortal, but the godkillers were altered too. At best, they would be an even match.

I was doing everything I could. Thassir needed to get that safe out, and quickly. Because I certainly wasn't equipped to hold off several godkillers at a time.

As if to underline that point, the one I was fighting got past my guard and sliced into the meat of my thigh. Pain seized me, like a dog shaking a helpless rabbit.

Blood dripped onto the road. I gritted my teeth but kept my breath. I swallowed.

A smirk lifted the corner of the godkiller's lips, showing off long fangs.

So confident, hm? I redoubled my efforts, but she stayed just out of reach, harrying me with sharp, shallow cuts. My breath was tight in my lungs; my stomach convulsed. The godkillers didn't have to slice my throat. They only had to wait until I needed to breathe.

And I needed to. In a moment I'd start to feel dizzy, and if I didn't breathe, I'd black out. Utricht would try to protect me, but I'd just be dead weight to him. I could hear the fighting behind me. "Two more godkillers," Utricht gasped out. That was all three for that cohort.

If I was going to die, I was going to take at least one more with me. The godkiller with the speckled wings closed in. I feinted, making it look as though I'd finally tired and lost my balance.

Both of them darted in.

I ducked down and hamstrung the gray-furred one. Never had much of a stomach for blood and killing, but I smirked right back at her as she stumbled screaming to the ground.

The blade of the winged godkiller hovered at my neck, and I froze.

"Do we take you alive or dead?"

Alive I'd still have a chance to find Rasha. And that was all my life was worth anymore. A gust of wind hit the back of my neck. Quick as thought, a clawed hand had seized the godkiller and tossed him into a rock.

Thassir towered next to me, black wings spread behind him, the safe tucked under one arm. He set it down. It took the god-killers a moment to regroup, and in that moment he'd taken out the one who'd been fighting Dashu, his wings buffeting the altered man, one hand grasping his skull and the other wrenching his wrist with a sickening crack.

There was none of Dashu's dancing elegance here. This was both efficient and brutal.

I pivoted toward Utricht and Alifra, certain that Thassir could at least hold his own, and knowing that Dashu would follow me into the fight. The other two were struggling. The missing guard had returned to the fight, and three godkillers circled like hawks, pushing Alifra and Utricht toward the wagon and looking for an opening to dive in. Three godkillers plus one guard against the five of us.

I darted toward the godkiller closest to me, digging into my pouch for more god gems. I was far from catching my breath, still gasping from my last effort, my chest and belly aching.

I swallowed two more as my footing faltered. And then I felt a sudden severing. It was like being in a room lit only from the hallway and having the door abruptly shut. I looked for Utricht, panic bubbling up my throat.

A godkiller's knife was protruding from his chest. He held his axe in limp fingers as he stared disbelieving at the metal piercing his flesh. The stone-skinned woman jerked her dagger free and Utricht fell. He was dead before he hit the ground. I could *feel* the life in him winking out.

"Utricht!" What use was there in calling after the dead? I knew there was none, that he couldn't even hear me anymore, but I couldn't help it. Only a few days I'd known him, and had started to feel as though we might become familiar, if not friends. Now he was gone.

Alifra was pinned against the wagon and Dashu was hurtling toward her, his expression panic-stricken.

Four of us against three godkillers and one mortal.

And I had no means to do magic.

23

Sheuan

10 years after the restoration of Kashan
and 571 years after the Shattering

The border between Langzu and Kashan

There are some who would give the old gods safe harbor.
To protect them from what they see as an overzealous
movement to eliminate them. These people must be turned
in for their own safety.

Sheuan lifted her gaze. The churning, dust-filled wall rose as
far as she could see. She wondered exactly how high it went,
how many birds could reach the necessary altitude to cross it
without getting caught by the aether.

This early, the road that led into the barrier was empty. She
peered into the dense, shifting brown as she put down her pack,
tightened her boots and sifted through the bag for Mull's filter. It
was an ugly contraption – she'd have to work with him on that
if he ever intended to sell them to the public. Several layers of
fabric were sewn tightly between two leather rings. She greased

the rubbery side of it that would lie against her face, just as Mull's notes had said to do. Then she fitted it over her nose and mouth. Kluehnn's-eye amulet swung as she bent her head. Mitoran's warning about Kashan and Kluehnn's precepts had prompted her, at the last moment, to hang it around her neck.

The cloth of the filter smelled strange – it was a proprietary blend, his notes had said. He'd been through several different formulations, testing them first by placing mice in cages covered in the cloth and putting them inside the barrier. His first experiments had ended in a lot of dead mice.

This final model was a blend of silk and a flaxen fiber only found in restored lands. It wasn't cheap to make.

In spite of the strange smell, she could breathe just fine. She settled the pack onto her back again and faced the wall.

She'd come this far. If she turned and went home, Mitoran couldn't blame her. She'd even approve. But Sheuan could already see the disappointment on her mother's face, and thought of how her family home would be sold, the Sim family elders thrown into the streets, their businesses pieced off to other clans.

Her mother had come to see her before she'd left, taking hold of her hands, her palms leathery and dry. There was familiarity there. Those fingers had once brushed the hair from Sheuan's face, had cradled her head as a baby.

For a sudden, desperate moment, she'd wished that her mother would stop her, would tell her to stay. She would not have the opportunity to take the trade minister position and to restore her family, but she would be alive. Her clan would continue to exist. Yes, they would fall into the dregs of society and would lose their estate, but at least most of them would still be alive. It could be a gentle thing, a leaf drifting from a tree instead of being plucked.

Please. Please don't send me out there alone. She'd wanted to cling to her mother, to lay her head on that thin shoulder, to remain in the safety of home. But she wasn't a child anymore.

Her mother had squeezed her hands. "Do the Sim clan proud. You *will* succeed, Sheuan. You will secure the trade minister position and our family's place."

Despair was a living thing inside her chest, gnawing at her heart. She clamped down on it. Of course she hadn't truly expected anything different. They had no other options. Her father was dead. Her mother was the head of the clan and deserving of all of her. They both had obligations.

She breathed in through the filter, the strange smells of it filling her nostrils. She pushed away the fear, that belly-deep want to be coddled and held and told that she *mattered*. That she was more than a bulwark holding back the tide. She would defend her family. To the last.

She closed her eyes and stepped into the barrier.

She had heard stories of what the inside of a barrier was like. Dark and churning, and filled with aether. Still, she hadn't quite been prepared for the actual sensation. It was the difference between knowing the ocean was cold and being tossed bodily into it.

She was surrounded by brown dust, her hands barely visible in front of her. Wind whipped at her hair and clothes. The air was thicker here, though, and it threatened to carry her along on a current to who knew where. No wonder all the guides were such hefty individuals.

Sheuan was not hefty. As far as she could tell, the filter was doing its job and blocking out the aether, but keeping her feet in front of her was another matter. She had to dig her toes into the ground to prevent herself from being thrown off balance with each surge. Her foot hooked into a piece of debris and caught. She knelt and felt something thin and long. As she tore it free from the ground and tossed it to the side, she could make it out more clearly. A thigh bone.

She could not panic. If she panicked, she'd lose all sense of where she was, and she'd no longer be able to tell which way Kashan or even Langzu was. She had to keep moving forward, to unerringly keep her feet facing in the right direction.

People had tried, over the years, to position guide ropes, to create paths. But these had always been worn or torn away almost as quickly as they'd been placed. The ground beneath her feet, which had been hard-packed earth in Langzu, was shifting sands inside the barrier. Her feet sank into it up to her ankles. And all the while air billowed up from below. Somewhere beneath the sand and the dust was cracked earth. Here, the cracks were small, but at some points in the barrier they opened into wide, uncrossable chasms.

Sheuan gritted her teeth and felt sand grind between them. She remembered the look on the Sovereign's face – he did not think she could do this. He knew their financial situation was dire, that Sheuan was young, that their resources were few. He was *expecting* her to fail, giving him an excuse to divvy up her clan's holdings to the other royal clans, maybe even to some of the noble ones – small favors to show his appreciation and win further loyalty. Either way, he would win. No wonder he'd risen to power.

She pushed forward.

Without her family, she would not have a roof over her head. She would not have food in her mouth. She would not exist. Her duty was to her mother, her family, her clan. They could only survive by watching out for one another, by setting the clan above everything else. Sheuan placed one foot in front of the other, repeating this like a mantra in her head. Her mother, her family, her clan. She breathed into the hot space of the mask, the moisture of her own breath beading below her nostrils.

One moment the darkness and the sand surrounded her, the next she was stumbling into a lush green landscape. She fell to her hands and knees and tore off the filter. Air had never smelled so sweet, like dew and the bright shoots of new plants. It took her a moment to orient herself. The road was now somewhere off to her left, barely visible through the bushes and trees. She'd wandered off course while she'd been inside the barrier.

Her lips firmed. She'd do better next time.

Beneath her feet, two ruts in the dirt marked the path a wagon had taken. The forest hovered three body-lengths away from the smoky barrier, as though maintaining a respectful distance from the wall of dust and magic. She spotted a small building nearly hidden in the trees. A tower rose above it and the treetops, and at the pinnacle she caught a glimpse of a figure, dark against the bright sun. She squinted but couldn't make them out.

Quickly, she stuffed the filter into her pack – they didn't need to know how she'd crossed. Mull's new technology was not yet public knowledge, and as cavalierly as she'd treated the other items in his shop, she intended to keep the filter under wraps. Then she waited to be greeted by the border guards. She didn't need to wait long.

Two guards came to meet her. They rode no mounts, though both of them walked with steady, road-eating strides. The taller one was built like a boulder and looked like one too – squat in appearance despite his height. His feet were wider and longer than seemed necessary; his legs were each nearly as thick as his torso. His skin was gray and cracked, though Sheuan had the suspicion that an arrow fired at him would merely bounce out of those crevices.

The shorter one still towered over Sheuan, her wings giving her the illusion of further height. They were dove-gray, feathers growing amongst the gray hair that fell over her eyes, sprouting at the edges of her eyebrows like seedlings. Her face was youthful and sharp, reminiscent of a stoat.

Her orange-eyed gaze passed over Sheuan. "You came alone?"

For a brief moment, she considered telling them the truth – that she'd walked through that barrier unassisted. But that was pride speaking. So she shifted, favoring one leg, shrinking, turning fearful and small. Sand and dust fell, glittering, from the folds of her dress. "I had a guide." She let a little breathlessness into her voice. "He made a mistake near the border. I couldn't see what happened. But he fell. I think he must have breathed in the air because he went stumbling deeper into the barrier. I could not convince him to step into Kashan." She held up her hands help-lessly. "I couldn't risk speaking and becoming poisoned myself."

There was no hint of pity in either guard's eyes, but nor was there disbelief. The rock-wood altered spoke. "The way is treacherous. A full fifth of the wagons coming through don't make it."

She'd had an idea of how dangerous passage was and knew he couldn't possibly know for sure exactly how many wagons made it through, but it was an opening to dig, and Mitoran had taught her never to pass one by. "Is it becoming more treacherous?"

"The aether churns." He exchanged glances with the winged woman. Something passed between them in that look, though Sheuan couldn't be sure what it was. He looked back to Sheuan and shrugged. She wasn't going to get more out of him.

She took a deep breath, knowing this next part would be criti-cal. "The way may be treacherous, but I am here at the behest of Langzu's Sovereign. He sent me here to speak to your Queen." Not *exactly* true. He'd sent her here to investigate the isolation of restored realms. She knew Mitoran was right, that the Sovereign would have already sent others to work this problem. So she'd done what she'd done best, insinuating herself into a friendly get-together at Liyana Juitsi's estate and poking around for answers. She'd needed to form a closer relationship with Liyana anyways in order to dangle that introduction in front of Nimao. She'd earned a reputation for connecting the right people, and she wasn't about to let that fall by the wayside.

What she'd learned had been disheartening. The Sovereign had already dispatched two expeditions of low-ranking officials to meet with the Kashani Queen over a trade agreement. Neither expedition had returned and they'd been quietly covered up.

She had to find a way to be different. Maybe coming alone would help, though she doubted it.

"Only you?" A slightly raised eyebrow from the winged altered was the only sign of skepticism she saw, though she knew they must be swimming in it. She might claim to have had a guide, but she hadn't claimed guards or any sort of entourage.

The Sovereign had met with Kashan's Queen only twice, once after her rather hurried election, and once a year after that. One meeting had taken place in Kashan and the other in Langzu. Both had been surrounded by so much pomp that Sheuan's father had remarked dryly that the circus had come to town. The prior Queen had been unseated by a vote of no confidence shortly before restoration. While many of Langzu's clans supposed the new Queen's rule might not be truly legitimate, they'd been happy enough to entertain her while she'd been in Bian.

Sheuan had only caught a glimpse of brown-speckled wings and a narrow-lipped smile.

She dug into her pocket. "I have the Sovereign's seal, given to me by his hand. He vested me with the authority for this meeting. I'll need an escort. Provisions."

They waited.

Her fingers searched the recesses of her pocket and found nothing but sand and dust. "I ... " She tried her other pocket, just in case. "I had it when I went into the barrier." Nothing. She could feel heat prickling at the back of her neck.

The rock man sighed. "A lot of trouble you went through."

She wasn't sure if he meant she'd gone to a lot of effort to simply come through the barrier, or if she'd gone through a lot to try and con them. Her lips went numb. No, not like this. She lifted the flap on her bag, searching the bottom frantically. The wind inside the barrier had tugged at everything, had tossed her about like a child in a stormy sea. "Wait. I have papers." The leather envelope was still there, half buried in dust.

She handed it over, her mind turning as they inspected it. The papers had her clan name on them and an image of a peach, her clan's seal. She was not one of the clanless of Langzu; she still had a position and some authority.

"I am Sheuan Sim." She shook off the mantle of the distressed traveler, donning one of seamless importance. "I may have lost the seal in the barrier, but I am still here to see your Queen at the Sovereign's behest."

The rock man cast a slightly pleading look at the winged woman, who gave a short shake of her head. He handed back Sheuan's papers. "I'm afraid you'll have to go back to the Sovereign and provide us with some proof."

Her tongue stuck in her throat. She let the humiliation wash over her and away; Mitoran had always taught her there was no space for shame in the game they played. It never helped, she'd said. It would only ever hinder her in reaching her goals. Kashan was restored, and Sheuan had seen enough of the altered wildlife in the Sovereign's castle to know that traveling without an escort here was asking for an unhappy end.

If she walked back into that barrier, she could make it through with the filter, she knew she could. But worse than the barrier itself was her mother waiting on the other side. She would look at Sheuan with a disappointment as vast as a mountain. "I'd thought we could rely on you. We have given you every resource we could afford."

It wasn't shame that she drowned in, not exactly. She could *feel* her mother's disappointment like her own, a bone-deep ache. But more than that, some part of her thought that this was what her mother *expected*. This was her only purpose and she had failed at the first test. The look the rock man cast her now *was* pitying.

No.

She would not turn back into the barrier. She would not give them that satisfaction. If she had to, she would die here. She tucked the papers back into her satchel but stepped toward the winged woman.

The woman took an involuntary step back. There was something in the way she moved, the way she clutched at her cloak. It hung about her neck, between her wings, so she had to hold it to keep it draped over her body. She was hiding something.

Sheuan took a step to the side, as though trying to get around the guards, and they both shifted in turn. She kept her gaze focused on the inside of the woman's cloak. The barest gleam met her stare. A violet glow that was not reflected light. A god gem.

Everything clicked into place. The woman before her might have truly been a border guard, but that only deepened the implications of her presence here. She was hiding a knife at her belt – a knife that had a god gem embedded in its hilt. She was a godkiller.

Which meant her loyalties lay with Kluehnn. Mitoran's words filtered back into Sheuan's mind. She'd told her to remember Kluehnn's precepts. She'd told her that Kashan was different now that it was restored.

Perhaps the rumors had all been true. Perhaps the Queen's election had been rushed through, the remaining officials intent on some agenda of their own, the Queen not a power in her own right but a puppet propped up by so many people moving behind the scenes.

Sheuan licked her upper lip, tasting the sweat forming there, grit catching on her tongue. If she fouled this up, she'd be meeting a very bloody and painful end. "Take me to the closest den." She kept her voice soft, but both altered stiffened as though she'd shouted.

The rock man frowned. "You will not be allowed inside."

A little thrill of triumph burst at the back of her throat, but this had only been the first step. She recalled the books she'd read, the letters, all forming the shape of Kluehnn's dens and their organization but never quite filling it in. Every government was expected to pay their tithes to Kluehnn, to worship him, but the dens existed almost on a different plane, the separation between the converts and the citizens sharply delineated. But there were ways in which politics and religion still interacted, each looking for ways to benefit from the other. Maybe this was how she did things differently, with the support of Kluehnn at her back. She mentally flipped through all the information she knew about Kluehnn and his religion, filtering down into the more obscure tenets.

She knew there was something in there about the dens being a safe place, welcoming to all who might wish to enter – at a cost. And there were specific tenets applicable to higher ranking political officials that provided assistance to them before taking them in. Low-level criminals might hide away in the dens, trading their lives for indentured servitude, but those who'd offended political leaders had to be dealt with more delicately. She couldn't ask to serve . . . there was another name for it. Ah, there it was.

"I claim the right of sanctuary."

The godkiller's eyes narrowed. "You don't have the standing to do so."

"I am a leader in my own country, my role important to the functioning of the government. My status is relevant. So too is the danger I am in. If I do not form a formal trade alliance with your new Queen, then the Sovereign has threatened to eliminate my clan, myself included. I claim my right to an assigned advocate who will help me to obviate my need for sanctuary. I have the political rank, and I am a devotee of Kluehnn If my grievance cannot be resolved, I will dedicate my life to the service of the den."

Amusement crept into the altered woman's voice. Her hand fell from her cloak, and it moved to reveal the knife at her belt. It was a threat more immediate than any from the Sovereign. "You are no true devotee of Kluehnn."

Sheuan's heartbeat clattered against her ribs and she clutched the eye amulet at her neck. She'd never been as devoted to Kluehnn as some of her peers, but she was devoted to learning. Mitoran had made sure of that. If she couldn't find out what the Sovereign wanted, she might be stuck in the den, spending her days performing whatever tasks the priests set her. She spoke in Old Albanoran, the words curling around her tongue. "I offer you not just my land, but my body. Let me be the vessel that brings you close to the surface, that gives you the way to break our world so that it may heal. Let me lead you from the darkness so that you may lead us from the darkness. Let me show you my gratitude in the very marrow of my bones, the beds of my nails, the roots of my teeth. I will hollow myself out so that you may have a home."

The winged woman gave a reluctant nod. "Tolemne's first devotion. And in his original language." She tilted her head to the side, her jaw moving as though she were rolling some morsel over her tongue. "Very well. Sanctuary for thirty days – the same amount of time it took Tolemne to reach the gods. If you cannot solve your grievance, you become one of ours." She beckoned Sheuan to follow her.

If these border guards would not provide her with an escort to the Queen, then Sheuan needed to find her own, even if that meant entering the bowels of the earth itself.

24

Hakara

10 years after the restoration of Kashan
and 571 years after the Shattering

Langzu - the outskirts of Bian,
under dicey circumstances

*The immigration system in Langzu is held up as a shining
example of a measured approach to refugees. Those who
can contribute materially to the economy and who pay the
proper fees are allowed to establish residency.*

*But Langzu's resources are already stretched thin. The
rest must face their fate with restoration.*

Utricht was laid out on the ground, and despite all my
fervent wishing, he did not rise. Two godkillers broke
off from circling Alifra to meet me, and I realized with a start
that I'd stopped moving. The godkillers said nothing as they
approached; they only, in unison, lifted their gem-hilted knives.
Sometimes the most intimidating thing is silence.

I felt my bowels go watery, my legs numb as I searched for

some escape, for some way we could get away with the corestone. The remaining guard rushed in at Alifra. Dashu lifted his sword to block his attack, though I could see his hand tremble with exhaustion. We weren't ready.

Even in this vastly outmatched situation, I couldn't imagine abandoning the corestone. It was the only leverage I had in getting Rasha back, and I would cling to it even as the hunters approached.

A clawed foot thudded on the ground next to Alifra.

I felt the breeze from his wings before I saw his face. Thassir. He hadn't flown off, though the scowl on his face said that he wasn't at all pleased to be back in the fight. With a quick pivot of his torso, he seized the guard Dashu had blocked and casually snapped the man's neck. He jumped into the sky again before landing next to me.

The god gems I'd swallowed weighed heavy in my belly, the wound on my leg aching, but not enough for me to stop. Hadn't gotten any more aether from Utricht before he'd died. Without the magic, the weapons in my hands felt like leaden weights. I was like a carcass hung up for the butcher.

Alifra backed into the wagon, any retreat cut off. If I ran, I'd be leaving both Alifra and Dashu to fend for themselves against three godkillers. Thassir was here because I'd made a bargain with him; I had no assurance he'd stay if I left. I was self-interested, I could admit that to myself, but I wasn't an entire monster.

Besides, I needed that corestone. "We can take them."

Thassir cocked his head at me, studying me with his black eyes like a crow studying some strange insect. "Utricht is dead. You can't use the gems."

I ignored him, using my dagger to cut a thin line on my hand, right over the wound where I'd bonded with Utricht. I held out my hand.

His wings snapped out, his gaze fiery. He crouched, his muscles bunched to spring into the air. I reached for him, expecting him to leap from the ground, for me to catch only air, but he did not move. I ended up clasping my bloody hand on his shoulder.

There wasn't any time and I didn't know what to say. I only knew that if I did not bond with him, I would probably die trying to get that corestone out of here. I wasn't even sure if, bonded, we could fight off the rest of the godkillers. I didn't know if he had the ability to summon aether. But I knew he was strong, and I knew I was as hard-headed as they came. If I just refused to die, I'd get out of here eventually.

He stared back into my silent, pleading gaze. Someone screamed and I knew a godkiller had struck either Alifra or Dashu. The other two crouched just out of reach, wary of Thassir's intimidating presence. My feet felt as though they hovered over the ground, my muscles tensed as I prepared to run toward the conflict, with or without him.

But I wanted this, I wanted this so badly. For once, couldn't he put aside whatever promise he'd made to himself not to get too deeply involved? He could break the bond later if he wanted to.

I held out my bloody hand.

"Hakara!" Alifra called.

So much wanting and needing all around me, and mine burned so brightly I felt my chest must be aflame. And here was Thassir in front of me, looking as though he sincerely regretted landing next to me, as though he'd rather do *anything* else except become my bonded partner.

It was only a moment, a fraction of a moment, but I saw something in his black, avian eyes shift as we looked at one another. Something in my face changed his mind. I didn't know if it was the pleading, the fear or the wanting – the endless wanting – but in a snap he'd broken his gaze away and had pulled a knife across his palm.

He grasped my hand in his, and quicker than I'd thought possible had pulled the shimmering aether from below to envelop our hands.

It seemed, in the safe house, that Utricht and I had stood with hands clasped for an eternity. The lamps had flickered, our breath echoed off the crates, a cat padded between us – all in the time it took for our bond to solidify.

This felt like two gears clicking into place, teeth intertwined, faster than thought. Thassir was there, his hand in mine, yet I knew I would be able to find him if he flew three realms away. "Use the gems," he said, his voice fierce. "Let us show the godkillers they have reason to fear."

I lifted my sword. Somehow the aether I needed was there in the next step, right where I needed it, Thassir anticipating my every movement. I breathed it in and felt the unfurling within me, the tingling as the god limbs overtook mine. This time I was prepared for the sensations. I bore down on the godkillers, trying to break their ranks.

For the barest moment, my courage flagged. These were godkillers. What was I except an imitation god?

But then I felt Thassir's presence at my back, a solid wall of strength to lean on. He might have been an altered and not a god, but he was enough. I slashed at the closest godkiller just as Thassir thundered into the next one.

Every move I made relied heavily on the strength of my arms and the speed of my legs; I had only a little skill. Thassir moved through the godkillers like a wolf – half brutal strength and half elegant movements.

He took one down, snapping the flightless wings at her back before breaking both arms. He seized the one I'd slashed at by the next. That godkiller tried to slice his arm with her blade, but he slammed her into the ground so hard I heard bones shatter. The godkiller who'd cornered Alifra bolted toward us, taking the opportunity to go for Thassir's hamstrings, but I blocked him with my sword.

Then Alifra was there, Dashu on her heels. The last godkiller took one look at the four of us, then turned and fled.

I breathed a sigh of relief, but Thassir sprang into the air, diving after that last godkiller like a hawk chasing a rabbit. In one swift movement he seized the altered man beneath his arms, lifting him higher, higher. He let him go and the godkiller fell upon the rocks with a crunch.

My breathing was still quick by the time Thassir landed back amongst us. Everything had happened so quickly, with unhesitating brutality.

He picked up the safe, tucking it under one arm.

Dashu squinted at the skies. "We go off road and hike back to the other side of the city. Tie up your wounds. We'll tend to them later. Kluehnn will want someone held accountable for the deaths of his godkillers and the loss of a corestone. Best we not give him an easy target." He glanced at Utricht's body, blinking a few rapid times, his mouth settling into a stony line. "Strip him. We can't leave anything identifiable. Leave the body. There's no time."

We moved quickly, all except Thassir, who watched me with an inscrutable expression.

I'd thought I'd never felt such power before when I'd worked with Utricht, but there had been an odd synergy with Thassir. I hadn't needed to ask; I'd known he would funnel the aether to me exactly where and when I needed it.

The path through the rocks and the withered forests of Langzuan was not even really a path. At least the heat of summer had eased somewhat, though sweat still stuck my shirt to my back. Alifra stopped every so often to check the position of the sun in the sky, to take note of a dry creek bed or a copse of trees. We kept to the lowest spots in the landscape, and even Thassir declined to take to the air. "We're too close to the place where it happened," he said when I asked, his lips tight. "They knew. They already knew." He moved very deliberately away from me after that, slipping artfully ahead each time I tried to walk abreast of him.

We stopped in a dip in the land that must have once been a pond. "No fires," Alifra said. "We keep quiet. They'll send scouts. We've got a head start, but Mitoran wouldn't want us taking any risks. Not when we're so close to getting back with the corestone."

She didn't mention that we'd lost Utricht. Maybe that was normal and expected in an operation such as this. We hadn't brought food, but no one complained. It wasn't uncommon to go without a meal in Langzu. Both Alifra and Dashu set to cleaning their blades, Dashu muttering words in a language I couldn't understand, stopping every so often to correct himself before continuing on.

Thassir found me before I lay down, dried plants crunching beneath my feet. The sun was just about to rise, the sky awash in the pale pink of a fading night. Insects buzzed in the yellowed grass around us, the tree we'd chosen to camp beneath scorched black by a recent fire. Something about the way he moved made my heartbeat quicken without my permission. I felt like a rabbit on the ground, the shadow of a hawk passing over me.

He held out one clawed hand. "Break the bond. I helped you when you needed it and now you no longer need it. This is not my fight and I do not wish to be bound to Mitoran in any way."

I hesitated, and did not place my palm in his. The way we'd

fought together ran over and over in my mind — the ease with which he'd pulled the aether for me, the way he'd seemed to know exactly where to place it, the way my courage had picked up as soon as I'd felt his presence at my back. "What if," I said slowly, and even with those first two words I saw the warning in his gaze, "what if we *didn't* break the bond. I'm not asking you to be bound to Mitoran," I followed up quickly, noticing the way his teeth pressed against his lips, the slight grimace that revealed their gleaming surfaces. I nearly expected a growl. "I'm asking you to be bound to *me*."

The glance he cast me was both skeptical and curious, though his lips closed over his teeth. "You're working with Mitoran."

"I'm working *for* her," I corrected. I cast my gaze at the sky, wondering why I felt suddenly shy. I wasn't shy. I was never shy. I licked my lips, swallowing my apprehension, feeling grief rise unexpectedly to take its place. "My sister ... When restoration came to Kashan, I was taken beyond the borders by a mining supervisor. He didn't let me bring her, and when I woke up, it was too late. They'd carried me to the other side and Kashan was restored. I'd ... I'd told her to wait. I made a promise." My voice cracked. "It was ten years ago. She was nine." Other words lingered at the back of my throat. She was small, she was kind, she had been there alone with no one to hold her or to comfort her when the black wall of smoke had overtaken her. She'd either been dissolved or had been altered, and it was killing me a little every day not to know which.

I had to know. I had to *know*. I watched the pink light turn to a burnished gold. "Others have told me that she's either dead or so changed I'd not recognize her. But she's Rasha. She's still my Rasha no matter what, and she'll be that way until she dies. I owe her more than *this*." I waved a hand over myself, the land, the sky and the world itself.

When I finally dared to look at Thassir, I couldn't judge his expression. The growing dark cast his face in shadows. "Mitoran said she would help you find her."

"Yes," I said. "But I don't trust her to keep her word. There might be a way I can get to Kashan myself. I could use your help."

"I'm not for hire."

"I know." I was caught somewhere between frustration and understanding, my teeth clenched so tight I thought they would crack. "You promised me you'd help me find my sister. And maybe helping me get that corestone was enough by your reckoning. I'm not asking you to join this cult or to try to change the world. I don't know how to explain. It's been ten years, but it's like living with a hollow next to me, a blank, empty space where a person should be. I was supposed to be there when she needed me the most. Instead I'm here, and it feels so wrong that I think either my mind or the world will break and I don't care which." I stopped, my words running dry. "Haven't you ever *needed* someone in your life like this?"

The fading light made sinkholes of his eyes. I could have been looking at a statue. He'd gone so still I couldn't tell if he even breathed. From my vantage point, everything about him seemed foreboding. I could have been gazing up the face of a mountain, trying to find an expression in its peak.

And then his right wing twitched, shattering the illusion.

"I will keep helping you," he said finally. "But only until you find out what happened to your sister. That, in my view, meets the promise I made to you. After that, you're on your own."

He didn't give me the chance to thank him. The sliver of the sun crested the horizon and he leapt, leaving me on the ground, feeling his presence wheel away into the sky.

25

Rasha

10 years after the restoration of Kashan
and 571 years after the Shattering

Kashan - Kluehnn's den

*Nioanen was a vicious and cruel god. Even Ayaz feared
him. With his lightning-forged sword, Zayyel, and his
broad golden wings, he bent the others to his will, threatening any who dared to oppose him.*

*No gods could be born unless others died, and he used
this fact to his full advantage.*

The winged boy's name was Shambul, and I hated him.

"Bait," he whispered as he slithered close to me, the
corner of his wing touching my shoulder in what I was coming
to realize was an intentional gesture.

"I am not bait," I hissed back. I clutched my bowl, waiting for
my turn at the food. We were in the eating corner of the burrow;
we rarely left. The burrow was our home, Millani had explained

to us. The other converts were our family. Did a person ever want to murder their family?

I prodded at the thought. It wouldn't be murder. Not truly. If we were a family, we were sharks in the womb, eating one another before only a few finally exited.

Shambul brushed his wing against my shoulder again and I jumped back, my face hot. His foot caught my ankle. I lurched into Khatuya behind me, barely catching a glimpse of her bark-covered face before I fell to the ground, my bowl clattering against the stone.

I grasped it, thankful at least that it had been empty, but Shambul leaned over me before I could get back on my feet. "So tall, but you're scared of me, aren't you?"

I stopped humming. I wanted to choke on my own breath. I'd been doing it again. Hakara's lullaby. It had no place here in these stone walls, away from the night sky and the tent and the sounds of the ocean. But I couldn't seem to stop humming it whenever I felt anxiety or fear. It was a liability, yet I couldn't let it go.

I bared my teeth, knowing that I was giving Shambul exactly what he wanted. He wanted to rile me up and I was letting him. It just made me stupid, and he was so much quicker and smoother than I was. He'd ask to spar with me at the next bout, and Millani would grant him that request. She always did, no matter how I protested.

Her words rang in my ears. *If you want to survive, perhaps you shouldn't complain you're being pitted against the best.* I wasn't Shambul's only target, but I certainly was his favorite.

"Next fight," I said, pushing myself to my feet, shoving a shoulder against his, "I'll take you down. Next trial, I'll kill you." Standing, I towered over him, even without the horns.

He only smirked. "Big words."

Something in me wobbled and I set my jaw, my teeth grinding.

All the other converts avoided looking at me. "Why do you *hate* me so much? What did I do to you?"

For a moment he looked startled. Then the grin returned. "Oh, my little sparrow, my little bait – you didn't do anything to me." He touched the wall beside us, running a finger along a crack. "And why *not* hate you?"

Voices came from behind the burrow's door. Shambul's wings twitched. He'd heard them too.

"Why choose my burrow? Why one of the neophytes?" Millani's voice.

"She needs an advocate and claims ties to the Sovereign. I can't risk going with anyone lower-ranked than that. We have to at least make an attempt. Most converts don't have enough fighting experience."

The door opened and we all pretended we were very busy doing other things or looking elsewhere.

Millani entered, her red tail whipping behind her. In spite of my hunched shoulders, her gaze landed on me. "You. Rasha. Come here."

I obeyed, setting my bowl back on my bed before Millani ushered me out the door. She took me by the upper arm, giving me a quick inspection before pushing me in front of the brown-winged woman before her. "Will she do?"

The winged woman only shrugged. "Follow me."

Mystified, I did as she asked.

The air close to the entrance of the den smelled fresh and sweet, with less of the earthiness I was used to in the burrow. I opened my mouth a few times to speak before deciding better of it.

"Her name is Sheuan Sim," the altered woman said as we reached the door. "She's from Langzu and she's claimed sanctuary here. She has thirty days to obviate the need for sanctuary before she becomes a permanent member of the den. Until those thirty days are up, you're to be her advocate."

She handed me a pack and a long-bladed dagger and opened the door.

"But what am I supposed to—"

Her yellow-eyed gaze seized mine. "Anything she asks."

And then I was being pushed into the open air, the pack still grasped between my claws.

A figure stood there, her back to me. Long, shining black hair was pulled into a travel knot at the base of her neck, though strands had worked their way loose. She was dressed in dark green embroidered cloth. The hem of her dress was covered in dust, and when she moved, a little more shook out from her sleeves.

"Sheuan Sim?"

She turned.

The light caught the edges of straight, slim shoulders, dappled shadows falling across her face. It had been a long time since I'd seen someone who wasn't altered. I'd forgotten how small they were, how frail they looked.

Then she met my gaze and I suddenly felt she wasn't frail at all – that *I* was the frail one. I felt taken apart by the mind behind those eyes, quick though her studying was. She didn't linger on my horns or my claws or even my teeth. She searched my face as though it were a map hiding something important. I choked down the tune of the lullaby before it could leave my lips, and cleared my throat. "I am Rasha. I'm to be your advocate."

She looked at my gray robes, the single eye embroidered on one shoulder. "You're a neophyte. I suppose that's what they think I rank. Can you fight?"

I nodded. But as her words sank in, my temper rose. Millani knew this would take me away from training. Thirty days! She was doing it to spite me. It would have been an easier thing to deal with if failure hadn't meant my death. I felt hot and cold in turns, dread and anger coiling in my belly. And *she* had the temerity to behave as though my rank displeased her?

I was as good as she was going to get and she should be grateful.

She nodded back at me. "I want to see your Queen. I need protection."

The forests of Kashan were filled with all manner of altered creatures. Most were dangerous, especially to those who weren't made for this environment. A sting from a nettle wasp might annoy me, but it would put someone like Sheuan Sim down for days, or it might even kill her. Packs of feline kinet wandered nearby; they'd find her easy prey, especially if she were incapacitated. I thought of the thousand ways she could easily die. Touching the wrong sort of flower, drinking from the wrong stream, stepping onto the wrong animal.

I didn't have to know much about politics to know they'd handed me a mess. "And you didn't bring your own protections? Your people had to have known this was dangerous."

She only stared at me, her silence cutting. She knelt and readjusted the ties on her boots, never taking her gaze from mine. "You are a neophyte. Your betters have assigned you to me."

Simple facts, simply stated. I wasn't in a place to question her. I set my jaw and felt my teeth grind.

The coldness in her face melted away, leaving someone breathless, vulnerable. "It's been a hard trip. I lost my entourage and I have a difficult task. Your den was the only place I could think of that could help me. Please. I need to get to the Queen and then back to your den."

I wasn't sure what to make of this abrupt shift. Her lashes fluttered as she looked down and away, as though ashamed. But did someone like her ever really feel shame for the way she treated those she deemed beneath her?

I swung the pack over my shoulder, strapped the dagger to my waist and started off into the forest, trusting she'd be behind me. "You're lucky. Things shifted during restoration. The palace is five days away. We'll have lodgings for some of it and we'll have to camp for some. There's a road. Here."

I'd only been to the town outside the palace perhaps a dozen times, mostly to gather supplies and tithes. The road was more of a trail than an actual road. Once there had been roads in Kashan. Now everything was overgrown, the plants that had once been a last gasp of green flowing over stone and wood. We were in the full-throated song of summer, long before the leaves turned the colors of fire. I followed wagon wheel tracks as they meandered through the brush.

Sheuan's steps sounded behind me.

We traveled in silence. I did my best to keep my focus on the path, on the sounds of the animals around us, stopping every so often to let dangerous ones pass. But I could feel the presence of the woman behind me, even just the thought of her eyes on me making the space between my shoulder blades itch. I wasn't used to being studied or watched. I was used to fading into the corners of rooms, an outsider to every conversation. Even when it had been just me and Hakara. There had been Hakara – sea diver, provider, protector. And there had been me.

We watched one another warily as we ate, exchanging only a few words. If she saw me as beneath her, I certainly wasn't going to start up a conversation. She could do so if she wanted to. Later, we spent the night at a small roadside inn without speaking, creaky beds on either side of the room.

It wasn't until the third day that Sheuan finally broke. She cleared her throat. "Kashan is different than it once was." Her voice was low, neutral. "The weather is . . . tolerable."

"It was restored. Just as Cressima and Albanore before it. Just as Langzu will be."

"A relief for some," she said.

The silence stretched again. Shambul was likely beating the other neophytes right now, gaining in strength as I tromped through the forest with an unaltered woman on my heels. "Kluehnn is merciful; restoration is the only way we can survive. He makes the world bountiful again."

I waited for her to speak some blasphemy, halfway wishing for it.

"He is indeed. It's beautiful here." There was so much that she left unspoken, things I somehow knew she wanted to say. In spite of the Kluehnn's-eye amulet at her chest, I didn't believe she was devout. There was something too slippery about her to be pinned to one religion, one god, one belief. She took in a deep breath. "What is it about me that makes you so angry?"

"You haven't exactly spoken to me either."

"And yet you're marching through the underbrush as though crushing it is your goal rather than getting to any destination."

I found my brow furrowing and tried to relax. Something about her made me feel as though I had to be on guard. I wasn't sure if it was her penetrating black eyes or the prim way she held her hands – I suspected palms softer than flower petals – or her straight but narrow shoulders. Her words sounded solicitous, but they felt as though they were attempting to pull something from me. She was the one who should be answering my questions, not the other way around. She had absolutely no idea how her actions would affect me, how my chances of surviving the trials were plummeting with every step we took. I deflected. "Why exactly are you here? Why come to Kashan? Why come through the barrier at all?"

"Because I had to. There are others relying on me. Will you answer me? Why are you angry at me? You don't even know me."

I scoffed before I could help myself. Didn't I? I'd seen the pamphlets for the Queen's campaign before the vote had come down. Pamphlets that promised things to the people in Kashan who mattered. The country's officials, the horse breeders, the wealthy merchants. Never to the people who were just trying to get by. Because we were nothing to the politicians.

"I know your type."

"Look at me." The snap in her voice had me turning before I'd realized I was doing it. She stalked toward me, closing the distance between us. "Is the problem me or is it something else? And don't pretend there isn't a problem. We both know there is."

She smelled like sweat and the remains of a perfumed bath. Everything about her was offensive. She was unaltered. She was pampered. She had no idea what it was like to be abandoned, to have to fend for oneself.

"It's both," I snarled. "You're not a devotee."

She clutched the amulet of Kluehnn's eye and opened her mouth.

I cut her off with a swipe of my hand. "Don't pretend. You're smart, you're practiced, you're polished. But you won't have me believing for a moment that you would become an indentured servant once this grace period ends. You're just here to use us. To use *me*."

Her brows lowered fractionally. "So you want me to care."

"I wouldn't believe it if you said you did. I've known people like you. You make promises. You don't keep them." A well of hurt was bubbling up and I couldn't seem to stop it.

"You *don't* know me." She didn't meet my anger with anger. Her voice was soft, and for some reason that made me take another step toward her. There was something simmering beneath that soft voice, and I wanted to poke at it until it emerged. That softness wasn't *her*. I didn't know how I knew it, only that I did.

I stuffed down the memories of the barrier and the rock and the smoky scent of the shadow wall. The image of Hakara's retreating back as she left me there. I could not seem to force my voice above a whisper. "Do you know what this task is costing me?"

Her lips parted.

And then she froze.

The grass behind me rustled. I smelled the creature before I saw it — like wet metal and rotting wood. Fear tingled through to the tips of my fingers, my hand hovering over the hilt of the dagger. I wouldn't be able to bring it to bear in time. Not against this foe. The paths were not safe. I should have been on my guard. I should have been paying attention to the road.

And now we both might pay the price.

26

Rasha

10 years after the restoration of Kashan
and 571 years after the Shattering

Kashan – on the road to Baatar-Un

*Nioanen was a weak and languid god, waited upon by
others. He could not fight Kluehnn. In the end, he never
stood a chance.*

I knew this beast by its smell.

Slowly, carefully, I pivoted until I could see it. It stood
in the path, its bulk blocking any possible passage. It was tall,
taller than I was, its legs long, four padded feet disappearing
in the grass. It had powerful shoulders, a heavy jaw and a long
face. There was something uncannily human in its expression,
its forward-facing eyes and its rounded ears. Mottled gray fur
covered it, though its face was bare. Dzhalobo.

Solitary predators, silent as shadows. I would have smelled it
earlier if I'd been paying attention. Usually they didn't stray this
close to the roads. I might be able to brush off nettle wasps, to

protect Sheuan from the venomous bites of grass serpents, but I was ill-equipped to fight a dzhalobo alone. If they consumed the flesh of an altered, they became stronger. These creatures had torn through entire cohorts of godkillers before, becoming more and more powerful with each kill. They were fierce, especially when protecting their young. The best thing to do was to avoid them completely, to never get close.

I'd lost that chance.

My heartbeat thundered in my ears, bile sticking in the back of my throat. This one might be sated. This one might not have whelped.

I kept my hand hovering over the hilt of the dagger, my other fingers spread to warn Sheuan against moving. If we stayed still, it might leave us be. Its yellow eyes stared at us, its mouth opening as it licked its lips. I spotted the brightness of sharp, serrated teeth. I tried not to breathe too loudly. And then, to my horror, I heard the lullaby Hakara had always sung to me filling the air.

Sheuan's hand shot out and grasped my wrist, her fingers tight. The song died in my throat. The dzhalobo took one step toward us. Another.

Almost imperceptibly, I felt Sheuan move behind me. Something clattered against the trunk of a tree to our left.

The creature's head whipped in that direction. Its muscles tensed. And then it was charging into the forest, some animal in the branches of the tree shrieking in alarm as it fled. The dzhalobo clawed at the trunk, snapping at the air.

We rushed past. I did not look at the dzhalobo. I did not stop, pulling Sheuan along when she didn't move quickly enough for my liking. As soon as the beast was out of view, we broke into a run.

Both of us were breathless and sweaty by the time we slowed

to a walk. The Kluehnn's-eye amulet she'd been wearing around her neck was gone.

Not a devotee, then. I'd been right. But I couldn't feel smug about it right now, not with my life barely still mine. "Quick thinking." I nodded to her grudgingly.

"I've read about the altered wildlife." Her eyes were wide and slightly glazed. Her fingers were still wrapped around my wrist. "I've only seen skins, teeth, trophies bought by the clans in Langzu."

"We were lucky. I didn't notice it before it was in the road. I attracted its attention. This was my fault."

Her breathing finally slowed and her gaze fell to her hand, clutching my wrist like it was a lifeline. She let her fingers fall, a flush rising to her cheeks. The crescent of her nails had left an impression against my skin. "I'm sorry. I didn't—"

"It's fine." I shrugged. "I've been through much worse at the hands of the others in my burrow."

Her dark gaze searched mine. I felt the questions she left unspoken. Why were we fighting one another? "Rasha." Something about my name on her tongue made a shiver tingle up my spine. "What *is* this costing you?"

Kluehnn help me, I told her. I couldn't say why. Maybe it was because I wanted, for once, to feel real to someone other than myself. Words spilled out of me as though I had been overflowing with them and just hadn't known it until now. I told her about the special attention Kluehnn had paid me, about Millani's jealousy, about the way she now treated me when she'd once felt like the only person I could trust. I told her about Shambul, about the first trial, about the killing and the blood and the spinning of my head.

"And now she's set me to be your advocate because she doesn't care that this takes me away from my training. She doesn't care that I've a limited amount of time before the second trial." I hadn't thought anyone could hurt me after Hakara, yet Millani had managed it.

I was walking again, my feet lighter on the ground but my heart thudding with each step.

Sheuan's careful footsteps followed me. "Your instructor may wish you dead, but I've no reason to. I can train you while you're busy being my advocate."

I sighed. "Train me in what? Pretty words? Dancing? The dining etiquette of Langzu?"

"Fighting techniques. Ones your fellow neophytes won't be familiar with."

I didn't know what to say. It was absurd. She was small. She was helpless. What could she teach me? Yet she spoke with such confidence.

"I am not everything you see at first glance," she said. "I may not trust you, but I need you. You may not trust me, but you need me too. Better for us both if we don't hate each other the entire time."

Some of the anger drained away. It was Shambul I was angry at. It was Hakara I was angry at. I slowed, allowed her to catch up. "Why exactly are you here? Why take such a risk?"

She looked into the trees for a while before speaking. This time, her voice was neutral, shadowed by no affectations. "My clan is on the decline. The Sovereign offered me a chance to protect them, but only if I find out why restored realms eventually cut off the unrestored ones."

I shook my head. "I don't know why. I would tell you if I knew."

"But someone at the palace might." Her dogged determination sparked memories of Hakara.

"Is your clan so precious to you?" I could taste the bitterness in my words.

She didn't look me in the eye. "They are everything."

Family had once been everything to me too. "And yet they sent you through the barrier to Kashan."

Her hands clenched into fists, her knuckles white. Not soft as flower petals, perhaps. "They had no choice. You cannot understand. We have obligations, people to protect."

I only shrugged, as though it didn't matter to me. It couldn't. When I'd finished advocating for her, I'd be back to my burrow, preparing for my second trial.

When the sun began to shine orange through the dappled leaves, I found a spot off the road to camp. They'd packed me a tent at least – only the one, though it should be large enough for us both.

Sheuan didn't wait off to the side as I set it up, as I'd expected; she was silently helpful, asking no questions, seeing where I needed assistance and filling the gap. She had her own bedroll, though when we placed them both inside, there was barely a gap between them. But as I moved to prepare some food, she grabbed my hand. "No. The light is still good. We practice. Just as I promised."

To my surprise, she hadn't been engaging in empty boasting. Her style of fighting was different, reliant more upon surprise than the techniques I'd learned. Hidden daggers, an unexpected elbow, using a person's attire against them. A necklace could easily become a garrote. Taking the time to observe an opponent. Getting them to engage in distracting conversation. I could see ways in which I could use these techniques when I sparred with Shambul again.

Sweat beaded her forehead. "Fighting is not the only thing you need to know to survive. Let me guess – the trials Kluehnn has you go through. They test your skills, but they also pit you against one another."

I didn't respond, my throat tightening as I thought of the cave, the dizziness, the blood on my hands. I'd had to. I hadn't had any other choice. I struck out and she blocked with her forearm, whirling to get inside my guard. The edge of her hand touched my throat. My pulse beat beneath that imaginary blade, her skin warm. Against all rational thought, I found myself wanting to lean into that touch, to yield, to let it expose the softness beneath. Instinctively, I grabbed her shoulders, my hands light. It didn't matter; I would have already been dead in a real fight.

Her eyes met mine. I could count her lashes. "It's an isolation tactic. It makes you not want to get close to anyone – what if you have to kill them later? What if they die? He wants to see which of you will rise to the top, while keeping you all loyal to only one being – himself. Can't have you making friends. You are his prized godkillers. You must be ruthless. What if, gods below forbid, you learned to talk to others? What if you talked to the gods and their descendants you've been charged with killing? No. You must obey without thought or question."

"That's not what it's about." Heat rose to my cheeks.

She took a step back and sighed. Her demeanor softened. "You don't have much time, and there is something to be said for focusing on the present. What is your problem right *now*? Your problem is that you need to pass these trials. And you'll have a lot easier time of it with others on your side. Will you have to betray them? Will you have to kill them?" She shrugged. "Perhaps."

She said it so matter-of-factly. I felt myself lowering my hands, drawing away from her. "That's cold." We squared away again, though I could see the thoughts swirling in her mind, ceaseless.

"Rasha." She ducked beneath a blow, touching my shoulder, forcing me to stop. "What is colder? Betraying someone you love out of necessity, or never loving them at all?"

I shrugged off her hand and went to prepare our food. We'd sparred enough. We ate in silence.

It was dark by the time we crawled into the narrow space of the tent. Neither of us apologized as we brushed against one another, limbs nearly tangling as we finally settled, our breathing filling the enclosed air.

I was about to fall asleep when she spoke. "What was that? On the path?"

I shifted, doing my best not to let my shoulder brush hers. "It was a dzhalobo. Altered wildlife. They—"

"No. Not the creature. The song you started humming."

My chest felt like a furnace. "It's nothing."

"Was it . . . a lullaby?"

I squeezed my eyes tight, knowing what would follow, knowing she would let out a laugh, that she would press at the soft space she'd found, not caring that beneath it was something painful and private.

But she didn't do either of those things. "You don't have to tell me if it makes you uncomfortable."

I started speaking almost before the last word had left her mouth. "It *was* a lullaby. Someone close to me used to sing it to me before we went to sleep. Before restoration. Before I was left alone." I wondered if she could sense the story behind those few words. If she understood, finally, why I'd joined Kluehnn's den. Why I loved him. He was all I had left. He was the only one I could really trust to always be there for me.

For a while, I was certain she'd fallen asleep. Then she spoke again. "Does it have words?"

There was something so gentle in her voice. Even as part of me screamed that she was a politician, that she was unaltered, that she was from Langzu and had her own agenda, I closed my eyes. Instead of humming, I opened my mouth and let the words flow out.

It had been so long – for a moment I was sure I'd forgotten them. But they left my lips as smoothly as they'd once left Hakara's. My voice was not as rusty or as creaky as I'd feared. I was a monstrous thing now, but my voice, it seemed, had not changed. It was a sweet tune, some nonsense about a horse that loved a boy and how that boy loved the horse in turn, and how the boy promised to feed the horse apples and sugar until the world had ended.

The last notes seemed to echo in the tent.

I opened my eyes.

Sheuan hovered above me, propped on her elbow. I couldn't see her expression in the darkness, but I could smell the sweetness of her breath. "The person who sang it to you. She hurt you. She hurt you in a way you will never recover from."

"Yes," I said simply.

"I know what that's like." Her hand slid from her side, hesitant fingers touching my cheek. I held my breath as she explored the harsh planes of my face, the roughness of the horns at my forehead, before her hand tangled in my hair. Everything felt light and strange, as though I wasn't truly experiencing the touch of her fingers against my skin. Why was she doing this? I couldn't think of a motive that made sense.

Her fingers tightened, her nails scratching my scalp. "I know what you think of me. You think I am ruthless, but that's just one side of me." Her voice sounded thick. Was she still angry? "You think I'm a liar because I do what I need to survive. Because I show everyone a different face. But Rasha, this is something true."

She lowered her head and pressed her lips to mine.

Her hands might not have been as soft as flower petals, but her mouth was. My nostrils filled with the sweet ginger scent of her, the faint smell of sweat. Without thinking, I curled my arms hesitantly around her, needing more. Wanting it.

Her hands disentangled from my hair, her palms pushing me firmly back down.

This felt ... *impossible*, yet her legs straddled mine, her hands cupped my jaw. I was stronger than her, yet I was completely undone, my body weak with need. In her grasp I was a mewling kitten. Her face lowered again, our breath mingling in the space between us.

She made me wait until I let out a soft, impatient sound.

And then she crushed her mouth to mine, fingers curling at my chest. She kissed me in a way that made me think she had done this before, many times, but I didn't care. I let her lead and she seemed to prefer it that way, looming over me, one hand going around my shoulders, the other searching lower. Her palm plied the space between my legs. I gasped, let her tug my head back to plant kisses against my throat. Before I could no longer stop myself, I pulled away, my breath heaving. I touched her cheek, one black nail at the corner of her eye. "You won't dissuade me from becoming a godkiller."

I heard her swallow in the darkness. "There's something to be said for living in the moment, don't you think?" Slowly, so I would have the chance to protest, she closed the distance and raked her teeth at the base of my throat. She whispered against my skin. "You're not a monster, Rasha. No matter what they make you do, no matter what you've done, you're not."

I closed my eyes and said nothing. And then I opened them and kissed her back with a gentleness I thought I'd long-since smothered. The warmth of her tongue flicked at my lips – a question – and I let her in. It glided against mine, a silken tangle in my mouth. Her palm pressed against my belly, sliding beneath the waistband of my pants, her fingers slipping inside me.

It felt like a new star was being born in my chest, a yearning heat flooding my limbs, pooling into an ache between my legs. I seized her face lightly as we moved against one another, wishing I could see her expression in the dark.

"You're beautiful," I whispered to her. It didn't cover the way I felt, the poetry that my body was speaking.

She let out a low, sultry laugh that undid me completely. Something about it made me think she was just as surprised by all of this as I was. I dared to brush my fingers against her breasts, to slip her shirt from her shoulders to explore the skin beneath. Her breath shuddered out as I trailed a claw along her collarbone, dipping my head to lick one brown nipple.

For a moment we froze like that, her fingers inside me, my face at her breasts. And then she took control again, her other hand cupping my chin. "Lay still."

"What if I can't?" My voice sounded frail, a thing that could be crushed with the slightest intent.

"Try." She pulled my pants down over my hips as her lips pressed against my neck. She lifted my shirt, trailing kisses across my torso and down to the junction of my thighs. My breath quickened and I fought the urge to writhe as she began to lick and suck, her hand keeping my legs spread apart.

She let me wind tentative fingers into her hair and I gasped her name, over and over. A litany in the dark, stronger than any I'd spoken to Kluehnn.

This, this could be enough. If I could live in moments like this, it would be enough. I would not ask for more than that.

I could not ask for more than that.

27

Mullayne

10 years after the restoration of Kashan
and 571 years after the Shattering

Langzu

*There are so many contradictions in the old texts. The elder
gods were weak, they were so strong as to be terrifying, they
were kind, they were cruel. Later texts elaborate on each
of these descriptions, agreeing on nothing. A god might be
said to have five heads in one book and three in another,
to have one sword, to have two, to have hunted mortals, to
have protected them.*

*So those who worship the old gods in secret choose to
believe they were kind.*

*Those who turn in their descendants to the dens choose
to believe they were cruel.*

*These days, truth is meaningless because truth is a
choice.*

Something wasn't adding up. Mull studied his notes from his workshop, comparing them with the copy he'd made of what had been written on the wall. His lamp flickered as he continued to translate the Old Albanoran. Imeah leaned into his side, her head pillowed on his shoulder. He could hear her breathing through her filter, shallow but steady.

She was growing weaker.

He tried not to notice when she stumbled, when she took his hand for help when before she would have waved him off. Even beneath the mask he could see the pallor of her skin, the way sweat beaded at her forehead at the smallest exertion.

But Imeah was never one to complain. Unlike Mull, she'd always taken her illness in her stride. When she'd first been diagnosed, he'd barked out a disbelieving laugh, saying that of course she would get a second opinion. Her family had the funds.

She'd held up a hand, her expression solemn, and he understood then that she *knew*. The diagnosis had only confirmed something for her; it had been no fresh revelation.

He stopped a moment to rest his cheek briefly on the top of her head, wishing he could smell the scent of her through his mask. Theirs was the comfort and familiarity of two aging dogs who had never been apart. Neither of them wished to be matched to one another, to the chagrin of both sets of parents, and their closeness had frightened off any other potential suitors. The clans of Langzu relied on marriages to one another to create alliances, to exchange lands and businesses, to smooth out disagreements. Then Imeah had been diagnosed and that hadn't mattered anymore.

Small blessings. Very, very small blessings.

She let out a little sigh and he lifted his head to focus on his work again, careful that he didn't disturb her position too much. The writing they'd found did not, to Mull's dissatisfaction, detail exactly how Tolemne and his crew had survived past the first aerocline. Some scholars had idly speculated that perhaps people were hardier then, more accustomed to the aether.

Mull rejected this hypothesis. It was, he felt, born out of a desire to see the past through the golden haze of a sunset – to paint it into a landscape where people had been stronger and wiser and more capable. As though the people of today could return to such glory if they only tried hard enough. Mull just didn't believe that people were that fundamentally different back then.

They'd broken the world; they'd burned away the magic in it, always inventing more comforts out of an abundance they'd thought would never end. And when the Numinars were few, they still couldn't stop themselves. Why would they, when they thought someone else would burn the last of the trees if they didn't? They were just as weak and craven as the people of today. Not that he thought poorly of people in general, but they *did* consistently fail to live up to their ideals, and he could state that as a fact.

"It's late, isn't it?" Imeah murmured.

"I can't be sure." The rest of the crew, including Pont and Jeeoon, were already curled into their bedrolls. "You should sleep."

She only let out a small sigh and tucked her arm in his. "Tell me what's bothering you."

"It's this." He pointed at his notes and then at the translation of the inscription he'd been working on. "All of my books say it's two thousand lengths to Unterra. Some of the information gathered comes from the time before the world was shattered, when better measurements could be made. But this inscription says it's two thousand two hundred twenty-five lengths."

"A small discrepancy."

"You'd think so. But if Tolemne was living post-Shattering, he would have been drawing much of his information from pre-Shattering sources. The same sources I've drawn from."

"Something lost over the years, perhaps?"

"All the records I've checked are consistent."

She reached out and traced the Old Albanoran he'd copied. "What does the rest of it say?"

He ran his finger over the relevant parts as he relayed it to her. "Some of it states the purpose of their journey. And some of it is prayers to the elder gods. Wishing for speed on their quest. Wishing for luck. Wishing for success."

"Then we can confirm it wasn't only Tolemne at that campsite." She shifted her head on his shoulder. "For some reason, I always thought he went alone. I know it doesn't make sense – just look at all the supplies we've had to lug down here – but when I hear the stories, they all emphasize the fact that he was alone when he begged Kluehnn for help."

"Perhaps he didn't start alone and only ended up that way." Mull felt the words seep into his bones like a chill winter morning.

"Then what happened to the rest of them?"

He opened his mouth to answer, to say something reassuring. A scraping sound emanated from the darkness. Some of his crew stirred. They all slept lightly down here.

Imeah's hand tightened around his arm. "Mull . . ."

For a moment he was sure it was just one of the crew members who'd gone to relieve themselves down a side tunnel. And then he heard a growl.

It was a rattling sound, like dried beans in a metal can. Something about it went straight to some primal part of Mull. He was already sitting, but he froze, his tongue a leaden weight in his mouth. It must have had a similar effect on Imeah, because her hand didn't move.

Only Pont, off in the darkness, rolled to his feet, unsheathing a blade from somewhere on his person as he went. "Mull," he said, his voice still fuzzy with sleep, "what's out there?"

The other crew members scrambled for weapons, tossing aside blankets. Someone knocked over one of the lamps and the light in the cavern dimmed. Mull unfroze, snapping his books shut and stuffing them back into his bag. "I don't know. We should be the only ones down here."

The footprint swam back into his mind, the four toes, the claws. The thing had been as wide as his two hands spread out, and just as long. There were fish living down here past the second aerocline; there could be other things as well, preying on them.

Something had happened to the rest of Tolemne's crew.

Mull reflexively pushed his filter inward, making sure it was set in place. Jeeoon peered into the darkness, a lamp in her hand. The cavern they were sleeping in was large and their light did not extend to all its depths. When no further growling echoed, she took a step forward, then another, her jaw set.

A slight widening of her eyes was the only warning.

And then she'd dropped the lamp and was darting back. "Run! Get out of here." Her voice sounded more than just a little excited, and that was what panicked Mull more than anything.

"Pont, take Imeah!" he called.

Before he could say another word, he saw what had caused Jeeoon such alarm. The lamp she'd dropped illuminated a scaly chin, saliva, thick and sticky, hanging in a string from heavy jaws. Empty sockets lay where its eyes should have been, scales covering slight indentations on either side of its head, which was nearly as big as Mull.

A clawed foot moved forward, knocking over the abandoned lamp and sending it rolling across the cave floor.

The giant lizard's head lifted and it sniffed the air. Mull caught a glimpse of flaring nostrils and sharp yellowing teeth.

Pont lifted Imeah, and then they were all fleeing through the cavern, seeking smaller tunnels. Mull seized the lamp he'd been reading by. If it couldn't see, it could only hunt by sound and smell. No one shouted after that; no one screamed. They scattered like mice before a cat, lamps swinging wildly, casting dancing shadows through the cavern.

The tunnel they'd arrived through was narrow — too narrow for a beast like that. They could escape from it through there. The latrine tunnel, too.

Pont had decided on the former. Another growl echoed through the cavern, setting Mull's nerves on edge. He'd brought Pont, but no one else here was a skilled fighter. Jeeoon could survive through sheer tenacity, and there were others who were passable. But fighting giant lizards certainly hadn't been on Mull's list of expectations when he'd put together this crew.

They were nearly to the tunnel when something scraped above them. Fear lit Mull's veins, putting fire in his lungs as he realized – there was more than one lizard in this cave with them.

A second lizard dropped from the ceiling, blocking the path between them and the entrance tunnel. It lifted its giant head, its gray scales glittering in the lamplight. Mull felt his fingers tightening around the lamp, knowing instinctively that it was the only thing that stood between them and being clamped between the jaws of the creature. Without light, they had no chance.

Pont set Imeah down before drawing his sword, the muscles of his back tensing as he lunged to meet the beast. "Get around it!" he called to Mull. "Take Imeah! I'll hold it off!"

Mull ducked his head as he approached Imeah, and she slung an arm around his shoulder. He wrapped his free arm around her waist and they climbed the rocks near the giant lizard, trying to give it a wide enough berth to avoid an attack.

Pont banged his sword against his scabbard, doing his best to attract the creature's attention. Its head swung in the warrior's direction. "Come on, I'm right here. I'll bet I taste a good bit better than whatever it is you've been eating."

Mull didn't linger to watch his friend fight. He pulled Imeah after him as they fled, her breath a shade quicker than his, her legs a good deal less steady. But he felt her steel herself against pain and exhaustion, pushing herself forward as quickly as she could go. They hobbled toward the tunnel like some dying three-legged creature.

Behind them, the lizard roared. Mull didn't know enough about lizards to know whether that was a roar of aggression or a roar of pain. He had to trust it was the latter. Pont wouldn't be so stupid as to throw himself at the creature as a sacrifice, would he?

And then they were inside the tunnel, trying to figure out how far they'd have to go before they'd be out of reach. They stopped a good distance away by some silent mutual agreement, and Mull swung his lamp about, checking back the way they'd come.

The lamplight was very quickly swallowed by the darkness, though he could make out the faint glow of luminescent fungus in the main cavern. He wanted to call out for Pont, to make sure he was well, but knew that would just put them all into trouble.

He had expected perhaps some giant spiders, some bats, some skittering insects. He hadn't expected to find creatures quite this large or quite this vicious. The ecosystem of the caves was much more extensive than he'd thought it would be, and it appeared some animals had adapted to living in the aether. Was the whole path that Tolemne had taken littered with such dangers?

The sounds of clattering and scrabbling claws emanated from the main cavern. Someone came careening out of the darkness.

For a moment, Mull shied away, bringing a hand up in front of Imeah as though that might act as a shield. His heartbeat fluttered and then quickly calmed as Pont's face appeared.

"Pont! Did it hurt you?"

The man swiped a hand through his sweat-slick blond hair. "No. But I couldn't hurt it either. I don't know if everyone else got away. I think so. Shit, Mull, did you see the size of those things? What are they *eating*? And is anything down here eating *them*?" There was a wild, panicked edge to Pont's voice.

"I wanted you to come in case we ran into trouble."

"Trouble, yes, sure. Trouble is two cutpurses in a back alley. It isn't giant lizards in an underground cave!" Pont strode back to the entrance of the tunnel, peering out into the darkness. "Still a couple lamps at camp. Mull, they're rummaging through our supplies."

Mull's belly lurched. They *needed* those supplies. Imeah let go of his arm and settled onto the stone floor. He turned, a different sort of fear coiling in his throat. "Are you all right? How are you feeling? Was that too much exertion?"

She waved him off. "We're not going back out there until the beasts are gone. I'm doing what any reasonable person would do – sitting and waiting and having a rest in the meantime."

Mull and Pont hovered over her awkwardly. Pont finally sheathed his sword and took a seat next to her.

"Didn't see anyone lying on the ground back at camp, so I'm assuming everyone made it to the tunnels," Pont said. He let out a long breath and then reached out to pluck one of the luminescent mushrooms on the ground in front of him. The air around it seemed to shimmer a little. Mull wondered if it fed off the aether somehow. There were so many things down here he could study. He could spend a lifetime doing so. If they got out of here alive.

Pont picked off bits of the mushroom, letting them fall to the

ground in a shower of blue-green light. It took a while for the
noise in the cavern beyond to die down, for them to be sure the
lizards were gone. Imeah had leaned her head back against the
cavern wall and taken the opportunity to sleep.

They ventured out like rabbits from their den, each step
hesitating and cautious, ears pricked for any sign of danger.
Only silence and the scuffle of footsteps from the other tunnel
met them.

"It's Pont," Pont said in a low voice. It carried, echoing off
the walls. "Me, Imeah and Mullayne – we're all accounted for.
Jeeoon, are you over there?"

"I'm here," her raspy voice answered. "The rest of the crew is
with me. Everyone is accounted for, no one harmed."

The camp was a different matter. Silently, they set to picking
up the pieces. The lizards had gone through it like two dogs
searching for a hidden treat. Bedrolls bore the marks of claws,
one cask of oil had been emptied onto the ground, and their food
supplies had been ransacked.

Mull took inventory of the food. Nearly half of it gone. They'd
built a large cushion into their supplies, just in case, but this was
more of a loss than he'd expected.

"Well, isn't this a right bit of a mess." Jeeoon set one of the
camp's lamps back up and relit it. "Seen a lot of things mining,
but nothing like that. Which one of you was expecting giant
lizards to come crawling out of the dark?" Mull couldn't see her
expression behind her mask, but her dark eyes glittered. She
spoke with a heavy dose of sarcasm, but guilt pricked him.

"I did . . . I did see a footprint back at the last cavern," he said.

Every eye turned to him, even Imeah's.

"You . . . what?" Jeeoon lifted her lamp as though it were a
weapon. "And you didn't think to mention it to me? To *anyone*?"

"I didn't know if that was what I was actually seeing. It was in the water and I only saw one – it could have been fossilized. It could have been from a long time ago."

"Clearly, it was not."

Imeah picked up their remaining food items, bundling them back into their bags. Her voice was breathy when she spoke. "What's done is done. If Mull didn't want to start panic and rumors over a footprint he wasn't even sure was recent, then I understand. Pont?"

Pont gave a grudging shrug. The rest of the crew glanced warily among themselves.

Jeeoon's eyes narrowed. "I'll thank you not to lead me into caverns where I can get my head bitten off while I'm sleeping. Anyone sees anything from now on, they mention it."

Pont held up a hand. "That's assuming we continue on. The way I see it, our food is nearly half gone. We're not equipped to fight monsters. We should go back to the surface."

Irritation flashed through Mull, chasing away the fear that had been there only moments before. Of course Pont would use any chance to return to the surface. "We've come so far already. Other than Tolemne, we are the first mortals to make it this far into the second aerocline. The next step is Unterra, the land of the gods. If we ration what's left of our food, we should have enough. And there are the fish in the last cavern. We could catch some of those. Pont—"

"No." The warrior pointed at him. "You don't get to decide this. Every time I put my life into your hands, I regret it. We take a vote. Everyone abides by the results."

The crew all nodded; even, to Mull's surprise, Imeah.

Pont peered round at them. "All in favor of going on?"

There were nine of them in total. Mull raised his hand first, his heart hammering in his chest. Three other crew members' hands went up. That was four. They needed one more. He looked to

Imeah. This whole expedition was for her. All he'd wanted was to find a cure for her, to help her get better, so she could finally live a normal life. If they could make it to Unterra, if they could ask a boon of one of the remaining gods, they could return together to the surface. It would be as though they were children again, running alongside one another in Langzu's markets, their futures stretching ahead of them like the ocean, full and unending.

"Imeah?"

She met his eyes, and he wondered if she pursed her lips beneath the filter, or if she frowned, or if she was giving him the slightest sad smile. She shook her head.

Without her, they didn't have enough votes. Without a will to live, she would die, and he'd be left to live out the rest of his years without her. It felt a vast impossibility, a gaping chasm he feared to look into. He would give *anything* to simply have this chance.

Pont grunted. "Really, Jeeoon?"

Mull whipped his head about to see Jeeoon with one wiry arm in the air. She shrugged at Pont. "He's right. No one's been down this far before. We can handle the lizards now that we know about them. We take turns on watch, put the food in the center of camp, cover it to dampen the scent. It's a setback. But all expeditions have setbacks."

Even the crew members who hadn't raised their hands nodded thoughtfully to her words. The mood was shifting, turning.

"You can't be serious." Pont pointed off into the darkness. "We are all going to die down here."

"Everyone abides by the results," Mull said.

"Fine." Pont scowled. "But by all the gods above and below, this time, Mull, I had better not regret it."

28

Sheuan

10 years after the restoration of Kashan and 571 years after the Shattering

Kashan – in the wilds

Do not take pity on the small gods. They may look like children but they are not as your children are. Your children will grow to be humans. Their children will grow to be monsters.

Rasha was already awake by the time Sheuan opened her eyes. Sheuan had pressed herself against the warm bare skin of Rasha's ribs. The altered seemed to run at a warmer temperature than mortals. By the quickening of Rasha's breathing, she seemed to have noticed that Sheuan had woken.

The girl was waiting for her reaction. Would she shy away? Quickly grab her clothes? Avoid Rasha's gaze?

Some other aspect of herself might have done so. There were so many reasons she shouldn't have indulged. She'd held herself back with Nimao; why hadn't she managed it with Rasha?

Something about the physicality of her, the nascent danger, all of it covering something sweet and yielding beneath. There was still time to correct this, to build the distance between them.

But some small part of her also acknowledged she might get some hidden knowledge on Kluehnn by being close to Rasha. That the neophyte might have lied about knowing nothing.

She hated that part of herself.

Still, she slid an arm over Rasha's torso and kissed her muscled shoulder. The girl relaxed at her touch, tilting her head so that her lips met Sheuan's hair.

For a while they just murmured low things to one another, soft compliments, observations about their worlds and their differences. Sheuan loved the lazy quality of the morning after – a time when she could forget all the worries piling upon her shoulders, to just exist in that satisfaction. Or at least, *she'd* been satisfied. She glanced up at Rasha to find a small smile. Good. They'd both been satisfied. Not that Sheuan had held any doubts. Well, maybe she'd had one or two. Altered physiology was different, but it wasn't *that* different.

People often let things slip at this time. For the first time in her life, Sheuan wavered. There was something about Rasha that made her feel protective. Something precious, like a flower that only bloomed one day a year when the sunlight was just right. She drew a pattern across Rasha's shoulder. "Kluehnn gets his due from the sinkhole mines. I've seen some of the gems among the clans. They're not supposed to keep them, but you know how the wealthy can be. Rules don't apply to them." Give some dangerous information, draw the person into your trust. "Even my clan, on occasion. But I heard one of the nobles talking about a large multicolored gem. I laughed at them. Does such a thing even exist?"

Rasha shivered as Sheuan let her nail trail across her collarbone.

"Yes. There's one in our den. Everyone came out to look at it before they carted it inside. They're real. Rare, but real."

Sheuan stored the information away. "Fascinating. I had no idea."

"We should get moving," Rasha said, pulling away.

Ah. Damn. The worst thing about living in the moment was that the moment always eventually ended.

The rest of their journey was much more companionable. Rasha spoke briefly of her life before restoration took her, of a family that it was apparent now no longer existed. In turn, Sheuan told Rasha about the clans, about the storied history of the Sims, though she spoke haltingly of her father. Sometimes the memories of him felt like old, dusty books that had fallen behind the others on a shelf. Sometimes they felt freshly pressed, as if the printer had just finished inking the page.

Something about their recent intimacy made the words she said to Rasha feel precious, made anew.

But she set all of that aside when they drew close to the palace.

She'd been to Kashan once as a child, in winter, and the cold sea and broad steppes had made an indelible impression on her. Her memories came to her in pieces – the warmth of the fur around her shoulders, the burning feeling of fingers unfreezing by the fire, the pungency of the mare's milk drink she'd been given, sliding down her throat. The Kashan she saw now was so different. The only reminders of the realm she'd known were the ruins they passed every so often, walls crumbling, the path embedded with red clay tiles that clinked beneath their feet. It felt like walking on the bones of a dead culture. That was what Kluehnn wanted, wasn't it? To change mortals into something else, to make them *better*. To ensure that no one repeated the mistakes of the past. But if this was what happened, if everything was made anew, what was Kluehnn saving, in the end?

The people were all changed, the landscape was changed, though presumably the government remained. For as long as Sheuan could remember, Kashan had been ruled by a selected Queen.

The dirt road widened, became gravel crunching beneath her feet. When she'd not been falling into Rasha's eyes, she'd been thinking. The two other diplomatic overtures had failed. The parties had not returned. They might have been overcome by the altered wildlife. That was a possibility. But they'd come here expecting the political landscape to be unchanged. They hadn't come with the backing of one of Kluehnn's neophytes. The right of sanctuary had been a desperate play, but it might now save her life and get her the information she needed.

"Is there a reason we've stopped walking?" Rasha was regarding her, one eyebrow raised, the other low, as though she was bracing for the response.

Strange, how this girl could already seem to read her so much better than anyone else had. She should have been wary of it, but she couldn't muster anything past the warmth of feeling seen. "I want to speak to the Queen."

"Yes." The word was stretched out like dough between two hands, nearly forming a question.

"I can't approach her directly. I need your help."

"You're about to ask me to do something illegal, aren't you?"

Sheuan flashed her a quick grin, though she found she couldn't hold it. "A little? Maybe? I don't know your laws. I can't approach the Queen directly. The Sovereign has already tried that." That godkiller at the border had been acting in an official capacity. "But you're a neophyte. I have the feeling they'll let you past. All I need is entry. I'll do the rest."

Rasha's mouth pressed into a thin line, but she nodded and looked to the sky. "It will be time for worship soon. I can join at the palace as a passing traveler. Godkillers are allowed to go any-where, as they wish." She beckoned Sheuan off the road. "And you can wear my robe over your clothes. Keep your head down."

Sheuan blinked. She'd expected more resistance. "You're a neophyte, not a full godkiller. Can't they deny you?"

Rasha frowned as she thought. "I'm not supposed to be out of the den. Neophytes usually aren't. They might just make assumptions."

Sheuan couldn't help but cast her a grin. "Ah, have I influenced you already? Sounds almost like something a politician would say." She stepped forward, adjusting the belt Rasha wore, bringing the dagger to the front. "Let's make this convincing then. Stand tall. Look confident. Keep your hand over the hilt of the dagger. Casually. Cover the spot where a god gem would be. They'll have no reason to question you."

Rasha shucked off her robe and handed it to Sheuan. Beneath it, she wore a sleeveless gray tunic that hung nearly to her knees, plain and pleated at the collar. "If this goes badly, I'm not the one they'll seek to punish. I'm acting as your advocate. They'll look to you. Do you understand?"

Well, that was one way to wipe the smile off her face. Still, she took the proffered robe. If she was going to find out what was going on and why, she needed to dig.

Rasha made a last few adjustments to Sheuan's appearance. "Wear your pack beneath the robe. Anyone glancing at you will think you have a small pair of vestigial wings. Most will just assume you're altered. We don't get many mortal visitors." She drew the hood over Sheuan's head, her hand brushing her cheek in a caress.

"We make a good team, don't we?" Sheuan felt a little breathless.

The look Rasha gave her was inscrutable, even to Sheuan.

The palace was as overgrown as the rest of the restored realm. Half of it descended into ruins; the other half looked as though it were making a feeble attempt to hold back the undergrowth. It stood at the top of a hill, a sheer cliff drop on the other side. A small town surrounded the palace, wooden walls erected to keep the more dangerous wildlife at bay. The streets were filled with altered folk, horns and wings visible above the crowd. By all appearances, this was a bustling place, no matter how strange.

Sheuan tried to look like she belonged as they wended their way through the streets, unconcerned by the giant, prickly fruits being traded in the market, the cages of birds with iridescent feathers, the animals that looked almost like horses but for their cloven hooves and shimmering green coats. Clothing was lined in furs she didn't recognize, coats styled to accommodate altered bodies. Scents assailed her – spices sweet and pungent, the musky sweat of furred altered who brushed too close, the wet smell of damp, clean air. Each time someone near her took a breath, she thought she might be discovered. Her own scent – sweet, gingery and faintly lavender – moved with her, wafting with each ripple of Rasha's borrowed cloak. Most of the altered were speaking Kashani, and the reminder that these people were still Kashani in this one small way left her with an odd pang, a feeling that she'd lost something important and couldn't identify what it was.

The gates of the palace were guarded, though the noise of the surrounding town seemed to stop just short of the threshold. The courtyard beyond looked deserted. No servants? No workers preparing meals and repairing the broken rooftops? No officials?

Rasha was careful to put herself between Sheuan and the guards. "I'm passing through and here for worship."

The guards looked them over. Sheuan kept her gaze low, standing close enough to Rasha to stretch her fingers and touch the back of her hand. She didn't dare. And then, at last, the one closest to them nodded and waved them inside.

She'd been here as a child, yet the palace looked almost entirely unfamiliar. She recognized little things – the faded rose color of the plaster walls, the doors into the main hall, one carved with a likeness of Lithuas, her silver hair in flowing locks around her, face lifted to catch beams of sunlight. The other had been haphazardly replaced with fresh, unmarked wood, the varnish several shades lighter and warmer than the carved one. Sheuan couldn't remember what had once been carved into that door.

The unmarked door was open.

While her memory served her images of crowded hallways, even the inner halls of the palace looked to be falling into disrepair. Plants grew from between floorboards; gaps in the roof above let in light and moisture. She caught a quick glimpse of a gray, furry tail before some unidentifiable creature disappeared around the corner.

Rasha grasped Sheuan's wrist, directing her down a narrow hallway. "The nave should be this way. It will be at the lowest point in the palace."

"And the Queen will be there?"

Rasha hesitated. What was she holding back? There was something – Sheuan could feel it. None of the books she'd studied had ever noted the Queen of Kashan having a strong religious affiliation. She was here to lead the people – and that meant both devotees of Kluehnn and those who were just trying to get by.

"She should be there." Rasha turned her face away.

They passed only two servants on their way to the nave, one carrying linens, the other uselessly sweeping dirt from the floor as more gathered in the corners. If the palace were a symbol of the old Kashan, then it was clear that restoration had won.

The nave itself was new. While plants wove around the

entrance, none of the roots had cracked the plaster. White and pink flowers closed as Sheuan and Rasha approached, shy of visitors. Sheuan did her best not to gawk. A rumble emanated from beneath the wooden door, the distant crash of waves against cliffs. The door opened at Rasha's touch.

Altered filled the pews, many ragged and looking in need of food or rest. They were still and quiet, their attention focused on the altar at the front of the nave.

A woman sat at a desk facing the altar, brown speckled wings catching the light filtering in from the windows high above. She wore a heavy red robe about her shoulders, the back draped low to give her wings free movement, the neckline embroidered with thick, brightly colored thread. Papers and books littered the surface of the desk. The altar rose toward the ceiling in front of the Queen, carved into the likeness of a tree, a pit beneath it. A spattering of bronze eyes covered the wooden surface, staring down at the gathered worshipers.

A man with long white horns stood at a pulpit in front of the pit. He wore a chain of eyes around his shoulders, marking him as a high priest, a den elder. When he spoke, his voice was deep and soft as the velvet night. "The world has changed from what it once was. Mortals broke it the first time. The gods refused to mend it. And I am here to ensure it is never broken again."

The room spoke in unison. "Kluehnn is the one true god. All others are false." Sheuan glanced over at Rasha and found her rapt.

"Children, my children – you must know how Kluehnn adores you. You are his creations. He has made you to thrive in this world he has built for you. He has made you to not repeat the mistakes of the past. You are neither mortal nor are you gods." His arms gesticulated, some gestures pleading, some grand.

Sheuan put her mouth to Rasha's ear. "I'm going to get close to the Queen, to speak to her when this is over. Distract the priest." She slipped away before Rasha could protest, walking with confidence to the bench nearest to the Queen.

The words from the pulpit blurred into one another as the horned man preached about obedience, about steadfastness. But more than anything, he raged against the other gods. No one had answered when Tolemne had begged the gods to do something. They'd all turned their backs on the surface world. Only Kluehnn had come forward. Only Kluehnn had heard this poor mortal's pleas. He'd traveled so far, he'd done so much to finally reach the realm of the gods. How could Kluehnn be the only one to answer him?

Every so often the crowd would chant an answer back. Each time the chanting increased in volume and fervor. Sheuan felt her throat go dry as she settled into a spot close to the Queen. The backpack beneath her robe shifted and she stifled the urge to scratch the sweat that trickled past her shoulders. If she stood and turned to face the crowd, she felt sure they would all *see* her and tear her to pieces. She didn't know what to say, how to act. But she could feel the energy of the altered folk around her, their anger rising. They hated the other gods. They hated mortals. They hated mortals like her.

Was this what Rasha had been hiding? She'd known that Sheuan would be walking into a death trap. She'd warned her in her own small way. Sheuan couldn't even tug the cowl of the robe down, afraid that any small movement would reveal herself.

After what seemed like forever, it finally ended. Altered filtered forward to receive something from the high priest, Rasha among them. Kluehnn's blessing, Sheuan's memory told her. A small bit of food, meant to nourish those who were hungry or suffering.

She sidled closer to the Queen, wondering if the other

delegations sent by the Sovereign had made it this far. She'd thought perhaps they'd run afoul of the altered wildlife, but now she wondered if they'd run afoul of the altered themselves. "Queen Kashan," she murmured.

The woman turned a little, her wing lifting, and Sheuan's breath came short.

The Queen's face was a mess of scars, a map of criss-crossing lines that led only to suffering. One lucid brown eye focused on Sheuan's face.

"*You* are not altered."

29

Sheuan

10 years after the restoration of Kashan and 571 years after the Shattering

Kashan – Bataar-Un, the Queen's seat

While the godkillers travel from realm to realm, they are never there right before restoration. For those who know where to look, this can serve as a warning.

There was something terrible about being caught in a lie, about being trapped in that inflection point between confessing and doubling down on it. Sheuan hovered in that space for a moment, her gaze locked with the Queen's, her heartbeat pounding at her throat, a flash of heat at her chest. To her right, the altered were paying last respects to the den elder before filtering out.

She didn't have enough information to go on, no indication as to whether she should confess to or smoothly squash the Queen's assertion that she was not altered. No one had heard what the Queen had said. So Sheuan did her best to sidestep it completely. "I didn't know the Queen of Kashan was so devoted."

The Queen's scars pulled as her mouth moved. "The Queens have always been devoted."

Sheuan's panicked gaze flicked to Rasha, who was the last in the line of altered. A line that was quickly diminishing. She focused, briefly, on the white shape the high priest fed into the mouth of the altered in front of him. But she wasn't here for whatever was going on in the nave. "You haven't always been devoted. The last Queen didn't even have an altar. All the books say so. This place was recently built."

"It was recently built because the last one fell during restoration." The Queen's gaze went somewhere over Sheuan's shoulder.

There would have been a sign of a previous nave and altar had there been one. Rubble, at the very least. The Queen would have been young at the time she'd been instated, but not *that* young. She would have noticed. She should have noticed.

"Forgive me, your majesty, but how can you believe that?"

The Queen didn't answer.

Sheuan had more questions – what terrible accident had befallen her to cause such scarring? Was she considering isolating Kashan from Langzu? Was it due to the churning in the barrier? Was there not a way their two realms could work together to overcome this? Or was it because the altered now distrusted their mortal brethren?

Two more altered in line in front of Rasha. *Stall for me*, Sheuan thought, wishing the girl could hear her. Hoping that she would understand she had to create a distraction. Sheuan might be able to divert the Queen from caring that she was not altered; she doubted she could do the same to the high priest.

She had to choose her words carefully. Mitoran's voice spoke in her head. *When you're pressed for time, start with the assumption, work backward.* "Why cut off trade with Langzu? Why not continue long past restoration? Our countries have often worked together."

The Queen's eyes focused on her for a moment before turning to the altar. "Kluehnn provides," she murmured.

"Kluehnn certainly isn't providing for Langzu at the moment. There are people starving in the streets." Sheuan's tone was sharper than it should have been, but she'd hoped to have more time, to find more information.

She'd expected the Queen to rebuke her blasphemy, but the woman said nothing. Yet she hadn't denied that Kashan would cut off Langzu. So at least Sheuan had a little more information to work with, if not the answers to her questions.

The sounds of a hushed argument reached her ears. She wasn't sure how long Rasha could hold the den elder off. The last altered were exiting. Soon it would only be the four of them in the nave, and he'd have to notice that someone had lingered and was talking to his Queen.

"Send altered to Langzu. Meet with the Sovereign in earnest. Keep our ties strong."

The Queen stared at the altar. "Traveling to unrestored realms is a weakness. One that must be burned out."

She shifted, and Sheuan heard the unmistakable rattle of a chain. Her blood froze. There had been too many strange things to see. She should have noticed how odd it was that the Queen sat at a desk in the nave when everyone else sat in the pews. She should have wondered if the Queen did all her work here, in this building. She should have then wondered – does she ever *leave*?

But then a brush of wind was at her cheeks and the high priest stood before her, his robes smelling faintly of cedar, his horned head limned with light. He had a face like an anvil – a heavy brow pressing down on eyes that regarded her with the same curious disdain one might give a spider on a pillow. Rasha stood at his shoulder, her face stricken. "You did not take Kluehnn's blessing."

He was holding something out to her. Feeling very much unlike herself, Sheuan reached out a hand and took it.

It was soft and spongy and white, like a piece of steamed bread. Again she stood on a precipice. There was still a chance they could get out of here undetected, and when she looked up into those steely eyes, she knew that trying to slide around this would result in too many questions. There was the chance it could kill or hurt her. She was not altered. She didn't think it was meant for mortals. But it felt like bread. She put it in her mouth.

He watched her as she swallowed it, like a parent waiting to ensure a child finished the last of their meal. It *was* steamed bread, with a grainy paste in the middle that tasted a little like sweet lotus root. Altogether, it was not unpleasant, though she wouldn't have paid good money in a marketplace for it either.

His hand seized her wrist. Rasha grabbed for his shoulders, but he wrenched away, dragging Sheuan toward the altar.

Toward the pit.

For one breathless moment she was above the pit. And then she was in it, falling, her breath short. She hit something. The ground? It was closer than she'd expected.

It was darker than she'd expected.

When she opened her mouth to speak, nothing came out. She wasn't sure whether her tongue was moving, or whether she had a mouth at all. There was no sound in the pit. Was it the blessing he'd fed her? Had she died here?

Think. She could think.

She put all her considerable willpower toward putting one foot in front of the other, toward lifting arms she wasn't sure was there, toward feeling for a wall. Toward climbing.

Sensation returned and she found herself with her fingers

curled around the edge of the pit. Someone was growling. She hauled herself out, her muscles aching.

Rasha and the high priest were locked together, her claws digging into his forearms, his horns near her throat. It was Rasha who was growling. Sheuan moved without thinking, her body responding the way it had when she'd encountered Nimao on the steps to the Sovereign's castle. She was ducking down, beneath the high priest's arm. One hand grabbing the robes at his chest. The other finding the hilt of Rasha's knife.

She didn't remember stabbing him, but in the next moment the hilt was jutting from between his ribs. His hands loosened from Rasha's leather vest and he sagged to the floor.

Her mind went immediately to next steps. She had a moment, so she waited, making sure she considered her moves before acting. Should have done so before, but seeing Rasha in danger . . . she'd lost her head a little bit. Mitoran had always told her to wait if she had the chance. She'd make fewer mistakes that way.

Well she'd already made one big one. The priest was dead. The Queen was a witness. And they couldn't very well kill the Queen without setting off some sort of incident.

Rasha's hands trembled. "You killed him. A high priest. A den elder. I . . . I helped you kill him. I'll be punished."

"He was going to hurt you." Sheuan flexed her fingers, feeling the wetness of blood against her skin. "I couldn't let him."

Rasha licked her lips and then put a tentative hand on Sheuan's shoulder. "Are you all right? When he threw you into the pit, I thought . . . "

"You thought I was dead," Sheuan finished for her. Carefully, she wiped the blood from her hands onto the inside of the administrator's robe. Then she stood. "This wasn't your fault. It was mine. You don't have to face punishment if we're careful."

Wobbly, but she could feel her feet, and that was a fair bit better than she'd been doing in the pit. Ah, this was not ideal. She looked to the Queen and found her gaze unfocused. If she'd witnessed the murder, she certainly wasn't giving any sign of it.

Sheuan wedged her hands beneath the high priest's shoulders. "Help me." For a while, Rasha only stared, her body still. Then she blinked and moved to help. Together they dragged his body next to the desk. Sheuan arranged his arms haphazardly. "The dagger. Can it be traced back to your den?"

Rasha shook her head. "It's not anything special. But they'll expect me to bring it back."

"Keep an eye and an ear out." Sheuan searched the desk, pulling open drawers. Each sent the scent of fresh wood and ink into the air. The Queen might not have been a puppet in the beginning, but Kluehnn's priests had made her into one. The puckered scars on her face – burns? Whatever the dens had done to her, it was clear that she was no longer in charge. Perhaps not even of herself.

Sheuan found a pen. Her hand brushed the pebbled leather cover of a book as she reached for it. They didn't have the time. They didn't. But she found herself opening the book anyways.

"Sheuan." Rasha said her name like a warning.

That only spurred her on. She flipped through the pages, a strange unease settling at the back of her neck. She *knew* this book. She had a copy in her personal collection. It was a history of Kashan, only – it wasn't the same book. In this one, Langzu and Kashan had never had strong ties. The Queens had always fervently worshiped Kluehnn, and they ruled by his mandate.

She shut the cover, her heart pounding wildly, a sudden fear gripping her. Had she been wrong about everything all along? Whose book was the right one?

"Sheuan." This time Rasha spoke her name with urgency.

She couldn't take the book and she didn't have time to

investigate further. She pulled Rasha's dagger free, wiped it on the inside of the robe and plunged the pen into the wound instead, wrenching it into the flesh until it looked as though it had caused the injury. Quickly, she sheathed Rasha's dagger back at her belt, looking them both over for spots of blood.

A few flecks at the bottom of the robe she wore. Rasha followed her lead, silently, as they rushed out the doors of the nave, doing their best to catch up to the altered who were leaving, to not appear out of breath. Sheuan scooped up a handful of dirt and rubbed it into the bottom of the robe just before they reached the palace gate.

And then they were through, into the bustle of the streets, her pounding heart and shaking hands the only evidence that the murder had happened.

Rasha put some distance between them when they reached the cover of the trees. "You've done this before, haven't you? Killed someone?"

Sheuan's teeth threatened to chatter. It must have looked that way – the swift clean-up, pinning the blame on the Queen. "No. That was the first. I have . . . training in how to deal with high-pressure situations."

And then Rasha was sweeping her into her arms with the air of someone carrying a precious, thin-walled vase. Her hands delicate, her grip firm.

Sheuan let herself fall apart. Emotional release was important, Mitoran had told her. It let a person leave those feelings behind. Her tears soaked into Rasha's sleeve as she regained some measure of calm. Distantly, she wondered at her own actions. Was she *this* practiced? *This* false? Was anything about her real, or was it all calculated – each and every emotion?

"I have to go back to Langzu." She didn't know for sure how to stop the isolation of Kashan, but she knew better now what was causing it. The Sovereign needed this information. She pulled away. Thirty days. She could stay, do more research into the den, say she needed Rasha for other tasks. But that would take the neophyte away from her training for longer, and while a part of her desperately wanted to stay close to Rasha, she couldn't afford to waste time.

"Will I see you again?" Rasha's voice was small, sad – such a stark contrast to the sharp teeth and claws, the horns atop her head, the fierceness of her brow.

Sheuan felt the masks fall into place. Layers of protection, of falsehood. This was why she resisted trysts with no purpose. She had no right to this altered woman. She had no right to her own feelings. "No," she said, turning toward the road. "Likely not. Take me back to the border, please."

She felt the emotional distance between them widen as they walked into the wilderness, the gravel path becoming dirt once more. A thing could be both true and a momentary distraction – she'd not lied about the way she'd felt being true.

Still, she couldn't help thinking, as she followed Rasha's broad shoulders, about the little girl who'd once been abandoned in a restored Kashan. Whom she was abandoning all over again.

An itch began between her shoulder blades.

30

Hakara

10 years after the restoration of Kashan
and 571 years after the Shattering

Langzu - the outskirts of
Bian, in the aftermath

*Perhaps, in some distant past, the old gods were kind.
Perhaps they gave to the mortals as much as they received
in return. But even gods can change over the many long
years.*

The funeral held for Utricht was heartfelt but perfunctory,
everyone moving quickly to the next tasks – sabotaging
god-gem mining, attempting to free more talented people like
me from the grips of Kluehnn's dens, digging into local politics.
There was no time to breathe.

I stared at the empty bedroll at night before falling asleep,
remembering Utricht's kind words, the way he'd stood up for
me against Mitoran. He'd had hopes, dreams, a sense of humor.
All of those gone and so easily forgotten.

Mitoran took possession of the corestone. They had to all be infused at once and then buried. The Unanointed's natural philosopher in Xiazen supposed that together they might have an amplifying effect, and besides, burying just one corestone would be an invitation for some rich clan to dig it up and take it. They had to be buried all at the same time; people in Langzu had to *see* their land changed.

I didn't know where Mitoran kept the stone, but that was how organizations like this were run, with as few points of failure as possible. She told me she'd sent a message to her people in Kashan, and I'd never been good at being idle, so I trained and I waited as the wound on my leg healed. The one on my arm had been shallow enough to only affect my god limb. If nothing else, these skills would serve me well once I finally found a way to my sister.

I watched Thassir on the main level of the safe house as he opened the window and tapped at the sill. Cats silently appeared, leaping to the window and descending into the room as though they belonged there.

I supposed they did.

Thassir never stayed in one place for very long. On one day I'd felt his presence somewhere in the city, and then in the wilds, and then there upon the roof at night, where he seemed to roost. He did always make sure to feed the cats, though.

I'd spent two sweaty, claw-marked afternoons helping him cart a few cats to an animal doctor in the city. I think the beasts and I had developed something of a silent enmity, though none of them seemed to hold a grudge against Thassir. They wound around his legs, purring when he reached down to scratch their heads. One, a rough-looking calico, flattened her ears as he extended his fingers with a piece of fish between them. I watched the grizzled street cat hiss and take a swipe at his hand.

"Is . . . is that how she shows love?"

Thassir looked at the flea-bitten beast the same way I looked at a fat stack of coin. He threw her several pieces of meat. "Rumenesca hates me. I respect that."

We seemed to have formed the same sort of respect, because he hadn't asked me again to break the bond. Not yet.

My ears pricked. Mitoran was talking to Alifra in the opposite corner of the room, her voice low. I could barely make out what she was saying, but I picked out enough. Her informant had returned. She'd made it through to Kashan. Presumably without a guide.

And Mitoran was leaving to meet with her.

I slid off my chair. Mitoran had bid me return the unused god gems to her, but I'd palmed one of them as I'd dropped the rest into the proffered pouch. Not like I hadn't done that sort of thing before. Hadn't had a plan at the time, but resources were resources, and I wasn't going to let one slip out of my fingers if I could keep a grasp on it.

So I had one resource. Two if I counted Thassir. And I was intending on counting Thassir right now.

Mitoran left through the front door.

"Can I speak to you outside?"

He followed me into the dusty street. The sun shone through a brown haze, bright enough to make me blink. But I caught a glimpse of Mitoran's back disappearing around a corner. Toward the inner city.

I seized Thassir's wrist and darted after her.

"What are you doing?" He didn't sound angry, not yet, caught in that moment of confusion. I pulled him after me, afraid we might lose track of her. She was wily, and she'd do her best to ensure she wasn't being followed.

"Mitoran. She's going to meet with someone who went to Kashan and back without a guide. I overheard her talking about this informant. Said she didn't have the money to hire one and that she had tried to dissuade her from going. But if there's a way to get to Kashan without a guide, I need to know it. What if I find out my sister is alive but I don't have a way to get to her? I can't just wait around."

My quick glance back told me Thassir was frowning. "Stop."

I didn't let go. "I can't. I took a god gem in case I needed it, but I can't use it without your help."

"Mitoran won't take kindly to being followed."

"What's she going to do? Kill me?"

His silence was not reassuring.

I turned the corner and caught a glimpse of iron-gray hair vanishing down an alley. I dug into my pocket.

In a flash, Thassir had his wrist out of my grip and was clutching mine in turn. "Don't." His eyes were fixed on something out of my field of vision. I let the gem fall back to the bottom of my pocket, casually turning the motion into a brush at the front of my pants as I followed his gaze.

A man was leaning against a building. He looked completely normal, world-worn even, with the scuffed-up countenance of a farmer trying to live off the land. Except for the blade at his side. That was a fair bit nicer and I'd wager sharper than a farmer warranted.

One of the Sovereign's enforcers in disguise? One of Kluehnn's devoted? Either way, pulling out a god gem would not have had a good outcome for me. Perhaps I would have been able to run away, but that would be yet another person who'd seen my face and wished me ill.

I peered around Thassir's shoulder. From a magical perspective, we might only be able to sense one another's presence, but any living being with half a brain could have felt the anxiety rolling off me in thick, roiling waves. "Shit. I lost her."

I'd lost her, I'd lost Rasha – all I could do was *lose* people.

He lifted his gaze to the sky and let out the most exhausted sigh I had ever heard. Then he pulled me into the alleyway we'd seen Mitoran disappear down. "Grab my back."

I did so, my fingers brushing the velvet soft feathers before settling around his neck. "You can't fly – she'll see us for sure. I need to find out who this informant is."

He didn't bother answering me. He seized the stone of the building beside us with his claws and began to climb.

This must have been what it was like to be the passenger on a squirrel's back. Quite a bit different from when he'd been flying me around. There was something pressing about the space in the alleyway; being surrounded by stone was just such a present reminder of how *hard* it was, how unyielding. How it might feel if I crashed into it from a great height.

Splat. Like an overripe fruit.

I grimaced and focused on where he was going, his muscles bunching beneath my hands as he climbed. We reached the rooftop and I slid down. He hunched at the edge and pointed. "There. She didn't go far. She changed her clothes."

Mitoran was at the gate to the inner city. Her clothing was finer; she'd done something to her hair. It was pinned up. She'd managed it all so quickly and she looked so different that I wondered how Thassir had recognized her. Were his black eyes also as sharp as a hawk's?

We crouched and hurried along the rooftops, Thassir helping me across wider gaps.

Mitoran stopped a couple times – once to remove her jacket as the day warmed, and another time for tea. We watched from the roof, taking turns peeking over the edge. Thassir cleared his throat. "What will you do if you find out how this informant got to Kashan? Will you wait for Mitoran's information or will you go yourself?"

"If I can, I'll go myself."

"Restored lands are dangerous. They're not made for mortals to live in."

I studied his figure, the black wings that he was, at the moment, keeping tight to his back. He'd lifted that entire metal lockbox, had *flown* it to safety. Maybe I couldn't do that, but I could do other things. "I'm dangerous too."

He let out a soft snort. "Hakara, you are not invincible."

It was the first time he'd said my name, and I was surprised that I'd noticed. I tilted my head to the side, struck by the sudden desire to pluck one of those feathers from his wings, to hear him yelp, to prove that he was not invincible either. "I don't care. It doesn't matter." The whispered words fell from my mouth recklessly, a wheel sent tumbling down a hill. "I'll go. I'll find a way."

I scrambled to the edge of the roof to take a peek, but Thassir grabbed my shoulder. His claws were sharp enough that one pricked through the thin cloth of my shirt, pressed against my skin. "Your life still matters."

"To no one but myself." Something made me add, "And I'd like to keep it that way."

I peered at the front of the tea shop. The table where Mitoran had sat was empty, tea still steaming at the bottom of her cup. Curse Thassir and his talk. I'd thought of him as silent and forbidding, but maybe that was just among the others. When we were alone, I somehow found myself confessing more than I'd intended.

It was the bond. It had to be. Either that or those raven-black eyes unnerved me more than I wanted to admit.

"There." He pointed again. Mitoran was weaving through a market – one last way to ensure she was not being followed. We started off again, creeping along the rooftops like thieves, the clay tiles baking beneath our feet. I could feel them through the thin soles of my shoes. The skin there would be red and tender after this, but would form more calluses.

Mitoran took one last turn and then she was sitting down at yet another tea shop, an outside seat off in a corner, where she wouldn't be overheard. Woman had to have a bladder of steel.

"Can we get to the tea shop roof without being seen?"

Thassir frowned. "If you learn the information you need to get through the barrier, and you find your sister, is that enough to fulfill my promise to you? Will you break our bond?"

"Of course I will. Do you think I *want* to be bound to you?" This wasn't exactly my ideal state of things either.

His feathers ruffled in a way that made me think I'd offended him. "I *am* powerful."

"Good for you. Having your presence in my head is still a burden to me. I asked to keep this bond for only one reason."

By the way he tucked his wings, I guessed at both annoyance and chagrin. Had someone tried to take advantage of him before? Mitoran, perhaps?

His wings fidgeted again. "Why are you looking at me like that?"

"Like what?"

"Like you're trying to peel off the layers of my skin with your eyes."

I stopped squinting at him and worked on finding a way to the tea shop roof. It took longer than I'd wanted or expected, but we managed by taking a longer route around. By the time we reached it, we had another problem. Thassir's eyes narrowed as he crested the peak of the roof. "Looks like our friend is here too."

The same man we'd seen back in the outskirts walked along the street. He'd shed the roughness like it was a second skin, his hair smoothed, his posture straighter, a jacket thrown on over his shirt. He'd either followed Mitoran or he'd followed us.

His gaze went to the rooftops.

I ducked away and Thassir shrank against the tiles, wincing at the heat of them against his skin. Well, that settled it. He'd followed *us*. And we weren't going to get any closer to Mitoran with a tail on our heels.

I crept over the peak on my belly.

"What are you *doing*?" Thassir hissed.

"Finding out who she's meeting with. The tiles are brown. My jacket is brown. If I keep low, he won't see me."

I moved as I explained, so by the time I'd finished, and Thassir reached out to stop me, I was already too far away. He'd have to creep after me, and those wings were just too conspicuous. I reached the edge, the sweat trickling along my shoulder blades and dripping from my neck. Slowly, I peered over the gutter.

Mitoran was sitting with her informant, though from this angle, I couldn't see their faces. I could tell her informant was young by the smoothness of the backs of her hands, but she wore a hat. Still, I was close enough to overhear some of their conversation.

"I didn't expect you to return. Didn't expect you to make it through, either. Is there a spot where the barrier is thin?"

The young woman's hands shifted. "If you're expecting me to tell you how I did it, you should know better. *You* taught me not to give away information."

Mitoran shrugged. "Can't blame me for trying. Tell me what you've learned since the last time we spoke."

The woman sighed. "I managed to make my way into one of Liyana Juitsi's social gatherings. The same petty rivalries. I can't decide if the Sovereign doesn't see it or if he chooses not to see it. After my conversation with him, I'm going to guess it's the latter. The Otangu clan is still trying to crush the Manado clan's silk business. They want to be the only brokers in Bian and they're royal, so they believe they deserve it. This time, they might succeed. They've somehow pushed their production quite a bit higher. Everyone is getting more desperate, more reckless. We're drawing closer and closer to restoration. The gap between restorations is narrowing. They can all sense it."

They spoke about the clan businesses, about recent marriages and alliances, about the current circulating gossip. Their conversation lulled, each of them sipping their tea.

The man with the nice sword strode up the street and around the corner, his gaze still flicking to the rooftops. I'd had to duck back a few times, my cheek pressed to the hot tiles. Thassir hissed wordlessly behind me. I ignored him.

Neither of them dropped their names, and the informant never turned her head in a way that let me glimpse her face. At last, she rose, tossing a coin onto the table for the tea.

I crept back to the apex of the roof. "The informant is leaving." I beckoned to Thassir before he could admonish me.

"I am not a horse," he said, even as he knelt to allow me to climb onto his back.

I pressed my knees into his ribs and pulled a lock of his hair. "That way."

I could feel the rumble of his growl beneath me, but he went. I had the feeling I was going to pay for this later, but always tried to never think *too* far ahead. Might as well get my little amusements where I could.

"I thought so."

It wasn't Thassir who'd spoken. My head whipped about faster than I thought possible. Mitoran stood at the edge of the roof, her expression stern. She straightened her cuffs. A strand of iron-gray hair drifted over her forehead and she tucked it back into place.

She wasn't old, but she wasn't young, either. Had she climbed the wall like Thassir? But judging by her expression, and by what her informant had said, she wasn't about to tell me how she'd gotten up here. One dark eyebrow lifted as she regarded Thassir. "I expected her, but *you?*"

He gave an uncomfortable sort of shrug, and for the barest moment I found him not intimidating at all. I took the opportunity to slide from his back.

I was caught – though that had never stopped me before. I was a fish on a line on the dry land of the dock and I'd keep flopping my way back toward the water. That might not have ever worked for anyone yet, but I could be the first one, couldn't I? "I wanted to know who your informant was. She made her way to Kashan and back without a guide, didn't she?"

Mitoran said nothing.

Damn. Of course. The old bitch wouldn't give me information, not without getting something in return. I narrowed my eyes at her. She narrowed her eyes at me. Thassir shifted uncomfortably by my side, and I was gratified that he didn't just up and leave. He certainly could have. She couldn't punish me – what could she possibly do? She'd already confessed she wanted my help. So we were at an impasse.

Something about her conversation with the informant clicked in my head, a piece of flint against steel. "The Otangu clan."

Mitoran blinked. She hadn't expected that.

"Their silk production increased." The broker I'd dealt with in the mining camps had mentioned something about the Otangus purchasing a rather unusual gem from him. Mitoran had said the corestones could increase soil fertility even more than the god gems when buried next to plants. "They have a corestone."

For a while, she just stared at me, then she uncrossed her arms. "Explain."

I did. It was a loose set of assumptions, but the more I spoke, the more it felt real to me. "Check on the other clans at the top of the hierarchy. Check when silk production increased. I'd bet my left arm the increase lines up with the information the broker gave me."

"That still leaves us with very little. Even if you're correct, we have no idea where in the Otangu orchards the corestone might be buried." I could see Mitoran considering it, the chance to obtain another corestone a temptation she couldn't resist.

"We already know the Sovereign only enforces the laws against the people he wants to. So get your informant to tip off Kluehnn's people. Make them do the work for us. And when they raid the Otangu orchards and find the corestone, we'll sweep in and grab it before they do."

"That is a *terrible* plan," Thassir said. Even crouched, his head nearly crested my shoulder. "You're inviting godkillers in. Last time we ran into them by mistake and were nearly all killed."

"Yes, so this time we'll be prepared," I said glibly. I'd tried to wheedle what I'd needed out of Mitoran. I'd tried subterfuge. Fine. If this was what it was going to take to ensure I had the means to rescue Rasha, then I'd keep bargaining with the head of the Unanointed. "I don't just want the messages to your people to find Rasha. I want passage to Kashan. I want to know how your informant got across."

Even from the corner of my eye, I could see the darkness of Thassir's expression. "We are *not* raiding the Otangu clan orchards and trying to steal a corestone from *godkillers*."

"What do *you* say, Mitoran? I found you another corestone."

She tilted her head, as though trying to figure out the origin of a strange sound. "You *think* you did. It's not enough." She'd drive a hard bargain; I'd known she would. "You know I want more than that. Once we obtain three corestones, I want you to use your abilities to infuse them with aether past the second aerocline. I have no one else. I want you to stick around. I want you as our linchpin."

Thassir's claws dug into the tiles. "We're not doing that."

I didn't look at him. "You find Rasha, if she's alive. You connect me with your informant. You give me one hundred parcels to fund my expedition to Kashan."

I hadn't asked for enough. I could tell by the way her tight expression relaxed.

"Done."

31

Hakara

10 years after the restoration of Kashan
and 571 years after the Shattering

Langzu – the outskirts of Bian

*The boats that never make it; the caravans that are lost
inside the barrier – they should have stayed. As that black
wall ran down on them, they should have made their peace
and stayed.*

Sweat slicked even the backs of my hands as I ducked and
swerved, the wooden weapons I carried feeling heavier than
they had any right to be. I needed the practice, especially against
someone who was stronger and more skilled than I was. Just like
a godkiller. I'd worked myself to the bone every day, until I felt
like I was swimming in a salt-soaked haze. Dashu had finally
agreed to spar with me, but he scoffed at my efforts, shaking his
head. Fighting him was like trying to wrestle an eel with my
bare hands; I couldn't pin him down no matter how hard I tried.

I'd never let the disappointment of others deter me. Without even hesitating, I darted in, aiming for his midsection. He blocked me and then dashed the wooden short sword from my grip in one easy movement. He pushed me back. "Always going for the killing blow."

"Why shouldn't I? It'd make the fight go a lot faster."

"You don't have the element of surprise. You're not as good a fighter as I am. It'll make the fight go a lot faster, sure, but it won't be going in your favor."

I swung for his neck with the knife in my remaining hand. He caught the wooden blade on the curved edge of his practice sword and wrenched that from my grasp as well, contempt curling the corner of his mouth.

I punched him, right in the smirk.

He fell back, his hand to his mouth.

"Are you sure about that?" I lifted both fists, keeping my feet light.

Dashu hadn't loosed his grip on his sword. In two lightning moves, he'd dispatched me, the wooden blade sliding along my neck and then jabbing my midsection.

It was my turn to fall back, my arm curled around my abdomen, coughing and dry-heaving.

"It's not a good idea to injure each other three days before your raid." Thassir's voice. For a man so big, he certainly knew how to sneak up on a person. I'd have noticed through our bond if I'd been paying attention.

Had I been avoiding him? Maybe. I knew he didn't approve of the bargain I'd made with Mitoran.

Dashu wiped blood from the corner of his mouth. "What's wrong with you?"

I swiped up my wooden weapons and returned them to the rack. "Innovation?"

"Well you'd be a dead innovator. My people like to tell the

story of Qutamil, who thought he could build a house in the ocean if he only erected a tall enough wall to keep the water out."

"And how'd he enjoy that?"

"He drowned."

I shrugged. "I was dead all the other times we've sparred, but at least this time I gave a little in return. Who knows, maybe Qutamil knew he was going to drown in the end and just wanted to do so in a nice soft bed."

Dashu shook his head in disgust and swept up the stairs. I should have called after him. Should have maybe apologized. If I kept up like this, he wasn't going to want to spar with me at all.

"He'll come back," Alifra said from the corner, cutting slices into a prickly pear. The sunlight from the window brought out the golden undertones of her brown skin, her freckles scattered like stars across her cheeks. "He knows what's at stake. He's just sensitive about his people and their stories." She glanced at my face. "Ah, he hasn't told you yet. He's from Aqqil."

I wasn't even sure exactly where on a map that was — wasn't even sure I knew of that realm at all — but I knew it must have been restored a long time ago. "So he's old. Incredibly old. Ancient. Would love to know what he does to take care of his skin."

Alifra rolled her eyes. "I meant his people are from Aqqil. He's one of the few of them left. They don't write things down; they tell stories. If you see him muttering to himself, that's what he's doing — trying to remember everything. That's how they keep their histories." She tucked a piece of fruit into her cheek. "Ask him sometime about those stories if you want him to warm up to you more. He'll talk your ear off and he'll make you learn some Aqqilan, but it doesn't seem like you have anything else to do besides training."

I squinted at her. "Are you speaking from experience?"

She took her time chewing and swallowing, carefully avoiding my gaze. "Dashu and I have known one another a long time. Nearly as long as I've been in Langzu. He was born here, you know. Not me. I washed up on these shores after trying to cross the barrier in a boat. Only one that made it." She pointed to her armor, her weapons. "Stole this first, from a rich merchant. Then this from some clan idiot who didn't know how to use it. This I got off the corpse of some poor sod in an alley." She shrugged. "The world's not fair, and I made it all a little more balanced."

Not like I was going to judge her after everything I'd done. And I had the feeling she'd just think it was funny if I tried to judge her for it. "So what's in all this for you?"

She gave me a face-splitting grin. "I get to steal from a god. And also, you know, the whole restoration thing. I'm done with it. I would actually take my chances on a boat again rather than wait for that black wall to overtake me." Her smile faltered a little. "Utricht was the best of us, you know. Only had good reasons for what he was doing. For *everything* he was doing. Dashu might be here to be part of his own story, I might be here to spit at Kluehnn, but he was here to do the right thing. He held it all together." Her gaze slid over my shoulder. "It's you that's got to do that now, because *he* certainly won't."

I turned to find Thassir glowering over the maps on the table, the notes. Mitoran was bringing in two more teams to our safe house tomorrow. They'd already been informed of the plan.

Two corestones. All we'd have to do after this one was find one more, then I could infuse them and be on my way.

"There is no way this works. This plan is foolish." His voice was low, his brow even lower. He tossed a few sheets of parchment back onto the table. "They'll kill us all."

I retrieved the sword and the knife from the rack, swinging them, running through some of the movements Dashu had taught me. Alifra gave me an approving nod. At least someone appreciated me. "If the plan is so bad, why don't you make it better?"

"Because there is no making it better. The den will send godkillers."

Alifra finished the pear, wiping her hands and knife clean on a rag. "Why are you so scared of godkillers, Thassir? Last I saw, you were ripping the arms off 'em." She imitated the way he'd torn into the godkillers at the wagon.

He grimaced. "I was not myself."

Her eyebrows lifted and she gave a theatrical shrug before walking out of the room, muttering in a voice so low I could barely hear it, "Maybe don't be yourself again then."

I focused on Thassir, letting my weapons drop to my sides. "Kluehnn's people will have jurisdiction to search the orchards. The clan won't resist. It's either we face a few godkillers or we face the entire Otangu clan when they catch us pilfering. If they've got a corestone, they'll already be on guard."

I felt him approach. "It's dangerous. You're not the only one going into this."

"They signed up for it." I whirled, giving him a mock salute with my wooden sword before I jabbed half-heartedly at his shoulder. He jumped back and batted my weapon aside. "Why are you continuing to help if you think it's such a terrible plan?"

"Because we made an agreement. I said I'd help you find your sister. I said I'd stay with you until you left this place."

I tested his guard again, this time more earnestly. A feint with the knife and then a slash at the legs with the sword. He ignored the feint and swayed out of the way. I knew he could snap the sword in half if he wanted to, but he was holding back. I circled him and he stood there only halfway entertaining my sparring.

"I'll be fair here," I said. "When we made that bargain, I

wasn't completely straightforward with you. You don't have
to keep your word. People break promises all the time, for less
reason. Yet you're still here, helping." I wasn't sure why I was
prodding him, except that if we were going to work together, if
he was coming along, we needed everything out in the open.

His jaw firmed. "I'm not. I'm just passing the time."

"I don't believe you. I don't know what's going on between
you and Mitoran, or why you've held yourself apart from the
Unanointed, but I believe there's a part of you that wants this
scheme to succeed, no matter how crazy you think it is. No
matter how much you claim not to want to get involved. So you
stick around. You dip a toe in once in a while, but you never
commit. You're afraid. But I know, deep down, you *want* the
Unanointed to bring greenery back to Langzu. On their own
terms, not Kluehnn's."

His wings snapped out, the feathers nearly brushing the walls.
"Wanting has nothing to do with it. You can spend a lifetime
wanting." He stalked closer, his eyes haunted. I thrust my sword
at his chest. He caught it. "Years and years until the world around
you turns into dust. But wanting changes nothing. Sometimes
things are as they are and nothing can alter the course."

He loomed over me, his wings smelling of sweetness and
musk, his jaw and his fists clenched. Everything about him was
taut. But my heart lurched when I saw the shine to his eyes, the
sheen of tears. I wanted to peel back his anger, his reluctance, his
sullenness – to strip his guard away from what secret vulnera-
bilities lay beneath. I would have done it with my bare hands if
it was possible.

I could not be gentle. That wasn't who I was. I jabbed at him
with the knife, but in a movement I couldn't follow, it was clattering
off into a corner. I didn't let that rattle me. I tugged at the sword,
but it was like trying to free it from a rock. "If you're coming with

me, if we're fighting side by side, how can I trust you if I don't know where all this hatred is coming from? You brood like a man who has nothing left to live for. I told you who I lost. Who did *you* lose, Thassir? A brother? A sister? A friend? A lover?"

He wrenched the sword from my grip, lunging out. I flinched back. But he didn't reach for me. His claws dug into the wall behind me, as though he were only just stopping himself from latching them into me. "I envy you." His voice was thick, dripping with some emotion I couldn't quite understand. "Yes, you. As ridiculous as you are. Always moving from place to place, from thing to thing, from person to person. You think I'm afraid? You are the one who is afraid. You know if you stop, if you stop to *think* for just one moment, your grief will catch up to you. It will make everything more real. So you just. Keep. Going."

I couldn't breathe. I couldn't feel my fingers around the wooden dagger. His hot breath gusted across my forehead as he spoke, and I felt the words burning me from the inside – a flame I didn't know how to put out. People think so often of despair as a hole in the ground from which you cannot climb out. But for me, despair was always a thing that consumed, leaving only ash and smoke in its wake.

The scratch of his claws against wood sounded in my ears. "At least you have hope. Some tiny, irrational sliver that she is still alive. I wish I could deny reality the way you do. Oh, I *wish* it."

I wanted to duck away but found I couldn't move. His wings darkened the space between us. His presence filled that corner of my mind and I found myself aware of how his hands were planted on either side of my head, the proximity of his body, the placement of his feet. "Stop." The whisper that left my mouth didn't sound like mine.

He let out a huff, a half-laugh. "Would *you* stop? Would you ever stop?"

I'd gone digging, yet somehow *I* was the one laid bare, my deepest fears dragged into the light. I licked my lips, felt them trembling. "Who did you lose?" I forced the words out.

He bared his teeth at me. "Everything. Everyone." He pushed away from the wall. "And some of us have no choice but to be still."

I didn't move from where he'd left me. My knees trembled, threatening to collapse. My teeth chattered briefly before I clenched my jaw. "I won't give up. Not until Rasha is back at my side."

"Thank you, at least, for telling me who you are. You're foolish. You're selfish. You're delusional. And I cannot be bound to someone like that. You're right. I shouldn't have to keep my word to you."

"Fine. Pretend you don't care. Pretend that you can't change anything. Whatever helps you sleep at night."

His gaze bored into mine, his mouth twisting as though he wanted to throw a dart right back at me. And then he snarled and turned, tearing one hinge off the door as he yanked it open. Dust and heat swirled into the safe house. The door slammed behind him, askew, the frame trembling.

I lifted a shaking hand to my face. Damn it. Was I *crying?* I sucked the tears back down. I could bond to someone else.

There had to be someone else.

32

Nioanen

40 years before the Shattering

Albanore - in the wilds

Kluehnn created the altered, and from the best of their ranks, he created the godkillers.

Nioanen wasn't sure how many of them made it out. In the panic of the retreat, he'd lost sight of friends and had seen others cut down. Irael had shifted into cat form – an orange tom – and had curled inside the ruin of Nioanen's armor as they'd taken to the skies.

Even the skies hadn't been safe, arrows and streaks of magic taking out other gods.

Sanctuary was gone. But he'd done as Irael had asked, hadn't he? He'd lived.

He sifted the silt from the water, wringing out the cloth to get the last drops. His knuckles were cracked, his lips peeling, his feathers dull. He wasn't sure if it was the environment or despair that had worn him at the edges. All he knew was that they were on the run – had been on the run for almost a year – and every furtive message they were sent from the others felt like a blip of light in a darkened room. It provided a small bit of warmth and illumination, but also gave them away.

Kluehnn was a predator, and he would hunt and hunt and hunt until every last god was gone.

Irael's hand touched his shoulder. She was in the shape of a young woman with short, dark hair today. There was still Irael's feline sharpness in her cheekbones and nose, eyes practically luminous. Nioanen would recognize her no matter what form she took, would love her no matter what form she took.

"We need to keep moving. Lithuas is working with Kluehnn. She's a shifter god and I just . . . I feel an itch at the back of my neck."

Nioanen had learned to listen to Irael's hunches. It was the only reason they were both still alive. He rose from the puddle, taking his canteen of newly filtered water with him. The landscape around them was barren, the skies stormy. The heat would break soon, but the coming rain would sit on the parched landscape, flooding it. The mortals couldn't seem to help themselves. They'd cut down that last Numinar, had fed its branches into their fires, had ignored the toxic billowing smoke in favor of catching the magic that spilled forth.

Perhaps some of them had tried to save the tree, or some part of it, but the end result was the same: the last of the Numinars was gone. And with it had gone the sap. The roots might still be in Unterra, sprouting beneath the warmth of the inner star, but here, on the surface, they had nothing.

Nioanen still remembered the days long past when they'd tapped the roots and sprouting branches far beneath the surface, refining and serving the sap at their parties the way the mortals did wine. Now all he had was a cask of the stuff and a dread that it would not last forever.

"Don't lose hope." Irael's touch was soft on his neck.

He knew he should not pull away, that he should accept this comfort, but he drew back anyways. "How can you say that? I lived through that battle, and so did you – but for what? The Numinars are dead, we are barred from ever returning home beneath the surface, and you and I – we cannot remain together. We're easier to find when we're not alone. You ... Irael ... " He stopped and took a deep, shuddering breath. "Your chances are better without me. You can shift and hide. I cannot."

Irael did not step away, though her expression was reproachful. "Is that what you want? For us to part?"

"No ... and yes. I can't bear to be the reason you were captured. Or killed."

She shifted into the big orange tomcat and leapt into Nioanen's arms. He caught the beast out of habit. "Nothing is certain. Don't borrow trouble."

"The world will never be the same. The Numinars are gone. The surface ... it's a wasteland."

"You're right. The world will never be the same. That doesn't mean it's not worth living in. And I make my own choices, Nioanen. You're worth it."

He held the cat close before springing into the air, the wind streaking past as he climbed toward the clouds. "I would argue with you over that, but I've learned I lose all our arguments. Fine. We run together. We wait, and we watch, and we see what this new world looks like."

"And we keep fighting," Irael added, his voice a shout over the wind.

Nioanen didn't answer, letting Irael's words drift away, hoping the shifter god would let it go. He'd watched friends cut down, their bodies hacked limb from limb. He wasn't sure he had the appetite to fight.

But he would do it. For Irael, he would do it.

33

Rasha

10 years after the restoration of Kashan
and 571 years after the Shattering

Kashan

*Nioanen was drawn to those who existed on the fringes.
He could be fierce, but only in his protection of the people
he saw as his. He was the god who defended those weaker
than himself, who summoned Zayyel to his hand whenever
the powerful sought to impress their will upon those who
wished to remain free.*

The second trial was quickly approaching. Some of us would
be promoted to acolyte, some of us would go to serve the
den in other matters, and some of us would die. If rumors were
to be believed, most of us would die.

But I could not put the thought of Sheuan out of my mind.
Her name repeated in my mind, conjuring those few moments
together in the tent, the scent of her hair, the touch of her lips. My
memories were only dim reflections of those actual sensations,

but I couldn't stop dwelling on them, as if I could somehow bring them to life if I only turned them over enough times. It was like being in love with a ghost.

She wouldn't come back. To her, our tryst had been temporary, fleeting. I could never know if it had meant the same to her as it had to me.

"Luck got you through the first trial," Shambul whispered into my ear as we took our wooden sparring weapons from the rack. "Don't expect it to carry you through this one. My father told me it's longer. It's harder. And bait like you won't survive."

I pretended I hadn't heard him as I pulled two daggers from the rack. He brushed a wing against my cheek and I ignored that too.

He turned his attention to another target. Khatuya stood with Naatar, the tall, skinny brown-scaled altered. Shambul jabbed at the girl with his blade, then tried to trip Naatar. The boy was surprisingly agile despite his gangly limbs, and he sidestepped the attempt. Shambul frowned and slapped him across the head with the flat of his weapon.

Millani leaned in a corner of the burrow, ignoring these petty disagreements. She only ever stepped in when it seemed as though someone was about to be seriously hurt. Kluehnn and the trials were to be our judge, she intoned, over and over. Not one another.

Yet it didn't feel as though she believed it.

Last night, a fight had broken out between two rock-wood altered boys, one with papery white skin and one with pebbled cheeks. By the time Millani had intervened, both had been streaked with red. Fights were breaking out more often these days, the tension rising with each day that passed.

Three days until the second trial.

And Sheuan, though she had continued to train me in her fighting techniques, had left me with only a passing parting kiss.

She knew she might never see me again. She knew I might die. Yet she'd left without looking back. I was always the one being left, wasn't I?

I clenched my teeth, trying to banish her from my thoughts. Not this time. I would get through the next trial, and even Shambul wouldn't be able to say it was luck. I would become an acolyte. I would make Kluehnn proud. He favored me? I would prove myself worthy of that favor.

Shambul was saying something to Naatar. Something about his family, how everyone knew they'd only become devout right before restoration. Naatar's face grew red with impotent rage. Everyone knew Shambul was the best fighter among us. During sparring sessions, he mowed through our ranks, one after another, sending each of us tumbling to the ground.

Khatuya stepped between the pair. "Yes, we all know your family is devout, and rich, and better than everyone else's," she said, her voice level. "We all know that *you* are better than everyone else."

Small, but brave.

Shambul's eyes narrowed. He seized the girl by her wrist, and though her skin was tough as bark, I saw her flinch.

Though I tried not to think of Sheuan, her voice filled my mind. *What is your problem right now?* My problem right now was Shambul and the upcoming trial. Inside, I quavered, but I had to make a stand or I'd be bait in truth.

I extended one of my wooden knives. "You. Shambul. Leave those two alone. Let's spar."

His gaze turned back to me. He sneered. "You're out of practice. You weren't here for the last few lessons Millani gave us. I'll go easy on you, bait."

I said nothing in return, already trying to find the focus of the deep woods, Sheuan opposite me, the calm of her voice juxtaposed with her lightning-quick movements. The touch of her hand as she guided me through different stances.

We faced off, and I felt more than saw the others finding sparring partners, lining up. Instead of watching them, I studied Shambul. His wings twitched in anticipation. His stance was easy, indolent, though I knew from experience he could tighten it in a moment. I noted his vise-like grip on his daggers. I wasn't sure if I'd made him uncomfortable by challenging him, or if he was worried about the upcoming trial – either way, he was on edge.

I could use that.

The knives felt at home in my hands. I'd been gone for ten days. At the time I'd been angry because I'd be missing valuable lessons. I'd never had a private tutor, so I'd needed those lessons, even if Millani hadn't spared me much attention. Sheuan had treated me, for those days, like I was the only person in the world.

She might have been gone, but she'd left her mark on more than my heart.

Millani pushed off from her spot on the wall, her tail lashing behind her as she stalked up and down the row of sparring partners. "Begin."

The neophytes around us leapt at one another. Neither Shambul nor I moved.

"You were pulled out of the burrow to advocate for a devotee." He looked me up and down, as though such a task might have left a physical mark.

"I was. I advocated for her successfully."

He snorted. "Surprising that it only took you ten days."

He was stalling.

I'd gathered all the information I needed. I feinted to the left and then went hard to the right. Shambul flinched at the feint and I caught him off guard. I struck him as hard as I could in the ribs.

I was bigger than him, though I often didn't realize it. He was better muscled, but there was strength in my bones I'd not been able to unleash at him yet.

He staggered to the side, clutching his injured ribs. Before he could recover, I seized one of his wings. Wings were powerful, but also quite sensitive in spots. I jabbed another dagger at the junction of feathers and flesh, then tugged hard enough to remove a fistful of gray feathers.

He screamed in pain and frustration, whirling and thrusting at my right shoulder. He hit me right in the soft spot between bones. I felt the flesh there giving way, the muscle-deep pain. Millani should have stopped the bout then, but she said nothing.

I should have expected as much. I turtled as best I could, lifting my arms to protect my face, crouching to protect my midsection. Still the blows rained down on me. Once in a while I sought to block one. I succeeded twice and then he broke through my guard and struck the side of my head, leaving my ear ringing and hot.

A few days with Sheuan was never going to save me against an opponent who'd been training most of his life. But that had never been the point of this exercise.

He kicked hard enough at my knee to knock me down. I stayed down – and only then did Millani call him off.

Three days from our second trial, and I was aching all over, my right arm tingling. I tried to wrap my fingers tight around my knife and found I could only hold it in a loose grip. Most other bouts were still going. Bouts with Shambul always tended to be quick and brutal. But I glanced up from behind the curtain of my black hair and noted with satisfaction that his hand had crept back to the spot on his ribs where I'd hit him, and one wing hung lower than the other.

I tried to rise and felt a pang in my knee. I gritted my teeth against the pain and tried again.

A bark-covered hand reached out to me. "I'd say you gave as good as you got," Khatuya said, "but we both know that's not true."

Naatar was behind her. He moved forward to help as soon as I'd taken Khatuya's hand. Together they walked me back to my cot.

"You'll have a bruise," Khatuya said, lifting my hair to check the spot where Shambul had struck me. Ringing still filled that ear. "Maybe a very mild concussion." She shrugged at my expression. "My father was a physician. Before." Her gaze went distant.

"Restoration," Naatar said, "took Khatuya's father. Took both my siblings. My parents were never the same after that."

"But we had food to eat again," Khatuya said quickly. "We aren't ungrateful. Kluehnn must take in order to provide."

Yes, just like the precept. Did he not offer sustenance and shelter to all his altered? Did he not care for us and protect us and make us strong? Better that some should survive than all of us die.

Naatar glanced quickly to Shambul and then back to me. "Thank you, by the way, for stepping in. And for your help during the first trial."

I gave him a quick nod, my throat tight, remembering for the thousandth time the way my blade had cut through flesh in the cave filled with aether. The way that feeling had traveled up my arm and burrowed deep into my heart. I'd done terrible violence. I'd done it to survive, but perhaps I shouldn't have.

There was a choice to be made here, I could feel it hovering behind my lips, flickering in my mind. Soon, the moment would pass and it might not come again. The bell rang for mealtime and three devotees entered the burrow, laden with trays of food. Already, the others were jostling, getting in line, trying to get the best spot. Everyone would be fed, but the last ones in line never had as many options.

Khatuya was turning away and soon Naatar would follow.

"We should work together," I blurted out. I kept my voice quiet, only loud enough for them to hear. There were few rules here, and there certainly weren't any rules against neophytes joining forces during the trials. There were limitations, however – trust being the foremost. I plunged on. "The second trial will be hard. We have better chances of survival if we work together."

"And better chances of stabbing one another in the back," Khatuya said. Her voice was wry, but her expression held no hint of amusement.

"So you would rather go into it alone? We make a pact. Us three. None of us leaves any of the other two behind. We go in together. We leave together."

Naatar's lips pressed together as he studied the wall. He was considering it, even if Khatuya was not. Perhaps they'd already formed an alliance between them. Perhaps they had already decided they didn't need a third member. But we all had something in common – we had all been picked on by Shambul. We all hated him. I hoped that thread was enough. The click of utensils against plates sounded from the dining corner of the burrow. No one was watching us. No one was listening. Even Millani had left. "And if there's an opportunity," I continued, "we kill Shambul."

Khatuya halted and pivoted back toward me. Something burned in her dark-eyed gaze. Whatever he'd done to me, I knew in that moment that he'd done worse to her. "I'm in."

Naatar shrugged, though the movement seemed forcibly casual. He couldn't seem to quite lose the tension in his spine, and his tail lashed behind him. "I'll make that pact."

I winced at the pain in my ribs. "Don't let him catch us

together. Don't let him suspect." They moved away from me. I'd get last pick of the food, but I wasn't about to fight for a place in line, not in my condition. Whatever was left would be enough to sustain me, and that was what mattered.

The next two days passed more quickly than I would have liked.

Neither Naatar nor Khatuya spoke to me again, though we exchanged quick, knowing glances. Shambul paid me back thrice for his injured wing. But I couldn't back down from his challenges, not anymore. I'd made a stand against him, and re-treating now would only make him redouble his efforts. By the time the morning of the second trial arrived, I'd added a black eye to my list of injuries. Nothing that would slow me down too much. Shambul's wing was on the mend, but I gathered a fair bit of amusement from the way he twitched it away each time I lunged for him during sparring.

My insides had tied themselves into knots. I barely slept before the trial, and from the creaking of cots and the shuffling I'd heard throughout the night, I was not the only one. The sounds of the forest filtering in from above, which had always lulled me to sleep, now sounded too loud and too harsh. Our morning meal was simple, with no choice bits for those who jostled to the front of the line. Only a grainy gruel, topped with herbs and a greasy, gamy meat. Devotees brought in leather jerkins and metal weap-ons, and we suited up in silence. Early morning mist seeped in from the hole in the ceiling above, the light gray, casting every-one in a ghastly pallor. The day was mild, but my armpits were slick with sweat.

Shambul shoulder-checked me as we formed into a line to leave the burrow. He cut very purposefully in front of Khatuya, his wings curled at his shoulders so she could not see around him.

Sometimes, in my kinder moments, I wondered what he'd

been through to become this way. I wondered if he had an exacting father, or a cruel mother, or a brother who leaned on him the way he leaned on the weaker members of the burrow. Perhaps he'd been taught that the only way to win was to dominate. Perhaps he'd been shown it.

But this was a competition with life-or-death stakes, and Shambul would never be my friend. I couldn't afford to be soft. Kluehnn had shown me that.

Millani led us through the deep corridors of the den, where the light from above faded and our only company seemed to be the sound of our breath and our footsteps. Stone leaned in from all sides. I thought I could feel the press of the first aerocline just below my feet. It smelled of dirt and metal.

Each step I took felt light, as though I were floating somewhere above my body, already a ghost. I couldn't seem to take a full breath.

Briefly, I closed my eyes. For Kluehnn. I would become a god-killer. I would prove to him that I was not as soft as he thought. I could be hard. I could be tough. I could be a person who took life without question or mercy.

Millani stopped in front of a door. With a small sense of relief, I noticed it was not the same door she'd led us to for the first trial. It was metal as well, though larger, two reinforcing bands across the middle.

"There is a small cave system past this door," she said. "Inside, there is a beast – we've trapped a dzhalobo. It attacked a nearby village and consumed two altered, which was when the godkillers had to get involved. It nearly killed one of them before we were able to capture it and bring it to the caves.

"Around its neck are three keys. This door will be locked behind you. Each of the three keys will open the door."

She looked us over, an eyebrow arching, as though she found

us all lacking. She had, after all, been through a similar trial and lived.

"Fifteen of you are entering this door. But only three of you can win."

She opened the door, the space beyond a yawning black maw. The air was cold and smelled of minerals. The drip of water sounded somewhere.

In the distance, a torch lit a shadowed wall.

One by one, we filtered inside.

34

Sheuan

10 years after the restoration of Kashan
and 571 years after the Shattering

Langzu

*Worship of the old gods continues to this day, if a person
knows where to look.*

She'd met with Mitoran at a local tea house after her return
from Kashan, updating her on the state of the clans and the
gossip she'd heard. She'd already sent word to the Sovereign, and
he'd requested to see her several days later.

Her mother was meeting with the head of the Risho clan
as Sheuan finished readying herself for her audience with the
Sovereign, though it seemed the meeting was just concluding.
She had a bit of time still, so she lingered by the open doorway
of her mother's office. There were too few servants here to gossip
and no clan elders to look at her disapprovingly. Besides, this was
what she'd been taught, wasn't it?

"Just think about it," Taelon Risho said as he rose from the cushion. "Thank you for the tea." They clasped one another's wrists before he made his way toward the door. Sheuan backed away to the corner. She didn't want to be seen here, especially when she wasn't sure of the content of the meeting. She tilted her hat over her eyes and busied herself with one of the few remaining paintings on the wall, lifting her hands to straighten it.

She felt the brush of air as Taelon Risho passed her on his way to the front of the estate. He did not even give her a second glance.

When she went into the office, she made sure to knock – loudly. Her mother had often accused her of sneaking up on her, and any suggestion that her hearing might not be what it used to be had ended in a verbal upbraiding.

Her mother looked up. She was sitting at a table on the opposite side of the room. The table itself was low, but it stood on a raised platform in a little alcove that overlooked the garden.

The relief that had crossed her mother's face when Sheuan had returned from Kashan had been real – Sheuan knew that much. And just a glimpse of that emotion had been enough for her to forgive all the harsh words. Her mother hadn't pushed her to go to Kashan because she'd wanted to be rid of her. It made no sense for her to want Sheuan's death or disappearance, yet fear and doubt always pushed her mind to travel down this unreasonable route.

She tilted her head in the direction Taelon had gone. "You met with Taelon Risho?"

"Nimao, his third son, has an interest in you." Her mother's lips pinched. "His clan is royal, which is more than I'd expect as far as marriage offers go. He offered Nimao to you in exchange for our pea-shoot farms outside of Xiazen."

The offer was less tempting than it should have been. For Sheuan it could have been a way to remove herself from this place, these obligations. It was mildly flattering, that the Risho clan saw her as something valuable, as worth having. Had Mitoran put Nimao up to it? She could have done it – a whispered word in an ear here, a suggestion there. Nimao might have been more interested in Liyana, but he was already interested in Sheuan; it wouldn't have taken much. She tried to imagine herself with him, taking his hand, leading him to her bed. The thought wouldn't coalesce. Instead, her mind took a quick dip into the soft brown of Rasha's eyes, the way her lips yielded beneath Sheuan's, the way her body, with all its potential for power and destruction, had responded to Sheuan's touch.

She shivered and turned the movement into a shake of her head. "You told him no, of course. We can't afford to lose another business."

Her mother's gaze was shrewd as she looked at her, but she nodded. "Did you send word to the Sovereign?"

"I did."

"Then you'd best meet with him."

No question of whether she'd succeeded or not. Was her mother's faith in her so strong? Or did she just know that either way, there was nothing she could do to change the outcome? Either the Sovereign would take her on as trade minister, or he would not, and the fate of her clan would be decided. She was already moving on to the next problem, papery hands shuffling through the documents on the table.

How lucky to be someone like Mullayne, absorbed into another life – one where he had no worries except how to keep his friend from dying. Sheuan had an entire clan to worry about. She spent overlong hovering across the street from the castle, trying on different expressions and discarding them. Should she appear cool, collected? Triumphant? Anxious? The Sovereign had enjoyed intimidating her during that last meeting. At last she settled on a steady neutrality, and introduced herself to the guards at the base of the stairs. They escorted her to the Sovereign's study and shut the door unceremoniously behind her.

The Sovereign stood with his back to her, gazing out the window at the dried-up lakebed just outside the city. "That was quick," he said, not turning around. "I charged you with finding out why the restored realms isolate from the unrestored ones – a mystery no one else has been able to solve. So, tell me, are you ingenious or are you incompetent?"

Sheuan bowed her head when he turned. She'd dressed well but without adornment – not that she could do otherwise. Her mother had pawned all their most expensive pieces of jewelry. But she still had the filter in her satchel, afraid to let it out of her sight, and even though she wasn't wearing it, it felt something like armor in this moment. "I'm far too modest to claim the first, and the second would be a lie. But in my short time in Kashan, I learned several things I think you should know about before I continue further."

He waved his hand at her. "Do tell."

"First, the government is unstable. The Queen is no longer in control of the border. It does not appear she is leading the country anymore. Which leads to my second point. Kluehnn and his dens are an even larger influence in a restored realm than we first considered. I believe the dens are in control of the government."

The Sovereign touched a finger to his desk as he approached her, as though wiping off a speck of dust. "None of this tells me why they will stop trading with us, nor does it help our predicament." His eyes narrowed. "I presume you do not come back to me empty-handed?"

She told him about her visit to the nave in the Queen's palace, the rhetoric against mortals and gods alike. She repeated the Queen's assertion that travel to an unrestored realm was a weakness.

He tapped her nose, lightly, an owner reprimanding his over-eager puppy. "That's a supposition only, my dear. That is *not* evidence. You cannot come here and tell me you have an odd feeling in your foot and that you know as a result we are headed to disaster. Give me clear-cut facts or give me nothing at all. Your father would have known better."

She clenched her teeth. She'd hoped this new information would impress him, would convince him to at least stay the reparations her clan owed. It had been more dearly bought than he knew. She had one more thing to offer, and though she knew that Mull would never quite forgive her, it was all she had left. "Do you want to know how I got to Kashan? How I came back? Why I am here giving you this information instead of staying there until I was sure I had an answer?"

A slight flare of his nostrils was all that told her he was *very* interested. If he knew how dire her family's situation was, then he knew they could not afford to hire a guide. Even if she had, by some miracle, scraped together a loan from another clan, she would not have come back with so little unless she'd known she could return again. He didn't judge her to be *that* stupid. Somehow the thought cheered her, because she knew that meant he'd respected her father at one point, no matter what had gone ill between them. He thought she might have inherited some of his shrewdness.

No point in holding back any longer. She'd teased far enough, and to pull back now would seem foolish and miscalculated. So she reached into her satchel and took out the filter. "I used this."

He frowned. Then he extended a hand.

Through some instinct she couldn't quite understand, she did not let go of the filter. Yes, it wasn't exactly her property, but it wasn't the Sovereign's either. "My cousin, Mullayne Reisun, designed this. It filters out the aether and allows you to breathe unsullied air. I passed through the barrier twice. No ill-effects. It's still difficult to get through, but I think most people could do it without a guide. This would allow us to trade more freely with Kashan. If we can pass easily to the other side, then can they really cut us off? Isolationism depends partially on the restored realm's ability to isolate. Even if they decide they no longer want to come to us, we can still get through to them."

The Sovereign had not withdrawn his hand. Slowly he reached toward the filter, his expression questioning. Sheuan nodded, and he took the edge of it between thumb and forefinger. He rubbed the seal and felt the layers of cloth wedged between. "Restoration is often described as a black wall, a cloud that sweeps over everything, changing it with a powerful magic. If magic is aether, could a person protect themselves from restoration with this?"

It was as though someone had poured a glass of cold water down the back of Sheuan's neck. She stood there, her hand still extended, an odd sick feeling rising in the back of her throat. She'd thought herself smart, worldly, wise. And she'd missed this completely.

Stupid Sheuan, thinking she could change the fate of Langzu by offering the filters to continue trade. The Sovereign wasn't just thinking about changing the fate of Langzu. What he was thinking would change the fate of the world.

Already her mind was hurtling forward. The materials for the filters were hard to come by – she'd gathered that much. They wouldn't be able to provide one to everyone in Langzu. Who would get one? The Sovereign and all the people he favored.

No one else.

What would it mean, coming through restoration unaltered? She should have seen this possibility. She'd been distracted by Rasha, by her own damned *feelings*. If she were a weapon, she'd

become dull in Kashan, her edges blunted by the presence of a
strong girl with horns and sad, limpid eyes.

"I . . . I don't know. I'd have to check with my cousin."

He withdrew his hand finally, and she was desperately re-
lieved he hadn't tried to take the filter from her. "Well, find out.
Quickly. Don't send word – speak to me directly. No one else."

She could feel herself careening, falling off into dark places.
More than once she'd played at this sort of unmooring to elicit a
solicitous response, but this was real, and she needed to find her
way back to shore. She grasped for an attitude that would fit,
found her features arranging themselves into a serious expression – one that spoke of secret knowledge.

This Sheuan knew more about the filters than the true one did.
This Sheuan had done all this on purpose. It was like donning a
cloak by the door; it warmed and protected her from the whirl-
wind of her thoughts.

"And what of the trade minister position?" The voice didn't
sound like hers. It was far too confident, given the situation. But
this Sheuan could not let that slide.

She almost expected him to get angry. She was young. She was
from a failing clan. Her father had allegedly robbed him. But he
only gave her a calculating look. "If this filter does what I think
it might, then the position will be yours. I'll forgive your debt,
advance your family a year of payment and protect you from the
other clans. Now go."

The filter was still in her outstretched fingers. She pushed it
into the bottom of her satchel, gave a quick bow and fled from
the room.

She couldn't fall apart, not yet. The corridors of the castle were
a haze. A guard escorted her from the Sovereign's study to the
entrance. It might have felt an unwelcome intrusion any other
time, but now she was grateful to have someone by her side,

thinking about where her feet should go. Because her mind was occupied by other matters, replaying the conversation with the Sovereign, trying to remember everything she'd read about the filters in Mull's notes.

As soon as she reached the street, she hurried to Mull's workshop. She'd closed it while she'd been gone. The doors were still blessedly locked, no sign of a break-in. Of course there wouldn't be. None of the other clans knew where Mull had gone or what new invention he'd taken with him. She entered quickly, locked the doors behind her. And then her legs gave way and she was sitting on the floor of the workshop, unheeding of the dust and grease.

None of it mattered. The only thing that mattered was the filter in her satchel.

She couldn't ask Mull about the properties of the filters. It didn't surprise her that he hadn't thought of this usage for them. He was so single-minded, so focused on two things and two things only: finding his way to the realm of the gods and healing Imeah. The filters were only a means to that end. The Reisun clan were used to his long absences, with their vague return dates. He often traveled, searching for cures or pre-Shattering relics or components for his inventions. He might have been fumbling and bookish, but he somehow always managed to have a good crew with him – he was the type of person others found themselves unintentionally orbiting, never quite getting as close as they might have wanted to. His clan always trusted he would come back.

She wished she knew when. How long would the Sovereign wait? How long could she stall?

She was panicking. The filters might not protect against restoration. That was only a possibility. She had to think this through, to use the information she had. Her breathing slowed.

The notes – she had Mull's notes on the filters. And he had a large collection of books and notes on restoration. Eyewitness accounts, speculations, diagrams – he was always writing and drawing. Sheuan liked to tease him about his strange calluses, the black and polished appearance of his right hand, the smudges on his fingertips.

Quickly, she pulled several tomes off the shelf, searching for and finding a sheaf of notes he'd made on restoration. Then she went to the box he'd hidden beneath the desk and took the journal of notes on the filters from there.

Her mother wouldn't expect her back for a while. Mitoran hadn't given her any tasks. She pulled down the shutter of the nearby window and settled in at Mull's desk to read.

Her shoulder blades began to itch again. Absent-mindedly, she reached back to scratch.

A small lump met her fingertips. At first she thought it might be a scab, and then a mole she'd forgotten about. But it was hard, moving a little when she pressed it. And oh, it *itched*.

It didn't feel like her fingernails that dug into her skin, that pressed and tugged until she felt a sharp pain and the sticky warmth of blood.

She'd gone to Kashan. Kashan was not for mortals. It was some sort of bug, she was sure of it, something that had crawled into the skin of her shoulder to stow away to Langzu. The thought made her dig more desperately. She knew that if she let it sit inside her a moment longer, she would be sick.

Her fingernails met a smooth surface, something that did not belong. She pulled.

The pain that erupted from the spot when the thing came free was fiery. It traveled down her arm, hugging the surface of her skin, making her shiver with both relief and dread.

She turned the object over in her fingers a moment, afraid to look at it. And then she brought it before her. Her hand was red with blood, the object slick with it, but there was no mistaking what it was. The little filaments that had escaped, the hard casing, the blue-black sheen.

A pinfeather.

35

Hakara

10 years after the restoration of Kashan
and 571 years after the Shattering

Langzu – the outskirts of Bian

Did gods ever commingle with mortals?

Thassir did not return. Mitoran was not as put off by his departure as I was. "He's more often gone than he is here. Usually he stops in only to look after his cats. Frankly, he was here more often after you arrived." She grimaced. Then she shook her head. "You're still bonded to him?"

"Yes." I could feel his presence somewhere far in the wilds. It was a faded thing, something I barely noticed during the day. At night, though, as I stared up at the ceiling of the room Utricht and I had once shared, the bond felt like an itch I couldn't scratch. I wondered if it felt the same way to him, or if he was able to blithely ignore it.

Probably the latter. It would be like him.

Mitoran had me practice with Buzhi, my one-time jailer. It

passed the time. That was one way to put it. For the third time this practice session, he summoned aether, his tiny white wings twitching. I saw the air shimmer to the left of me, tried to catch it before it dissipated. Utricht had been steadily competent. Thassir had been a miracle worker. Buzhi was . . . well, he didn't have the best aim.

I wiped sweat from my brow as I whirled to face him. "Try again."

He was sweating just as much as I was, the effort it took to conjure the aether clearly getting to him. His face had a pinched, tired look to it. Was he truly the best Mitoran had to offer?

"You're not moving in predictable ways," he snipped back.

I threw my arms out wide. "Am I *supposed* to be moving in predictable ways? How do you think that's going to look to a godkiller?"

Alifra let out a little half-laugh. She was working on something else off in the corner. Traps to be triggered once the godkillers located the corestone.

"It's your job to figure out where I'm going to be, isn't it? If I'm charging off with god-enhanced legs and arms, I can't very well stop to give you directions." I was needling him. I knew it. He knew it. Couldn't seem to stop. Maybe it was the way he always nodded along to everything Mitoran said, like he'd thought up the words coming out of her mouth. Or maybe it was the way he seemed to look down on everyone who wasn't altered. Or maybe it was the way he insisted that even though those wings of his couldn't carry him anywhere, they could be dangerous in a fight.

I don't know — it was a whole lot of things, really. I found myself picking apart each one of his behaviors, fascinated and annoyed and disgusted by all of it.

He wasn't so bad. To someone else he might even be likable. I could admit that. But he felt specifically bad *to me*, and I didn't think I could explain that to him without starting a rip-roaring fight.

We were leaving for the orchards tonight and I was still bonded to Thassir.

As though the thought of him had triggered some response, I felt him move. He was approaching. Quickly. I tried to let it go, to move through another attack. I was sparring with Dashu and he never held back.

I got a slap on my ribs in response. The aether Buzhi summoned hit me right in the face, but if this had been a real fight, I would already have been dead.

Even if Thassir was moving toward me, that didn't mean anything. He had to travel around – to eat, to find places to sleep, to fly.

But he was approaching in a straight line. I beckoned to Dashu again, urging him to attack me. He readily obliged. I blocked the first blow, Buzhi conjured aether in the right spot, then I fell for a feint and received a jab in my gut.

I backed away, rubbing at the spot.

"This rate you'll not last two blows against a godkiller," Dashu said. "There are Aqqila stories of people with worse odds triumphing in the end, but I think their enemies are always painted as stupid." I was getting the feel for him now. He didn't say it to be unkind, and I shook my head ruefully.

"I'll have god-enhanced limbs."

"Yes. And they've got godkilling blades."

He was right. They might not completely neutralize my new magic, but they certainly put us on more even ground. Fine, less than even, if I was being honest with myself. I'd not gone through three deadly trials to earn a blade. At least, those were the rumors I'd heard about godkillers. That they had to rip out each other's throats to earn the dagger.

I stepped back, breathing hard. "Let's try again in a bit? Something's on my mind."

"Better get it off your mind before tonight." But he tucked his curved sword into his belt and took a piece of cactus fruit from the bowl on the table. Buzhi left the room without a word to me, or even a glance. Maybe he found me as infuriating as I found him. Couldn't see why, though.

Thassir was nearly here. Now that I took a moment to think about it, of course he was. We had a bond to break. He would at least have the decency to do that before I went out on this mission. Wouldn't leave me hanging, no partner to help me fight.

Still, when he burst through the door close to dinnertime, his wings ruffling and his dark hair a storm cloud about his face, I felt something like surprise. Shouldn't have been a surprise at all, not with his presence creeping about in the back corners of my mind. Yet I still felt a little off kilter as he ducked his head through the door frame. Everyone turned to look at him.

He drew a dagger from his belt and approached. For a moment I wondered: should I be scared? Couldn't quite muster up fear, no matter how big he was. There was a feeling *like* fear running along the back of my tongue, but it didn't really match.

He held out his hand. There was something in his gaze – something distant and final. "We break the bond before the orchard mission."

I only nodded.

"Cutting it rather close." Buzhi was behind me, and I knew from the tone of his voice that his arms were crossed.

"I am here. That's what matters."

I drew my own dagger, aware of everyone watching us. It had felt almost like a sacred act when we'd bonded. This felt something less. But weren't all endings like that? Abrupt?

His gaze flicked behind me to where I knew Buzhi was standing. "Who are you bonding with for the mission?"

I jerked a thumb back at Buzhi and watched Thassir's eyes
narrow. "You're doing this on purpose."

I was well and truly mystified. "Doing what? Bonding with
someone so that I don't get killed right off?"

"He cannot draw aether past the second aerocline. His aim is
inaccurate."

I wasn't going to argue with any of that, but I only shrugged.
"I don't have any other options."

"Tell Mitoran to choose someone else."

"Mitoran isn't here, and she's not returning until it's time to
leave."

Thassir bared his teeth. "You cannot take *him*."

I tilted my head. "Didn't realize we had that kind of relationship. You telling me what I can and can't do. Last time we talked,
you stormed out that door and wanted nothing more to do with
me. So let's just get this over with and you can stop crawling
about in the back of my mind. It's not pleasant, you know."

"You think *I* enjoy it?"

This admission, that the bond had itched at him too, was so
satisfactory that I smiled. Gave him a little teeth in return. Felt
like the wrong thing to do in the moment, but gods *below*, it was
good to know he wasn't as impenetrable as he liked to appear.

"Buzhi is what I've got, and it's that or my own little mortal
limbs up against godkillers. I don't think I need to tell you which
I prefer."

Slowly, his lips curled back over his teeth, pressing together.
"Fine. I'll go. We stay bonded for this mission."

I wanted to tell him to take his moodiness, his refusal to get
involved, to take his whole *self* and just leave me to this job. That
was what he wanted to do, wasn't it? My sister and what had

happened to her was my business – it wasn't his problem, even if he'd felt a little bit of pity for me when I'd first confessed it. Even if he'd given me his word he'd help.

But I remembered the way it had felt when we'd worked together, the power and weight of the aether he'd conjured for me, the way he'd seemed to know exactly where I would step, where I would be.

I was approaching a passable fighter with a bit of practice. With the god gems I was quite good. But when I'd fought with him as my bonded partner, I'd felt unstoppable.

Damn – just wasn't fair. Whatever weird guilt he was feeling, I had to use it. I needed him more than he needed me. "Just this mission," I confirmed. "Only because the Unanointed could use your help."

He let out a soft snort, as though he could see right through my words. Probably could. Probably knew exactly what I was thinking. But when it came to finding my sister, I'd long abandoned any sense of pride.

He gave a curt nod and then retreated upstairs, his heavy footsteps creaking on every tread. Everyone in the room turned to look at me.

"Well, you're welcome, I suppose. He's stronger than any of us and we've got godkillers to get past for the second corestone."

"And if you two fight like that when we're in the orchards, we'll all be dead," Alifra muttered as she raised a cup to her lips.

She'd pitched it loud enough for me to hear, but I ignored her.

I tried to get some sleep, thought I was failing miserably, but then Alifra was shaking my shoulder and my room was dark. I couldn't remember the sun setting, so I must have slept at some point.

Mitoran was waiting for us downstairs, accompanied by another team. I spotted their arbor and their bruiser right away. The arbor was tall, with branching antlers; the bruiser was short and lithe and missing her legs below the knees. The arbor pushed a wheeled chair, but his bruiser was currently strapped to his back in a contraption that she could easily step in and out of when she had a pair of gem-grown legs. The antlered one was Gamone, the short one was Keka. Their pest was a narrow-faced teen who gave Alifra a nod. She pinched his cheek in response. "I trained him," she said. "Since he was little." He shrugged her off with the rolling eyes of a boy who had no clever response. And their vine must have hailed from north of Cressima – unusual, these days. A long-bladed spear jutted over one shoulder, just below a shield, and his hair was a shade darker than fresh snow.

They'd come from Xiazen, a coastal city. Eight of us.

Mitoran waited until we'd finished sizing one another up. "My informant tipped off one of the dens. The godkillers should arrive shortly before we do, though there may be some delay. So you might have to wait. The orchards are guarded by several Otangu clan men and women. Five in total, though they have the means to call in reinforcements. That's why you must be quick."

All information she'd told us already, but by the glassy looks on everyone's faces, we needed the refresher. Thassir stood behind me, black wings tucked at his sides. It was like standing with my back to a wall.

We crept out into the night, Alifra taking the reins of a covered wagon, the rest of us packed into the back – even Thassir, who was too large to approach the clear skies above the orchards without being noticed. We rolled out of Bian and toward the surrounding farms.

I noted the way Keka and Gamone held hands and wondered if that was common between bonded partners. How strange, to always know where the other person was. I cleared my throat. "You two – have you fought godkillers before?"

Gamone inclined his antlered head, his horns brushing the curved tops of Thassir's wings. Thassir shifted uncomfortably but said nothing. "Yes, and killed them too. That's why Mitoran asked us to accompany you. If we succeed, according to Keka's calculations, we only need one more corestone."

"Your calculations?"

"I've been doing the research," Keka said, nodding eagerly, "though Mitoran has helped. We've seen how large a radius of soil an infused god gem can affect. I've experimented with the corestone you retrieved, and our initial suppositions were correct – an infused corestone has a magical radius ten times that of most god gems. So if we further extrapolate, and assume you can infuse a corestone with even more concentrated aether, we can cover a large portion of Langzu. I can't know for sure, but there may also be a multiplying effect when the infused stones are close together. Even with that effect, it won't be enough to cover everything, but it will be enough that we should be able to live off the land indefinitely instead of starving. We can steal the gems Kluehnn is collecting for restoration. We can break our pact with him."

Gamone squeezed her hand. "Once we change Langzu, we can convince other unrestored realms to follow in our footsteps."

My shoulder was pressed against Thassir's ribs, and I felt him let out a long, deep sigh. But when I looked to his face, it was too dark to make out his expression.

The moon was high by the time we arrived at the Otangu orchards. They were walled in stone, and as soon as we could see the walls, we abandoned the wagon and crept away from the road.

It would have been easier if Langzu had not already been so desolate. The landscape was flat and dusty, rocks and scrub providing scant cover. Dashu led us forward and then made us stop, adjusting direction, squinting into the darkness. Bushes and trees had sprung up near the walls, fresh new growth damp beneath my feet. It seemed the corestone's power had extended beyond the orchards.

Alifra only had the time to set one trap before Kluehnn's lackeys arrived.

Early.

36

Hakara

10 years after the restoration of Kashan
and 571 years after the Shattering

Langzu – the Otangu clan
mulberry orchard

*The oral histories of the Aqqila peoples have been passed
from one generation to the next, through barriers into new
realms, though with each restoration, their numbers become
fewer. Their stories say that the god Irael once had dalliances
with mortals. But oral histories are flawed and we must rely
on what is written – in ink, in charcoal and in stone.*

Thassir was right. The den sent godkillers. I counted four.
In one sense, their early arrival was a blessing – the
guards converged at the entrance to the orchard to greet them,
and we were able to rush to the wall opposite, climbing and sitting atop it like a ghastly set of statues. The orchard trees were
lush, the leaves shielding us from view. Thassir had to crouch so
low he was nearly lying down.

In another sense, it meant we were behind in our plans.

"Shit," Alifra muttered into the darkness. "We won't get to it before they do. We didn't finish laying out the traps."

They would find the corestone and they would converge upon it before we could set up a distraction. "I counted four godkillers," I said. "There are eight of us."

"And five Otangu guards with more probably in reserve. Plus godkillers move in packs of three, meaning there are at least six," Dashu reminded me, smoothing a hand over his goatee. "Eight against at least eleven isn't good odds, Hakara. And I can guarantee you, in spite of your most fervent wishes, the godkillers are not stupid."

He was right. They weren't good odds. "We can be quick. Thassir can fly. We go in, kill the godkiller with the corestone, and Thassir flies it out."

Thassir's voice was a rumble in his chest. "That leaves everyone else scrambling to escape a walled orchard while there are godkillers on their heels. I won't do it."

I bit my lip. The corestone was right *there*, somewhere in this orchard. We were too close. "What's better? Getting it now, or trying to retrieve it from a den filled with godkillers? This is our chance."

Dashu let out a sharp breath. "You're right. Much as I don't like to admit it, we won't have many better opportunities. We've been lucky to hear of two corestones in so little time. And restoration is getting closer. The whole of Langzu can feel it. It's worth my life if you all agree it's worth yours."

Everyone gave grim little nods, and a part of me sank, curling within myself. I wasn't fighting for their cause. I was fighting for one person. But wasn't that enough? Didn't that still mean something?

Thassir, next to me, tensed. He always seemed tense, but he'd gone from log to boulder. I followed his gaze and saw a slim black cat picking its way through the orchard. "It's close to the trap."

Alifra let out a soft groan. "It's going to spring it."

"Let it," Dashu said. "It's just a cat. We go down there now, we risk being seen."

Thassir was already pushing himself up.

"Thassir," I said, my voice low and filled with warning. I knew that look in his eye. I'd seen it each time he'd grimly picked up one of his cats and taken it to the doctor, unheeding of the needle-like claws latched into his forearm. "We are not stopping to save a cat. We are *not*."

"We stopped," he said simply, dropping his legs over the side of the wall. "We are saving the cat."

And then he was gone, and I had only the soft slip of feathers against my grasping palm before my hand was empty. I cursed beneath my breath. I cursed Kluehnn, I cursed every elder god whose name I could remember, I cursed Thassir's mother, his father, all his ancestors and all his possible future children.

We were two steps off track and quickly careening into the unknown.

Dashu held out a hand to forestall any of the rest of us from creeping into the orchard. He gestured at the walls. "Stick to the plan. Keep watch. Spread out. Whoever sees the corestone uncovered, go in for the attack. The rest of us will do our best to pull the other godkillers and the guards away. Hakara. Keep an eye on Thassir."

Everyone else moved, creeping away from the spot we'd climbed to. I was rooted to my place on the wall, watching Thassir as he ducked beneath the branches, silently moving toward the cat, moonlight limning his rolling shoulders. Something about them captivated me, and I had to tear my gaze away to watch the godkillers below conduct their search.

My lips went numb. Dashu was right, there were six god-killers. One must have been crowded in with the others, short enough to escape notice. Another appeared out of the darkness, finished with whatever business had taken her away from her brethren. And they didn't split up to canvass the orchards. They were measuring the green grass on the ground with their hands, one of them writing notes on a piece of parchment, another holding a lamp to provide light.

They weren't moving about haphazardly. They would uncover the corestone together. Which meant our odds had worsened considerably.

I couldn't see Dashu through the darkness and the trees. We had no further direction. Brush rustled as the godkillers strode toward Thassir. Thassir moved unerringly toward the cat.

By all rights, I should have just sat there, let the scene play out. Would the cat spring the trap or would one of the godkillers do it?

And then I was down the wall, the grass brushing my shins as I crept after Thassir, doing my best, in vain, to be just as quiet as he was. The cat was lingering near the trap Alifra had placed, tail lashing, crouched in the grass. I'd nearly reached Thassir's side when it pounced on something.

Both Thassir and I froze. It had come very close to the pressure plate Alifra had covered with a thin layer of dirt. That thing was meant to hurt godkillers. The little beastie wouldn't stand a chance. Neither would we.

The grass nearby rustled. We both hit the ground right before the godkillers appeared out of the darkness, one of them carrying a lantern. Blades of grass partially obscured the view, but they stopped at a nearby tree. One of them began to dig. I reached out and touched Thassir's ankle, squeezing so he'd know I was there. He glanced back at me before focusing not on the godkillers, but on that damned cat.

It wandered closer to the pressure plate.

"Thassir," I hissed, risking the sound. I *knew* he'd heard me, but he didn't even flinch. "It's a *cat*. Don't even—"

For the second time that night, he slipped out of my grasp. He was surging out of the grass, he was darting forward, he was sweeping up the cat beneath one arm. The beast yowled and all six godkiller heads whipped in our direction.

At least we were no longer careening into the unknown. We were knee-deep in a shit-filled creek with no obvious way to get to shore.

Without even speaking, two of the godkillers peeled off and drew their knives.

I pushed myself to my feet. No use trying to hide anymore. My hand went to the pouch with the god gems, but I stopped myself before I could clutch it. Thassir had saved the cat from the trap. Which meant no one had tripped it yet.

As though he could sense exactly where my mind had wandered, he cast me a glance. He lifted the cat to his mouth and kissed its head as it growled.

Gross. The thing was probably absolutely *covered* with fleas.

But I knew from the look Thassir had given me that he was thinking exactly what I was. They might have drawn their knives, they might know we were up to no good, but these godkillers didn't know who or what we were yet, and there was no reason to let them know until we'd seized the advantage.

"Cat jumped the wall," I said with my best wobbly smile. "Had to get it back. Sorry."

They stalked toward us, giving no indication they'd heard me at all. Thassir took a couple steps back, his wings down as he tried to shrink himself into something a little less imposing. I took his arm as he came abreast of me, adjusting his stance, making sure the pressure plate was right between us and the godkillers.

I held up my hands. Had to look real pathetic so they'd just come straight at us instead of circling for a better position. "We're just nearby farmers."

One of them looked at the short sword strapped to my belt, hesitated, a frown pulling at the brown scales on his cheeks.

Only one thing for it. I pulled a gem from one of my pouches, tossed it back, and turned to run at the same time Thassir did. And the godkillers, like dogs watching fleeing prey, did what came naturally to them. They pursued.

Aether surrounded me, and I took in a deep, sharp breath of it.

I heard a soft *click* as one of them stepped on the pressure plate. White powder burst from the tree above, dusting the air around them.

And then it exploded.

I stepped to the side to protect Thassir, letting the brunt of the explosion hit me. I'd taken one of the invincibility god gems. For a split second, the heat of it seared my back. And then I felt only warmth, like a spring breeze. Thassir was next to me as soon as the heat and light died away, leaning down to let the cat free. His mouth stopped near my ear. "Are you—"

"I'm not hurt, thanks to you. Quick thinking."

"Only following your lead." Was that quirk to the corner of his mouth a smile, or just a trick of the light? Not important. I turned to see one godkiller falling to the ground, engulfed in flames. The second one was patting out a fire on her arm.

Behind them, I caught the first glow of the corestone from the hole the other four godkillers were digging. Quickly, I tossed two more gems into my mouth. And then I was hurtling forward, unable to reverse my momentum. The corestone was there and I would have it in my hands if it killed me. I would have it in my hands and I would give it to Mitoran and I'd find Rasha.

One of the godkillers was lifting the corestone out of the

ground. Another peeled off to confront the guards. The penalty for smuggling god gems was death. The Sovereign might not have cared to always prosecute the smugglers, but Kluehnn was different. The guards might not have had anything to do with it. They might not have known. But that godkiller would find a way to make them give up the names of those who *had* known.

Four. That meant I was only facing four, and one of those still nursing a burned arm. For now, at least. It wasn't what we'd planned on, but it was better than six.

The aether surrounded me – Thassir doing his part, no matter how much he disapproved. I took a couple quick breaths and then sucked in the bitter taste of seawater and held it. My ribs and hips begin to itch. The god limbs sprouted, their strength flooding through my veins. I plucked the sword from the scabbard at my side and darted forward.

The godkiller with the gem tried to dodge, but she was too slow. She screamed when I hamstrung her. I felt Thassir take flight behind me, heard rustling in the distance as the others rushed in.

The corestone fell from her limp fingers and I caught it.

Eight Unanointed against four godkillers and five guards? Time to find out how shit those odds really were.

37

Hakara

10 years after the restoration of Kashan and 571 years after the Shattering

Langzu - the Otangu clan mulberry orchard

The aether barriers exist in the ocean too — far out at sea, churning the surface and sending sprays of water into the air. Is there easier passage beneath the waves? Perhaps, but no safe way to get a ship across.

It turned out that eight against nine still wasn't great odds, no matter how you tried to cut things. Especially when four of those nine were godkillers. I'd hamstrung one of the three I was facing, but that was mostly because I'd had the element of surprise, and the remaining two looked none too pleased by my appearance. There was another behind me, probably recovered from her burned arm; I'd have to trust Thassir to take care of that one. One of the godkillers in front of me set down his lantern in a matter-of-fact manner, as though he were merely putting it aside so he could eat a meal.

I wasn't up the side of a mountain with no shoes, but I certainly wasn't wearing a good sturdy pair of boots, either.

The other two converged on me as the third ripped her robe and tried to staunch the bleeding with a makeshift tourniquet. Neither of the two approaching me bothered to help their fallen comrade. I had the corestone in my hand and I couldn't have felt more like a person holding a bloody hunk of meat in front of two hungry wolves. They'd take my hand with it, they didn't care.

One rock-skinned altered, and her partner with a pair of short, sharp horns. Funny how two very different-looking godkillers could still have the exact same expression. Brows lowered, lips thin, jaws clenched, they circled, their blades flashing orange and silver by the competing lights of moon and lantern.

I put my back to the tree, tucked the corestone into a pouch and pulled my knife free, breath still held, weapons at the ready.

They darted in as one.

I barely managed to block their daggers. I didn't have the same coordination in my left arm as I did in my right. Gods below, I really was shit at this. The one on my left seemed to immediately sense this weakness, whirling away from my block and granting me a thin cut across my ribs. My belly chose that moment to spasm, urging me to breathe.

The hiss of pain that escaped my lips didn't feel like my own. My breath went with it, my strength and speed sapping away as my god limbs dissolved into smoke. I gasped in another breath, trying to get enough air, trying to clear the spots from my gaze. I couldn't keep a close eye on both godkillers, and there was a smugness to their grim expressions that told me they knew it. Some silent communication seemed to pass between them as they darted in.

I was beginning to think I'd gotten lucky in my previous fight. Very lucky.

And then I felt the breeze of Thassir's wings, and he was wedging himself between me and the godkillers, black feathers brushing against my arm. He seized the wrist of the horned one, wrenching it with a sharp crack.

I didn't have time to watch their fight. Pulling two more gems from the pouches at my side, I swallowed them during the reprieve, then leaned over my knees, doing my best to catch my breath, my heartbeat thudding in my ears.

Thassir swiped his free hand over the face of the rock-skinned godkiller, forcing her back as he punched his claws into the horned one's arm. The latter screamed, his blade falling into the grass, the violet glow of the gem in its hilt the only thing still visible.

A quick quirk of Thassir's finger and the air around me shimmered. I didn't know where the rest of my team was at, where the other team was. But we had the corestone. We just had to get out of this alive. I took in a deep breath, felt my arms and legs strengthen. And then I swept past Thassir's wings and attacked the rock-skinned godkiller.

For someone who looked like a living boulder, she moved with surprising swiftness, her speed nearly a match for mine. She whirled and pivoted, blocking each blow, leaving my knife hand numb with the force of the clash. I stabbed blindly with my sword and scored a hit on her forearm.

Her thick skin made it barely a scratch.

In return, she struck, I blocked, and she caught my dagger by the cross-guard. A flick, and she sent it flying into the air and into the grass. I was down to my sword, but I was better with my dominant hand anyways. I rushed at her, trying to put an end to this quickly.

She grabbed my wrist, pulled me in and met my stomach with her knee.

All the breath went out of me in one *whoosh*. Sick rose in my throat as I struggled to take another breath and couldn't. I should have had more time, but my breath was gone and the divinity in my limbs dissolved into smoke. I had more gems in my pouch, but my fingers fumbled as I tried to reach them. I finally managed to suck in a breath, barely blocking a killing blow. Thassir's shoulder brushed mine and I risked a glance his way.

The godkiller I'd hamstrung limped toward him from behind.

Without thinking, I darted between Thassir and the tree, leaving my back exposed. A searing pain hit me across my shoulder blades. The rock-skinned godkiller had caught me with her blade, though I wasn't sure how bad it was. I blocked the hamstrung godkiller's weapon, her scaled face grimacing as she tried to bear down with her knife.

I kicked the hamstrung leg, hard, and she fell to the ground. Without even thinking, I stabbed down. My sword entered her chest and I pulled it free, then whirled to see Thassir was now occupied with both the horned godkiller and the rock-skinned one.

My gaze landed on the orchard wall, the dark line of it nearly invisible against the night sky. I could run right now. The godkillers and the guards were occupied with everyone else. I could climb that wall and escape into the brush. Take the wagon. I knew, in a flash of clarity, that Mitoran wouldn't upbraid me for leaving them. I would bring her the corestone. She had other people across other cities, all of them ready to answer her call. And weren't they willing to die for this cause? If I stayed here, the corestone remained at risk.

But Thassir had come to help *me*. I gritted my teeth. Damn having no pride but still having a conscience.

I rushed back into the fray, my sword held in a weak grip, my back still stinging. I tried to edge past him to help, but he spread his wings, blocking me.

And giving the two godkillers more surface area to attack.
They went at it with relish, cutting at his wings as though they
were trying to give them a nice trim.

Feathers fell onto the grass at my feet. The corestone was a
warm weight in the pouch at my side. In the distance, I could
hear the clash of blades elsewhere in the orchard, grunts and the
occasional shout. "Let me past!" I demanded. All this effort to
help him, and he was going through a good deal of trouble to stop
me. Should have just run off into the night after all.

"You're hurt." His voice was perfectly neutral.

I finally pushed aside his wing. "Not that badly." In truth, I
didn't really know *how* badly. It didn't feel great, but I was still
moving. I swallowed two more gems and Thassir summoned
the aether.

Breath. Breath. Long breath.

He was holding his own against the godkillers. The one with
the broken wrist had switched his dagger to the other hand.
Thassir's wings snapped shut and he lunged forward, dodging
a swipe from the one on the right. He seized the one on the left,
ignoring the dagger she stabbed at his side. I darted in to push
the other godkiller away from him, striking hard with my short
sword. Might have been injured, but the horned godkiller had a
broken wrist and a torn-up arm.

He fell back, just as Thassir sank his teeth into the rocky
woman's shoulder. Bones crunched and she shrieked. Claws
raked across her torso. For a moment, I lost my concentration. There was something so savage, so *animal* about the
attack. I should have expected it from him, yet I hadn't. Part
of me had seen him as mortal, as like me, even when he was
so clearly not.

I flinched back from a thrust barely in time, the horned godkiller's dagger catching the front of my tunic. My enhanced legs

were quicker than my natural ones. I tried to fall into the rhythm of fighting, but the wound on my back was beginning to burn.

I could have been mortally injured – I didn't think I would know until I died or this fight ended.

And then Thassir was bodily lifting the godkiller I was fighting, one hand holding him in place, the other gutting him.

Would it offend him if I was sick? I was used to the brutality of the sinkhole mines; I was not used to the brutality one person could visit upon another.

For a moment we stood, our breathing ragged, listening for the others. The godkiller I'd left to my arbor earlier, the one with the burned arm, lay in a crumpled heap to our left. The lantern on the ground still burned, casting an eerie light upon Thassir's face.

Then footsteps came careening out of the darkness. Dashu and Alifra, Dashu's face wet with blood. Followed by Gamone with Keka strapped to his back.

No others.

Gamone shook his head at Alifra and she crumpled, a fist to her mouth. The moan that left her didn't sound human. Dashu was there in a flash, lifting her. "Grieve later. We grieve *later.*"

I knew from the panicked, empty looks in their eyes that the remaining godkillers and guards were dead. No more blades clashing against one another, no grunts, no shouts. We'd been fortunate to make it out with so many of us alive.

Yet there was a thickness in the air that told me this wasn't over.

Dashu clenched his jaw. Alifra got her feet beneath her again, putting a hand to his arm to let him know she could stand on her own. Blood covered the front of Dashu's jacket, though I couldn't tell how much was his. "Do you have it?" he asked.

I nodded.

He and Alifra exchanged grim looks. They felt that tension too. But we were lucky. We'd made it through with our team intact. A cool breeze hit the back of my neck, licking at the sweat that had gathered there. I shivered.

Something shuffled in the trees, the low hiss of a thing being dragged across grass and brush. We weren't alone in this orchard. Not quite yet. Dashu glanced at Gamone and Keka, lifted his sword and gave me a nod.

I tossed the pouch with the corestone to Gamone. "Get it out of here. We'll buy you time for an escape."

Instinctively, I moved closer to Thassir and found him doing the same, until his wing brushed my shoulder. Dashu and Alifra took up position on either side of us and a little in front. My heart hammered against my ribs. It could have been one of the Unanointed, injured and unable to speak. But whatever was moving toward us did not have a friendly feel.

And then a *thing* emerged from the trees.

38

Hakara

10 years after the restoration of Kashan
and 571 years after the Shattering

Langzu - the Otangu clan
mulberry orchard

*People have traversed the highest mountains, have forded
angry rivers, have cut paths through the thickest brush.
They find their way through the barriers. The way is dangerous, but they always do.*

The thing that emerged was a mass of bone and wiry tendons.
It crept along the ground on eight clawed hands and feet,
with four barbed tails waving in the air like tentacles, too many
eyes and mouths embedded into its body. Its skin had the roughness of tree bark or stone in places, and was pale and shiny in
others, horns bursting forth in random spots. It was even larger
than Thassir. Three round black eyes peered at us from above a
mouth with row after row of needle-sharp teeth.

"Come for a corestone, have you?" Its voice was softer than

I'd expected, with all the depth and darkness of a sinkhole. All
three eyes tracked over my shoulder, in the direction Gamone
and Keka had fled. "Ah, you have already procured it. You really
think the Unanointed's plan will work?" None of us responded.
One of the three eyes narrowed at me. "You. You're *interesting*.
There's aether lingering in your blood. More than most mortals
can handle."

Alifra tossed me an extra knife, which I caught gratefully.

What was this? An odd-looking altered? A godkiller? It certainly wasn't from the Otangu clan.

"Kluehnn," Thassir said. He pulled a dagger from his belt, the
first time he'd seemed to want a weapon in hand.

This was Kluehnn? I'd thought the god would tower over me,
speak with a booming voice, not be this – yes, fine – somewhat
terrifying lump of flesh in front of me. I thought of the god I'd
seen on the pike, who in spite of his state seemed just a little bit
more than everything surrounding him. Who might have looked
like he'd belonged in the realm of the gods but certainly didn't
look like he belonged on the surface.

This didn't look like it belonged anywhere. This looked like it
shouldn't have existed at all.

The creature's eyes flicked to Thassir, and then all of them
widened at once.

Thassir didn't give it time for conversation. He darted in,
dagger raised. Kluehnn rose from his crouched position, arms
outstretched, claws and sharpened barbs glinting in the lamplight. A second mouth ripped open on his belly, larger than
the one on his face – a slathering thing that undulated with his
movements, one thick tongue barely visible behind rows of teeth.

He met Thassir's attack with surprising speed, barbed tails
lashing out.

Alifra drew her little crossbow, firing off three bolts in quick succession. Dashu whirled out of the way of a clawed hand and brought his curved sword down on one of the barbed tails.

And I was standing there like an idiot, useless blades held in useless hands. Quickly, I tucked the knife back into my belt, grabbed another two god gems and tossed them back.

Thassir, occupied as he was, lifted a hand. Aether surrounded me, lifting the hairs around my ears, making me feel for a brief moment like I was swimming. I breathed it in, sucking down as much of it as I could, feeling a fizzing in my blood as the gem and the aether reacted.

My god limbs sheathed my mortal ones as I joined the attack. I charged in next to Thassir, aiming for the bulk of the body.

It was like fighting three people at once. Kluehnn had too many arms, too many limbs. I tried to focus on one or two at a time, using my strength and speed to tear at him. I managed to cut off one arm, to injure another, and then my stomach was spasming and I was whirling away, trying desperately to catch my breath. Thassir stood over me, always aware of where I was and how I was moving. I leaned against him as he fended off the monster's efforts to get to me, too weak to do anything else.

Dashu filled the gap, Alifra doing her best to keep Kluehnn from being solely focused on him. Dart-like knives sank into the fleshy bulk of the thing, joining the bolts she'd already landed.

And Dashu *danced* with that blade of his, flowing into an attack and then out again into a defensive posture with the grace of a sapling bending in the wind. If I was a bruiser, then this creature was too, its movements filled with strength and speed. Dashu could only deflect; he didn't have the power to take an outright stand.

I gasped in a few more breaths, trying to figure out the balance between jumping back into the fray to help my team and steadying my breathing so I'd have more stamina. They were all doing their best to protect me, and I'd nearly left them here to face this god alone.

I pulled a couple more gems free, noted I had only two more each for my arms and legs, and swallowed them. Thassir summoned the aether. I took in a breath.

The fizzing in my gut began, strength rushing back into my arms. I ducked back into the fray, batting away a claw that was harrying Alifra. She gave me a brief grateful nod and then I pivoted toward Dashu. Two barbed tails were left, weaving in the air around him. Sweat shone on his forehead as he shifted to avoid their stings. The sweet smell of trampled grass floated into my nostrils, mingled with scents of loam and blood.

I pushed forward and the beast shifted, putting its body between me and Dashu. Every cut I'd suffered began to throb, the one on my back reminding me of its existence each time I ducked away from an attack. I couldn't tell if it was blood or sweat or both that stuck my tunic to my skin.

"I've got this!" Dashu called.

He hadn't. Anyone could see that.

My heart was pounding; I hadn't caught my breath enough. Spots swam in front of my eyes. I hacked at Kluehnn's body, unheeding of the mouths, the sharp teeth, the raking claws. Dashu had taken the time to train me. He'd stood up against Mitoran for me. He was part of my *team*. I was their bruiser and I was failing them. The arbor's job was to protect me, and my job was to crush the enemy, to get us all out of there alive.

A flutter of black feathers and Thassir slammed into the beast's side, giving me space to move past. The smaller mouth latched onto his left wing. Thassir grimaced, trying to pry it off. The larger mouth was close, lips fumbling as it tried to pull Thassir's arm and torso into its maw.

If it killed him, it would kill me.

"Go," Thassir shouted at me. "I can handle this."

I went.

One of the tails lashed out at Dashu, narrowly missing his face. Another one drew back.

I spun into Dashu, pushing him out of the way. One of the barbs struck me in the back of the neck but I ignored it. That was a problem for future-me. Present-me just needed to get out of this situation alive, and then I could start worrying about poisons.

I sidestepped another tail, slicing it off just before the barb.

To my left, Thassir was prying the beast's mouth from his wing. I caught a glimpse of a bloody wound before he sank his dagger deep into the thing's eye.

It staggered back, a high-pitched keening in the back of its throat. Unceremoniously, it dropped to the ground, its sides heaving twice before it was still.

I let out my breath, smoke rising from my limbs. My hand slapped over the wound on my neck. It was already burning. Turned out future-me was a lot closer to *now* than I'd thought.

The orchard seemed to spin around me.

Blood dripped from Thassir's wing, black in the dark of the night. He looked to the sky. "She's been poisoned."

I opened my mouth to say something, to refute it, but I'd somehow fallen to the ground, the earth pillowing my head. I seemed to have forgotten how to make words. The only thing that left my mouth was a low hiss.

Dashu swore. "I don't know where that thing came from. I don't know if more are coming. I don't know what it was."

"There won't be." Alifra's voice. "May not be part of your histories, but I heard about them in Albanore. They're rare. Thassir, take Hakara. Find help. Dashu and I can make our own way back. We'll meet up with Gamone and Keka."

Thassir's deep voice again. "The others . . ."

"Are dead," Dashu said. "Gamone and Keka wouldn't have left them unless they were sure. We can't do anything more for them. There will be more godkillers coming, or more of the Otangu clan. Either way, Alifra's right. Do what you can for Hakara and we'll regroup."

Footsteps scratched the earth next to my ear. Thassir bent over, lifted me into his arms and sprang into the air.

The night was warm, the sky deeper than the ocean at night. The wind slipped around me like the currents. I couldn't care about how far we were above the ground. My head listed to the side, the stars spinning around me.

I tried to tell him I was fine, only a little dizzy. A slurred "hnnnggggh" escaped my lips. It seemed like the right thing to say at the moment, to keep him from worrying too much. Was I ... worrying about him worrying? I let out a wheezing laugh, which only seemed to deepen the crease between his brows.

He landed in a small copse of stunted trees, setting me down on the thin, drying grass. Time seemed to pass both too quickly and too slowly. He leaned over me, and I became aware that I could see his face. A small fire was lit beside us. When had he done that?

A hand touched the back of my neck with surprising care. I saw two versions of his face, both frowning. The burning dissipated, though the warmth remained. "It's shallow," he said, relief coloring his voice. "Sleep it off, Hakara."

Perhaps I'd already died. He'd never been so kind to me. He *hated* me. He had only come along because of some unspoken guilt.

And he'd called me by my name again. It sounded sweet on his tongue, and though I knew he couldn't be Kashani, he spoke all the accents and tones in the right place. I wanted to tell him that. I wanted to tell him thank you.

But his words swept over me like a command.

I wasn't sure when the line between wakefulness and sleep blurred.

Consciousness returned through individual sensations. First, the sun leaching red through my eyelids. Then the smell of burning wood and the coppery scent of blood. Then the feel of feathers beneath my cheek.

It was that last one that woke me fully, that brought every painful wound back to the forefront. I opened my eyes and found Thassir already awake next to me, his black eyes gazing into mine. For a moment he looked startled, and I thought he might rise from the ground and leap into the air, hissing and growling like a cat cornered in an alley. But he didn't move. From his stillness, I didn't think he even breathed. One wing was spread out so that I lay partially pillowed on it. The other one was stretched over us like a canopy, protecting our faces from the sun.

How long had he been lying here like this? All night?

I couldn't seem to hold his gaze for long. I found my eyes flicking to his wing, to where I'd seen Kluehnn biting him. He'd bound the wound, but red seeped through the bandage.

I scrambled to my feet, remembering the other injuries he'd suffered at the godkillers' hands. "You're hurt. I . . . " I touched the back of my neck. The spot where the barb had pierced the skin was a little swollen, but nothing more. The wound on my back ached, but when my fingers explored it, there was no bloody crevice like I'd expected, only a tear in my shirt and a shallow wound. Had I imagined the depth of that pain?

"He poisoned you, but you slept it off. You didn't get a full dose."

"Sure felt like a full dose." My fingers returned to the spot on my neck, rubbing. "Your wing." Without thinking, I touched the bandage. "You shouldn't have flown with it like that. There's water nearby. I should clean it."

He twitched the wing away, grimacing, though I couldn't tell if it was with pain or irritation. "I already did that."

"It needs a fresh bandage." I didn't know why I cared. I'd gotten what I'd come here for. The second corestone was on its way back to Mitoran. Thassir didn't want my help.

I reached out and he moved his wing away again.

"Leave it alone."

Gritting my teeth, I tried once more. This time, I anticipated the direction he'd dodge and seized the joint between my hands.

He bared his teeth at me, a low growl in his throat.

"Well now, you're just like your stray, Rumenesca, aren't you?" The reference to his cat seemed to startle him into silence. "Don't give a damn what's good for you. You can hate me, as long as we respect each other." I seized the end of the bandage and began to unwind it. "Why don't you want me to change this?"

He pulled his wing away and redid the wrapping. "I don't like to be touched," he said slowly. "It's nothing to do with you."

I wondered, not for the first time, how long he had been alone. The altered tended to live longer than mortals. Not as long as gods, but long enough that I wondered which realm he'd been born to, how long he'd orbited the Unanointed, helping them without ever truly diving in.

"I'm sorry." I wasn't sure what else to say.

"Kashan is not the first realm I've seen restored. And Langzu won't be the last. I have watched the march of refugees from one border to the next. After a while, it all starts to feel meaningless."

"And that's how you want to see it?" I could have pressed harder, challenged him more, but I was bone-tired and he'd saved my life. I supposed it didn't hurt sometimes to be gentle.

He grimaced. "I know what others would say. I've heard it a thousand times before. That I could make a difference, that I could turn the tide, that I – only one person – could stand against Kluehnn and we could change the world in a kinder way."

"Mitoran tell you that?"

He let out a soft snort. "She's far too practical. It's the ones like you. The ones who would throw themselves into a storm to scream at it, believing that would make it stop."

There was something in the way he looked at me that made me want to hide, to burrow under a blanket or sink my head beneath the waves. I wasn't sure if it was because I felt too perceived, or because I felt he was pinning traits on me that didn't belong. I wasn't here for the Unanointed and their goals. I was here because it was the best chance I had of finding my sister. I didn't care about standing against Kluehnn or changing the world.

I pressed the spot on the back of my neck. It felt like an old bruise. "You do what you want. I won't tell you what you should and shouldn't do. I've had enough people telling me that in my life. Not going to do it to someone else."

He cleared his throat. With a heave, he pushed himself up from the ground and held an arm out to me. "We should get back to the safe house."

And I, because I really could *not* let things go, reached up as though to wrap my arms about his neck, and instead seized the bandage at his wing and pulled – quick, sharp.

It fell away and I saw immediately why he hadn't wanted me to touch his wound. I saw why he might not have wanted to join the missions of the Unanointed.

There was fresh blood oozing from the bite, and it wasn't only red. It shimmered beneath the light of the sun.

God's blood.

39

Mullayne

10 years after the restoration of Kashan
and 571 years after the Shattering

Langzu - Tolemne's Path

Aether is thicker than air, and depending on the part of the world can feel warmer than the ambient temperature. In most places, except in the barrier, it settles into the ground, forming into two distinct layers.

The trek was longer than Mull had expected. He'd estimated the vertical distance between the second aerocline and Unterra, but there was no telling how steep the caverns would be, how much they would wind or even backtrack on their way down. The filter was chafing him. He stopped every so often to reapply grease, though he longed for a clean bed, a washbasin, a breath of air that wasn't polluted by his own stink.

Every time he took new measurements, his face flushed, sweat prickling at his forehead. If his calculations about the density of the aether past the second aerocline were correct, then they were edging closer and closer to the top end of his estimations.

He was the one who'd wanted to continue on, and he was *still* feeling the drain of it all. If this was how *he* was feeling, how were the others? How was Pont?

Pont's broad shoulders nearly spanned the width of the tunnel they walked down, his now considerably lighter pack strapped to his back.

"Should we stop to eat soon?" Mull said. His muffled voice echoed through the tunnel. His hair, which he now regretted not cutting before they'd begun this journey, floated at his cheeks, tickling his skin with every turn of his head.

Pont only grunted. He'd gone from full conversations with Mull since the vote, to scattered sentences, to this. Just grunts and nods, though he mostly avoided him as much as he could.

The rationing probably hadn't helped. They'd tightened it up over the last day, when it had become clear that finding Unterra was going to take longer than they'd first considered. Jeeoon had caught some fish from the underground lake, and they'd cooked pieces of it slowly over the lantern flames, salting the rest of it. It was a pleasant change from the dried and cured rations they'd brought with them, but it had only lifted everyone's mood temporarily.

Down here, in the dark, it was easy to become morose.

"Pont?" Mull tried again, reaching out to touch his shoulder.

Pont shrugged him off, shook his head, and then rubbed the spot Mull had touched, as though it had left an itch. "Never should have agreed to the vote."

"We all agreed to abide by it. Even you."

"I . . . " Pont squeezed his eyes tight, then opened them again, as though trying to clear his vision. "I know I did. But that feels so long ago now. We can't . . . we need to consider turning back."

"We still have enough rations to make it there and back. We can do this." Mull didn't know why, but he was suddenly talking to Pont as though he were coaxing a child. There was something newly fragile about his friend's demeanor.

It was the crushing weight of the stone and the aether, that was all. They were bubbled safely in their filters, but being surrounded for so long by darkness, not seeing the sky . . . He didn't want to save Imeah at the cost of losing Pont.

"Give it one more night." He patted the big man's shoulder again, and again Pont brushed him off and rubbed at the spot.

"Just make sure Imeah is well," he said.

Imeah looked as well as someone in her condition could. Perhaps it was the density of the aether, or she was on a streak of good days, but she barely used her cane down here. She didn't seem well, not exactly, but she seemed stable, and that was more than Mull could hope for at the moment.

Jeeoon called from the front of the column. "Boss, there's another cavern. Big 'un." She lifted her lantern and let out a low whistle. "You should come see this."

Mull and Pont exchanged quick glances – they'd continue this conversation later – and then Mull was slipping past the other members of his expedition, finding his way to the front.

The cavern was indeed large. Jeeoon's lantern light didn't carry far, but the walls of the cave were covered in a softly glowing moss. It limned the edges of her face in blues and greens. At first, Mull thought this was what she'd wanted him to see – the bioluminescent plant life, the beauty of light in a place that should have been perpetually dark.

But that wasn't the sort of thing Jeeoon found beautiful. She seemed pulled to dark and deep places, the harshness of stalagmites, the eerie countenances of ghostly cave scorpions. Bioluminescence just wasn't *her*.

She patted his arm with the back of her hand. "Yeah, yeah, it's pretty. But look at *this*." Her lantern swung toward the wall closest to her.

Another campsite was laid out there, a few discarded items off to the side, the rocks cleared and leveled. Something was carved into the wall in Old Albanoran. Mull lifted his own lantern, stepping quickly to the carvings.

They were on the right track. He checked the rest of the message, reading it silently to himself.

We have come so far already and of the six of us, we have only lost two of our number. If anyone is reading this, know that we made it here. That we have tried so hard.

There is one more barrier before Unterra.

He read the lines over and over, unsure how accurate his translation was, if he was failing to take into account certain connotations or word combinations. One more barrier? What could Tolemne have meant? In all the readings he'd done, the research into Tolemne's Path, there had been only vague descriptions of the tunnels, the repeated claim that the way was dangerous, the first aerocline, then the second.

And then there was Unterra.

The breath turned cold in his lungs. Tolemne had set out with a party of six. Only he himself had made it into Unterra. He'd reached this point with four remaining members.

If their stories held any truth, and he'd petitioned the gods alone, then he'd lost three more between here and his goal.

Mull became aware of Jeeoon beside him, leaning in as though she couldn't help herself. Too close. She swayed toward the wall, her nose nearly touching it, before swerving away, as though suddenly realizing she'd stepped in too far.

Her hand went to her arm in a jerky movement.

She scratched.

Mull felt the bottom of his stomach give way, the sudden sensation of falling. He reached for her shoulder, but he was too late.

With a strangled cry, she darted toward the crew. For a moment, he thought she might run past them. He thought they might have the chance to correct things. But then he caught the flash of a knife by the light of the lanterns, and she was in the thick of them.

She tore off her filter.

He should have noticed. He'd been so preoccupied with Pont, had attributed his foul mood to the length of their travel through the second aerocline. He'd ignored the way Pont had rubbed at his shoulder; he'd ignored the tickling at the back of his own neck. He'd been so *confident* in his own genius.

Someone screamed. Blood spurted.

"Mullayne!" Imeah called out.

Mull had always wondered, in idle moments, what sort of person he'd be in a crisis. During those daydreaming afternoons, sitting at his desk, pen in hand, a breeze from the window ruffling the papers before him, he'd find his thoughts uncoiling and meandering away from his work. He'd imagine terrible moments in great detail, trying to prompt himself to an emotional response. Each time the scenarios would slip away from him as he turned back to his books and his notes; he could never quite pin them down. Would he run away from the danger or would he run toward it?

The cavern tilted around him, his feet seeming to move of their own volition toward Jeeoon. Maybe he would never know, because this was wrong. Jeeoon had never been dangerous; he couldn't think of her that way. This had never been among the terrible things he'd imagined.

He might have even gotten himself killed for his bravery. But then Pont was there, stepping between him and Jeeoon, short curved blade in hand.

She whirled to face him, teeth bared, red with blood that Mull couldn't determine the source of. It wasn't *her* behind those narrowed eyes. He wanted to pull Pont away. There'd been some horrible, terrible *mistake*. He wanted to stop this awful, violent momentum.

He couldn't. He'd frozen up at last.

Jeeoon attacked Pont, slashing the air with cuts meant to maim and kill. He slid away from the blows, flowing around them like water.

It was over in one swift, brutal moment. Pont was standing behind Jeeoon. There was a blade jutting out from just below Jeeoon's ribs. She slashed weakly at the air, her body refusing to believe it had been stopped.

She slid to the ground and Mull rushed to her side.

"Jeeoon." He felt so helpless. There was nothing he could do. He wasn't a doctor; he had only basic field medical training. He just wanted her to know she was not alone.

She stared back at him, her breathing becoming more and more shallow. He could hear the wetness of her lips as she opened her mouth, but she said nothing. After a while, he became aware that her eyes did not blink, that the breath had stopped rising and falling in her chest. He had the vague thought that he should have *noticed* the moment when she'd passed, that there should have been some clear dividing line between life and death.

Someone was sobbing. He looked up to find one of his crew members sprawled on the ground a little ways from where Jeeoon now lay, his throat torn open by Jeeoon's knife. His blade was still sheathed; he'd never had a chance.

Mull was going to be sick.

And then he *was* sick, his face too close to the stony cavern floor as he lifted his filter to spew the contents of his stomach into a small hollow. He had the presence of mind to push it back onto his face, and the sour smell of his breath threatened to send him into another spasm. He swallowed.

A hand was on his shoulder. Imeah. "Mull. Mull." Her voice seemed to be reaching him from a great distance. "*Mullayne.*"

It was like waking from a nightmare that had somehow become true in the middle of the night. He needed to haul himself out of this. He needed to keep moving, to find safety. The cavern was silent. They were all waiting for him, waiting *on* him.

"The filters. They're failing." He wasn't sure why or how. Theoretically, they should have held. The particles of aether were too large to pass through the layers of cloth. Practically, they were not holding, and it was the practical part that mattered.

If they had only begun failing recently, it was fair to assume time played some role. They had, in some way, been worn through.

The eating and drinking. If they'd been lifting their filters to eat and drink, perhaps the aether had begun to cling to the insides, still potent even as time had passed. Perhaps they'd been breathing it in, a little at a time, without knowing it.

He couldn't know for sure, but it was the best explanation. Already he was thinking through modifications he could make, ways he could test the modifications. He pushed the thoughts aside. What mattered was here and now.

He had packed more filters as backups. Hands trembling, he pulled his pack off and rifled through it. "We never had the chance to test them at length past the second aerocline, and not for eating and drinking while using them. If we find another source of water, we can wash them — that *should* clear any aether clinging to the insides. For now, we use the spares."

Seven crew members, including himself. Six extra filters.

The man who'd been sobbing stood up. His black hair was pulled into a slick tail, his wide-set eyes puffy with grief. "This is more than just a setback. You expect us to keep descending? Jeeoon was our caving expert. She's *dead*. So is my friend."

"We're almost there." It sounded desperate, even to himself. "We can each ask a boon of the gods."

"If there are even any *there*. Maybe they all went to the surface a long time ago. Maybe all of them wanted to conquer the mortals."

"Mull." Pont had pulled his sword from Jeeoon's body, its blade still wet with her blood. He held it loosely at his side, as though he wanted more than anything to forget he held it at all. "We've gone far enough."

What was that even supposed to *mean*? How could they have gone far enough when they hadn't accomplished what they'd set out to do?

"I trust him." A woman spoke up from the back. "We honor our dead. We keep going. We all knew this was a risky expedition. No one's done this since Tolemne's time. But we've found his path. We've seen his words. I'm not ready to quit."

Everyone began speaking at once. Pont shouted to be heard, but no one stopped to listen. Mull's world shrank to the vomit on the ground in front of him, to the feel of Imeah's hand on his shoulder.

He knew, with sudden clarity, that he might not be the sort to run toward danger. But he was the sort who would walk steadfastly into it if it meant saving a friend.

Jeeoon was gone. He couldn't change that. But he still had power over Imeah's fate.

"We go on." He spoke quietly, but the noise around him ceased. "We make a cairn for the dead. Quickly. And then we continue on to Unterra." He lifted the filters, proffering them to the others. "By the time we finish building the cairns, breathing clean air will have cleared the effects of the aether. We can switch them so no one is left with a faulty mask for too long."

Pont shook his head, but he accepted one of the backups, took a deep breath and replaced the filter he'd been wearing.

The dead man's friend shook his head. "You're fools. The lot of you." Then he lifted his lantern and stalked back the way they'd come, following the length of string.

Imeah leaned against Mull. She didn't take a fresh filter from him, but she didn't refuse when he pressed one into her hand. Her gaze was still fixed on the end of the tunnel where the man had disappeared into the darkness. "He won't make it, Mull. You have to know he won't make it back. Not alone."

He wanted to argue, though he knew she was right. What was he supposed to do? Run after the man? Beg him to reconsider? Give him one of the filters they so desperately needed?

"He made his choice," he said, and his voice sounded distant even to himself. "So have we."

40

Rasha

10 years after the restoration of Kashan
and 571 years after the Shattering

Kashan – Kluehnn's den

*The gods could perform miracles given aether and time.
Natural philosophers scouring pre-Shattering documents
have categorized these into four types: shifting, making,
changing and augmenting.*

Our breathing echoed off the cave walls, a faint dripping
in the distance. I made my way to Khatuya's side, saw
Naatar next to her. "We act together," I whispered. "We can't
afford to wait or hide."

The others were already moving. I caught a glimpse of
Shambul, his wings twitching as he ducked beneath an outcrop-
ping. No one strode forward with any amount of confidence. A
dzhalobo was formidable; few godkillers would be able to defeat
one on their own.

But someone had to fight it to get the keys off it. If we waited here, we might never get the keys. If we waited, we might die anyways. We were better off chancing the beast. Naatar's trembling shoulder pressed against mine.

The tunnel opened up into a cavern, multiple dark recesses indicating further tunnels.

The neophytes scattered into the darkness. Naatar groped along the wall; we followed behind.

He whispered to me in the darkness. "My family *did* only become devout after restoration, but what Shambul didn't mention was that my father once fought a dzhalobo. It came rampaging through our small village. It was soon after restoration; we were still rebuilding. A godkiller happened to be close by. My father killed it with her help. Without that godkiller, he would have died and the beast would have eaten us. It's one of the reasons my family became devout."

We turned down a tunnel, the soft orange glow of a distant lantern illuminating the entrance. A rattling growl emanated from below. I couldn't tell what direction it was coming from. Everyone froze as we listened to the sound echoing, bouncing from wall to wall. I had no illusions that this place had been built for easy navigation. The den had lanterns aplenty. They'd made these tunnels dark and damp and confusing for a reason. It was all a test. Every loose rock and cold drip from above was part of it.

Every turn we took led us deeper into the maze. Naatar seemed to be picking tunnels at random, but neither Khatuya nor I protested. I had no idea where we were or even how we would find our way out again.

"They kill large digging animals and take over their burrows. This place might seem like a burrow to them," Naatar said.

Khatuya sniffed the air. "We're going down."

"As deep as we can."

I tapped the blade at my side. "We'll find the dzhalobo at the bottom?"

Naatar gestured as we walked. "They'll want this trial to be as hard for us as possible. My bet is that the beast has whelped. It makes them more aggressive."

"But it also makes them more vulnerable," I said, understanding. I remembered the solitary one Sheuan and I had encountered on the road. I'd seen a group of them before, thankfully from a distance. A mother and her pups.

Khatuya pursed her lips. "Do they care for their young?"

"They do. If we can find the deepest part of these caves, we can find the place where she's made her nest. We find her offspring, we find her vulnerability."

Naatar turned down another tunnel. I heard the soft gasp before I caught the flash of steel, embedded in his side, piercing the leather armor and the brown scales beneath.

"Good to know that." Shambul's gaze fixed on me. "Hello, bait." He pulled his blade free.

In the next moment, Khatuya and I were standing between him and Naatar, our knives drawn.

"Leave him," Khatuya said. She wasn't afraid of Shambul. She should have been. "If you value your life, you leave."

Another growl echoed through the tunnels.

Shambul eyed us, his face smug. "If you take a key, the rest of the neophytes will come after you. I'm doing you a favor by cutting loose the weakest member of your team." He faded back into the darkness.

I dropped to Naatar's side, pressing a hand against his wound. Blood coated my fingers, slippery and warm. He grunted, teeth clenched in pain. "Should have been paying more attention. He's right. As soon as one of us gets a key, the rest will attack. This isn't just about fighting the dzhalobo. This is about fighting one another."

Again. It always seemed to come down to that. The treacherous part of my mind, the part that sounded suspiciously like Sheuan, wondered how Kluehnn could care about us and still set us against one another. I pushed the thought away. It wasn't my place to question. He was doing this to make us stronger, to see which of us was capable of rising to the top. Should he instead send us out to kill gods completely unprepared?

Khatuya tore her sleeve from her arm, using it to bind Naatar's wound.

We were wasting time. I knew it – both of them must have known it too. The longer we lingered over Naatar, the longer we stayed here, the more likely we'd lose our chance at the keys. What was my problem right now? That was what Sheuan had said. My problem was that Khatuya and I couldn't defeat the dzhalobo alone, but Naatar would slow us down.

"We have to leave him."

Khatuya shook her head.

I took Naatar's arm. "You go back to the door. You wait there for us. If we can get you a key for you, we will. If we can't, then waiting there is the best chance you have of avoiding getting caught by the dzhalobo or another neophyte. You'll still make it out alive."

"But not as a godkiller." His voice was thick with bitterness. I would have felt the same way. To survive that first trial only to be relegated to outreach or administrative work. Most neophytes would rather die trying. And they did.

I stood, glancing up and down the tunnel, knowing there were other neophytes probably close by. "We don't have good options here. We only have ones that are not as bad as others, and that's the truth of it. Khatuya, you're with me."

She hesitated.

"Unless you want to stay with him?" The edges of my voice

were sharp. I could feel myself shifting, changing into someone I didn't know. The person Kluehnn believed me to be.

Necessity. This was about necessity.

She rose to her feet and came with me. We left Naatar groaning on the cave floor. His wound wasn't fatal; we'd stopped the bleeding. He had a good chance of making it back to the entrance.

The tunnels seemed to close in around us. My horns scraped the ceiling as we ventured forward, always trying to find the path that led downward. And all the while, the growling became louder.

Left, right, middle, left. I tried to keep track of the turns we were taking, tried to memorize the texture of the walls. I glanced back and saw Khatuya doing the same, her cracked lips moving silently.

Lantern light shone from a crack ahead of us. The growl seemed to emanate from beyond; a dark shape briefly blocked the light. Khatuya's hand gripped my shoulder. For a moment, I thought she might have done so out of fear, but then I realized she'd seen something I had not.

It wasn't a crack ahead of us, but another of the neophytes, blocking the entrance into the dzhalobo's burrow.

My hand tightened around my knife. I lifted a finger to warn Khatuya to stay where she was. The two of us together might create too much noise. Whoever it was, they were focused on the beast. So I crept forward.

The beast growled again. I used the noise as cover, darting forward, seizing the hair on the back of the neophyte's head and putting my knife to their throat.

It was another horned altered, like me. Gamgai – that was his name. He had an inordinately square jaw, a flat nose, a heavy brow. While I was tall and long-limbed, he was short, built like an iron teapot. I watched his expression in the dim light. He didn't shout. He had that much of a survival instinct. We were too close to the dzhalobo. But he licked his lips, his mouth trembling.

I leaned toward his ear. "I'm not here to kill you. I'm going to let you go, and when I do, you tell me everything you've observed."

He gave a short, quick nod. I released him.

He licked his lips again, his gaze going back to the narrow opening before us. "There is more than one way into its den. I think there are other neophytes in other tunnels, waiting to attack. Someone already tried."

I peered past him into the cave.

A hulking shape crouched in the middle of the space, all gray and shaggy, her too-long legs folded beneath her. Her strangely human-like face searched the tunnels and then her nostrils flared and she growled again, lips pulling back from sharp white teeth. The familiar fear struck me, that feeling of being in the presence of a thing that would not just kill me, but *consume* me. There was already a body at the dzhalobo's feet, a tangled mess of bloody limbs, the face chewed beyond recognition.

I tried to focus instead on the chain around the creature's neck, the three keys dangling just out of reach. In the nest of soft, downy fur beneath her, a few small shapes wriggled.

The heavy muscles of her shoulders tensed and relaxed as she gazed at the openings into her lair and sniffed the air. Shambul was in one of those tunnels, I knew it. He wouldn't attack the dzhalobo; it wasn't his way. He'd wait for someone else to do the work, and then he'd try to take the keys. He'd sparred with all of us. He knew our weaknesses, knew how to best us.

At least he did one on one.

A plan formed in my mind.

I put a hand on Gamgai's shoulder. "Truce? Khatuya and I are working together. If you join us, there will be three of us."

I caught a glimpse of Khatuya's face from the corner of my eye, and even in that quick look I could see the shock, the disgust. What did she think of me now? I'd stopped Shambul from bullying her and Naatar, only to turn on Naatar when it seemed to suit me. But I knew she didn't have a choice at this point. She'd followed me far enough; she'd follow me to the end.

Gamgai nodded. "Should we try to take down the beast ourselves?"

As soon as it appeared we had an advantage over the dzhalobo, the others would rush us. We would be like a flock of birds fighting over the tossed scraps of someone's meal. "No. We have to play this carefully." I explained what I had in mind and watched both Khatuya and Gamgai's faces go grim.

"It's not a great plan," Khatuya whispered into the dark, her voice tart. I was starting to understand that she *was* afraid; anger was just how she made herself feel less so.

"It's not," I admitted. "But it's the only one that has a chance of working. Unless you want to kill the beast and then fight Shambul and every other neophyte afterward?"

Both she and Gamgai shook their heads.

"Then we do it this way, and we hope for the best."

All three of us lifted our weapons, and I slipped to the side to allow Gamgai and Khatuya to pass me.

They entered the cavern with the beast.

All her hackles rose, claws extending from her massive paws, her teeth bared. A thread of saliva dripped into the nest she hunched over. One of the pups within made a soft squeaking noise. Neither Khatuya nor Gamgai even glanced at it; their focus was on the dzhalobo.

Khatuya stopped short in front of her, while Gamgai circled to the right. As he moved to its flank, she darted in with her knife.

She didn't have the same indolent grace as Shambul did. She

didn't flow around the dzhalobo's attacks, ducking out of the way with barely a hair out of place. Her fighting style was fiercer, frenetic. Her knife moved in barely seen flashes. I couldn't tell when she'd made contact and when she hadn't.

But I did see the single red drop fall from the dzhalobo's face.

She'd drawn first blood. The beast might not have noticed, but I was watching when Khatuya took a deliberate step back.

I held my breath.

Another low growl filled the air, the sound seeming to reverberate in my bones. A clawed foot moved forward as the creature followed her, leaving part of its nest exposed. I wanted to run. I wanted to run blindly all the way to the door we'd entered through, to pound on it until my fists were raw. Instead, I stepped into the cavern.

Immediately I felt exposed, the leather armor I wore as useless as see-through rags. Every brush of air against my skin was a reminder of how many vulnerable places I had. Gamgai circled, moving toward the space the dzhalobo had left between herself and the wall. He was smaller than I was, I'd explained. This role suited him best.

I didn't envy him. But then I didn't envy myself.

The three keys around the creature's neck clinked together as it took yet another step toward Khatuya. Its claws had marked her leg, leaving blood running in rivulets into her boots. I hadn't even seen it attack.

I had to keep my focus on my goal, on the squirming shapes huddled in the fur on the cave floor.

We had to time this correctly.

The dzhalobo moved another step forward and Gamgai wedged himself between the creature and the wall. He glanced at me. I gave a quick, short shake of my head.

Not yet. As soon as the beast turned, she would know what we were up to. Dzhalobos were not stupid. We had to let Khatuya take the brunt of her attack, for just a little longer.

She caught my eye as she took another limping step back. The weight of her pain and fury hit me like the heat from an open oven. She thought I was going to sacrifice her – just like Naatar.

She was going to run.

All well-laid plans fall to pieces in the end. Seeing them through is only a matter of seeing how well one can hold together those pieces, to keep too many from scattering into dust.

"Now!"

Gamgai surged forward, his blade leading the way. He pushed the creature clear of the nest. The dzhalobo whipped about, snapping at him. Khatuya, who had taken a few steps toward the tunnel, swayed back. Together, they attacked, forcing the beast to field them both at once. If I hadn't known any better, I wouldn't have noticed that Khatuya had tried to run at all.

But I had my own task to complete.

I plunged my hands into the warm gray mound, my heartbeat pounding in my ears. The velvet-soft feel of new fur met my fingertips. I seized both pups and pulled them to my chest.

Khatuya and Gamgai were already moving toward the tunnel we'd entered through. The timing was all off. They'd be through it before I could get there. I had to run. I had to be quick.

Shambul stepped from another of the tunnels, his sword lifted. He stretched his wings, blocking my path. We hadn't executed this correctly, and he had seen his chance. I had one pup in each arm and an angry mother who would soon find out someone had stolen her young.

She would come after me. She would kill me. And while she was trying to recover her pups, Shambul could kill *her*. He didn't fear the other neophytes coming after him. Everyone knew how good he was in a fight. Everyone would be wary of him, and there'd be two keys left to scrap over. He could stroll right back up the tunnels to the door, unmolested.

He wanted to make me pay for the injury I'd given him in our fight. He was still slightly favoring that wing. I would have taken a grim satisfaction from that if I'd been in any position to do so.

"Bait," he mouthed at me, his lip curling in a smirk.

The dzhalobo sniffed the air. She whirled from her pursuit of Gamgai and Khatuya, tail lashing, her growl like boulders cracking against one another. We watched as she stalked toward us.

"Shambul." The fool actually looked at me instead of the beast. All the fighting prowess in the world and not two intelligent thoughts to rub together.

I tossed him one of the pups. He caught it in his free hand, with that same measured grace. He moved instinctively, reactions trained into his limbs, bypassing his mind.

The pup yelped.

I was moving even before the dzhalobo attacked. She seized Shambul's wing between her teeth. He brought up his sword, too slowly. She was already shaking him, jaw clenched, blood spattering the cave floor. Something crunched as I squeezed past. He screamed.

I didn't care. I was into the tunnel, Khatuya and Gamgai just ahead of me. We ran together, up, up.

As soon as she was done with Shambul, the dzhalobo would come for me. The soft shape in the crook of my arm guaranteed that. And she knew these tunnels better than we did. She might have trouble with some of the tighter spaces, but we had her pup. She'd scrape past even if she had to leave skin behind.

None of us spoke. I only once let out a breathy "No. The left one." Only a brief hesitation before Khatuya decided I was right.

Behind us I could hear raspy growls. They sounded as though they were getting closer. My breath ached in my throat. The tunnels seemed to tilt around me, my head fuzzy and floating somewhere above my body.

We weren't going to make it. We'd taken a wrong turn somewhere.

And then the tunnel opened into the cavern near the entrance. Relief flooded through my veins. We'd broken the plan and somehow it had still come together in the end.

But it wasn't over. Not yet.

I pivoted as soon as we reached the tunnel leading to the heavy iron door. "Here. We make our stand here."

The three of us faced the cavern and waited for the dzhalobo to arrive.

41

Nioanen

5 years after the Shattering

Albanore - a small house on the mountain above the city of Billoste

Ayaz the Cutter kept to himself even more than Nioanen did. While Nioanen was known for making things more than they were, Ayaz bettered things by removing — cutting away weakness and impurities.

But cutting was seldom without pain.

Irael was late. Nioanen tried not to let the delay bother him; she had been late coming home before. It was in the shifter god's nature to be fickle, to happen upon interesting things and then forget the thing that had brought her there. Her movements were as fluid as thought, flitting along loosely interconnected paths before finally idling back to their origin.

Ever since the Shattering, his anxiety had increased. Kluehnn had devised a way to send the aether churning up from the ground, breaking the surface into a hundred different realms. Nioanen remembered the shake of the earth beneath his feet, the screams of terrified mortals, the feeling that everything was ending. The world had changed, its people split and isolated from one another. The gods could pass through these barriers with little issue, but doing so with such ease raised questions. He stirred the pot for the thousandth time; it did not need stirring. The laundry was done, the garden tended to. He'd checked the traps, the roof, the buried stash of glowing gems. He had nothing left to do but wait.

"You must be careful," he was always telling her. "You must remember what we are."

"How can I forget?" she would say tartly. "You remind me every chance you get. Maybe I'd *like* to forget, have you thought of that?"

He would fall into a still, sort of clumsy silence, and then she would sigh, rub her temples and drop a kiss on his shoulder, or his wing, or whatever spot of him was close and available. "We've built something here."

"It's fragile."

"I *know*."

The hinges of the door creaked, a squeak that would respond to just a little bit of greasing. He had the brief thought that *this* was something he could have taken care of while he'd been waiting, but then Irael was strolling through the door, a basket under one arm. She'd not left with a basket.

She looked like a mortal in this form. Red curly hair tied into a knot at the base of her neck, a few loose tendrils at her cheeks. Sweat beaded on her forehead; freckles spattered across her crooked nose and cheeks in the whorling pattern of a piece of knotted wood. She was round, and stout, and beautiful – an oak tree with foliage bright as fire.

She put a hand to her hip. "Well, I'm back, so you can quit worrying."

He went to her, cupping her face, her shoulders, the swell of her belly. "Who said I was worrying?"

"The polish on the silverware says you were. I think it's blinding me from here." She let him pull her into his arms, a pleasant crinkling at the corners of her eyes as she smiled.

He leaned down to kiss her. The basket mewed.

He halted, his lips still puckered. He'd forgotten about the basket.

Irael pulled away. "He was alone, Nioanen. His mother had abandoned him. I couldn't very well leave him there."

His wings twitched. "A cat."

"A *kitten*."

"We have enough mouths to feed, and soon we'll have another."

Irael sighed, shrugging her shoulders as though casting off a cloak. "I miss being able to shift at will. You don't know what it's like. I feel ... wrong and I'm stuck like this until the baby comes. This is a distraction. A cute one. It helps." She set the basket on the table, dipped a hand in and pulled out a mewling brown tabby beast. Its paws waved in the air and she cradled it in her arms, kissing its head.

He could hear it purring even above the crackling fire.

"You're frowning." Irael gave him a mocking pout. "Is it the delay, or the pet?"

"Both. What happens when Kluehnn or his godkillers come for us? He's restored his first realm. His plan is in action but he still fears us. We can't build a home here, Irael."

"So our child will never have a home?"

It had the cadence of an old argument. He *wanted* to build a home here. Irael knew that. But they had to be able to pick up and leave at a moment's notice. They could never truly get comfortable. They couldn't afford to start adding things they would hesitate to leave behind.

She set the kitten on the table – *that* was something he'd have to set rules against going forward – and then leaned over it. The kitten rubbed along her wrist but she didn't move to pet it.

Something was wrong. "What have you heard about the rest of our brethren?"

"Another dead. Ophanganus."

Not a surprise. He'd had the long face and horns of an antelope; they'd all done their best to send support along their fractured chain, but he couldn't blend in the way many of them could. It didn't help that he'd gone about indiscriminately murdering mortals despite the protests of the others. Ophanganus painted them all with one brush. They'd destroyed the world, he'd always said. With his anger focused outward, he'd never stopped to think about his own role in matters, the way the gods had let it all happen. He had permitted the roots of his soul to spread into bitter soil, doomed to eventually wither. "Any others?"

"No. Rith and Chaunette had a second child."

"Is that wise?"

"No, but then neither is what we're doing."

They looked at one another, and he could see the thoughts passing through her mind the way they passed through his. The same thoughts. The same worries and hopes and dreams. The kitten mewed again.

"This child will be born on the surface," she said. "They will never know their true home. They will never swim in the Agonian Sea. They will never bask in the light of the inner star. They will never run through fields of tintean or pluck darkshine berries from the deep caverns. If I am trying to build a home here, it is only because I want our children to have what we had. It's not fair that we have so much less to give them. I've thought often of what we've lost and I've grieved that. But I haven't finished grieving what our *children* have lost. They will grow up in a world that is told to hate them, and they won't ever understand why."

Irael was the fighter; Nioanen was the one who always teetered on the edge of giving up. But he could be the one who fought. For her, he could. "Kluehnn has altered the mortals with restoration. They look more like us now, and as the number of altered grow, it'll be easier for us to hide. It's a chance. We'll take back our home someday. We'll take it back for our children, or our children's children. If Kluehnn still fears us, there's a reason. We just have to find out what it is."

She reached out to pet the kitten. It wound between her forearms, rising to nudge her chin. She let out a soft huff of a laugh. "You're right. But until then, I want to make this our home. I want to try."

He went to her and kissed the top of her head. "Fine. The kitten stays."

"Muffincheeks stays."

"Oh dear." He marveled at the touch of her cheek to his chest as she leaned into him. "Someone should have stopped us from having a child. Who knows what we'll name them?"

"I have a name."

"Oh?"

"We don't have to use it."

"You're carrying the child; I think you have the right to name them. Just not Muffincheeks. Promise me."

She laughed. He loved the way her laugh took over all of her, in any form. Her shoulders shook. When she could take a breath again, she looked up at him. "Thassir. I'd like to name them Thassir."

Nioanen tightened his arms around her. "I think that's a perfectly acceptable name."

She took his hand, placed it on her belly. "Feel that?"

Something moved beneath his palm — some indistinguishable limb.

"I think the child will have wings."

42

Hakara

10 years after the restoration of Kashan
and 571 years after the Shattering

Langzu - the farmland surrounding Bian

*In the tales, Ayaz and Barexi once quarreled. In the middle
of the night, Ayaz went to Barexi's bed and cut him to a
thousand pieces. He scattered the pieces across Unterra and
into the mortal world.*

*The stories say Velenor took pity on the Stag, that she
put his arms back together, and from there the arms crept
across the world, finding each of his bloody parts. Except
for one. A whale swallowed Barexi's smallest finger and
became a behemoth.*

*When you see Barexi painted, he is always missing the
last finger of his left hand.*

I stared at the shimmering blood on Thassir's wing, wondering
why I hadn't considered it before. He *looked* like one of the
altered. Sure, he was big. Sure, he was powerful. But even the

god I'd seen on the pike with his guts spilled out over the ground
had an *aura* about him.

Thassir didn't have an aura so much as a storm cloud.

All I could think was *You lied to me* and *You're a god*. "You lied
to a god" was what ended up coming out of my mouth.

His face screwed up in confusion.

And I couldn't help it. I laughed. It sounded hysterical. Maybe
it *was* hysterical. I hadn't just dragged a big, powerful altered into
this mess. I'd bonded myself to a god.

I was losing it. No, I'd lost it a long time ago.

"Mitoran has partnered with *a god*? Does anyone else know?
There are so many people who'd like to kill you right now. Or
to at least collect a nice bounty."

His wing twitched away, his teeth bared. "Don't you think I
know it? Do you know how long I've avoided godkillers? Only
to have you force me to face them. Only to have you force me to
face Kluehnn."

"I didn't force anyone to do anything. I persuaded."

He gave me a hard look.

"I *strongly* persuaded."

With an annoyed huff of breath, he turned away from me and
began walking from the copse of trees. As though that would
accomplish anything. But he wasn't flying off without me, and I
supposed I should consider that in his favor.

He must have heard me following him, because he spoke
without turning around. "I didn't lie to you. You never asked."

"What, I'm supposed to randomly go about asking people if
they're gods? Let me at least look at your wing."

"I'd prefer that you didn't."

"I know you're upset, but you're hurt. Even gods can be hurt."

He stopped. "You think I want this? I didn't want to be bound
to you, and this – this is *worse*. I can break our bond but I cannot

break this knowledge out of you. It's there until you die, and as long as you have that knowledge, you can turn me in to the godkillers."

I climbed over a fallen log he'd merely stepped over. "But you killed Kluehnn."

Now it was his turn for hysterical laughter. "You think that was Kluehnn? You think I could just kill him, simple as that?"

"But if you're a god, then shouldn't you be able to . . . "

He sighed, as though he were having to explain to a child that money was not something he was just given by bankers any time he asked. "Kluehnn is not one being anymore. He has split himself into many aspects, and those aspects are in every single realm. I killed only one of his aspects. It's like thinking you destroyed a colony of ants by stepping on a few workers."

He'd stopped walking at least, though he seemed unaware he'd done so.

"Can't blame me for thinking so. I'm just a tiny little mortal, aren't I?"

His glare could have shattered glass. "So you keep telling me. But you're not. You're a thorn. You're the spine of a cactus driven deep, where you cannot be dislodged, but where you cause pain with the slightest jolt."

I put a hand over my heart. "I've moved you to poetry. A god."

His eyes narrowed. His wings spread. "Are you not afraid of me?"

Some primal fear tingled along my spine, waiting for claws or teeth to sink into my skin. I swallowed it down. "Can I tend to your wing?"

His teeth clenched, he stalked toward me. I almost backed down. I almost did, but then he sat on the log and spread the injured wing in my direction. The bandage was askew, the shimmering blood lending an odd shine to the black feathers.

He had no aura, no brightness to the air around him. I wasn't sure why.

I pursed my lips and got to work.

Altani and I had often cleaned one another's wounds after particularly dangerous dives. She'd have rope burns on her hands, or I'd have suffered scrapes I couldn't remember earning. Those sessions had many times devolved as hands wandered, as lips pressed to scratches and caused quickened breathing.

Not where my thoughts should be going at the moment.

I matter-of-factly cleaned the wound with water, doing my best to not look at his face. Were my cheeks burning or was it just the heat of the rising sun? I was not the sort to *blush*.

I had no clean cloth, so I blew on his wing to dry it. His feathers ruffled. A sharp intake of breath. A stillness I couldn't quite describe. I caught a glimpse of goosebumps on his shoulder. I imagined reaching out, tracing the path of that prickled flesh, following my fingers with my lips.

I swallowed, the sound loud in my ears.

"By all rights that wound should be sewn shut." I kept my voice brusque as I wrapped the bandage around the injury, tucking it between feathers so it wouldn't be in the way.

He pulled away as though offended. "I'm a god. It will heal quickly."

I leaned back, using the opportunity to put some distance between us.

"We need to return to Mitoran, and quickly." Thassir beckoned for me to approach. So much for distance. I'd forgotten he was my means of transportation.

"Are we not going to discuss the fact that you're a god?" But I went to him again and wrapped my arms around his neck. "Who else knows?"

"Mitoran. And that is all. I'd like to keep it that way."

"Just don't piss me off."

He didn't laugh. I could *hear* his teeth grinding. But then he was in the air again, flying as though he hadn't been injured at all.

We made it to the edge of Ruzhi before dark. The safe house there was in the basement of an old restaurant, the space widening into a maze of catacombs. Dashu had explained that the Unanointed had painstakingly excavated some of the ruins — a long process of digging and carting dirt out into the wilds. Flaking paintings of a landscape that seemed foreign graced the walls. Metallic contraptions that carried people through the air, machines that turned mud and garbage into elaborate meals, buildings that soared into a sky with only a trace of yellow haze. And in the distance, an enormous tree that dwarfed the surrounding forest, a glow seeming to emanate from within it. Our ancestors had truly fucked us all, hadn't they? Pre-Shattering ruins at least provided a convenient hiding spot. So good job on that, ancestors, I supposed.

Mitoran was there to meet us. "Well?"

No worry over our sorry state, over the fact that only Thassir and I had returned. She was all business.

"Well what?" I snapped back. "Well here's some food and a warm bath? Well where did everyone else go? I'll tell you where they went. They're all dead."

She was still for a moment. "All of them?"

I finally relented, though I was pissed off enough to wish I could have left her thinking we'd lost the corestone forever. "Gamone, Keka, Dashu and Alifra are on their way back with it. They should be here soon. The others are dead. Thanks for asking."

Her mouth pressed into a thin line. She didn't like being spoken to this way.

I couldn't bring myself to care. "That's two corestones. Now tell me what you know about my sister."

She sighed. "Nothing yet. But likely soon. These things take time."

I was already moving past her, trying to find some place to escape to, some place where I could hole away.

"We found the location of a third corestone."

I stopped in my tracks.

"My informant pried the information out of one of Kluehnn's acolytes. It's deep in the heart of one of the dens. This den is also one of the final destinations of god gems. We take the corestone. We take the gems. We fix some of the land here and we stop restoration from occurring."

This wasn't an Otangu clan orchard. This was . . . *a death wish.*

I didn't turn to face her; I strode away. I didn't know what to say, how to process this. The underground cavern had several rooms and I stepped into the first one that appeared unoccupied, shutting the door behind me.

It wasn't enough. I shoved the little table at the bedside, wedging myself between it and the bed, sinking until my butt hit the floor. I buried my head in my hands. I could wait. There had to be another corestone. This was too soon; I wasn't ready. We'd lost half an entire team in the orchard. We'd almost lost more of us.

All reasonable objections. But I felt the pull of it, the need. Rasha's face pressed close to mine as we told one another stories beneath the blankets of our tent until we fell asleep. I missed Mimi and I even missed Maman. But missing was not a word I could use to describe Rasha's absence. It was a sinkhole in the midst of my life, always threatening to swallow up the rest of it.

The door creaked open. "Hakara?" Thassir's voice, uncharacteristically hesitant.

Of course. He'd always know where I was.

He stepped into the dark, enclosed space. I heard the door shut behind him.

"I'm going." I said it before he could attempt to dissuade me.

His feet scuffed against the floor as he approached. "Counterpoint." His voice was soft. "Don't go."

I wove my fingers into my hair. It was greasy. I couldn't think how long it had been since I'd washed it. "Thassir—"

He talked over me, as though he were afraid that if he didn't speak now, he would never be able to. "It's dangerous. Wait for another opportunity. Mitoran can't make you go. Better yet, find another way into Kashan. You don't need to be involved with the Unanointed."

"What? Would *you* take me?"

His feathers ruffled, his expression suddenly uncomfortable. "I . . . It's not safe for me to do so."

"And it's safe for you *here*?" I threw up my hands in frustration. I'd spent ten years trying other ways. If I'd had legal status in Langzu, perhaps I could have found another route to Kashan, but even my false papers had been taken from me before I'd had the chance to really use them. I'd never had the opportunity to exist in Langzu on my own terms. Maybe if things had gone differently, what Thassir was saying would have made sense. But I thought of another unbearable ten years. "I can't wait any longer. I have to go."

I watched his feet appear in front of me, the black tips of his wings nearly brushing the floor. "You are pinning everything you have, everything you *are*, on *hope*. Have you ever considered that Mitoran is lying to you? You think someone with your talents just wanders around Langzu every day? She would tell you anything to get your help. She knows what you want to believe and she is taking advantage of that."

My fingers curled around my shins, nails digging into my flesh. My ears rang. "Are you sure?"

He sighed. "I cannot know for sure, but don't be naïve.

Mitoran has always held her own goals as paramount. You think she cares about you finding your sister? Or does she care about infusing the corestones?"

If Mitoran was lying about sending people to find Rasha, if she was lying about her resources, then I had nothing. I was back where I'd started – only now I was involved with the Unanointed and wanted for so much more than just my abilities and my illegal status. I couldn't let that be true. "It's the only hope I have. I have to *try*."

I felt the slight change in our bond as he shifted back, a low tension in the magic that tied us together. "You *always* run headlong into everything, refusing to believe that sometimes you do not have control. Rasha is lost to you, but it was not your fault. The supervisor took you. You were young. You cannot seem to admit that you had no power in that situation. Sometimes we just don't have that sort of control. Not even over our own lives."

And then he was moving for the door, a dark, angry cloud of black feathers.

"It didn't happen the way I said it did." Something within me had broken open and was bleeding soft words. Thassir halted.

It was a truth I'd only ever allowed to exist in the early-morning hours, when I was alone and awake, staring into a darkness that gave me no indication of time and place. But I'd always – *always* – pushed it away again because it was a truth I didn't know how to live with. My voice didn't feel like my own. Why was I telling him this? I'd never spoken it aloud, yet the words felt pulled from me. I wanted him to know – to know how ugly I really was. "It *was* my fault. Guarin didn't knock me out. I passed out from holding my breath, from trying to prove to him I could be part of his crew. And he took me with him. When I woke up, we were inside the barrier. It was dark inside, dust and debris swirling, the wind howling like an animal. I could have gone back. I could have tried to go back to Rasha. But I didn't."

There was nothing else to say. I fell into the hollow the words had left, diving into the black.

Thassir should have left – and maybe that was why I'd told him, so he wouldn't just angrily storm off but would leave for good. He had helped me, but in the end, this was my problem to fix. And he was right: I'd killed enough people with my recklessness.

A hand touched my knee. He was there, kneeling in front of me, his bright, dark eyes trying to find mine through the curtain of my hair. His fingers were warm, the heat of them leaching through the cloth. "Hakara." He'd never spoken my name so gently.

I lifted my head, letting my hands fall back down. My fingers grazed the back of his hand. I had the brief impression of soft skin before his gaze trapped mine.

"You were only a child. You were alone. You were scared."

How strange, to have someone forgive me when I could never forgive myself. It was easy, perhaps, for him to say, when he'd not abandoned the person who'd relied on him for everything. When he'd not left behind the person to whom he'd been both a parent and a sister.

His hand gave my knee a gentle squeeze; his wings hovered above us, blocking the harshest of the lantern light. A gleam still cut through to his eyes, reflecting a flame in their depths. I watched it, fascinated, unable to look away, to feel anything but the warmth of his skin. "You put too high expectations on yourself." His voice caught on the last word, as though there were something he'd meant to add after but had stopped.

My mouth felt dry. "Why shouldn't I have high expectations of myself if not meeting them means losing the only person I give a damn about?"

His eyelids fluttered. It was like watching someone in the moment they were hit by a poisoned dart. A slight flinch, the slow realization of pain.

Some part of me wanted to take it back. I brushed my fingertips against the cold floor and wished it was his hand again. But to what purpose? We were bonded, but Utricht and I had been bonded too. I hadn't wanted Utricht to die; I didn't want Thassir to die. Did that mean I cared about him? Perhaps I did, in whatever way I was capable of. But I had to keep my focus on what mattered, always.

Had he drifted closer, or was I so caught in the raven-black of his eyes that it only felt that way?

"You have to acknowledge the truth," he was saying. His lips barely moved. "Your sister was very young when restoration hit Kashan. In all likelihood, one way or another, she is dead. And Hakara – it is not your fault."

I waited for the rush of anger at his words. She *was not* dead. Anyone who supposed so was wrong, was only trying to hurt me in the only way they knew how. There was no other way to hurt me; nothing else could bring me down. But he hadn't said it to hurt me.

And for the first time in my life, I had no angry rejoinder, no swinging fists. The knee where Thassir's hand lay was the only warm part of me.

I pushed him away, my lips numb, scrambling to my feet. Clenching my teeth, biting back the shivers that threatened to overtake me. I tried to find that heated spark within me.

There were only ashes.

My hand fumbled at my belt. I didn't know how I got my knife free without cutting myself. I think I would have cried if I'd had any tears left in me. If I'd not wept them all when I'd awoken on the Langzuan side of the barrier.

I nicked my palm, held it and the knife out to Thassir. "Break the bond."

He took the knife wordlessly.

"Do it."

He cut his own palm, held it out. I pressed my cut to his. Some swell of emotion swirled in my belly as our hands met. The warmth of his fingers enveloped mine, his claws only lightly touching.

I put my other hand atop our clasped ones; I couldn't seem to stop myself. I watched the breath in his throat catch. All I had to do was take one step toward him. I knew that would break down whatever wall I was building between us. I could see us falling into one another in ways both familiar and strange, the warmth of his skin against mine, the softness of his feathers beneath my touch.

But the aether shimmered around our hands, and I felt the magic take hold. The bond dissolved, a cube of sugar lowered into a warm bath. A soft, sweet taste at the back of my tongue, and then it was gone.

I swept from the room. Mitoran saw me hurrying toward the stairs to the main floor. She rushed to stop me. "Hakara—"

"I'm out. Find the last corestone yourself."

I climbed the steps two at a time, and it seemed I must have had some reserve of tears after all, because something warm wet my cheeks.

I fled into the streets of Ruzhi, the afternoon sun too bright, too hot. And as I hurried away, my hands buried in my pockets, I could not tell how far I was leaving Thassir behind.

43

Sheuan

10 years after the restoration of Kashan
and 571 years after the Shattering

Langzu - inner Bian

Kluehnn created his own armies to fight against the gods from below. He protected the people of the surface world, driving back the old gods with peerless fury. He diminished their numbers.

Yet there are still gods who would see his reign overthrown, who would seek to overrun every single realm above.

Mortals must remain vigilant.

If she didn't think much about the pinfeather she'd pulled from her back, well, Sheuan had other things to occupy her. She'd fled from Mull's workshop to her family home, holing up in her room with the prototype filters, the tile floor cool beneath her folded legs. She leaned her head back against the bed, trying to clear her thoughts.

Every path she could see was dark, obscured by fog. She'd broken Mull's trust. She'd brought the filters into the light, had used them for her own ends, had even paraded them in front of the Sovereign. And this was the least of her worries. Theoretically, *theoretically*, they'd protect someone from restoration. A person could smell the desperation on the streets these days. Animals starved in alleyways as the people of the city hoarded what little food they had left. The cities of Langzu had become a study in contrasts – castles rising above the populace in gilded tiles and carved stone while the dead bodies of the less fortunate were hauled into the dry lakebed to burn. Even the highest-ranking clans must have seen the smoke growing thicker by the day.

Mitoran had never tried to proselytize to Sheuan; they had too much respect for one another for that. And Sheuan couldn't understand the Unanointed's goals. Even if they managed to somehow change the Langzuan landscape, nothing they did short of restoration itself would change things fast enough to save everyone.

Either way, people would disappear. People would die.

Holding the filters felt like holding cards she could add to the deck at will. Mull really *was* going to kill her when he got back. If he got back. If he wasn't dead already.

She only had two ways to uphold her bargain with the Sovereign. She could hand over the secret of the filters, affirm they could protect against restoration. Or she could lie, say that they would not protect against restoration. And they might not – she couldn't be sure without a test.

Her door creaked open.

She knew it was her mother before she even looked – only her mother would enter without knocking. Quickly, she stuffed the filters back into the bottom of her satchel. Somehow she knew her mother would demand they hand over Mull's secrets to the Sovereign, and this was Sheuan's decision to make.

"You've been hiding." Her mother's mouth was pinched at the corners, the circles beneath her eyes a shade darker than Sheuan remembered. "It's been days, and I've given you your space. What did he say?"

Sheuan focused on a loose thread on her bedspread – the golden end of a pheasant's tail. It had been a long time since Langzu had seen this kind of pheasant. There wasn't a lot of preparation she had to do before lying – because it never was completely a lie. It was only a version of the truth some version of herself would have told. The words came to her easily as soon as she had the right mindset, and she could slip in and out of those as easily as she changed a pair of socks. "He said the information I brought back was not enough. It was speculation, he said. Conjecture. No hard evidence."

Her mother let out a huff of breath and sat at the end of the bed. For a moment, Sheuan thought she might reach out and stroke the top of her head. She could nearly feel the touch of her hand there, like a memory of a moment that had only just passed.

But instead she sat ramrod straight, her gaze on the wall, the look behind her eyes calculating. "You have to go back. You have to go back to Kashan and look for more evidence. You're close, Sheuan."

It shouldn't have unbalanced her at all. She'd expected this. Yet hearing the words sent her stomach off a cliff, crumbling into the sea. She'd only just returned from Kashan. It was a miracle she'd made it there and back at all. "You don't even know how I got there."

Her mother looked at her then, shrewd eyes studying Sheuan's face. Her voice was quiet, precise. "If I asked, would you tell me?"

She should have wanted to. She should have wanted to confess everything that had happened to her. They'd been that close, once. But time and obligation had formed wedges between them. Sheuan didn't answer.

"The fact is that you got there, and you came back unscathed. You can do it again."

Now Sheuan thought about the pinfeather she'd pulled from her back, the insistent itching between her shoulder blades, the way she'd washed her hair and had found fibers in it she hadn't recognized.

She hadn't been through restoration. Yet something was changing in her. Some magic was flowing through her blood, an unwelcome hitchhiker from a time she'd rather forget. Was it that darkness in the pit alone that had caused it?

Her mother was looking at her, and Sheuan thought she saw a modicum of concern there. For a moment she wanted to tell her everything. To pull down the back of her dress and show her the angry red marks, the spots where she could feel black pinfeathers pressing at her skin. To unburden herself.

And what would that do, except burden her mother instead? She could see, in her mind's eye, the dawning horror on her mother's face, the understanding of the true cost of all this. And even as Sheuan thought about it, she knew that if she found out this cost was acceptable to the clan's matriarch, it would only crush her. Her mother had been prepared to see her dead, after all. Would a slow alteration be any different?

She was the only daughter of the Sim clan. She was the pillar upon which everything else rested, and she would not crack.

"You would have me go back." Her voice was steady; she was grateful for that.

"Girl, do you want to be the cause of our family's ruin? When our elders are thrown out on the streets, when I am burned in the lakebed, dead from starvation, you would know you could have stopped it. Is that what you want?"

Exhaustion settled into the marrow of Sheuan's bones. There wasn't any reason to fight this. Why was she even trying? As soon as she'd kept the filter in her hand, as soon as she'd decided, in that moment, not to hand it to the Sovereign, her fate had been set. How could she betray Mull's trust even further? How could she hand over the filters to the Sovereign and give him that sort of power?

She would go back to Kashan. There was no third path.

This time, she had to return with clear answers, with evidence, with a way to keep as many of the Langzuan people as possible alive and content until restoration came.

"It is not what I want."

Her mother let out a breath, her gaze going to the ceiling, her hands fussing in her lap. Had she thought Sheuan would say anything different?

In the end, she was a dutiful daughter. "I will go back. Give me until tomorrow. I need to rest and pack my things." She hesitated. "If I don't come back, tell Mull I'm sorry."

Her mother gave her a questioning look, but then Sheuan was rising, and she took the hint and stood too. She smoothed her skirts, then clutched a lock of Sheuan's hair between her fingers. "Tuck that beneath a cloth when you're in Kashan. Your ends are splitting."

She left the room, closing the door softly behind her. Wordlessly, Sheuan touched the lock of hair her mother had lifted. There was a patch there, soft as feathers, fibers interlocking. With a shudder, she let it drop.

Sheuan made for the border in the morning. She'd written a note to the Sovereign, telling him where she was going, telling him she could not get a hold of Mull at the moment, telling him she expected to hear from him soon. It might have been easy to lie in person, but it was even easier to lie on paper – the words inked and final, with no room for nuance or rejoinder.

It took her three days of walking and cart rides, the dust gathering in her hair, the heat of the sun scorching the back of her neck and making her head pound. The summers seemed to grow longer and hotter every year. The fires would start before long, making the air stink of smoke. She had to peel her pack off her back when she found inns to rest at for the night.

She didn't bring money to pay for a bath. But most people in Langzu were used to stinking, to being sweaty and dirty and uncomfortable.

No one gave her a second glance. No one recognized her.

It was late morning when she reached the barrier, the shimmering, dust-filled wall fading into the hazy sky. The sun was rimmed with a brown halo, the light a golden yellow. She walked a little ways away from the road, fitted the filter to her face and went back to Kashan.

Even though it was the second time, the green of the landscape and the clear blue of the sky shocked her. It was like she'd spent her whole life in a room lit by only one lantern, only to stumble one day into the light.

She didn't have a plan yet, so she set out for the den. The way was dangerous, but she'd trekked it with Rasha. She knew something of how to avoid the dangers – even if she could do little to protect herself against them. It would be better to have a guide. Her thirty days of sanctuary weren't over. She could still ask the den to spare Rasha for a few days.

If the girl had survived the second trial. Her feet moved a little faster at the thought.

Of course she'd survived. Only three from each burrow became acolytes; only three moved on to the final trial. Even if

Rasha wasn't one of those three, she would have made it through. Sheuan shouldn't have cared. She tried to make herself into a person who didn't. But her feet kept moving, her heart pounding with every step she took.

And there was the matter of the rhetoric in the dens. She could dig, she could learn more about whether that intense hatred of mortals led to restored realms cutting off unrestored ones. She told herself all these things even as she knew that walking back into that den meant walking back into a danger she couldn't quite comprehend.

Everyone in the ravine stared at her as she made her way toward the cave. She did her best to ignore their gazes.

It took some time to sort things out once she'd announced herself. No one quite knew what to do with her, so the devotee who'd greeted her was replaced with another, who also didn't know where Rasha was, until finally Millani appeared at the entrance, her tail lashing.

"Back again?" In spite of the strangeness of her face, Sheuan could read annoyance in her voice and her tightened lips. "If you're here for your advocate, she is in her second trial."

"I have several days left of sanctuary," Sheuan said by way of explanation. Inside, she was panicking, thinking of Rasha facing down whatever danger awaited her. The girl should have left with her. There were altered people in Langzu. Sheuan could have pulled strings, she could have gotten her legal status in the country. Rasha wouldn't have had to go through with this, putting her life on the line.

"Fine," Millani said. "You can wait in the burrow until she's done." She beckoned Sheuan to follow her into the darkness of the den. "If she lives."

44

Rasha

10 years after the restoration of Kashan
and 571 years after the Shattering

Kashan - Kluehnn's den

*Velenor liked to say that the mortals respected beauty, but
only insofar as they couldn't turn it to their whims. They
called her the Glittering One, and she was that, her dark
skin and even darker eyes glimmering beneath the light of
the sun. She used her power to make, and though she knew
how to forge a blade and how to create castles, she was most
. fond of flowers.*

The dzhalobo flowed into the cavern, keys jingling around
her neck, her teeth bared, spittle foaming.

We were tired, Khatuya was injured. We were not the finest in
the burrow; we all knew it. But there were three of us and there
was one dzhalobo. And all of us knew how to fight. I set the pup
down and drew my blade. As soon as she turned her attention to
her offspring, the three of us attacked.

I went straight for her neck. The chain there was heavy and we wouldn't be able to break it, but the links that held the keys were small, and the skin of her neck was softer. A strike against either would help us.

Her head whipped about quicker than I'd anticipated. I barely managed to dodge. Her teeth scraped a path against my forearm, leaving me shaken but unhurt. It was distraction enough for Gamgai to score a cut against her leg before spinning away out of her reach. Khatuya lunged at her flank, too slowly.

I'd promised I'd see Khatuya through this, that we'd stick together. I let my blade bounce uselessly off the creature's thickly furred chest. She veered away from Khatuya and struck out with her claws. I slid to the side and they connected with my shoulder, fiery lines of pain traveling up my arm. I gritted my teeth and breathed through the sensation. I couldn't afford to slip.

Gamgai was surprisingly agile given his build. He darted away, avoiding the dzhalobo's claws, and then drove his knife into the meat of her thigh. She screeched, the sound threatening to freeze me to the spot. I forced myself to move, stiffening my trembling limbs, going straight for her neck. My blade sheared through the rings holding the keys and into the beast's flesh.

Hot blood spurted. The wound on my shoulder flared with pain as I pulled back, as I scrabbled for one of the keys. In an instant, Khatuya and Gamgai were there too. We each snatched up a key.

"Quickly." Gamgai turned to the corridor where the door lay.

I could hear footsteps echoing through the caverns, my triumph tempered by fear. The neophytes might have been deterred by the dzhalobo, but she was dying now, and we were injured.

They wanted the keys. We all wanted the keys.

The torch was still there by the door. So was another neophyte, who'd decided the best strategy was to tackle whoever made it back with the keys. Naatar was on the ground near the door, a bloody trail behind him on the ground. He was still alive, though his lips were pale.

The other neophyte approached nervously, her blue scales glittering in the light. There were three of us and only one of her. She hadn't considered that when she'd thought about her strategy. I'd known the neophytes would end up breaking into loose alliances; not even Shambul could have defeated the dzhalobo on his own.

I glanced at Khatuya, saw her gaze fall on Naatar. They'd been close from the beginning. We were primed to be hardened, to be tough, to love no one but Kluehnn. Yet I'd asked them both to trust me.

There were only three keys.

You are stronger than you tell yourself you are. Kluehnn's words filtered into my mind, urging me to act. Gamgai and Khatuya were right in front of me, blades drawn, daring the other neophyte to fight them.

No time to reconsider. Only time to act.

I put the flat of my hand on Gamgai's back and pushed him into the other neophyte's blade. It sank into the soft flesh of his belly. Only a little ways; there'd been no conviction behind her stance.

It was enough.

I seized Gamgai's wrist and wrested the key from his hand. I did not look at his face; I only caught a glimpse of gaping mouth, of agonized eyes. I gave the key to Khatuya. "We enter together. We leave together."

The surprise on her face melted away, replaced by an emotion I didn't recognize. Fierceness? Pride? Determination? She held my gaze and gave me a brief, firm nod.

We moved at the same time, a silent understanding between us. We seized Naatar beneath his arms, hauling him to his feet, carrying him between us. Khatuya shoved the last key into his hand. He must have still been conscious, because his fingers closed weakly around it. I glared at the scaled neophyte and she backed away. The way to the door was clear.

I slid my bloody key into the lock and turned it. The door groaned as it swung open. Millani was there, face neutral, chin lifted, three acolyte robes draped over her arms.

We left together. As one.

I heard devotees and a few godkillers rushing into the cave after us to clean up the mess we'd left behind, to deal with the dzhalobo if it was still alive. Millani handed us each a robe and we shrugged them on over our bruised and battered bodies.

This was supposed to be a victory. It didn't quite feel that way. I'd done what I'd needed to – living in the moment. But now I felt pulled inexorably toward the past, to the moment when I'd put my palm to Gamgai's back. He hadn't deserved it.

At the same time, I felt the solidarity between Naatar, Khatuya and me. I'd kept my promises and we'd emerged the victors.

We wound our way back through the deep tunnels of the den, close on Millani's heels. There would be one more trial after this, and though I tried to savor our victory, I couldn't help but think of the future. We'd meet with Kluehnn again before being given this last challenge. Most godkillers made it through the final trial, though I knew from the rumors that it was an all-or-nothing task. Either all three of us completed it, or all three of us failed.

There would be no possibility of becoming a devotee who served the den if we failed. The penalty for failure was death. I took in a deep breath, ducking beneath a ledge so my horns wouldn't scrape the stone.

We were on a different path than the one we'd taken to the second trial.

"A minor tunnel collapse," Millani explained, glancing back at us. "They'll have it cleared up eventually."

So the rumble I'd thought was my imagination making the dzhalobo out to be even more frightening had actually been real. Tunnel collapses were rare in restored dens, but they did happen. Restoration firmed up the soil and led to fewer sinkholes. We'd be allowed into the deeper tunnels soon, once we passed the last trial.

A room opened up to our right. I caught glimpses I couldn't make sense of. There was a hole in the floor of the room, much like the one I'd seen in the nave and in the room I'd spoken to Kluehnn. All around it were stacks of crates. Several chained mortals loaded books into the crates.

I'd seen these crates moving in and out of the den. I'd never thought they'd be filled with books. Bright lanterns lit one corner of the room. I caught the glimmer of a needle. The mortal there was sewing the binding together on an enormous tome.

And then we were past it, and I was left with more questions than answers. Millani had not even turned her head.

Why books? There were too many and of too many different shapes and sizes to simply be religious tomes. Did all the crates like that hold books? If so, that meant there were hundreds of books being brought to the den and being sent out again.

Khatuya raised an eyebrow at me, but Naatar was too badly injured to care. We'd find out eventually, as soon as we became godkillers. So I held my tongue.

Millani opened the door to the burrow, waiting for us to step through. It would be much emptier than it had once been, with only three occupants down from twenty-two.

Sheuan was waiting on my bed.

45

Sheuan

10 years after the restoration of Kashan
and 571 years after the Shattering

Kashan – Kluehnn's den

Refugees from other realms are all remnants of dead cultures. Whatever exists beyond the barriers is not the same. The people are not the same. Lifestyles and customs that were created to survive post-Shattering fade away.

Some Kashani in Langzu may still drink fermented mare's milk. They may still note Evensday on their calendars, the holiday during which the first Queen was selected. But now they live in hovels on the outskirts of cities. They blacken their hands with the mines.

It was with no small measure of relief that Sheuan watched Rasha step into the burrow. One horn was chipped, and blood stained the front of her armor. She couldn't tell how much of the blood belonged to the altered woman. An acolyte's robe was draped over her shoulders, long and dark gray, an eye sewn onto each shoulder.

She'd made it through the second trial.

Two others accompanied her, though one acolyte was seriously injured.

"Naatar needs to be seen by a physician," Millani said. "Rasha can stay here and do her advocate duties. Khatuya, come with me. Kluehnn will want to see each of you."

Khatuya and Naatar drew away and the door shut behind Rasha.

For a moment, Sheuan just stared at her. Neither of them spoke. She wasn't sure whether she should lift her hands from her lap or leave them there.

"I'm an acolyte now," Rasha said. Her lip was bruised and split, and Sheuan felt the odd sensation of being pulled back to a time when she'd kissed that unblemished mouth. She frowned. Still pretty, in a wild and dangerous way, even when the crease between her brows deepened. "What are you doing here?"

"The information I brought back to the Sovereign was not enough. He's still threatening my family."

"So you're back for more." It wasn't what Rasha wanted to hear.

Sheuan *knew* what she wanted to hear – she'd spent years studying what to say to put a person at ease. She also knew that crossing that boundary would be pointless for them both.

She should have gone to the palace, no matter how dangerous the journey would have been alone. She should have dug for more information there instead of coming back to the den. Well she was here now. She ran a hand through her hair, watching dust fall onto the floor. "I'm the only one left my family can depend on. I didn't know what else to do. I should have gone somewhere else, I know. I'm sorry."

"No." Rasha stopped her. She limped down the steps toward her, stopping in front of the bed. "I'm glad you came here."

And with that, the boundary was broken. How strange – that someone Sheuan had seen as young, as naïve, could be braver in this way than she was. She took one of Rasha's hands. "My cousin left me in charge of his workshop. I found the filters he'd made. They can get you through the barrier without a guide. I've done it several times now." She took a deep breath. "I told the Sovereign about them. He asked ... he asked if they could protect a person against restoration."

Rasha's claws twitched. "Can they?"

She hadn't told her own mother, yet she was telling this girl she'd had a one-night tryst with. "I don't know. My cousin has gone on an expedition and I don't know when he'll be back. I read his notes." She swallowed. "I think they might be able to. But I haven't told the Sovereign that."

"And if the filters do protect against restoration? He will help your family?"

"He'll promote me to the trade minister position and advance my salary to my family. The Sim clan would rise in the ranks once more. I know what he would do with this new technology. He would dole it out to those in his favor. He would let them fight over it. He would make them pay dearly for it. And everyone else ... they would be left to face restoration with the same uncertainty as before. If Kluehnn punishes Langzu, the wealthy clan members won't be the ones who suffer."

Rasha was still. "And is that what you want?"

Sheuan watched her face, but her expression was like stone. She couldn't figure out what to say, what persona Rasha wanted or needed. "Help me figure this out. Just ... If I do, tell me you'll come back to Langzu with me. The Sovereign can protect you." She couldn't comprehend the words that were coming out of her mouth.

Yes, she could help Rasha. She could get her set up with a life in Langzu. But what would that mean for them? She knew she wasn't offering out of the goodness in her heart. She was offering because there was something about Rasha that tugged at her, that made her feel for once that she wasn't pretending.

Rasha's thumb moved over the back of Sheuan's hand, tracing tiny circles across it. How could Sheuan have left her here the first time? She wasn't sure she'd be able to do it again.

"It's not about protection," the acolyte was saying. "I want to become a godkiller. That's who I am. That's everything I've worked toward. What would I have instead if I followed you back to Langzu? A few short years before I had to flee restoration again. I belong here."

It was unfair, Sheuan knew it, but she lifted Rasha's hand to her mouth and kissed the back of it. She let her lashes flutter across her cheeks as she murmured against the girl's skin. "Are you sure?" She'd use every weapon at her disposal. She'd thought she'd left Rasha behind, with maybe only a stray lingering thought or two, but the moment she'd laid eyes on her again, she'd felt caught.

Rasha twisted her hand in a movement Sheuan couldn't follow, but in the next moment, she was holding Sheuan by the shoulder. She reached out with her free hand and seized a lock of Sheuan's hair. "Are you sure *you* belong in Langzu?"

Her hair — the patch with the silken texture of feathers.

Sheuan rose to her feet, pulling away. The place between her shoulders itched again. She wondered if that blackness in the pit at the Queen's nave existed in the den as well. If whatever particles were in the darkness below filtered into the air above. Was she breathing it in even now, furthering her alteration? "Should I keep looking for the cause of isolation, or should I give the Sovereign the secret to making the filters?"

Rasha scoffed, and now Sheuan could read her face. One brow

up, one down, the skeptical twist to her mouth. "Is this why you came to me? Is this why you sought me out again? You really don't know what the right thing is to do?" Her fists clenched, and Sheuan saw flakes of dried blood break free. "Do you not have any convictions? Any sense of yourself? Or do you have only your family and your duty?"

Sheuan had told her that what had happened between them was real. And then she'd left her. She lifted a hand as though she could forestall any further anger. As though their quarrel could be smoothed away. "I can understand why you'd be upset."

"Can you? I don't think you can. The only things you can understand are your family and your duty. These are, after all, the only things you care about."

"That's not true. I came back."

"Only because you were *sent* back! And then you come here and ask me to go to Langzu with you, as though I don't already have a life and a destiny here."

"What sort of life? They send you to your death, over and over."

Rasha's eyes blazed. "And yet I am still here."

"You don't have to do this to prove that you're strong!" The words rang out, echoing from the walls.

Something flickered across Rasha's face, a shadow without a name. She took a step toward Sheuan. Her voice filled the silence, soft as velvet. "Your family. Your duty. Can you not care for anything else?"

Sheuan had to tilt her head back to meet her gaze, and she drank in the sight of her. The broad shoulders, the curving black-tipped horns. The soft brown eyes. The sharpened teeth. "Rasha, what would you have me *do*? Just tell me. I'll do it." She knew as soon as the words left her mouth that they were the wrong thing to say. She felt her truest self when she was around Rasha, yet her truest self made the most mistakes.

Rasha's mouth tightened. "I won't be your substitute family. I won't be that. You don't say it, but I can see how much you resent them. They're holding you back in so many ways, no matter how much you love them. Do you think I want to be *that* to you? To tell you what to do so that you can both love me and resent me?"

Her breath was warm against Sheuan's face, her lips only a moment away. All Sheuan had to do was lean in, cup the back of Rasha's head in her palm, press herself into the girl's body, strip that filthy armor away. Rasha's heartbeat must have been a mirror of Sheuan's own, kicking wildly like a horse newly to pasture. Sheuan wanted to consume the sweetness of her, to bury her face and her hands between Rasha's legs. To stave off the decision to another moment, another day.

Before she could even make that choice, Rasha whirled and went to the door. The air she left behind her was cold, smelling of sweat and copper. The door shut behind her before Sheuan could recover, her head swimming with desire.

She sat back on the bed, trying to make sense of what had happened. Rasha would not come with her. Rasha would not help her make this decision.

After what seemed like forever, Millani returned.

"Rasha?" Sheuan asked.

"Having her wounds tended to," the godkiller said. There was something displeased and wary in her voice. Her tail lashed like that of a nervous cat. "She won't be back. She's requested you be assigned a different advocate. And as she has new . . . duties, I've granted that request."

A different advocate? The thought settled like a pit in Sheuan's belly. She had the feeling whoever was assigned to her next wouldn't take as kindly to her poking around in the den. "I only have a few days left of sanctuary."

Millani's yellow-eyed gaze met hers. "Then you should be

prepared to either become a lifelong member of this den or return home to face consequences. I can escort you back to the ravine. Your new advocate will meet you there. They'll find a tent or an alcove for you. Any further business you need to conduct can be completed outside."

So she wasn't to be let back into the den at all. Numb, Sheuan followed Millani through the tunnels and back to the ravine. The sky was shockingly bright. Was it still day? It felt as though hours had passed.

She didn't wait for the new advocate. She went straight back toward the border. Rasha hadn't wanted to make this choice for her, yet in a way she had. What else could Sheuan do except give the filters to the Sovereign? The thought slicked her stomach with unease. But it was the only way she could save her dying clan.

Perhaps she was imagining it, but the way back felt easier, her feet steadier in the cracked landscape of the barrier. She emerged into the yellowed landscape of Langzu only a little out of breath.

Would she ever see Rasha again? She pushed the thought away. Rasha had abandoned *her* this time, not the other way around. Yet she couldn't find any anger. Instead, there was only exhaustion, and the feeling of a purpling bruise deep in her chest. They'd had several wonderful, perfect days together. She would have to live with that.

Her mother wasn't there when she finally arrived home, dusty and travel-worn, which she was eternally grateful for. She could only imagine her look of disappointment at seeing Sheuan back so soon. But there was a letter on her bed when she set her pack down.

The envelope was blank, but she recognized the handwriting when she unfolded the parchment. Mitoran.

Contact me when you return. There is someone I promised a favor to.

46

Hakara

10 years after the restoration of Kashan
and 571 years after the Shattering

Langzu

*The Aqqila claim that before the mortals began burning
the Numinars, gods used to visit the surface far more often.
That they were involved in our wars, in our treaties, in the
fabric of our lives.*

There has never been as miserable, as sorry a wretch as me.
I had a few coins left clinking in my purse, and though I
should have used them for lodging, I used them instead to smoke
and to drink, until I was a stinking, sodden mess, the last cus-
tomer in the tea house. The workers eyed me, wondering if I'd
leave or if they'd have to kick me out.

I made them kick me out, of course. Not with words, but with
hands and lifting and one judicious foot to my lower back. Is it
really kicking someone out if you don't kick them?

My cheek pressed into the dust and the cold stone. That plus the slamming of the door sobered me up a little. Not enough to take the edge off my self-pity, but enough to get me on my feet and moving.

I frowned, my head swimming. I'd collected a second core-stone. The way I saw it, Mitoran might not owe me the money or the guide, but she owed me a meeting with that informant of hers. I'd make my way back to collect, but I was still wearing shame like a blanket. It would take some time for me to shake it off and return to my usual bravado.

The streets of Ruzhi were dark and growing darker as people extinguished their lamps. Should I go back to the safe house, sheepish, asking for a place to stay for a couple nights? Or should I chance it on the streets? I found myself reaching for that connection with Thassir, that invisible thread. It was well and truly gone. I had no idea where he was, though I was convinced he was curled up in some comfortable hollow in the wilds, sleeping dreamlessly.

My teeth clenched as I replayed for the hundredth time the things he'd said to me. My fingers twitched as I wished for a drink in my hand, a way to forget. Instead, I made a fist, fingernails leaving half-moon impressions in my palm.

I *hated* him. Him with his black-feathered wings and his black hair and his black eyes. With his shimmering blood and his rumbling voice and his rough hands. With his sadness and un-expected tenderness beneath. I let my fingers unclench. Maybe I didn't hate him. This wasn't his fault. It was mine. It had always been mine.

I put my back to the wall of the nearest building, sliding down, uncaring of the dirt that had accumulated there. I was a mess already; what was a little more?

Two of the Sovereign's enforcers turned the corner, their stiff blue vests dulled to gray by lantern light.

Through some miracle of good fortune, I'd never run afoul of them, though I really should have. The sinkhole mines were always a bit of a lawless place, filled with gambling, fighting and whatever exotic drugs we could get our hands on. And of course there was the flourishing black market in god gems. Enforcers had a sort of selective blindness, though, and never seemed to notice how many illegal refugees worked in the mining camps.

I scrambled to my feet, doing my best to look respectable. My shirt was damp with either sweat or liquor – I wasn't sure which – and my hair, half out of the tail I'd put it in, stank of smoke. Ah well, the whole city stank at this hour. Too many bodies, too much heat, too much garbage piled in alleys. I might not stand out too much.

Both enforcers focused on me, like two hounds sighting a hare. They marched straight toward me. I hesitated for a moment, wondering if I should run. Wasn't really in any condition to do so.

I tried anyways.

The string of curses I let out when a hand wrapped about my arm would have made Rasha hide her face, her cheeks burning.

"You're out past curfew," the man said. "Name?"

"Only by a few minutes. It's Hakara." No clan name. They wouldn't have expected one, and it wasn't as though I could fake it.

His partner wrinkled her nose, her hand on the short sword at her belt. "She stinks. Vagrant?"

I gave her the most indignant look I could manage. "I have a home."

They exchanged glances. "Papers, please," the man said.

Ah, and there was the sticking point. Never did get those legal papers made, and it wasn't as though Mitoran had offered. They'd been harder and harder to come by the longer I'd lived in

Langzu, and the longer I'd lived in Langzu, the more I'd needed them. I'd come here with nothing. And being a sinkhole miner wasn't really the sort of job that would allow me to petition for legal status, not without substantial funding.

I patted my empty pockets. "Do you really expect me to carry them on my person? What if someone tried to steal them?" My Langzuan was perfect now, but my face still held that hint of Cressiman. Any enforcer with half an eyeball could see I didn't quite belong.

They nodded to one another. It was what they'd expected. I'd tried to run, after all.

I'd always feared this fate – being caught as an illegal tres-passer on Langzuan soil. Living and working and earning money in a country that wasn't mine, could never be mine. I didn't belong in Kashan anymore, but I didn't belong here either. There was no place for me and no one who cared that there was no place for me. All they wanted was for me to be *not here*, and they didn't care what that meant about where I ended up.

In this case, it meant the cell in the back of a wagon, along with two other miscreants. One was in the throes of some drugged stupor, laid out where I could trip on him, dead to the world. The other had bird-quick eyes that darted about the cage as though she could find some escape if only she looked hard enough.

I settled onto the bench, letting despair blow its smoky way across my body. Maybe I'd get back to fighting in a little bit. Maybe not.

She's dead.

Thassir's words echoed in my mind. It was the first time I'd really allowed myself to believe it. I let my head rest on the wooden wall of the wagon, drifting off to sleep as it moved into the night. Every so often the enforcers would stop to empty our latrine bucket, to toss us some questionable-looking food.

The stinging heat woke me on the fourth day. Would have thought a covered wagon would be cooler, but instead it seemed to trap the warmth inside. I stank, the other two occupants stank; we were all just swimming in a cesspool of our own bodily odors.

A knock sounded at the wagon door. Something in the haze of my waking made me think it wasn't the first knock. "Hakara." The female enforcer's voice. And then quieter, "Look, I don't know if she's going to answer and I'm not going in there."

Another knock, louder and more assertive than the first. "Do you want to be tossed into the barrier or do you want to talk?" A woman's voice, with more authority than I could muster even on a good day.

With a groan, I forced myself to my feet, stepped over the man on the floor, who somehow was not dead yet, and peered through the bars on the door.

The woman standing there was short and dark, with sharply slanted brows and a mouth that would have been generous had her lips not been tightly pressed. Her gray dress was cut to reveal slender but surprisingly well-muscled arms, and though the floral embroidery at the front was rich, it was in an older style, and threadbare at the shoulders.

She looked me over. "Let her out," she said, her gaze not moving from my face.

The enforcer shifted nervously from foot to foot before unlocking the door.

"I'll take custody of her."

"That's . . . highly unusual. She doesn't have papers and we found her—"

"Did she murder someone?" The woman's voice was quiet, though it had the tenor of distant thunder.

"Well, no."

"Rob anyone?"

"No."

"Then release her to my custody and I'll deal with the lack of papers."

Before the enforcer could protest yet again, I pushed the door open and stepped into the sunlight. Gods below, it was bright! How long had I slept for? My tongue felt like a metal rasp; my eyes like someone had poured glue into them.

"Hm." The woman looked at me as though she'd bought a rotten fruit she couldn't be bothered to return. "Follow me."

We were on the outskirts of Bian. They'd probably spend the day here picking up more miscreants. The enforcers always did like to have a full wagon before they dumped criminals into the barrier. That was the Sovereign. Say what you wanted about him, the man was efficient.

I let myself be led like an obedient dog for a little ways before stopping. The woman had keen hearing, because she stopped shortly after I did, pivoting to face me.

I gave her a bow. I wasn't an idiot. I could see she was clan blood, no matter how worn the shoulders of her dress were. "This is where we part ways."

Her eyes narrowed. "Says who?"

"Says me." Whatever the reason she'd freed me, I wasn't keen on finding out. I'd already been nearly imprisoned by godkillers and had been pulled into working for the Unanointed. I wasn't about to make myself into a victim of a *third* faction.

She stalked closer to me. Shouldn't have let her, but she was pretty, and I was a bit weak for pretty. "Mitoran told me she owed you."

Ah shit. Wait, I *was* keen on finding out. "You're the informant."

She hissed and took my arm. "Are you always this thick?"

I rubbed at my forehead. "Only when I've spent the past four days with terrible company in a wagon that smells like piss."

Her nose wrinkled. "Somehow I doubt that's the only time." She led me into an alleyway, checking both ends and the windows above. "I'd take you somewhere you could get a bath and something to eat, but you're in such bad shape, I can't be seen with you. Mitoran said you wanted to talk to me."

Everything sharpened, burning off the last vestiges of sleep. "You went to Kashan without a guide."

She hesitated, then, "Yes."

"Tell me how."

"I ... can't."

"Can't or won't?" I would break this woman if I had to. I seized her by the shoulders. She gave me an affronted look but did nothing. Her feet shifted beneath her into a more defensible position, almost imperceptibly, telling me she was doing me a kindness. So. She could fight. "Look, I don't have any money. Obviously I don't. But I need to get to Kashan. I heard Mitoran say your clan's funds are dwindling, that you couldn't afford a guide. So tell me how you did it."

She looked sorry for me, and I hated that. She wasn't allowed to feel sorry for me; the only one who was allowed to do that was me.

"It's not my secret to tell."

I could have torn her hair out. Or mine. Both. But Thassir might have been right that I rushed headlong into everything without taking a moment to think. "There has to be a way. Go ask the person whose secret it *is* to tell. Or take me with you the next time you go."

But she was shaking her head. My fingers dug into her skin a little and I was rewarded with a quick, sharp cuff to the ear.

Her entire demeanor changed from prim authority to

brimming danger. "You will not handle me that way." Her eyes bored into mine. "Why are you so desperate?" One more sweep of that assessing gaze. "You lost someone."

I thought of those early days after restoration, when I was still recovering from aether sickness, when I could hear some of the people who'd made it through begging for word of those they'd left behind. Eventually those crowds had thinned out, and by the time Guarin had moved us along, there were only a few strays at the barrier.

I hadn't even been one of them. And I'd spent the rest of my life trying to make up for that. "My sister. Everyone tells me she's dead." I let her brush my hands away as though they were merely annoying flies, watched as she pressed her fingers to the bridge of her nose. "Who are you?"

"Mitoran's informant. That's all you need to know." She let out a sigh and dropped her hand. "Family, hm? Let me think. There may be a way I can help you."

47

Sheuan

10 years after the restoration of Kashan and 571 years after the Shattering

Langzu - the outskirts of Bian

Much of what mortals had pre-Shattering has been lost. Their buildings, their churches, their technology – all of it lost to time and disaster.

Sheuan had promised Mitoran she'd hear this woman out; she hadn't promised anything more. She should have left her in the alleyway – probably to get arrested again, but that wasn't exactly her problem, was it? Instead she found herself entertaining, actually entertaining, the idea of loaning the filters to Hakara so she could find her sister. She had enough problems on her plate, everything revolving around the filters. Loaning them out? It was ridiculous. She'd never been this soft.

Maybe it was because there was something about Hakara that made Sheuan feel soft. Logic and statistics dictated that her sister was dead. Half the people disappeared during restoration.

And Hakara had never heard anything from beyond Kashan. Sometimes the remaining altered found ways to send notes to loved ones in other realms, though that took money.

It had been ten years. But she said nothing.

Hakara leaned against the wall, running her hands through hair that looked as though it hadn't been washed in a very, very long time. Her voice was as ragged as her appearance. She looked entirely wrung out, like she had nothing left to her except one single driving force. "You were going to tell me that she's dead, weren't you?"

"I . . ."

Her eyes squeezed shut. "People have been telling me that ever since I got to Langzu. To move on. To forget about her. Because she's gone." She cracked open one eye, as though she couldn't bear to look at Sheuan fully. "You know, I used to start fights over that." She pointed to a scar on her forearm, another on her knuckle. "Little gifts from those times. I say this like it was a long time ago. It *feels* like a long time ago.

"I've been spending so much of my life trying to get back to her. It's the only thing that's mattered to me. I lost focus on everything and everyone else. How could I care about the people around me? Things would have been different if I *could* have left her behind, if I could have accepted that she was dead. I could have had a life – an actual life. People say it like moving on is a choice, when I still have no answers."

Sheuan felt as though she'd swallowed a mouthful of icy water. Her chest hurt. She thought about her family, her clan. She'd dedicated her whole life to them, to trying to correct the mistake her father had made, or not made. She was her clan's weapon, the last blade standing between them and the other clans, which hovered like vultures. There was nothing outside of that. "That doesn't mean your life hasn't meant anything."

She wanted to believe it. If she could save her clan, she would believe it.

Yet there was a part of her that wondered what her life could have been like if she'd thrown her obligations aside. She could have taken Mitoran's offer of marriage to Nimao. She could have let her clan fall to the vultures, to the Sovereign. She would have been safe, with a fresh new future to look forward to. Was she a blade, or were they a crooked old hand, dragging her down?

Tawny eyes looked at her from beneath a curtain of dark brown hair. "Doesn't it? I have nothing to show for all those years." All the fight had gone out of Hakara. She looked like an entirely different person. "You won't give me whatever means you used to cross the barrier, will you?"

"No. It's not something I can give away."

"Even if I killed you for it?"

Sheuan let out an amused huff of breath. "I'm an informant for the Unanointed. I know what that means. You'd have to do a lot to break me, I'm afraid." Except all the Sovereign had to do was to threaten her family and she'd foolishly spilled half of Mull's secrets to him. To be fair, she hadn't quite understood what she'd been offering. And maybe she *was* getting soft, because instead of just leaving Hakara in the alley, she put a hand on her arm. "I may go back to Kashan. Who is your sister? I can at least have notices posted in the border towns that you're looking for her."

"Rasha. Her name is Rasha. She looks – or she *looked* – a little like me, only smaller. She was only nine then. I don't . . . I don't know what she would look like now. Not after restoration."

Sheuan couldn't breathe. There were too many things she wanted to say at once; all the phrases got jammed up at the back of her tongue, vying to be let free. Her first thought was: *So I haven't gone as soft as I'd thought*. There was something easy and familiar about Hakara. They had similar mannerisms, the same quirk of the lip when bothered. How had she not noticed it before?

But Rasha wasn't an uncommon name. It could have been someone else. She couldn't be sure. Not yet. She tried to temper her conclusions.

Hakara's eyes narrowed, the tears there threatening to brim over. "Why are you looking at me like you've just swallowed a mouthful of too-hot tea?"

"I met a Rasha in Kashan. She's probably not your sister. I'm likely wrong. Just—"

And then the woman was weeping, her teeth clenched as though the tears were causing her physical pain. "You'd better not be lying to me. You had better *not* be."

There was a way to find out. "Do you recognize this?" Sheuan hummed the lullaby Rasha had sung to her that night in the tent. That one, perfect night before reality had intruded.

Hakara seized her shoulders again, and this time, when her fingers dug into Sheuan's forearms, she didn't strike the woman away. "That's it. That's the song our Mimi sang to us. She's alive. She *is*." A moment ago, Hakara had looked a husk of a person, a desiccated corpse baking beneath the sun. Now all the life flooded back into her. She was shaking, gulping sobs escaping each time she tried to say anything more.

Sheuan had always known how to read what a person wanted without asking. So she gave it. "She's changed, yes. A horned altered. She's tall, and strong, and while she has black-tipped horns and sharpened teeth, she has a sweet face." *And sweet lips*, her traitorous mind whispered. "She's well." She let that information settle, let Hakara absorb it, because the next part would not be so easy. Let her live in her unfettered joy for a moment longer. The woman was holding onto her as though she were the only thing keeping her upright.

Finally she caught her breath and met Sheuan's gaze.

"There's more," Sheuan said. "She survived because one of Kluehnn's dens took her in. She's devoted herself to him, to becoming a godkiller."

"They have trials." Hakara's grip hadn't lightened. "They're deadly."

"Yes. She survived two trials. There's one more left."

"I have to go. I have to go to her. Get her out." She was searching the walls as though they might yield a way through the barrier, to Kashan.

Sheuan squeezed her arms in return, bringing her attention back. "I tried that already. She didn't want to come with me."

"Well I'm her sister." Some dawning realization crossed Hakara's face. "Wait, what exactly are you to her? Why did you try to get her to come back?"

The day was already rather hot, wasn't it? Or was the heat in her cheeks from another cause? "We were friends. *Are* friends still, I hope," Sheuan said hastily. It was a harmless lie, but throwing her romantic interest into the mix with a protective older sister didn't feel the best idea at the moment.

Hakara let her arms go. She waved a dismissive hand, her lips pressed together. "The Unanointed are planning to raid one of Kluehnn's dens."

Sheuan remembered the information she'd pried out of Rasha, and delivered to Mitoran. She had thought the Unanointed would find another way, send a spy after the stone, or wait to see if it was moved. Passage for an entire raiding party through the barrier would be difficult. This didn't seem wise, but Sheuan wasn't Mitoran and she wasn't privy to the same information. She closed her eyes. "They're going to raid Rasha's den. In Kashan."

"Ah shit. Ah, Fuck." Hakara clenched her fists. "I have to go with them. The Unanointed. It'll get me into Kashan on their coin and I need to be there if they're raiding the den Rasha lives in. For all I know, if she's nearly a godkiller, she'll be part of their defenses. She might be killed. I have to do what Mitoran wants. I have to be their linchpin."

Their linchpin? Sheuan had wondered exactly what Mitoran's plans were, and over the years she'd pried little pieces of information free. Now everything seemed to be crashing together at once — the Unanointed's plans, the discovery of the filters, the restoration of Langzu itself. Things were shifting faster than she could keep track of. There were too many threads at play here, leaving her feeling lost on a giant loom instead of picking her way deliberately through it.

"What is she trying to do?"

"So you don't know either? Just an informant, telling her what she wants to know." Hakara lifted her shirt a little, sniffing and then grimacing. "The gems she's been having us steal. The corestones. She wants me to infuse them. She thinks if I can infuse them with aether from past the second aerocline, they'll be powerful enough to restore the soil in Langzu. And if they manage to steal enough of the god gems that Kluehnn's collecting, he won't be able to enact restoration here."

An ambitious plan, and one worth sending an army of Unanointed to Kashan. "The air will still be hot and hazy. The land won't heal overnight."

"Yes, but half the population won't have to disappear."

But what was better for the clans and for the Sovereign? If the Unanointed succeeded, the land might be more livable, but life would still be difficult. If the filters could forestall alteration and disappearance, then half the general population might be a cost the Sovereign was willing to pay to return the land to lushness in one fell swoop.

It was one of the few pieces of information Mitoran didn't have.

And Sheuan wasn't about to give it up. She stepped away from Hakara and felt she'd narrowly avoided falling off a cliff.

"I wish you the best of luck. With your sister." What she wanted to say was *Find her. Keep her safe. Tell her I care about her. Tell her she doesn't have to be a godkiller to prove herself. Tell her that she is enough.*

But Hakara had already shifted her gaze to the end of the alleyway, focused on the distant buildings, as though she were looking through them and across the vast landscape to the barrier itself. "I'll need it. I'm going to do what I should have done ten years ago. I'm going to bring her back." She looked briefly to Sheuan. "Maybe you'll get to see her again."

Sheuan doubted it, but she kept her mouth shut. She watched as the filthy, stinking woman strode out of sight, her footing sure, her gaze unerring.

She firmed up her jaw, feeling just as determined. She had her own decisions to face.

48

Mullayne

10 years after the restoration of Kashan
and 571 years after the Shattering

Langzu - Tolemne's Path

If the barriers are created due to cracks in the earth that allow the aether to churn to the surface, why do we not see this same phenomenon at sinkholes?
What mechanism continues to force the air upward?

In the early hours of the morning, when he lay awake while everyone else slept, Mull thought about the crew member who'd turned back. Had he died yet? Had his filter failed, or had he been dragged into the lair of one of those giant lizards?

The farther into the depths they went, the stranger the world around them seemed. Their hair floated around them like halos, luminescent vegetation casting sickly green and blue light across their faces. They were nearly out of oil, so they'd stopped using their lanterns. There wasn't any need.

At least they had enough food. There were fewer of them now with two people gone, one of them dead.

Jeeoon. She'd only just been entering middle age when they'd first met, her wiry arms bronzed by the sun. They'd never been close friends, but he'd come to rely on her.

Now he never could again.

He shifted on his bedroll and heard Imeah sigh next to him. He got up, pacing until everyone else awoke and packed up the camp. They should be there soon. They should be at Unterra. The way the books described it, it was a massive hollow in the center of the earth, a bright, shining sphere at the center. It was warm, and so vast that it sometimes rained. The gods lived there, and one of them would grant him a boon. It was what had happened for Tolemne, though he'd had to ask a great many gods.

It would be simpler for Mullayne, he was sure. He wasn't asking for the surface world to be restored. He was asking only for the means to save his friend.

Pont stood silently at his shoulder and Mull handed him a fresh filter. He doled out the rest of the supplies until everyone had exchanged their filters. Then they marched on, down into the dark. They only had to stop once to check the map. At this point there were fewer branching tunnels. The one they followed opened periodically into larger caverns but always went eventually in one direction: down.

At least their packs felt lighter past the second aerocline. Mull had always been good at finding positives when it suited him.

"This had better not be all on my behalf," Imeah said, her breathing heavy as they turned a bend.

"It's not. The crew isn't here for you," Mull said. "I'm here for you, but we all want to see Unterra. No one has been this far before. No one except Tolemne."

"It had better be worth it," Pont said from in front of them. Ever since the lizards and Jeeoon, he'd led the way.

"It will be," Mull said.

They passed into a cavern lit by scalloped glowing mushrooms on the ceiling, the ground damp and lighting up blue with every step they took. Some unidentifiable furred creature fled as they approached. It was beautiful down here, more so than he'd anticipated. He'd tried to get some sketches in his journal, but the light was low and he'd only ever been a mediocre artist. He *was* correcting the map when he could, making his own version that showed the appropriate distances.

They left the cavern and entered another long tunnel.

Pont stopped. Mull and Imeah nearly ran into him.

"Light a lantern, Mull." There was something odd about his voice, like he'd stuffed a whole egg into his mouth and was trying to speak around it.

"We don't have much oil left. We should save—"

"Light one."

Mull peered into the darkness, trying to see what Pont saw. He'd never had as good eyesight in the dark. Imeah handed him a lantern and a tinderbox.

The crew behind him were murmuring. Or was it grumbling? He didn't want to think too hard on it. His fingers trembling a little, he lit the lantern and handed it to Pont. Wordlessly, Pont took it and lifted it in front of him.

Mull saw it first, and from Imeah's quick intake of breath, he knew she'd seen it too. There was a dip in the floor in front of them, the way suddenly steep. It would be easy enough to traverse, even with Imeah, but that wasn't the issue.

The air at Pont's feet *shimmered*.

Another aerocline. A *third* aerocline. That ... couldn't be possible. Nothing in all of Mull's books had ever said anything

about a third aerocline. There were only two, and then there was
Unterra. That was accepted knowledge at every school in every
realm he'd ever heard of. That was the shape of their world.

Yet he stared at the way the air shimmered on the floor and
he couldn't think of any other explanation. No strange gases, no
biological reasons. He took off his glove, brushed past Pont and
knelt.

When he touched it, when he pressed his hand past that
shimmer, he could feel the density of the aether. The air was
heavier down there. It was like placing his palm into a bowl of
warm water. He lifted his arm and almost had the urge to flick
his fingers dry.

"It's another aerocline," he said, his voice cracking.

"Another one?" someone behind him said. And then they
were all talking and then shouting. He thought he heard someone
weeping.

Pont seized his arm, his masked face close. "Mull, we have to
go back. We don't know how much farther this layer goes. We
don't know if we'll ever pop out in Unterra. What if Unterra is
gone? What if it was replaced by *this*."

"That wouldn't make any scientific sense. And if you look at
the circumference of the world and how far we've gone, taking
into account how large Unterra must be, then—"

"Scientific? This is *magic*. They're falling apart. Come to your
senses," Pont hissed.

Mull glanced back at the remaining crew. There was no deny-
ing that Pont was right. One of the women was indeed sobbing.
A man had rested his forearm against the wall and was leaning
over, breathing hard. Another stared vacantly at the aerocline as
though he'd retreated into some safe place inside himself.

"We've made it this far."

Pont shook his head. "You know I'd do anything for you. I'd

follow you anywhere. But that's because I trust you to make wise decisions. You're smart. Smarter than I'll ever be." He tapped his temple. "Think about it. And be *smart*."

He turned away and went to the crew, patting shoulders, asking everyone if they needed any food or water.

"Mull?" Imeah took his arm, and he realized he'd started staring at the aerocline too, as though he could see past it and into all the dangers they still might face. He wanted to turn back, to go back to the light. Even his love for Imeah couldn't make that desire disappear entirely. But something else pulled him forward. He *could* save her. And the filters were still holding now that they'd learned to change them out. They'd just have to sleep in shifts, change them more frequently. And if there was a third aerocline, what else didn't they know?

The pull of that forgotten knowledge was stronger than a fishing line and a hook he'd already swallowed.

He faced the crew. "We should sleep on it. Let's not make any decisions now. I can tell you confidently that we're close to Unterra, though. Even by our greatest estimates of the world's circumference, we've traveled far. Unterra once held all the gods. If we turn back now, we'll do so with many unsolved mysteries haunting our hearts. We'll never know. We're close to answers. We're *so* close."

He'd never been great at reading people. Had his speech inspired them? Terrified them? He couldn't tell, and at the moment, he was too tired to care. Jeeoon's death had weighed him down ever since they'd left her cairn. He carried it with him like a second pack.

They set up camp in the preceding cavern, and Mull used a little of their remaining oil to light the pages of his journal. He redid his calculations, allowing for an even larger world, for some error in the distance they'd traveled. Even at his most conservative, his calculations said they were close. Even if there *was* a third aerocline, they were close.

He waved off the food he was offered, chewing the end of his pen instead.

"Mull," Imeah finally called from her bedroll. Everyone else had long since gone to sleep. When had that happened? He couldn't be sure. "Get some rest."

He put down the pen, not without a great deal of hesitation, and then unrolled his mat next to hers. She patted his arm as he closed his eyes. It was the last thing he remembered before he fell asleep.

It was quiet when he woke up, quieter even than it had been the previous waking. He blinked bleary eyes. He felt well rested, and they'd all gone to sleep before he had. So why was no one stirring? Something was wrong.

Fear squeezed his heart, forcing him bolt upright. Imeah still lay next to him, her breathing slow and even. Pont was there too, and Mull felt the fear ease a little.

But everyone else was gone.

They'd left in the middle of the night. Just upped and left. Mull threw off his blankets, running his finger along the seal of his filter to make sure it hadn't come loose in the night, that he wasn't hallucinating. "Imeah! Pont!" He wasn't sure why he whispered – only that he couldn't quite get enough breath.

Both of them stirred. Pont was up first. He threw his blankets aside as soon as he saw. "*Fuck.*"

Mull quietly assessed as Pont chucked his bedroll at the ceiling, as he paced, as he screamed at a wall. The crew had taken nearly all the supplies. They'd only not managed to take all of them because Mull had kept some in his personal pack, which he'd slept next to.

What was left? A few extra filters, some salted fish, some

pickled vegetables and some rice. Imeah helped him go through it, laying out the rations, counting out the number of days they would last.

Pont sat on a nearby rock, letting out a long breath. "We are *fucked.*"

And for once, Mull couldn't find it in himself to disagree.

49

Hakara

10 years after the restoration of Kashan
and 571 years after the Shattering

Langzu – Bian

*The altered are blameless. They are changed beyond their
original states into something wholly new. All the mortals
are flawed. All the gods are flawed. But the altered are
Kluehnn's children and are the true inheritors of this world.
Do not fear them, for they are what you will become.*

Rasha was alive. She was alive and I knew where she was. I
desperately wanted to find a way through the barrier now,
to run straight to that den, to finally see her again. We'd spent
longer apart now than we'd spent together, but I felt I would
know her even if she were in a different skin.

I found Mitoran in the Bian safe house. It was stuffed to the
gills with other Unanointed; there was barely any room to
practice or to spar. It seemed she'd already begun gathering the
raiding party for the den, and there was little enough space on

the main floor. But they let me in and let me wipe down with a washcloth before I went to talk to her.

"There are more of us coming," she said when I looked around the room. "We're throwing everything we've got at Kluehnn."

I thought of the aspect of Kluehnn that Thassir had killed, the way it had nearly murdered all of us. I thought of the godkillers. That den would be full of them. "A lot of them will die."

Mitoran gave a quick, short nod. "Yes. But this fulfills our two end goals – taking the power of restoration away from Kluehnn by stealing his god gems, and bringing some measure of prosperity back to Langzu. If we can get that last corestone; if we can infuse them all, then it will have been worth it. Compare our potential casualties to the number of people who will die during restoration. Someone has to sacrifice. Someone has to fight back." She leaned over a table, weighing out god gems to check their sizes. "It's a long way from Ruzhi to Bian, yet you came all the way here. Have you changed your mind, then?"

I wasn't about to just meekly return. Thassir's words were still ringing in my ears, still banging about in the useless hollow of my heart. "Is Thassir here?"

She watched me. "He left soon after you did and I don't expect him here for the raid. He comes and goes as he pleases. He always has."

Damn him – I knew I'd said harsh things to him. I knew I'd broken our bond and had stormed off. But this was the worst time he could have chosen to disappear. How could I go into Kluehnn's den, how could I search out my sister, if he wasn't there with me?

Maybe he'd still come back. Maybe he'd be willing to renew our bond and to take on this last mission with me.

I hesitated. Even if it meant going into the depths of a den?

Even if it meant throwing himself into the midst of the godkillers and perhaps even Kluehnn himself? He was a god.

I'd grown too accustomed to having him by my side. I cast Mitoran a suspicious glance.

"Did you really send messages to Kashan to look for my sister? Did you even try, or were you always going to hold that over my head until I did what you wanted?"

She sat back, setting down the red gem she held between her fingers. "Don't believe everything Thassir tells you. We've known one another for a long time. He's been at this a long time. And time can hone hope for some people while it embitters others."

I wanted to tell her that I knew – that I knew Thassir was a god and that I knew that she knew. But I kept my mouth shut. There were too many listening ears.

"I sent messages to Kashan. I had to check the information I was given, after all." She pulled a folded piece of paper from her pocket and handed it to me. "If you'd waited instead of running off, I'd have had the chance to give this to you."

I unfolded it. There were sketchy details written on the page. Sightings of a little girl near the border where I'd crossed, alone. A horned altered. That matched what Sheuan had told me. Someone had seen her taken in by a scaled woman.

And that was all.

"It might be her, and it might not be," Mitoran said, her hands clasped serenely in front of her. "But I keep my word. Didn't my informant seek you out?"

I frowned. "She did."

"Yet you believed Thassir." She sighed. "He looks tough on the outside. He seems hardened. Yet beneath he is the sort who gravitates toward those who need the most care. He doesn't want you to go after your sister or even to capture this third corestone, because he doesn't want you to get hurt. To him, you are like one of the stray cats he's picked up and given a home. He cannot help himself."

I didn't want to believe her. I couldn't help *but* believe her. There's something particularly humiliating about having someone else's perception of you picked apart in a way that shows you how little they truly think of you.

He was a *god*. I was a mortal. We'd never been partners, not to him. To him, I'd been something small and weak in need of rescuing.

"We won't wait for him." Mitoran scooped the gems up and divided them into the nearby pouches. "If you want to come along, you'll have to bond with Buzhi."

They were going to rush into that den – the same den where my sister lived – and they were going to ask no questions and take no prisoners. They had two goals: the corestone and the god gems. If I wanted to stop Rasha from getting hurt, I *had* to go. Even if that meant forgoing Thassir's prowess. Even if it meant bonding with Buzhi.

"Tell me where he is."

She nodded upward, toward the sleeping rooms. "Your team is waiting for you."

I found them in the room I'd shared with Utricht. Alifra was tucking her various daggers and crossbow bolts into her vest, checking and rechecking how easily she could pull them free. Dashu was sharpening his blade with a whetstone, stopping every so often to test its edge.

Buzhi sat by the open window, his brow furrowed in concentration, his fingers spread before him. The air above them shimmered – aether he'd summoned from below. He let it blow away, took a breath, closed his eyes and had another go.

It took a moment, but the air above his hand shimmered again, like the heat distortion from a fire.

"Mitoran told me I could find you here."

His head snapped up. His fist closed. The aether dissipated. He let out a quick huff of breath. "I'm trying. I'm getting better." His gaze flicked to the ceiling, to the rooftop where Thassir often liked to sit at night. "I'm not him. I don't know how he does it. He seems just like a big, lumbering menace, but when he moves … when he calls the aether from below … it's like he's suddenly someone else."

He really had no idea. That was Buzhi – skirting close to the truth but not quite finding it.

I needed to stop thinking of him this way if we were to be bonded. We'd need to work together. "We had a falling-out."

Buzhi snorted, and I suddenly wanted to wring his neck. "I'm surprised it didn't happen sooner. He's not easy to get along with."

Neither was I.

He eyed me. "I'm your last choice for an arbor, aren't I?"

I tried on a rakish smile and felt it wobble at the corners. "There's nothing wrong with a little desperation if it nets us the corestone, is there?"

"If it kills as many godkillers as possible," he responded, his face grim.

"If we have the story of this day to pass on to our descendants." Dashu ran his finger along his blade and then, satisfied, kissed the flowered hilt and slid it back into its sheath. Then he pulled something from a pouch at his belt. "I made these. Something to give our new bruiser in case you didn't come back. To help them feel welcome." He handed a little patch of cloth to each of us. I brushed my fingers over the one he'd handed me. Two crossed swords were embroidered on it in black, the stitches as neat as Dashu's footwork. I glanced at the others – an arbor for Buzhi, a wasp for Alifra, and a vine for himself. I wasn't bonded to any of them, but I felt a thread of connection between us, frayed and thin, but there.

Alifra's gaze was distant as she held her patch, her hazel eyes unfocused. "What's the point? Our team keeps changing. We keep dying."

Dashu put a hand on her shoulder. "One more corestone and we can stop restoration in Langzu. We grieve later."

There was something desperate in Alifra's eyes when she finally looked at me. "What if we don't take enough god gems and we can't break the pact? What if restoration happens anyways?"

For a moment we stared at one another. I wasn't here for the corestone. I wasn't here to stop restoration. I could be truthful with my team for once. "My sister. I found out she's in the den we're raiding. They took her when she was a child. I have the chance to get her back."

Buzhi stood. "I had a brother who was like you – able to use the aether with the gems. But no one came to rescue him the way we did for you. They took him to a den. I never knew which one or where to find him. No one hears from the ones who disappear. No one ever hears from them again, and it's been eight years. I know he's dead. Your sister is not."

All of the Unanointed had a reason to hate Kluehnn. Just not all of them hated him because of restoration.

Alifra's lips tightened almost imperceptibly. "She is one person, but she still matters. She matters to you."

Dashu nodded, as though it were decided. "Then we go. We get her back. Together."

My throat tightened. I was their bruiser, I'd failed them multiple times and here they were, standing behind me, supporting me. It was more from them than I deserved. I tucked the embroidered patch into a pocket.

Buzhi pulled the knife from his belt and nicked his palm.

I took my knife and did the same. He wasn't Thassir, but he was all I had. And I'd dived into sinkholes under hairier conditions.

"I can shake on that." We clasped hands and he pulled the aether from below.

The magic sparked in my blood.

50

Rasha

10 years after the restoration of Kashan
and 571 Years After The Shattering

Kashan - Kluehnn's den

Altered who flee into unrestored realms must keep fleeing.
For if restoration catches them a second time, they lose all
reason, their bodies twisting into nightmares.

It shouldn't have hurt so much. Sheuan had already left me
once. This time I'd been the one to leave her. But there was
a part of me I couldn't seem to smother, a part that wanted to
believe that the little time we'd spent together would somehow
overrule her devotion to her family. Yet we hadn't spent enough
time together. We didn't know one another that well.

We'd met the other survivors of the first two trials – the lucky
ones who had only one last task to complete before their ascension
as godkillers. They'd all seemed fiercer, more prepared than we
did. When they stared at us I wondered if they marveled at how
we'd made it to the end. Had they banded together, or had they

each managed to take a key on their own? Beneath the bandages, beneath the corded muscle, I wondered if they were as damaged as we were. There had been only two other burrows and only six other surviving acolytes. One final trial. Killing a god.

Millani had granted me leave from my role as advocate. Not that she'd had much choice. After our welcoming ceremony, we would have to travel to find a god. We had to follow the clues we'd been given. I couldn't do both that and my advocate duties.

"Our godkillers have sensed traces of aether coming from these directions." Millani stood over the last remaining table in our burrow, pointing at the red pins on a map, at the lines drawn from them. The three lines converged near a small farming village. "You'll take a team of god killers with you and you'll investigate. The team will not be assisting you directly. Often, when we find a god, cleansing is necessary."

Khatuya and Naatar stood on either side of me, Naatar still a little pale from his injury, but healing. Altered were hardy like that. I could feel the tension wafting from both of them, Khatuya's rough brown shoulder brushing against mine. Naatar's tail swished anxiously behind him.

Millani pushed away from the table. "The rest of the details can wait until after the welcoming ceremony." She beckoned us to follow her into the tunnels.

Two turns later, and I knew the path we were taking. We were headed to the nave of the den, where everyone went for worship. I'd been there a thousand times before, had listened to the high priest preach, had eaten Kluehnn's blessing. This time felt different. I swallowed past a throat gone suddenly tight.

I could do this. I could take this next step toward that dream I had, the one I'd made myself – the one of a knife in my hand, of my own power, of being the one who protected instead of the one who needed protection.

I held my head high, let Khatuya and Naatar see: I was not afraid. Slowly, as we entered the nave, as we saw the other six acolytes who'd survived, I felt the tension uncoil as they took their cues from me.

Each of the other two groups had their own leader, and together the burrow leaders led us to the altar, to the pit that stood before it.

Darkness swirled within. My stomach dropped. I thought of the wall of black that had swept over me as a child, the way I'd ceased to exist. There was something primal about that fear, even though I'd come back from it. What if I didn't come back from it again? Or what if I ended up like one of the twice-altered?

Millani looked down into the pit, lantern light glittering off the red scales of her cheeks. She didn't look afraid, merely respectful. She'd been through this once. She'd come out the other end. If she could do it, so could I.

"It's not the ceremony we need to worry about," one acolyte whispered to another, though she sounded more like she was trying to convince herself. "It's the godkilling."

A shout echoed from somewhere in the caves. All the acolytes exchanged nervous glances, yet none of the godkillers reacted to it at all. Another shout. The sound of clashing blades.

And then Millani was before us, offering us Kluehnn's blessing. "Swallow it."

We were all used to Kluehnn's blessing. I opened my mouth and did as I was bade. This blessing was different. I could feel the weight of it on my tongue, something heavy beneath the soft bread. I swallowed.

My belly fizzed, an odd sensation. I looked to Khatuya, to see if she felt it too.

A hand pressed to my back, and before I could protest, it pushed me into the pit. I had the brief impression of Naatar and

Khatuya falling in as well, flashes of light and color and a surprised gasp.

The world went black.

There was no pain this time, only a soft awareness, like a breeze against my face. I had the simple thought *There is nothing to be afraid of* before I sank into the black, letting it blow me into so many pieces like dust into the wind.

Then a hand grabbed me by the wrist and I was in the nave again, Millani pulling me out of the pit. Everything felt a little brighter, a little sharper. Khatuya and Naatar were already there, looking as dazed as I felt. How much time had passed?

The rear door to the nave slammed open.

A man stood there, gasping, blood covering the rocky surface of his face. "The Unanointed! We're under attack!"

51

Mullayne

10 years after the restoration of Kashan and 571 years after the Shattering

Langzu – Tolemne's Path

Pre-Shattering relics are few and expensive to get a hold of. What little we have left paints a fascinating picture – a world of realms between which travel was simple and trade and ideas flowed.

"We have to go on." Mull heard his own voice and it didn't sound like his. He was shaking, trembling as though he were cold. His voice, however, was steady and assured. He stirred the rice he was steaming over the flame. Only a little. Just enough.

Pont pointed toward the tunnel they'd discovered yesterday. "That's another aerocline right there. Don't talk nonsense. Everyone left for a reason – because they were scared you'd try to get them to go down into those depths."

"And they took most of the food," Imeah noted.

Mull removed the pot from the flame. "There could be more food past the third aerocline. We found fish before, and there were the giant lizards. We could find more further down. And we *must* be close to Unterra by now."

"Could be? *Could* be?" Pont squeezed his eyes shut. "Do you hear yourself?"

But he wasn't asking to go back. He hadn't asked yet to go back. They all knew, though none of them had said it aloud, that the food they'd been left with wouldn't last until they made it back to the surface. They could go hungry for a little while, but Imeah would need her strength to make those climbs.

And the mystery beckoned.

In all the years Mull had known Pont, throughout all their expeditions, he was aware that in spite of Pont's complaining, the same sort of urge burned below his breastbone that burned in Mull. That need to *know*, to find something no one else had found.

Each time Mull had thought he'd found Tolemne's Path, Pont had grumbled and groused, but each time he'd finally caved and joined Mull's expedition. He spoke so often of the dangers, but half the time Mull suspected he complained because they *hadn't* found the path yet. Because he yearned for it.

Pont was still seizing his hair, shouting at the wall, waving his arms about in grand gestures that had long since ceased to alarm Imeah or Mull.

"Pont." Mull said his name quietly.

The big man stopped and turned to look at his friend.

"Do you want to go back, or do you want to go on?"

Pont's hands fell back uselessly by his sides. He looked like a rind that had been emptied of fruit. His gaze flicked to the tunnel where the third aerocline waited. "No one's ever been this far before. Not since Tolemne's time. And we're finding things no one's even dreamed about. What lies deeper down? Does Unterra even look the way our books describe it?" He sighed and rubbed his forehead. "I don't know, Mull. I just don't know."

Mull glanced at Imeah.

She held up her hands. "Oh no, don't look at me. I won't make this choice for you. You and I both know I've been following along to indulge you, darling."

"And you would go along only to indulge me further?" He tried to keep the frustration from his voice and failed.

She only gave him a wan shrug and picked up her cane, clearly ready to go in whichever direction he bade.

This was not what he'd expected. This was never what he'd wanted. But the third aerocline was right there and they were close to Unterra, he knew it. He closed his eyes. "We go on." The words echoed in his jawbone, trembling to the very soles of his feet. They had to *know*. They had to *see*.

Pont nodded in a grim sort of way, no complaints left on his lips. It seemed right—as though fate did exist. The three of them, heading down into the great unknown. The only thing Mull might have changed was the lack of Jeeoon. She should have been there with them. She'd always been a core member of their team.

They ate first and switched their filters out for fresh ones. Pont carried the majority of the supplies, his broad back easily bearing the weight. Mull took the rest of the food, as well as Imeah's bedroll. Imeah walked free of hindrance, and even though her filter obscured her mouth, Mull knew her teeth were gritted. She'd been pushing herself so hard to keep up. She must have been exhausted.

He offered her his arm, which she gratefully accepted, leaning into him as they followed Pont into the tunnel.

The third aerocline lay there shimmering. The way beyond was brightly lit, the tunnel walls coated with bioluminescent moss and fungus; they wouldn't need their lanterns. There was such a sharp delineation between the glowing life in the second aerocline and past the third that Mull thought his earlier supposition must be right – that the plants and fungus down here fed off the aether. But he didn't have the time for experiments.

Pont turned back to them, offering a hand to Imeah. Wordlessly, she took it, and the three of them stepped into the third aerocline.

Mull didn't feel anything different, not at first. The shimmering surface of the aerocline rippled outward, breaking and dissolving in spots as they descended into it. There was no change in temperature. It wasn't until his hands submerged that he felt the difference. The air was thicker, viscous, his fingers encountering a slight resistance as he moved them. And it *was* warmer, only slightly. His arms were lighter. Imeah's head submerged first, her long black hair drifting with her movements.

He took in a long, deep breath. The air in his filter still smelled clear. They'd have to change out the filters more often here.

There were calculations he could do that gave him some idea of the concentration of aether in the second aerocline. Research had been done at sinkholes, papers published that he'd been able to read in the clan libraries. But nothing spoke of the third aerocline, so he wasn't sure of the concentration of aether here.

They'd have to err on the side of caution.

Pont held a breath and blew out their lanterns, then placed his filter over his nose and mouth and breathed sharply out, clearing as much aether as possible, before sealing it back onto his face. "Everyone all right?"

Mull wanted to laugh. *Everyone*. As though there were more people than just the three of them. But he nodded, as did Imeah. The green-blue glow of the moss at their feet bathed their faces in an eerie, sickly light.

They marched into the darkness.

His map was of little use here. There were no more tunnels marked on it, no notes. They'd gone beyond that. Twice they found themselves at a fork, but a quick scouting proved the other way impassable or a dead end.

He found his mind turning in impossible circles, trying to calculate things he had no reference for. How large was their world? Everything said it was round. If that were so, given the estimated circumference of the planet and the estimated circumference of the hollow within, how far would they have to travel? How far had they traveled already? What was the difference between those two numbers? Was it possible there was a fourth aerocline?

It didn't matter. They were committed.

He tried to focus instead on the feel of Imeah's hand on his arm, the sound of their breathing, the way his floating hair tickled the backs of his ears.

Pont let go of Imeah's hand, absent-mindedly scratching his shoulder.

Mull held his breath. "Pont." His voice sounded strange this deep down, floating through the thickened air, distorted. "How do you feel?"

Pont's hand froze.

He met Mull's gaze. Fear was filling his eyes to the brim, widening them. One eyelid twitched. "I don't know. I can't tell if the itching is because I've been without a bath for so many days or because of something else." A drop of sweat ran down his forehead and into his filter's seal. "How bad is the air down here, Mull?"

Panic fluttered in Mull's throat. He stuffed it down, trying to get his stomach to settle. "You should go back."

"Back?" It came out as a snarl. "After everything you've put us through, you want me to go *back*?" Pont stopped, swallowed.

He shuddered. "I . . . It's happening to me, isn't it? Everything is swimming. The light down here seems too bright."

The rope. Mull had a rope. He pulled the coils free from his pack, his fingers trembling. Imeah's hand left his arm. "We have to tie him up. We have to take him back."

The hair on Imeah's forehead was plastered to her skin. "He's too big." She held up her cane in limp fingers. "I can't carry him – you know I can't."

Dammit. He *did* know. Were his scattered thoughts just the result of a heightened emotional state, or was it the aether, sliding beneath his mask, digging its claws in? The metaphor felt too real to him. The skin around his mouth prickled. He couldn't think about that.

"First step is to immobilize him. We think about the rest later."

Pont held his hands up. "Quick. Before I can't help myself."

Mull wrapped the rope around his wrists, and then his forearms for good measure. Pont was bigger and stronger than Mull and Imeah combined. More than anything now, Mull wished he'd taken him up on those fighting lessons he'd always offered. "You should know the basics," Pont had told him, over and over.

"With these arms? A man like you could snap me like a twig."

"It's not always about strength."

But Mull had always shrugged and smiled and waved him off. He'd had better things to do.

Right now, he couldn't think what those better things had been. All he could think was that those techniques might have helped him save his friend's life, and he'd *wasted* that time and the opportunity for knowledge. All he had now was a rope and two arms his mother had once described as akin to dried noodles.

"Mull." There was more sweat beading on Pont's forehead. "No matter what happens. No matter what I do – you know that I love you, right? We've always been like brothers."

"Stop. Tell me when we're back in the light of day."

Pont let out a long breath.

Mull put a hand to his shoulder. "Slow your breathing. You're a big man. You take in more air than Imeah and I do. I should have known you'd fall to it first. And the lantern ... you shouldn't have lifted your filters to blow it out. Imeah – do you see anything ahead?"

She was already moving, her cane thumping against the moss as she made as much haste as she could further down the tunnel. If Unterra was ahead, if it was *close*, they could take Pont there instead. The air in Unterra was clear of aether, according to all the books Mull had read. Unless those accounts had been wrong too.

He tightened the knots on the rope and then began to wind the loose end around Pont's upper body. At this stage of aether sickness, he should have been afraid of his friend, but he found he couldn't be. They'd spent so many nights together on the hard ground, backs pressed to prop one another up when they'd been on watch duty. Telling jokes to keep one another awake. Another day, another night, another expedition.

Pont swallowed, his breathing quick in spite of Mull's warning. "I don't know how much longer I have left. I think I can *smell* it, Mull. It's not bad. It's actually ... nice. It smells like my grandfather baking pies by the heat of the vents back in Cressima. Sulfur and sweetness."

Mull fumbled in his pack. "Take in a breath. I'm changing your filter."

Pont nodded and breathed in. Another drop of sweat fell to his chin. His bound hands tightened, his right hand the palm of his left.

In the first aerocline, it took time for the aether sickness to settle in. This was happening so quickly. Too quickly.

Where was Imeah? Mull needed to know what direction to

move in, and quickly. Before he had to fight Pont to get him to save his own life. He pulled the filter off Pont's face and held the fresh one over his nose and mouth. "Breathe out. Sharply."

Pont obeyed. Mull's fingers felt too clumsy as he pressed the filter to his face and tried to tighten the straps.

Something glinted in the depths of Pont's eyes.

No.

The big man surged forward and up, knocking Mull to the cave floor. He towered over him, his breathing heavy.

The filter slipped from his face.

Mull thought he'd known despair before – several times on this expedition. But this was the first time he wished he'd turned back. He wished it as hard as his body could manage, his bones aching with it. He should have turned back. He should have. *He should have.*

If someone had held a knife to his friends' throats and told him he had to choose Imeah or Pont, he would have picked Imeah. He would have hesitated, he would have wept, but he would have chosen her.

But there was no errant hand here, no third party with a blade. There was only him and his desperately foolish choices. He'd thought he could have them both.

Pont charged him.

Mull scrambled away, trying his best to keep his breathing level even as he wept, even as fear prickled in his limbs and chest.

He couldn't fight Pont, not even with his hands bound. A foot kicked out, trying to catch his ribs. Mull barely rolled out of the way. "Pont. *Please!* Fight it off a little longer. Just try."

Pont's chest heaved, a growl in his throat. He stopped his attack for a moment to try and work himself free. One of the knots started to slip.

"Stop, don't do that. Don't—"

And then he was attacking again, with feet and teeth and heavy shoulders. Mull lifted his arms to protect his face. Pont bit his wrist, and Mull stomped hard on his foot until he let go. Whatever Pont had smelled, Mull couldn't smell it. All he could smell was sweat and blood.

The world shrank to the battering of Pont's body against his. The glow of the surrounding vegetation flashed behind the darkness of his friend's silhouette. His head spun. Both ears ached. This was what he deserved in the end, wasn't it?

"I'm sorry." He couldn't hear his own words. Pont didn't seem to hear them either. He took a brief step back, his muscles straining.

The knot around his body slipped. His arms came free. He lifted both fists and brought them down hard on Mull's head. Someone was screaming. Or was that just the ringing of his ears? Everything faded to black.

He couldn't breathe. It took him a moment to realize that the beating had stopped, that Pont was slumped over him, his weight pressing him into the cavern floor. He squirmed, trying to get out from beneath his friend. The glow of the cavern appeared once more in his vision and he had the presence of mind to put a hand over his filter, keeping it on his face as he wriggled free.

The hilt of a knife protruded from the back of Pont's neck. Imeah stood over him, her face stricken.

52

Hakara

10 years after the restoration of Kashan and 571 years after the Shattering

Langzu - the border

The clans of Langzu say their families were chosen by Barexi to lead. Chosen for their intelligence, their strength, their kindness. Their right to the land, to its people – all passed to them by divinity. Now there is no Barexi. Now there is the Sovereign, and he holds the clans in his fist.
He decides who rises, and who falls.

The way through the barrier was a fair bit uncomfortable – worse than I remembered. Maybe it was because back then I'd been just a kid and had been carried halfway through. I'd also been out of my mind with aether sickness, so the details hadn't been exactly clear to me.

I was sober this time, and every grain of sand and dust that struck my face and eyes was an affront. We were swimming in it, trying to stumble our way through a current that was doing its best to buffet us into oblivion. I held tight to the guide's rope, my breath held, my heartbeat slow and steady in my breast.

It was further than I'd remembered too, but it was easy enough for me to keep from inhaling the aether. I watched the back of Buzhi in front of me, the white of his vestigial wings as he walked out of the barrier, until that was the last thing I could see of him.

I followed him into the light.

Everything about the world smelled wrong. It was green here, so green and overgrown that I couldn't quite comprehend it. I fell to my knees, touching the soft grass that grew close to the border.

"Keep moving!" Mitoran shouted.

I half rose, stumbling out of the way. More of the Unanointed came out of the barrier, the rope still clutched between their fingers. Our guide was pulling them through, keeping the rope taut.

Someone I didn't recognize was consulting with Mitoran – a rock-skinned altered with a sharp-edged face. Undoubtedly one of the Unanointed's agents in Kashan. Other than her, no one was here to greet us. This wasn't an official border crossing.

It would take us longer to reach the den through the dense undergrowth of Kashan's restored forests, but we could do so unseen. The winged woman looked us over, mentally tallying our numbers as the last Unanointed came through.

There were at least a hundred of us; Unanointed from every part of Langzu. Langzuan natives, refugees from Kashan, from Cressima, and possibly some from Albanore. There were people of every kind, from every level of society. It had surprised me at first to spot a few Langzuan people I *knew* must have been from the clans – their clothes plain but just a little too fine for normal wear. What did they have to gain by throwing their lot in with the Unanointed? From what I knew, the clans all worshiped Kluehnn to some extent. But perhaps the same fire burned in all people – the desire not to be beholden to a bargain they did not make.

We made our way toward the den.

Mitoran's Kashani agent stopped us every so often, scouting ahead, making sure the way was clear. Everyone was instructed to keep their hands as close to their sides as possible, not to touch any of the strange flora and fauna we saw. One woman was stung by a flying black insect and quickly died, blood-flecked spittle staining her cheeks, but that was the only bit of excitement. One of the altered was stung as well, but he brushed off the effects as though he'd merely been bitten by a mosquito.

This world was not hospitable to mortals. The mortals gravitated toward the center of the group, the altered cushioning us from the dangers of the restored world.

We stopped just short of the den, dividing quietly into groups. We would attack in waves, the first group meant as a primary diversion, pulling as many godkillers as possible into the ravine. The second group would drive them away from the entrance and attack from above, mostly with magic and ranged weapons. The third group would go straight into the den, causing havoc as they searched for the infused god gems. They were the secondary diversion. And the fourth group – my team's group – would try to find the corestone. We had no maps of the place, but we knew at least that the god gems would be kept past the first aerocline so they'd retain their infusion.

Mitoran crouched farther up, between a gap in the trees. She lifted her lantern and flashed the shutters. Once. Twice.

The first group surged forward.

Is there anything so grueling as the wait before a fight? I crouched in the brush and shifted from foot to foot with nervous energy, even though I was meant to be doing my best to lie low and stay quiet. Didn't want the den to catch wind that the first wave was only that – a first wave.

Buzhi watched me as I turned to picking the dirt from beneath my fingernails. Should have been practicing my breathing. Should have been looking to Mitoran for the signal. But really, that was what everyone else was doing. Wasn't like I was going to miss the whole crowd around me upping and disappearing into the woods.

"Are you very calm or very nervous?" he asked. "Because I can't tell."

I shrugged. "It's not the fight that's getting to me."

Three groups ahead of us. I knew that Rasha was bigger now, probably even bigger than I was, if she was altered. But I couldn't stop imagining her as I'd left her the last time, her brown eyes wide, arms wrapped around herself.

I turned to look at Alifra, because I was tired of looking at Buzhi. There was something vacant in her black-eyed gaze. Wherever she was, she still wasn't with us. Dashu gave her concerned glances, but if he'd tried to bring her out of it, it hadn't worked.

"Hey." I snapped my fingers in front of her face. "You ready? You wanted to steal from a god, right? What's better than taking the god gems and a corestone right out of one of his dens?"

The grin she flashed me evaporated as quickly as morning dew on a hot day. "That wasn't the full truth. The Otangu orchards . . . their pest . . . that wasn't the first time I'd failed a child. I didn't . . . I didn't come alone on that boat. I had a daughter."

Something in Dashu's face shifted, then broke along well-worn lines. He'd never heard this before. She'd never told him.

She was somewhere in the past, caught in a memory. "There's no pity in Langzu because it's not undergone restoration, so why would I tell anyone? I know what people would say. That I should have stayed in Albanore with her because the way was dangerous. That she was just a baby. That I shouldn't have taken her on that boat. But half the people who stay disappear, and there were two of us, me and her. I took the chance. Babies can't swim. Did I try to save her, or did I just let her go? I don't know. I'll never know."

With the care of someone removing the shell from a hatching egg, Dashu reached out and tucked an errant piece of curly hair behind her ear. "I'm sorry. Grieve now." His voice was so low I nearly didn't catch the words. "Grieve now and use it when we fight."

She ducked her head, took in a breath and nodded, her hand finding his. And then, just as quickly, she pulled away, as though she couldn't bear his comfort for too long.

Buzhi touched my arm. I really didn't like the man, but I didn't shrug him off. "We'll find your sister."

"Supposed to be finding the corestone."

"We can walk and think at the same time."

I tilted my head, my nose wrinkling. Wasn't really the best analogy. This was entirely different, wasn't it? My sister and the corestone could be in two entirely different directions.

But then Mitoran was signaling for the next wave.

My breath quickened. I steadied it, pressing my palm to the space below my ribs. The third wave went right after that. There'd be a short pause, and then we'd dive into the ravine after them. Utricht had always held the team together. That was my job now, and though I didn't feel up to the task, I tried anyways. "We've all lost people to restoration. We've all lost pieces of ourselves. Now we've got the chance to take something back. Ready?" I asked.

All three of them were with me now. They each gave me a firm nod, even Buzhi.

Maybe he wasn't so bad. Maybe I'd only disliked him because frankly I disliked most people. Sure, he was a little incompetent, but he was trying, and I knew he'd do his best to protect me.

He looked to my fidgeting feet. "I guarantee you I'm more ready than you are."

Well, maybe he was still an asshole. In spite of myself, my gaze fixed on Mitoran's silhouette ahead. The shutters flashed. I surged to my feet.

Our route followed the third wave, circling around to where the scout had told us the den's entrance was. Fighting was still raging in the ravine, and shit, it didn't look good for the Unanointed. Blood caught the fading light, coating rock and dirt. One god-enhanced arm was lying on the ground, a thin layer of smoke rising from the skin as the fingers twitched.

The godkillers had formed tight formations and were managing to hold their own. I scanned their number desperately, searching for Rasha. A part of me wondered if I'd even recognize her after alteration and so many years. The rest of me knew I would know when I saw her. I would *know*. And she wasn't here.

The other two waves *had* done their jobs. The way to the den's door was clear. We used the ropes left by the previous wave, descending to the bottom.

It was a short drop, nothing like diving a sinkhole. Yet my belly swooped like I was descending into the depths of the earth. The entire fourth group was made up of teams – arbors, bruisers, vines and pests. The door to the den was askew, and we pushed past it into the den itself.

This was where our information remained nebulous. We weren't sure where the corestone was, but Mitoran had told us to check the nave first. It had to be a large cavern.

There was no sign of the third wave as we searched, but they'd left their mark. Blood and the scratches of blades marred the walls; here and there were discarded or lost weapons, pieces of armor that had been dropped or cut free. We weaved silently through the tunnels, checking passages and caverns. I kept my breathing deep and steady, trying to make sure I was getting enough air before we ran into someone.

But there was no one on our path.

The skylights above disappeared as we descended into the deeper parts of the den, the tunnels lit only by lanterns, a few of which had been destroyed or had gone out. Somewhere, echoing through the tunnels, I heard the sound of fighting.

We stepped into the nave. It couldn't have been anything else – a carved wooden altar at the end of it, covered in eyes and mouths. I hadn't quite expected the cavern to be quite so damned big. The light here didn't extend to every corner, leaving a vast blackness into which I stared but couldn't make out anything.

What I could see wasn't comforting. There was a hole in the floor. A sinkhole.

"Do you think they toss people in it?" I whispered to Dashu. "Do you think if someone says, 'Kluehnn isn't actually that great', they say, 'Oh well, into the pit with you'?"

He gave me a sidelong glance as the rocky altered in front of me said, "Quiet!" in a low voice.

"Eh, *you* be quiet, why don't you? There's no one here."

The rocky altered pointed to the hole in the ground and I couldn't fault him for his logic. We couldn't see into the hole, so who knew if anything was hiding down there? I didn't.

The altar stood behind the hole, and on it was a box. I thought, if I squinted, there was a glow at the seams of it.

"I'm going to take a look."

Buzhi swiped for my arm, but I slid out of his reach. I heard his footsteps hurrying to follow. That was what a good arbor did, wasn't it? Watched out for their bruiser. Someone had to scout the way, and we couldn't just stand around wasting time. Unanointed were dying left and right, all to give us this chance. And the quicker we found the corestone, the quicker I could infuse it and pass it off to someone else. Rasha was down here somewhere, and she was at risk.

I glanced down the sinkhole as I skirted around it. Darkness as far as I could see, with only the faint glimmer of gems in the depths – a sprinkling of barely visible stars. If Kluehnn was in there, I couldn't see him. It should have been a comforting thought, but somehow it wasn't.

The altar itself was simple, brutal in design. No traps I could see, nothing stopping the box from being grabbed. Not like they would have expected thieves in a den full of godkillers.

I opened the box. Only one small green gem within. No corestone.

Godkillers flooded into the nave in formations of three. Fifteen in total against our twenty. Fair odds – except we were in their nave, in their den, and we didn't know the layout of the tunnels.

Shit. Shit shit shit.

The rocky altered drew his blades. "Go," he called to me from across the hole. I knew what he was thinking. I was Mitoran's linchpin. I was the only one among us who could infuse the corestones with enough power to complete the plan.

I grabbed Buzhi's arm, nodded to Dashu and Alifra, and we ran. Past the altar, toward the only other tunnel leading into the nave. A narrow space, wide enough for just one person at a time.

Three godkillers were blocking it, one standing in front of the other two.

I think I knew before I even fully took in her face. She was half covered in blood, none of it her own. Her hair was the same shade I remembered, her eyes the same golden brown. Her face was longer, her teeth sharp. The black-tipped horns at the crown of her head swept away from her forehead before curling inward. She was frightfully tall, nearly as tall as Thassir, though not quite as broad. Her height was the lankiness of a crane or a heron, though her corded muscles spoke of a strength those birds did not possess. I could not see the other two godkillers; they were a faded halo around the only person who mattered.

All my breathing exercises, all the effort I'd taken to keep myself calm – they meant nothing. My throat tightened, my eyes hot.

"Rasha."

Her fingers loosened on her knife, the hilt nearly dropping from her fingers. Her lips moved soundlessly, though I caught the shape of them. *Hakara.*

I tried to speak, had to clear my throat. If my team was still behind me, I could no longer sense their presence. The whole of my attention, my world, was focused on Rasha. On this moment.

The sound of clashing blades brought me back to myself. "You look . . . you look well." It was a stupid thing to say. The worst thing. Ten years, and this was all I could manage? She'd been altered, her body changed against her will. And I hadn't been there for her through any of it. "I'm here. I'm here to take you home."

For a moment, I thought she might run to me, throw her arms around me. That was what I'd imagined in tear-soaked dreams that had dissolved into hard, hot days. She took a half-step forward as though drawn to me against her will.

And then her jaw firmed up. She closed her eyes and took a breath, then opened them. "Where do you think home is exactly? Langzu?"

"You can get through the barrier, we can work together, get a house—"

"Until restoration comes for Langzu too. I'm not welcome there. I will never be welcome there the way I am here."

I hadn't cared about restoration until now. The only thing I'd had the space to care about was finding Rasha, and now that I had, my mind fumbled forward. "It doesn't matter; we'll be together. *I'm* your home, Rasha. I'm here to rescue you."

"I don't need rescuing, and *this* is my home." Her fingers tightened around her dagger.

The world was slipping away from me, leaving me in a cold and empty place devoid of light and sound. I kept talking, trying to find some way back to solid ground. "I did everything I could. I tried to come back for you sooner. You have no idea how hard I've been working to find you again."

"No." There was a tone of finality in the word, and it cut me cleaner than any blade. "I know you." She shook her head. "You didn't try hard enough. If you really cared about me that much, you would have found a way. You *always* found a way."

She glanced over my shoulder to where the fight was taking place, to where I could hear a low, sinister growl echoing up the sinkhole. "You are a weakness I cut out of me, piece by piece. And then I burned those pieces. I don't need your protection. I don't *want* your protection. What was I ever to you except something to give you purpose and meaning? The only one who has ever really cared for me, who has never abandoned me, is Kluehnn."

I was crumbling. I was dust dissolving into the sea, becoming the great deep cold of the ocean itself. I'd always believed myself capable of anything if only I threw myself at the problem hard enough. It was a story I'd told myself over and over through the long, hard years of sinkhole mining. I'd blamed my abandonment of Rasha on Guarin because I couldn't face my own role in it. It was easier to be angry with him. He'd deserved some of my anger; why not give him the whole lot of it? Until Thassir, I'd always shied away from the truth.

I stood there, helpless and hopeless, as the Unanointed died behind me, as they died above me. Frozen by the shattering of this long-held dream. Everything would be all right if I only found Rasha again, I'd told myself. I could fix things. I'd always thought I could fix things.

But time had not stood still, and she had stopped waiting for me.

She lifted her knife. The two godkillers behind her did the same.

"Rasha, please." I couldn't breathe. How could I fight if I couldn't breathe? How could I fight *her*? I couldn't. There was no way I possibly could. I would let her kill me.

"You shouldn't have come."

Something within me broke. I was that young girl again, waking up in the barrier, the dust and dirt swirling around me. I could taste it on my lips, the aether coursing through my blood, the salt-water smell of it filling my nose. And Guarin with me over his shoulder. He must have felt me stirring, because he'd patted my leg in a way I was sure now was meant to be comforting. He was an asshole, he was cruel, but he was never as bad as I'd wanted him to be. His grip was loose. I'd known in that moment that I could have slipped free.

I hadn't.

"You're wrong about me," I said. Rasha hesitated, and I pressed on. "I'm not as strong as you think I am. I *have* tried to find you. I passed out when I tried to prove to the foreman I could hold my breath long enough to work as a diver. I woke up in the barrier, thrown over his shoulder. He didn't know where to find you, so he did the best he could. When I woke up, I had a choice – I could have given up my life trying to get back to you. Or I could choose to continue onward. Maybe it was weakness, maybe it was something else, but I didn't turn back.

"I would give my life for yours. But that wasn't the choice that was offered to me. I had to take care of you after Mimi and

Maman were gone. I think I forgot that I was still so young. And some things – big things – were still out of my control."

I wished Thassir were here. I wished he were at my back. I hated accepting that I didn't have control over everything, yet accepting that was the only way I could forgive myself. And I had to forgive myself. Even if Rasha couldn't.

She hummed a few notes of a song I recognized. The lullaby Mimi had once sung to us. The one I'd always sung to Rasha. Something had shifted in her expression and in her stance. "I did miss you," she said. "For so many years. I missed you so much. I always looked up to you. I always wanted to be like you."

I reached for her. "Get us out of here. Help me find the corestone. Come back to Langzu with me."

She touched her fingers to mine. It was a light touch, as though she wanted just to be sure I was real. Then she shook her head. "My place is here. It's been ten years, Hakara. For you, maybe, it was not as long. But I was nine when you left me. No matter what happened in the past, the outcome is the same: we are on opposite sides. I won't yield. Will you?"

And then her fingers darted for my wrist, seizing me in a surprisingly strong grip. Before I could react, she'd yanked me forward, sending me tumbling to the floor behind her.

I caught a glimpse of a flashing blade.

Her blade.

Blood spurted from Buzhi's neck. His face widened in surprise, and then I felt the bond within, born only three short days ago, break.

53

Sheuan

10 years after the restoration of Kashan
and 571 years after the Shattering

Langzu - the outskirts of Bian

*Irael, the God of Many Chances, was rarely worshiped in
a group setting. He visited his miracles on mortals quietly,
in the dead of night or the early hours of the morning. He
looked for those whom all others had forsaken or had given
up on.*

*In their darkest hours, Irael would come to them. He
believed in the inherent goodness of mortals, never content
with only last chances. The oral history of Aqqil says that
it was Irael's steadfast attention that changed Lisha the
Orator from a drunkard, a cheat, and a liar into a queen.*

Mull's workshop was up and running when Sheuan
dropped in. Business was brisk, in no small thanks
to her. Nimao had spread word of the contraptions he'd bought,
and she'd seeded the rest of the clans with whispers of the other

things they could find. She wanted to feel satisfied, but the filters weighed heavily in her satchel.

Mull had told her that some of his inventions weren't ready for public consumption, yet she'd forged ahead anyways. It felt inevitable, like as soon as she'd opened that box, her path was set – to the Sovereign breathing down her neck and her out of her depth.

The workshop foreman nodded to her as she entered, and the workers only glanced up briefly before returning to their jobs. The scent of sawdust and hot metal filled the air. Sheuan picked her way deliberately past them to Mull's desk. The notes on the filters were still there in the box tucked away beneath its surface.

She wasn't sure if Mull was just too trusting, if he'd truly vetted his workers *that* well, or if he was just so preoccupied with other things that security had slipped his mind. She'd have to talk to him when he returned, or at least write him a note, if he refused to speak to her. All it would take was a spy from a rival clan to steal some of his trade secrets. Or even a spy from the Sovereign. He wasn't above that sort of subterfuge.

She tucked the sheaf of notes next to the filters in her bag and made her way back through the streets of Bian. Back home.

Her mother was waiting for her at the door. "Well? You went to Kashan and returned again. Did you get what the Sovereign wanted?"

"Not exactly." She'd done her best in Kashan, to do exactly as the Sovereign had asked. As her mother had asked. But that path was now closed to her. She was the only one holding the secrets of Mull's filters. Until he returned, she was the only one. The power of it sifted through her veins, making her feel both terrible and free. "I did not find the evidence he wanted, or a way to stop isolation."

Her mother's hands went to her hair, her lips trembling. "You have to go back. Again. You have to."

Sheuan stood firm on the threshold. Inside, she was shaking, unsure whether it was with fear or anticipation. "I could die."

"Think of everything our family would be losing, the way our clan will be disbanded if you don't do something. All our elders out on the streets. Some of them murdered by rival clans after their years of loyal service. Every business we worked so hard to build pawned off. We put all our hopes in you! We put all our money into you!"

"I didn't ask for you to do that."

"This isn't just our legacy. It is *yours*. Is this what you want everyone to remember you by?"

And beneath those words, Sheuan could sense the unspoken ones. Better to be remembered dying in an attempt to make things right. Better to be remembered as dutiful, as steadfast, as unwavering in her devotion to family and clan.

Her thoughts flashed to Rasha, her golden-brown eyes, her serious lips. The hesitancy of her hands when they'd lain together so markedly different from the hard set of her jaw when she was angry. And she'd been angry with Sheuan the last they'd seen one another. The first time Sheuan had left her with only a slight pang, so why did it hurt so much to be the one left, even when they'd barely spent any time together?

What would Rasha say if she could see her now? She knew exactly what Rasha would say, with a certainty that stilled the shaking in her soul. Rasha would tell Sheuan not to listen to her mother, to do what she damn well felt like.

And what did she feel like doing?

If she dug through each layer she'd accumulated over the years, each trait she'd assumed to survive, there was something pale and new beneath, something that was yearning to break free, to uncurl, to find the sun.

She had always existed to serve others, to bear the weight of that guilt and responsibility for her family. What if she stopped? And not in a way that was meant to serve Mitoran and her shadowy goals, but in a way that was meant to serve herself? She was gifted, everyone had always told her so, and her training had only enhanced those gifts. What could she accomplish if she used those gifts to further her own aims?

"No."

The word rang out in the entrance hall. She caught a glimpse of their one servant scurrying across from one doorway to the next, unwilling to be caught in the crossfire. "I'm done. I am not going back. I will no longer be the one bearing all the responsibility for this family. You want to dig us out of this hole? Go to Kashan yourself."

Her mother's eyes widened, her mouth opening as though the words were a slap. She took two swift steps toward Sheuan, and for a moment Sheuan thought she might *actually* slap her. But she only stood there, her gray hair as frayed as her sleeves. "Do you think I wanted my only daughter to be used in such a way? Do you think I orchestrated all this to weigh you down? Oh, I'd rather your father had never worked for the Sovereign, I'd rather he'd never been caught embezzling, had never been executed. I would have seen you grow up with the sort of worries most children have. Instead, I have watched you bent to one purpose. You think I wanted this? I am your *mother*.

"But this is what the world has demanded. This is what has to be done. Do not talk to me of suffering and responsibility. You think you've suffered? You haven't suffered until you've watched the person you care about the most suffer. Until you must send them marching toward danger because everyone is waiting for you to *fix* things. Look at me! I am old." Her face was inches from Sheuan's, her eyes glinting and red-rimmed. "It cannot be me."

Every emotion imaginable tumbled inside Sheuan, a tangled skein that could not be undone. She couldn't tell if what her mother was saying was true, if she believed it, if she was only saying it to turn Sheuan back to the one task she'd always been set to: saving their clan. There was no way to take a step back, to judge the woman objectively; their lives were intertwined in a way that let past feelings weave into the present. They would always fall into these same patterns, play out the same scenes over and over. Her mother had never said this to her before, yet there was the feeling of familiarity, a shoe falling into a footprint someone else had left behind.

No one could hurt Sheuan the way she could.

Had she been so unfair and so callous – not considering what she was putting her mother through? Had she been selfish and self-centered, thinking only of her own repressed desires and not the desires her mother had put to the side?

Yet she'd been a dutiful daughter. She'd put on that face, had worn it day in and day out, layering the other masks on top. She'd worn it so long she'd thought that was her true self – a woman who would always put her family above herself.

"I have always done as you've asked," she said slowly. "I have tried so hard to be everything you and our clan needed me to be. And now, when I balk, you still can't give me a moment's consideration. You don't even see me anymore, do you?" That *was* unfair, because Sheuan hadn't seen herself either. But it was true – they both knew it.

She watched the shift in her mother's expression, the sinking knowledge that she could not rely on Sheuan to save them. The flickering light of desperation snuffed out – what was the use? She steeled herself against the flood of guilt, let it wash over her. She turned.

"Do not walk away from us." Her mother's voice trembled,

echoing against the empty stone walls. "Do not walk away from *me*. Sheuan, we need you."

She didn't look back. She only pulled Mull's notes from her satchel and tossed them into the fire by the entrance.

Her life was her own. And she would make decisions she could live with.

54

Hakara

10 years after the restoration of Kashan and 571 years after the Shattering

Kashan - Kluehnn's den

Relics tell us that Numinars existed in every realm, and natural philosophers suppose they must have adapted to each environment. Some suppose they used their magic to establish a foothold in unfriendly soil. Some suppose there were different varieties of Numinars, which would explain how depictions of them vary slightly from culture to culture.

I had a score of godkillers to my back, a broken bond and a dead partner, and an empty tunnel ahead of me. Deep down, I'd always been a survivor, someone who took action first and took stock later. My feet were moving before my mind had even had the chance to agree that yes, running was a good idea.

"Let them go." Rasha's voice, a deep echo from dark places, barely reached me.

Dashu and Alifra followed me. Through the narrow gap and

into a wider tunnel. Every tunnel that was heading back up, back toward the surface, seemed to be filled with fighting. Every time the three of us tried to stop for a moment to catch our bearings, footsteps sounded from behind.

And what use was I? I had gems in my pouches but no means to use them. Even if I'd run into another Unanointed I could partner with, I was too out of breath to be much use. Rasha had killed Buzhi. She could have killed me, but she'd spared me and killed him.

I'd left her again, but it sure as the gods below didn't feel like an abandonment this time. She'd wanted me to go. She'd wanted me to escape. It was the only thing that kept me going. Rasha was now strong and fierce and more than a little frightening, but there was still a hint of that girl beneath. Underneath everything she was still soft and kind. I had to believe it. I had to live to believe it.

So I pulled a lantern from the wall and fled into the deeper parts of the den, Dashu and Alifra at my heels, unquestioning. The sounds of fighting faded behind us. The tunnels here were darker, the lanterns interspersed at greater intervals. I stopped, my hands on my knees as I tried to catch a moment's rest. Dashu came abreast of me. "How much deeper can we go before we run into the first aerocline? Do you think the corestone is still in here, or was it all a trap?"

I opened my mouth to respond. Footsteps sounded again behind us. We exchanged panicked glances and darted into the nearest doorway.

It opened up into a cavern, stalactites and stalagmites dotting the space, creating eerie, lumpy pillars. A pit lay at the end, the space beyond so dark I couldn't tell if there was another tunnel or just a wall. It looked as though no one ever came down this deep. I had a sense that if I lifted the lantern over that pit, I'd be able to see the shimmer of the first aerocline right at the lip.

"You're still alive."

I whirled about, my sword in my hand before I remembered drawing it.

Mitoran stood at the entrance to the cavern, a winged altered at her shoulder. She was in armor, a long, thin-bladed sword in her hand. She held it well in spite of her age, and the lantern light caught the glint of red on its edge.

"You should be more surprised that *you're* alive," I said. While Mitoran had never told me her background, she'd always struck me as more of a planner than an actual fighter.

Alifra's feet shuffled behind me. "We weren't all so lucky."

Mitoran looked us over. "Buzhi?"

I shook my head.

She reached into the pouch at her side. I saw the glow before she even lifted the corestone out. "We found the last one. It cost us a great many lives, but we found it. You're the only one we know of who can infuse it using aether from beyond the second aerocline. We need to get you out of here. Follow me." She led us toward the dark end of the cave.

My heart was still raw from Rasha's rejection. Thassir had left. Buzhi was dead. I'd gone so long expecting someone else's presence in the back of my mind that I felt oddly empty without it. Everything about me felt empty. I had no purpose now except this.

"Hurry. We retrieved the god gems, but most of the Unanointed are now dead."

Most of them were dead. They were dead? I was trying to crank a rusty gear in my head, knowing that if I just pushed hard enough I could break through. Dashu, Alifra and the winged altered were following Mitoran. Following her to the other end of the cavern, where there was presumably a tunnel that led up and out.

Because she somehow knew.

We all wanted to believe it, didn't we? That we'd accomplished our mission, that we were somehow survivors of this massacre, that our leader would do as leaders in the stories did and get us out of this colossal fuck-up. It was a comfort. It let us feel, at last, safe.

But if I'd learned one thing in my twenty-five years, it was that life was never safe. It was messy, it was unpredictable, it gave us things we did not deserve and did not know how to handle. Alifra with her drowned daughter. Dashu with the weight of a dead culture on his shoulders. Thassir, hiding his godhood lest he be hunted down and killed. And me, given the responsibility to care for my sister when I'd been little more than a child myself, ill-equipped yet doing my very best. My best hadn't been enough.

I wanted to believe this was over. Wanting could drive a great many things. It could not keep us safe.

I cleared my throat, something like panic squeezing icy fingers around my heart. I had to dig, and I dreaded what I would find. I put a hand out to stop Dashu and Alifra from continuing forward. Dashu gave me a questioning look. But they trusted me now – they both did.

"We didn't have a map of the den. That's why so many of us died. We didn't have a map, Mitoran."

Mitoran stopped. Her head turned so I could see one dark eye. "I saw someone headed this way and they never came back. There has to be a way out."

It seemed reasonable.

Dashu's voice sounded in my ear. "We can't have this argument later?"

I held up a hand. Other jagged pieces were rising in my memory, uncomfortable edges I couldn't explain away. The picture they made when I put them together didn't match the one before me now. She'd made it all the way down here without so much as a scratch. She'd conveniently found the corestone. Her reluctance to have Thassir involved. The way she'd so quickly changed her appearance when I'd trailed her to the meeting with her informant. I didn't know how these pieces added up, but I didn't like how they were looking.

The rusty gear in my head finally cranked ahead. It flung me into dark and silent waters, the shock of it freezing the breath in my lungs. "You wanted them to die. The Unanointed."

Her soft snort echoed off the rock formations. "Did you hit your head? That's a wild accusation."

And I was probably the only one crazy enough to make it. Alifra and Dashu didn't speak, and I knew they were stopping, examining what they believed they knew about this woman.

In one swift movement, Mitoran had changed her grip on the sword, plunging it into the torso of the winged altered next to her. The woman spat blood, her startled cry a gurgle.

Mitoran jerked her sword free and strode toward me. Everything about her shifted and changed with each step she took. The gray faded from her hair as it took on a silver sheen, she grew taller, her eyes gleamed the same color as her hair.

I knew her. I'd seen the hidden altars, carved with her many shapes. "Lithuas." My own blade felt useless. I might as well have been holding a stick. She was an immortal goddess, one of the seven elders. And I was . . . well, I was Hakara. I was sweaty and tired and absolutely filthy. It didn't get much more mortal than that. I might have had Dashu and Alifra at my back, but without a bonded partner, I couldn't act as their bruiser.

I couldn't match her. I'd never be able to match her. I could train as hard as I could and she'd always still be a hundred steps ahead of me. "You're supposed to be dead."

Her voice was flat. "I'm not. Now do as you're told and come with me."

If I did that, she would kill Alifra and Dashu. And somehow, I found myself caring. "Kluehnn took mercy on you? Is that how it happened? You said you'd work for him and he spared you? Rolled over just like that?"

She gave me a bored look. "You have no idea what it was like or what happened. I don't care whether or not you approve."

"Have you always been the leader of the Unanointed?"

"No. But Mitoran died long before you ever met her." She barked out a short laugh. "She had wild ideas. Grand ambitions. She and Kluehnn might have gotten along had she not pitted herself against him. But it makes no sense for us to let that ambition go unchecked. By taking over whatever resistance forms in each realm, we control casualties. We can direct that energy, use the resistance to help us find the corestones and the mortals who can infuse the gems with concentrated aether." She seemed so satisfied with her own cleverness.

Alifra's voice was choked. "And then when you're done using us, you kill most of us off."

Lithuas only shrugged a shoulder. She looked me up and down. "Come with me. Infuse the corestones. Help Kluehnn use them to restore Langzu. That's your purpose. What else are you going to do?"

We'd thought all along that the god gems enacted restoration. I licked my lips, my voice feeling rusty. "I thought ... The god gems ... ? That's why he collects them." Every realm, funneling god gems to the dens. All the sinkhole mines. The punishments for smuggling and selling them. There was a reason. There had to be a reason.

"What does it matter?" Dashu put a hand on my shoulder, his gaze fixed on Lithuas. "She'll only lie to you. She's lied to all of us. Lithuas, Bringer of Change. The stories of this day will call her Lithuas the Deceiver. We take a stand against her. You don't have to do what she says."

I shrugged off his hand and set one foot in front of the other, following her into the darkness. She gave me a small nod before turning back around, her sword still out and at the ready. Alifra let out a small, dismayed sound. What else *could* I do? I was as stubborn a mule as had ever been born, yet what choice did I have? I'd lost Rasha. I had no bonded partner. I was as broken as a shattered teapot, not worth the effort to put back together.

I had nothing. Nothing except my determination and my sheer will.

And you could say what you liked about me, but I'd never gone down without a fight. I elbowed Dashu, kicked at Alifra's foot. It was all the warning I gave them. I'd have to trust they would follow my lead. I thrust my sword toward Lithuas's back just as Dashu lifted his blade and Alifra cocked her crossbow.

Lithuas was a god, older than the Shattering. She sensed my movement, whirling to face me. But my thrust had been a feint, and I shifted, cutting the pouch loose from her belt instead. I grabbed for it. Lithuas brought her blade down toward my torso.

Dashu blocked her sword, their weapons clashing with a sound that rang through the cavern. Alifra's crossbow clicked, sending a bolt straight into the woman's shoulder.

Get in, get out, make it quick. I pulled away, thankful that at least I didn't have to hold my breath this time. The pouch was heavy in my hand, the corestone within glowing faintly through the fibers. I poured it out into my hand and held it up.

"Stop!"

Lithuas froze and then backed away from Dashu, her gaze focused on the glowing stone in my fingers. Blues and reds and greens and colors of every kind glittered from its surface. It was as big as the end of my thumb and I was still afraid I might accidentally drop it.

"Hakara." She drew out my name lazily, her silver hair like waterfalls on either side of her face. "What do you think is going to happen here? I'm just going to kill your friends and then take that stone back."

She was right. I couldn't stop her. She hadn't used any magic yet, and if the tales I'd heard of what gods could do were even halfway true, I was in enormous trouble.

"Yeah, I can't stop you." I shrugged. "But I can slow you down. And you know what? I'm spiteful enough to do just that."

Before she could make any sort of retort, I did the stupidest thing I could think of. I shoved that corestone between my teeth.

And swallowed it.

55

Nioanen

11 years after the Shattering

Albanore – a small house on the mountain above the city of Billoste

Rumenesca, the Mother, appears in the origin stories of most civilizations – a kind and nurturing presence who helped people through hard times. One who offered crucial knowledge to help them grow.

"Rumenesca is dead." Irael stood at the door, his face grim, snowflakes still caught in his red-gold hair.

Nioanen froze, his fingers still halfway submerged in the dough on the counter top. He thought he might always remember this moment: the feel of the flour on his hands, Thassir playing with a wooden boat on the floor, dark wings spread wide. The fire crackling, a cat curled on the hearth. The smell of freshly cut rosemary.

And Irael at the door. Irael at the door with terrible news.

They'd been falling one after another this past year, the gods who had fled. Rumenesca had come to see them only a few days prior. She'd held Thassir in her lap, pressed her cheek to his, lamented the fact that she'd never wanted babies, because he was so sweet. If only gods could come fully formed. He'd pushed her away only half-heartedly, protesting that he was six years old and not a baby. And now she was dead.

Nioanen pulled his hands free from the dough, brushing off the remnants and the flour. They'd made this place a sanctuary, but it couldn't stay that way any longer. "We have to go."

"We can't." Irael went to him and took his hands. "We've been making progress. There's the magic you've been working on. We can push Kluehnn back. There's still a chance."

A chance. Always Irael chased chances; he was made of hope and luck. Nioanen couldn't be the same way. He was steadfast, and stern, but they'd always found a way to see eye to eye. But they couldn't risk Thassir.

The boy began to cry as Nioanen's words sank in. Irael shifted into an orange tomcat, winding around his wings, rubbing his cheek against his shoulder. Thassir quieted, his arms snaking around the beast. "I don't want to go."

"Hush, we're fighting back. We might not have to leave."

Nioanen stared at the dough he'd abandoned. It might as well have been in his throat. There was a stickiness there that was making it hard to swallow. "He's tracking us down somehow. Rumenesca was always careful. She blends in. And he still found her."

Irael purred, his voice a low rumble. "They're all coming here in two days. Surely we can wait two days. Practice the magic again, and then we'll meet with our brethren and go to the caves." He looked up at Thassir, who scratched his chin. "The boy doesn't want to leave home."

"He's a child. He cannot make decisions for us."

Thassir gave him a woeful look. Any look his son gave him was magnetic; Nioanen found himself on the hearthstones with the rest of his family, a hand on the boy's black hair. "I need to keep you both safe. This is just a place – and we can find other places. I cannot find another Irael. I cannot find another Thassir."

He fondled Irael's ears, and they both knew he was acquiescing. They could tell at a glance what the other one was thinking. "Practice," Irael said. "And maybe Thassir won't have to live in hiding forever."

Nioanen had never been good at theory – that had been Barexi's purview. But he knew that one of Kluehnn's great advantages was his ability to exist in multiple bodies at once, and if he could sever that connection, the gathered gods could strike back effectively. They could establish a foothold.

Nioanen's strength was augmentation, but he knew he'd have to use change in order to sever that bond, and he'd always had a hard time wrapping his head around change. He summoned aether from below, letting it suffuse him, the magic separating in his blood into something usable.

He idly changed the tarnished silverware to untarnished, the dried herbs hanging overhead into fresh ones, the blue curtains into green. Even these small things were an effort. Perhaps if he were older, or if he could spend time again in Unterra, he might be able to do more. It had been so long since he'd breathed that air, since he'd bathed beneath the warmth of the inner sun. He'd forgotten that feeling of power, of invincibility. Everything about him was diminished on the surface. But then he'd still have to crack the theory of it. How could he change that bond in a way that would effectively sever it?

By the time he'd finished, Irael and Thassir were both asleep in the larger bed, Thassir's wings curled about his shoulders, Irael sprawled out beside him. Every part of Nioanen felt weak and worn. He rubbed at his eyes before rising from his spot by the window to pace once more around the room.

He was still missing some element. It wasn't practice he needed. It was something else.

All their years spent below, isolated except for periodic trips to the surface – they were suffering for it now. They'd grown complacent, convinced of their superiority and of their place in the world. They'd forgotten their roles, their duties. And they'd paid for it. Their children were paying for it.

Kluehnn had to be stopped. That much was clear. But even if they defeated him and returned below, they'd have to make changes. Things could never return to the way they were before. And they shouldn't. They had to send regular emissaries to the surface, they had to work together with the mortals. They couldn't continue to exist in two separate spaces, because the truth of it was, the world was all one space. He could see the vague shape of it in his mind, but the danger had always been too immediate, too large to focus on anything else except survival. Except the next step on the path.

He went to sleep in their son's room, though he had to draw his knees up and tuck his chin to fit on Thassir's bed. He could sleep fine with Irael – he'd been doing so for decades now – but sharing a bed with Thassir meant a tiny, sweaty body next to his, kicking out randomly in the middle of the night, fluttering wings and small whimpers. He couldn't do it without waking still bleary-eyed and unreasonably angry. He would save them all the trouble.

His thoughts as he drifted between sleep and wakefulness turned to Unterra, to the long, lazy days he'd once spent under the light of the inner sun. It was hard not to dream of something better, especially for their boy. Nioanen thought of Thassir's dark wings and hair, the way his mouth quirked into the same smile as Irael's, the burgeoning magic he'd been displaying more and more often as the years went on. He was gifted – any child of two such powerful gods was bound to be. But more than that, he was *theirs*. He was exhausting, but he was laughter and light and Nioanen would do anything to give him a better world than the one he'd entered into.

Something scratched at the door. In an instant, he was alert, his heart pounding.

A hinge creaked. He rolled out of bed silently, landing on his feet, his wings tucked close to his back. Someone was here inside their house in the middle of the night. He had no hope for a gentle wanderer. This person was here to kill him and his family.

Nioanen turned the knob and pushed the bedroom door slightly open. A woman was creeping through their home, her gaze surveying the drying herbs, the embers in the hearth, the gems glowing in a pouch by the window. He couldn't see the color of her clothing, but the cut of it was tight, efficient, layered with studded leather. She moved with quiet, feline grace, every step deliberate and quick. It was dark, but he caught the gleam of something in her hand by moonlight. A knife.

Though her movements were silent, he heard a small huffing sound. She was sniffing the air. He watched, a growing sense of dread tickling his spine. Her sniffing led her to the spot Nioanen had been sitting in as he'd practiced his magic.

This was how they'd been tracked. Kluehnn had discovered a way to find the gods through their magic. And Nioanen, practicing over and over, had led Kluehnn's agent straight to his family.

He should have argued harder for a peaceful life, for hiding longer, for waiting until Thassir was grown. At the same time, anger sparked in his belly. This was his home. And Kluehnn dared send one woman to try and kill them? They were gods. He should have come himself.

Nioanen stepped into the waning light from the hearth. He hefted the poker, let it drag across the stones. The woman whirled at the sound. He could see now that she was one of the altered, a small pair of horns at her forehead, barely visible beneath her cowl. Her pupils were vertical slits in large blue-green eyes.

There was a gem in the hilt of her blade. A glowing gem. Nioanen was immediately wary. If she could smell his magic, she would have also been given other advantages. He wasn't sure how Kluehnn had managed it — creating new worlds, new peoples, new creatures. Even with the power he'd accumulated, it must have taken years of study and research.

He had to be careful. "You were looking for me. Well now you've found me. What is it that you plan to do?" He spoke loudly enough that he hoped Irael and Thassir would wake, that Irael would take the boy and flee.

Muffincheeks had already gone into hiding, no hint of even his striped tail from beneath a cushion. Somehow he'd had the good sense to know that danger was on its way, even before Nioanen had.

In all their contingency plans, they'd run together. They'd had time before an attack. They'd even taken the cat. But she'd bypassed all their traps, all their alarms. He didn't know how, and that frightened him. He could come to grips with dying. That wasn't what scared him. But even when Thassir had hit his head as a baby, his wails had made Nioanen restless with the deep, abiding need to go back in time, to prevent such harm from ever happening. It stabbed at him in ways he couldn't quite explain.

He circled the woman, putting himself between her and the larger bedroom — the one where Irael and Thassir slept. She wanted to kill gods? She'd have to get through him first.

The step she took toward him appeared casual until it did not, flowing straight into a blinding attack. Her knife seemed to be in several places at once, that was how quickly she moved. Kluehnn could not make gods, but his altered were nearly as strong and quick, straddling the space between mortal and immortal.

Nioanen blocked the blows with the poker. It was heavy, wrought iron, but in his hands it was light as one of his flight feathers. And then, before she could step back, he brought it down hard toward her head.

She parried it just in time, though it still caught her shoulder. She grunted at the impact before sliding back out of his reach.

"Why did he send *you*?" Nioanen asked. "If he wanted to kill us, why not come for us himself? You are no god." She had no godly aura; she was merely one of Kluehnn's imitations. She could not kill him.

She lifted the knife, and the violet glow of the gem in the hilt caught Nioanen's eye again. There was something strange about that knife. But he stood his ground. She could cut him all she liked; the wounds would bleed, but that was not enough to kill a god. She could sever his head from his body and his lips would still speak.

It wouldn't be pleasant for him, but even in the stories, the mortals had once burned a god and spread his ashes, only for the ashes to gather and form back into the god.

What had happened to Rumenesca was different. What had happened to the others was different.

The knife caught his upper arm, a thin line of shimmering red breaking forth. But she'd come within his reach, and he slammed the poker as hard as he could into her ribs. He felt, with satisfaction, something crack.

The door hinges creaked again.

Another would-be assassin entered, this time a man with brown-feathered wings, much smaller than Nioanen's golden ones.

Very well. He could take both of them on. He reached down, down, grasping the aether close to Unterra, pulling it up and into his home. It was intoxicatingly sweet. He breathed it in, felt it infuse his blood. He cast his hand toward the floor and augmented the roots that he found, until they burst forth, forming a wall between him and his attackers. A small part of him wanted to lament the floorboards – he and Irael had spent so long building this place without the use of magic – but then a voice was at his ear.

"The knives, my love." Irael was there in his young man's form, a long, thin sword in his grasp. "They're blessed in a way I don't fully understand. They can kill us."

Already the man and woman were hacking through the roots, pushing them aside. So this was how they'd fallen so quickly, one after another. Kluehnn had created more abominations – altered who could smell the signature of a god's magic. Altered with knives that could kill gods. Godkillers.

The roots slithered out of his way like snakes. Nioanen seized the woman's arm as she cut one of them free, squeezing her wrist so hard he felt the bones grinding together. With a growl, he wrenched the knife from her grasp and used it to cut her throat in one quick, vicious movement. The other godkiller had already pushed his way through, and Nioanen pivoted to face him, speaking to Irael at the same time.

"Get out of here. There are more important things to protect." He didn't want to say it, to give this godkiller any more information than he already had. Irael nodded, then fled back into their bedroom.

Nioanen summoned more aether from deeper below. This was the most powerful aether, but it was also the most poisonous. Gods had more fortitude than most, but he'd still have a slight headache for days after this. But it wasn't the time for caution. He'd rip these godkillers apart with his bare hands if he had to.

He used some of the aether to summon Zayyel. Smoke coalesced around his right hand, forming into a shimmering blade. The rest he used to push his blade's augmentations even further, making it sharper, harder, the silver fire inside hotter.

The godkiller stepped to meet him.

The man was just as skilled as his late comrade had been, moving with a swiftness that startled Nioanen. He had to quickly change his mindset, to pretend he was fighting another god. He couldn't afford complacency or to underestimate his opponent. The knife the godkiller held was curved, and his movements reflected the shape of the blade. He drifted from one attack into another, ceaseless, like the waves curling toward the shore.

Nioanen used his superior size and strength to his advantage. Each time he blocked a blow, he did his best to push back, to interrupt the man's follow-through. He had the height, the longer reach. And the man was tiring more quickly than he was.

He quickly shifted tactics, dodging instead of blocking, instead of using his weight to press back. He had patience, and patience in a fight was often an advantage. The godkiller over-reached on an attack and Nioanen stepped to the side, bringing his blade down on the man's back. An ordinary blade would have been slowed by the leather, perhaps even deflected by the metal studs. But Zayyel sliced through cloth, flesh and bone as though they were all made of the same soft stuff.

The godkiller didn't have the chance to scream. He slumped to the floor, dead before he struck it.

Nioanen's chest heaved as he let his hand fall back to his side, the tip of his blade touching the wooden floor. He'd killed them both. Rumenesca hadn't been so lucky. They'd have to leave this house, find another place to hide. When they met with the others in two days, they'd have only their belongings on their backs. At

least for a time they'd been able to give Thassir the semblance
of a normal life.

The window of their bedroom was open, cold air and snow
blowing in, flakes landing on the rumpled sheets. He should go
after them, let them know they were safe. Thassir wouldn't be
dressed for the weather outside.

He froze on the threshold of the room.

He was one of the strongest gods, but even Kluehnn had
known that Irael and he were together. He'd seen them at that last
battle; he would have known there was the chance the godkillers
would face more than one god when they came to this house. If
they'd gotten through to the door without triggering any of the
traps, they would have had time to scout the way, to understand
what they were dealing with. There should have been more godkillers marching through that door. He knew it.

He couldn't fit through the window, so he strode to the front
door, wrenching it open and plunging into knee-deep snow. Irael
was strong too. He would watch over Thassir. Irael could change
into a dozen shapes.

But Irael had never been as good in a fight as Nioanen was.
Nioanen was all brute strength and unwavering force. Irael was
subtlety and grace – the sort of god who skewered his enemies
better at a party than on a battlefield. He could fight, though, of
course he could fight.

Rumenesca had been able to fight, too.

Nioanen stumbled through the snow to the back window,
following Thassir's small and quickly fading footsteps. He was
too young to fly, the muscles of his wings not quite developed. A
couple more years and he'd be able to take to the skies. His mind
was going in circles; it would not be quiet until he found them.

He spotted them in the snow, half hidden among the rocks of
a ravine. His heart jumped. "Irael," he dared. The wind carried

away the sound of his voice. Neither of them moved. Neither of them glanced up. By the time he was close enough to touch them, he knew.

The snow had already begun to cover the shimmering blood that stained the ground. Both had been cut neatly at the throat – quick, efficient. Irael's body was covered in wounds. He had fought. He'd fought to the last. The aura around them was gone. They were dead in truth.

He couldn't help but wonder, in that moment before the pain truly struck, whether Irael had died first, or if Thassir had – if Irael had felt the blade across his throat knowing he would not be there to protect Thassir. Or if he'd had to watch it being drawn across Thassir's throat. He wasn't sure which was worse.

The pain finally flooded him, his bones and chest aching. Footsteps marked the snow, leading away from the bodies. He didn't count how many. They must have gone to scout further ahead, to see if there were any other gods they should kill. But they'd circle back to check on their comrades at the house. They'd find him here in the snow.

He wanted to let them find him. To die with the only two people who had ever really mattered to him. He would never again kiss Thassir's forehead or stroke Irael's hair, suffused in the golden light of a dawning day. They should have had an eternity. Instead they had this.

Voices sounded in the distance, carried on the winter wind. He picked up both small, frail bodies, holding them to his chest.

He ran.

56

Hakara

10 years after the restoration of Kashan
and 571 years after the Shattering

Kashan - Kluehnn's den

There are other stories of other gods, though Kluehnn takes part in none of them. Not all gods interacted with the surface world. Some spent their entire lives in Unterra — living, breathing, dying — with not a care for the mortals above.

My belly was on fire, though not the kind that could burn. I felt warmed from within, like I was the fire. The weight of the corestone felt like a physical thing, my feet dragging as I took another step back from Lithuas. "You want three infused corestones? You can wait until I shit this one out."

She marched toward me, her sword tight in her hand. I lifted my arms instinctively, trying to protect Dashu and Alifra. But she didn't seem to care about them. "You *idiot*. You'll die first, and then we'll have to find a new linchpin."

Die? My knees buckled. The world was swimming around me. A bright golden glow surrounded Lithuas when I looked at her. Couldn't tell where it was coming from. Maybe it was the glow of the gem from within. I found myself bringing my hands before my eyes, examining the bright veins beneath my skin. Were they glowing too?

Somehow I was on the floor, my cheek pressed to the cold stone. My gaze focused on the cave entrance, where several godkillers had shown up. None of them glowed gold like Lithuas, but my vision was hazy nonetheless. Was this really how it would end for me? Making one foolish, impulsive decision? I'd bought time, I supposed. They'd have to cut the stone out of me. By that time they'd have to get a new linchpin.

At least I'd gotten to see Rasha again. At least I knew she was alive.

Lithuas stood over me, her expression disgusted.

A growl echoed through the cavern. Shouts. Screams. The sounds of rending flesh – so loud it was as though it was happening right next to my ear.

I blinked and Lithuas was gone. Had I dreamed her standing over me? I couldn't tell if this was what happened when you died – if everything just went strange and thick. The burning had extended to my limbs, every bit of me feeling as though it was being consumed to feed the corestone. And then I turned my head and saw *him*.

Thassir was there, though he didn't look the way I remembered. He was haloed in gold, the brightness of it filling the cavern. I couldn't see anything else as he tore through the godkillers. He held one by the throat. He was gutting another with a sword engulfed in silver flames. I'd never seen this expression on his face. Even when he'd been killing the godkillers at the orchard, he'd merely looked grimly determined. Now he was

alight with anger, his teeth bared, eyes wide, every muscle of his arms tensed, claws clutching the leather grip of the sword so tightly he was bound to leave marks.

I'd been surprised to find out he was a god; now, as I watched him, I wondered how I could have ever mistaken him for one of the altered. He ripped through them with the vicious grace of a cat chasing down its prey. I didn't think I'd ever seen something quite so beautiful.

Hot tears pricked at my eyes. Were my tears glowing too? Trust me to get sentimental at the end. The godkillers were all dead. Thassir stood there, chest heaving, facing down Lithuas.

"I've watched you restore realm after realm because I made a promise to someone I loved. I've made half-hearted attempts to help and told myself that was enough when it was not. I've twisted myself into knots trying to fulfill a promise that no longer has any meaning. Escaping death and living are two different things. I stopped knowing that difference. It took a mortal to remind me."

Was he talking about *me*? I would have sidled up to him with a grin and poked him in the arm until he glared at me – if there wasn't a sword-wielding god between us and I wasn't lying on the floor actively dying.

"I'm willing to die for this, Lithuas, even if you are not."

Grand words and two gods about to have a bout. And here I was, useless as an old dish rag, skin glowing like an ember in a fire, my life sputtering out just as quickly. Not really how I'd envisioned my exit. Thought I would have had a good lay, a good drink, a smile on my lips as I spent my last moments making rude gestures at the ground below my feet.

Something shook the cavern, sending dust down from the ceiling.

The world seemed to be fading around me, narrowing to a

single beam of light. I wanted to stay, to at least see how this fight was going to shake out. I wanted to see if Thassir made it out alive, if he killed Lithuas – she deserved it.

Hands touched my shoulders. "Hakara."

It was Thassir. I blinked. Everything was shrouded in gold, his wings spread around us in a protective arch. Couldn't see much, but could feel my eyelids move. "I'm sorry about what I said to you before. Don't ask me which part. All of it. What's this about a promise?"

His hands froze on me and then he was leaning over. Whatever had happened, everything had gone silent. Someone groaned. I caught a glimpse of his face.

Same frown he always had. "We can talk about that later."

"I know you, you won't tell me anything."

Footsteps sounded. I caught a glimpse of Dashu and Alifra above me. Dashu put a hand to Thassir's back. "More coming. We'll hold them off. Get her up and running. We need our bruiser."

Thassir nodded, and then his palm pressed to mine. I didn't feel any pain, but he must have cut me. Faintly, in the back of my mind, I felt the bond between us re-form. It was like stepping into a room I'd once lived in and finding nothing at all had changed in the interim years.

"You cannot give up. You are the most stubborn woman I know."

"It's too much." I didn't even sound like myself. When had anything been too much for me? I thought of Rasha, who'd turned her back on me when I'd finally come for her. "Sometimes giving up is the right thing to do."

"Yes," he said, his voice rumbling through me, "sometimes it is." His hand squeezed mine. It felt cold in my too-hot grasp. "But not now. Now you have to fight. Dashu and Alifra need you."

I don't know what it was – if it was because he was telling me this and he didn't look angry with me, not anymore, or if it was because I knew he was right. It was too late for me and for Rasha, but it was not too late for others, and I could put all the considerable force of my will into something I knew mattered.

So I fought. I fought to stay, to live, to hold and contain the power that was coursing through my veins. My fingers spasmed. He was still holding my palm against his, even though the magic had long since dissipated. "You came back to me."

"I'd always intended to."

"Even though I made you really angry?" I found my thumb caressing the back of his hand, a touch just to be sure he was there, that he was real.

"Maybe because of that."

"Don't leave like that again. Please." I was fighting, but I was losing the fight. I could feel the world, briefly sharpened, fading again, no matter how hard I tried to keep it in view.

Thassir's head lowered. "I won't. But *you* can't die like this. Not like this. I never should have bonded with you in the first place – we both know it. But you asked me to, and I couldn't stop myself. You asked, you *wanted*. And a part of me wanted in return. Because being near you was like putting my hand to a licking flame, and I knew – I *knew* – being that close would thaw parts of me I'd let freeze over the many long years. Your team needs you, yes." He paused, hesitated. "But Hakara, I need you too."

He . . . what? Before I could register what was happening, his mouth pressed to mine. His lips were warm and soft; he brought my hand to his chest, where I could feel the beating of his heart. This wasn't exactly the lay before I died I'd been thinking about. But people were fighting. I'd damn well make this kiss worth it.

I found some last bit of strength and twined my fingers in his hair, pulling him closer to me. It was soft as silken down feathers in my grasp. My hands were greedy, wanting to feel more of him, the heat of his skin, the hard muscle beneath. Thought I'd known before what it had been like to drown in desire, to dip my head beneath that ocean's surface, to hold myself there in that place of wanting.

I hadn't.

The feel of him against me, solid and heavy, made every thought in my mind turn effervescent, until there was only a bright fizzing – a single, pure note. It vibrated through the core of me, until I was nothing but desperate need, I slipped a hand beneath the front of his shirt, curling my fingers against his skin, wanting to tear the cloth from his body.

Didn't have the energy. Already my arms were growing weak again, the corestone inside me taking over. Then something poured into my mouth from his, tasting like oysters, fresh from the sea. I breathed it in without thinking. It was aether, thicker than I'd ever felt it before.

Strength flooded into me. The corestone's magic, which had felt unmanageable before, simmered. I captured it, contained it, held it within me.

Thassir was gone by the time I opened my eyes. Somehow, the clash of blades sounded even louder in my ears. My skin wasn't glowing anymore.

I pushed myself to my feet. Lithuas had survived whatever magic Thassir had done, and they were fighting again, their movements nearly too quick for me to follow. And the ragtag band of remaining Unanointed were taking on an aspect of Kluehnn that had climbed out of the pit. It was larger than the one we'd fought in the orchard, its horn-covered head scraping the stalactites. Pale patches of skin flashed from between bark-like protrusions. No barbed tails this time, but spines and thin, clawed arms undulated at his back, like a bug that was trying desperately to right itself. Two Unanointed were already dead. Four remained.

He'd been right. They *did* need me. And I'd been focused inward for too long.

I pulled two gems from my pouch and swallowed them. Aether rose to meet me as I ran, Thassir knowing exactly what I needed even as he engaged in his own fight. I breathed it in and held it.

My arms strengthened. My feet moved quicker. I pulled the sword from my belt and threw myself into attacking Kluehnn. He was covered in mouths with sharpened teeth, but he was covered in eyes, too. I aimed for those, doing my best to duck out of the way of his claws. Dashu and Alifra fell in with me, cutting at the surrounding claws, clearing a path.

My sword sank deep into one of the black eyes on his front. I jerked the blade out. Shimmering blood spurted.

I whirled away as his teeth tried to latch onto my arm, Dashu weaving in to take my spot, Alifra at a distance, firing a crossbow bolt into another of the beast's eyes. Usually Thassir would have been there, taking the hits for me as I breathed, before moving in for another attack. But he was occupied. I felt the heat of some ancient magic at my back as I lunged in again, my lungs burning.

I thought of the peaceful quiet of the ocean, the way it closed over my head, distant whale song in my ears. My stomach spasmed, but I felt the blood retreating to my core, a fresh reserve of strength unlocking. I held my breath and slashed at Kluehnn's face, catching him right above the mouth. He roared, rearing up, his myriad arms and legs waving in the air like an ant's antennae.

The woman next to me sucked in a breath, her partner stepping in to give her space. Kluehnn fell back down and seized the altered man's head between his teeth. Screams filled the cavern as long, sharp teeth punctuated his skull as though it were an overripe fruit.

The woman's god limbs disappeared. She swallowed two more gems. No bonded partner. No aether. I let out my breath, retreating a little so I could recover and pull two more gems free. I swallowed them and stepped in close to her. Aether surrounded us and she gave me a grateful nod as she breathed some in. I did the same.

Dashu flowed out of the way, giving me an opening. I gritted my teeth and plunged back in. I parried teeth and claws once, twice. Quick as thought, I seized a clawed hand with my god one, pulling until I felt the arm pop loose. I jabbed my sword into another eye.

Kluehnn roared.

When it came down to it, Rasha's abandonment was a little my fault, a little Guarin's, but mostly Kluehnn's. He was the one who'd thought restoring the realms was the best way to solve our problems. He was the one who thought killing people and separating families was an acceptable cost to pay.

I let my breath out, more than a little lightheaded. I danced to the side. "I'm going to hunt down all your pathetic aspects. I'm going to stab all of them in the eye. I hope you have a thousand aspects. I hope those thousand have a thousand eyeballs each just so you can feel this pain that many times."

My god limbs faded. I needed a moment to catch my breath, but I wasn't going to get one. I spared a glance and saw through my flickering eyelashes that Thassir was still fighting Lithuas, their blades locked.

I tossed back another couple gems. Last two I had. I slipped out of the way of another attack, my pounding heart aching, before Thassir pulled the aether for me. The salty taste of the air slipped past my nostrils and down into my lungs. I closed my throat. There was a hammer in my head, trying to break its way out from behind my eyes. I ignored the pain and drew another dagger from my belt. Another set of god limbs encased my own. I leapt for the top of the creature, aiming for its face, where its largest eye lay. I plunged my sword as deep into it as I could manage.

Its largest mouth seized my right leg. Razor-sharp teeth dug into the muscles there.

I forced the tip of the blade further in, the muscles of my god arms straining. My hands grew cold, blood retreating to my core. That was the problem with being so good at holding your breath. Once you hit a certain point, the danger wasn't in being tempted to pull in a breath. The danger was being tempted into not breathing at all.

If I took a breath now, I'd lose my enhancements. I'd lose the only advantage I currently held. So I clung to Kluehnn's clammy flesh with my mortal hands, and I pushed the knife past the soft tissue of the eye, felt the tip scrape against bone.

And then I found the opening at the back.

I pressed.

As Kluehnn screamed, I fell.

57

Rasha

10 years after the restoration of Kashan
and 571 years after the Shattering

Kashan

*Magic is not a gift; it is a responsibility. The mortals could
not handle it. The gods wasted it. Kluehnn is the only one
who has ever used it with any meaning.*

The ranks of the den were thinner these days. The
Unanointed had freed the infusing mortals, so there was
a scramble to find more. And the clean-up of the den itself took
time – mounting new doors, burning bodies, washing away
blood and guts. Training of godkillers had been suspended.

But Kluehnn's worshipers were nothing if not efficient.
Though the Unanointed had killed the aspect of Kluehnn that
lived in the den, the den elders assured us another was on its way
from below.

I kicked at the stones on the path, watching them tumble over
one another. A nearby bird paused in its song.

Khatuya and Naatar walked at my shoulders, neither of them talking. It had been a long twenty-two days. Someone could have told me it had been two years and I would have believed them. But eventually Millani had come to our burrow and told us to pack.

Several other godkillers walked behind us, a team to purge the village. They'd come from another den; many of the godkillers in our den had been killed by the Unanointed.

I rubbed at the back of my neck, wondering if a person could truly feel someone's gaze on them, or if I was only imagining the scrutiny of the godkillers behind me.

Had anyone other than Khatuya or Naatar seen me let Hakara go? I'd said nothing about it and the two of them had followed my lead. As much as everyone tried to pretend that life in the den was continuing as normal, I'd heard the same rumors as the others. A god in the depths of the den. A god who had been working with Kluehnn.

Insects buzzed in the trees around us, echoing the frantic, unceasing noise of my thoughts. If there were no true gods except for Kluehnn, if we were meant to hate and kill the gods here on the surface, if they were working to usurp the mortals he claimed to protect, then why would he be working with another god?

The rumors had quickly dissipated after the fight, as though someone had opened a window and wafted the words away. I never knew where they originated from, only that I'd heard them from so many lips the day after the fighting had ceased, and those lips had quieted not three days later.

And Hakara claimed to have come for me.

My mouth tightened. She should have stayed in Langzu. She should have moved on with her life, forgotten about me. It was what I'd always thought she'd done. Instead, she'd said she'd spent the past ten years trying to find her way back to me.

Lies. Manipulations. She was with the Unanointed. She must have learned somehow that I was still alive, that I was becoming a godkiller, realized that she knew someone on the inside. She must have thought she could use me to her advantage.

It had been ten years. We could not be the same people we'd once been. We could never go back to that. Stupid for her to think she could move me at all. But she had. She'd moved me enough not to kill her.

A hand touched my shoulder. Khatuya. I startled out of my reverie, met her gaze. Her head tilted subtly toward a fork in the path.

I'd almost walked straight past it. At least I knew I could count on her and Naatar. We'd been through the worst together. We'd fought and we'd killed and we'd nearly died. No one else could understand that. Not even Hakara.

I sniffed the air as I turned my head, searching for the scent of aether. It tingled at the back of my mouth. I'd thought I'd have to train this new ability of mine, but I'd taken to it with the instincts of a duckling tossed into the water. We were going in the right direction. I looked over my shoulder at the six godkillers behind us. "Continue on to the village. Purge it. The god dwells by the river." I pointed into the trees. "Find us there if we don't finish first."

The woman in front nodded before they all brushed past us.

Naatar let out a breath when they'd moved out of sight. "Why do I get the feeling they're here as much for us as for the purging and the godkilling?"

"It's the final trial," Khatuya said. "We're not godkillers until we complete it. We're still acolytes. Some fail at the last task."

"It can't be as difficult as the prior two." Naatar scoffed as he said it, though he somehow managed to fill the sound with anxiety.

We were all equipped with multiple blades, including the godkilling knives we'd been given on loan. I touched the hilts of three of them, lingering on the one with the violet gem. "Let's go." I wasn't in the mood to offer platitudes or reassurances. My belly swam with unease. The god seemed the least of my worries. If someone else had seen me let Hakara go, if someone had heard her say she was my sister . . .

Dew-encrusted grass brushed our knees as we walked into the forest, leaving my leggings damp. Although both sides had suffered heavy losses, the aspect of Kluehnn had been killed. Whoever had done it had escaped. I couldn't be sure that meant we had lost, but it felt like a loss. And I couldn't *know* that Hakara had survived. But I had a feeling. I'd always seen her as too stubborn to die, though perhaps that had been a younger sister looking up to an older one, basking in the feel of her invincibility.

Or maybe she was just that, and it had been her who had plunged the blade into Kluehnn's eye. My memories of her were filled with her easy smile, the strength of her wiry arms, the defiance she spat at anyone who thought a young orphan girl was an easy target. It seemed like something she might do.

We crept toward the river. A tent was there, racks to hang and dry gutted fish. If the god wasn't there, he would be nearby.

"You've come to kill me."

I whirled.

He stood behind us in the forest, his antlers brushing the branches above his head. "Kluehnn sending children to do his work for him. What a shame." His voice was the soft rasp of a cat's tongue. "I only wish to be left in peace."

Khatuya pulled her godkilling knife free, a long-bladed dagger in her other hand. Naatar followed suit, his tail lashing.

"I don't know what you've been told, but I am only here to

make more fish in the river so the villagers can eat. Life in a re-stored realm is not as easy as Kluehnn likes to say it is."

I didn't move. Nothing about this made sense to me. He said he wanted to be left in peace, he was here helping the villagers. If he had a longer plan in place, a plan to take the surface world, nothing about it was apparent yet.

You must not speak to gods. They will only deceive you, twist your words until you doubt yourself. This is their way.

I should have drawn my knives. I should have rushed headlong into a fight with this creature. He was a god. I was a godkiller. It was the way things were done – the way they had always been done. But Sheuan had already instilled more doubt in me than I'd thought possible. This god couldn't hold me, couldn't make me believe I was the only thing that mattered in the world. He couldn't ask me to leave the only home I'd really known and make me feel if I took one step more, I might fall over that cliff into an entirely new life. What more could a god do that Sheuan hadn't?

I shut my eyes tight. These were blasphemous thoughts. In the darkness behind my lids I saw a face: a girl with horns and bright green eyes, a meat hook through her shoulder.

My eyes flashed open. What was *that*?

The words left my mouth before I could reconsider. "How long have you been here, in this village?"

Both Khatuya and Naatar froze. I'd broken one of Kluehnn's precepts, one of his most important ones. I'd committed blas-phemy. Naatar's whisper was hoarse. "Rasha, he won't tell you the truth."

"It's a simple enough question." There was no turning back now. I was committed to this path. I tilted my head, regarding the god. He was not young.

His gaze swung between us, his golden eyes considering. "I

have been here for three years, helping these people. Kluehnn has not."

"He offers sustenance," Khatuya said. She set her gaze on me, as though she were only speaking to me and not the god. As though she were engaging in a battle for my soul. "Anyone who goes to worship is taken care of."

"And I ask nothing in return for my help. Which do you think the villagers prefer? You think they want to eat in your dark halls, to listen to your hateful rhetoric? Or do you think they want help freely given, without obligation?"

Naatar was watching my face. "Kluehnn says gods will attempt to deceive. They will make you doubt." He was pleading with me, hoping I would turn back.

But I could see the shape of the path in the dark and I wanted to know where it ended. "The villagers here worship you."

"I did not ask them to."

His ears flicked. A scream carried on the wind, the faint smell of smoke. He let out a huff of breath, like a startled horse. And then his lip pulled back, revealing sharp teeth. "The people here have done nothing to you. You cannot mean to—"

Khatuya leapt forward, her godkilling knife held low. She'd always attacked first in our practice sessions, using the element of surprise and her smaller size to her advantage. I should have foreseen that. Naatar followed, as he always did.

I only hesitated for a moment before I pulled my blades free. My first obligation was to them. I wasn't sure when things had shifted during the second trial, but they had.

The god no longer seemed in the mood for talking. The scent of aether tinged the air. Out of nowhere, a bolt of lightning struck the ground, sending an impact wave outward, throwing Khatuya off her feet. He'd missed her, but only just.

Naatar still hurtled forward, and I joined him, circling around as he lashed out with his knife. The god jumped out of the way, his hands summoning more aether from below.

I struck out at one wrist. The god slid out of reach, but whatever magic he'd been pulling together dissipated. We had to keep moving, to keep attacking.

This was why godkillers worked in groups of three. This was what we'd been trained for. The god's dodge put him in the way of Naatar's knife, and the scaled altered scored a cut against his shoulder blade.

Shimmering blood dripped to the forest floor, pattering against dried leaves.

But the god didn't have only magic. He pulled free the knife he used to gut fish. He ran his hand along the blade and it lengthened into a sword.

Not exactly the sort of fight I'd been hoping to have. I'd been hoping to sneak up on him, to deal with him by the clear banks of the river. Instead we were in a forest that he knew best, and he'd had fair warning.

He was a better fighter than all three of us. I bounced off each attack, his blade pushing me back, chasing me to dig into the gaps between my leather armor. He wore no armor, yet I found it much more difficult to score a hit on him. The wound Naatar had given him was shallow, though it kept bleeding.

Khatuya was on her feet again. We circled him like hungry wolves, darting in each time he seemed to regain his bearings. He pulled more aether from the ground between attacks, his free hand reaching out, making a fierce wind that brought the surrounding trees down on top of us. Wood creaked, branches rustled. I had to leap to the side to avoid being flattened by a trunk.

Naatar was not so lucky. A branch caught him on the shoulder, a sharpened end piercing into flesh. He groaned.

Khatuya and I ignored him. The only way to save him was to end this, and quickly. Had Millani knowingly sent me to my death? This god might have only been in this village for a few years, but he looked old. Perhaps he'd gotten tired of waiting for godkillers to hunt him down. Perhaps he was here to die. He didn't quite seem ready.

My heartbeat fluttered as I stepped over a fallen branch, the ground beneath my feet suddenly grown treacherous. The god flowed over the trunks and branches without even looking at his feet. I had the sense we were no longer the wolves; that he was a cat, ready to deal with prey that had dared wake him.

I slashed at his arm at the same time Khatuya ducked within his reach, her blade reaching for his leg. He lifted his free hand, lightning balled within it. He was going to kill one of us, I knew it; I just didn't know which one of us it would be.

"Aluviel!" A girl's voice, crying out.

The god hesitated.

Khatuya hamstrung him.

He fell to his knees, his mouth open but no sound escaping. I cut his wrist where he held the blade. The sword dropped from his hand. And then, without stopping, I plunged my godkilling knife into his throat. Hot blood spurted over my palm. I turned my head to see the girl running away through the forest.

"We should go after her," Khatuya panted, her knife still shimmering with the god's blood.

I shook my head. "That's not our job. We get the body ready to transport back to the den. We help Naatar. Purging is everyone else's responsibility."

Khatuya nodded.

Naatar clenched his teeth as we pulled him free from the tree. The wound would need stitches, but we bound it to stop the bleeding. By the time we'd lifted the god's body from the ground, the other godkillers had finished purging the village. Smoke had joined the clouds above, gray against white.

The leader of the other group helped us to lay out the sling, to lift the tall, lanky body of the god into it. His dark eyes stared sightlessly at the sky above, his mouth still open as though in surprise.

"It went well?" the godkiller asked. He ruffled the feathers on his gray wings. Something about the way he stood reminded me of Shambul.

"Yes," Khatuya said.

Naatar only nodded, his hand at his shoulder.

I drew myself up to my full height, pleased that the other god-killer had to look up to meet my gaze. "He's dead, isn't he? Let's get back to the den." I hefted the knife that was on loan to me and realized that not once during the fight had I hummed Mimi's lullaby. A surge of triumph filled me. "I want a knife I can keep."

Khatuya and Naatar fell into step behind me.

Neither of them had said anything about the blasphemy I'd committed. Of the way I'd broken the precepts.

Of the words I'd spoken to a god.

58

Mullayne

10 years after the restoration of Kashan
and 571 years after the Shattering

Langzu - Tolemne's Path

*Different realms have different beliefs surrounding death.
Some believe your spirit goes to Unterra, waiting to be born
into a god's body. Some believe your spirit and your matter
return to the world around us. Some even believe your spirit
goes somewhere entirely different.*

*Me? I'm a practical man. When I close my eyes for the
last time, I expect it will be akin to sleeping.*

Pont was dead, his eyes open, glassy and staring.

"Mull, I'm sorry, I'm so sorry." Imeah was weeping,
leaning hard on her cane, her body swaying as though she were
hanging by a thread. "I had to."

Mull couldn't think. He didn't have enough energy to speak.
He just reached into his pack and pulled out the fresh filters,
holding one out to Imeah.

They changed their filters.

As he took in a deep breath, he noticed a smell, just as Pont had said. But to him, the air didn't smell of baking pies – it smelled of Imeah's hair, faintly floral and woody.

The air in the fresh filter was noticeably different, smelling of spit and the dampness of cloth that hadn't been allowed to properly dry.

"You had to," he said when he could manage to speak again. "It wasn't your fault." It was his. He couldn't quite believe this was how Pont's life had ended. He kept expecting his old friend to take a breath, to pull the knife from his neck. How could he grieve something he couldn't quite believe?

Imeah's hair floated in front of her face as she knelt next to him. She shook her head to clear it away. "I went farther down. Mull – there's a camp there." She reached into Mull's pack, pulling out his journal and pen. Quickly, she wrote something down. "Another wall carving. I don't think ... It's not ... " Her gaze flicked back the way they'd come. "He lost everyone else in his party. Tolemne was the only one who made it to Unterra. But that's not the only thing that's different from the stories. All our books were wrong. He didn't stay in Unterra. It's not an outgoing camp. It's an incoming one. He was on his way back to the surface."

"Why?" In the stories, Tolemne had always stayed among the gods. The world would be restored by Kluehnn; his mission had been completed. In the stories, he had lived out the rest of his days in a magical paradise.

She shook her head. "There's more. I wrote it down as best I could. But you have to go back while your filters still work. We don't have enough for us both to continue. Even if we change them more often, the others will need to be washed and dried. Only one of us can go on." She took his hand and squeezed it. "It has to be me."

"You don't know how far it is. What if you don't make it? What if you die down here?"

"Mull." Blue light glinted off her brown eyes. "I was always going to die."

Somehow it struck him differently here, down in the dark, so close to their destination. Jeeoon was dead. Pont was dead. And still he'd clung stubbornly to the idea that Imeah – *Imeah* – would survive. He would make her live. But now he couldn't believe it anymore. He was trying to grasp a stone in a river when it had long since been carried out of reach. The pain of it was physical, radiating to his fingertips. He couldn't breathe. "I've … I've made all the wrong decisions from the start, haven't I?"

"No. We each made our own decisions." She was kneeling on the moss-covered floor, pulling at the straps that held Pont's filter in place.

"But you told me no."

"And then I changed my mind. I knew you were going to come down here anyways. It's never been just about me." She stuffed some of the extra filters into her bag, her breathing heavy. "I know you, I know how an idea takes over your mind and won't leave you. This discovery – you've been wanting it all your life. I wanted to be a part of it. I could have lived out my last days on the surface in comfort. But I'd always have been wondering whether you were coming back. I'd always have been wondering what was happening to you. I'd always have been wishing that you were at my side."

Mull wanted to reach for her, to stop her, to ask her to speak less so her filter would last longer. "I wouldn't have left you."

"You would have. Maybe not physically, but your mind would have been far away. You would have been a lesser version of yourself. Better to be down here with you. Better to know. I can think of worse ways to die. For a slim moment there, you gave me hope. You gave me the chance to see something new. And most of all, you gave me more time to spend with you."

She touched his cheek, her eyes dry. "Now take Pont's pack and get out of here."

"I won't." He was still fighting that current, trying to wish the river in a different direction.

"You will. If not for yourself, then for everyone who deserves to know the truth. Go. Before your filter fails. Don't make me try to fight you off."

That got him moving. He grabbed Pont's bag, pulling it onto his back. Imeah was already halfway down the tunnel, her cane thumping, her steps slow but steady.

"Imeah!" he called after her.

She turned her head, briefly.

"I love you."

"Darling, you'll feel awfully silly if one of the gods takes pity on me and I live through this." She sighed. "I love you too. But you already knew that."

And then she was off into the dark, and Mull was rushing back through the tunnels toward the third aerocline, feeling as though he'd left some important part of himself down in the depths of Tolemne's Path.

But Imeah was right. All their stories were wrong. Their books were wrong.

Tolemne had returned to the surface.

And he had to find out why.

59

Sheuan

10 years after the restoration of Kashan
and 571 years after the Shattering

Langzu – inner Bian

*Without the Sovereign, the people would rise against the
clans. Without his tight fist, his judicious doling out of
food and privileges, Langzu would fall into chaos before
restoration. He has kept the realm in a holding pattern.
Though some of his methods have been harsh or deemed
unfair, he and his enforcers have ensured that Langzu will
have the largest population possible when it finally faces
restoration.*

May he live through it.

Sheuan strode into the Sovereign's castle like she belonged
there. And really, in a sense, she did. He would want to
speak to her. The guard at the gate asked her name before letting her in, and then she was quickly escorted to the Sovereign's
dining room.

He sat on a cushion on a platform, the dining table a fair bit larger than the ones Sheuan had been accustomed to. His table was a veritable treasure trove of riches – fresh fruit, a steaming whole chicken rubbed with spices, a plate of noodles that smelled strongly of sesame.

Her stomach growled so loudly she thought she could hear it echoing off the wooden pillars. But she was here, at last, and under her own power and confidence.

The Sovereign did not invite her to sit. He did not even look at her. He was engrossed with both his food and a book he'd laid next to his plate.

"You're back," he said, turning a page.

"I am."

"That was quick." A pause before the last word, a slight emphasis. One eyebrow lifted, his lips tightened. He did not look up from his meal. "Again."

"I do not have any more information about isolation, or about how to stop it. But I can tell you about the filters my cousin made."

He closed his book with a snap, setting it gently to the side. His chopsticks, too, he laid down neatly next to his plate. "Then tell me."

"No."

She let him sit with that for a while, until the guard at the door shifted nervously from foot to foot. When she finally spoke, it was without any of the inflections she was used to employing, without any of the personas or masks she'd donned in order to please people, to flatter them, to make them feel as though she were just like them.

This was Sheuan as she was.

"I am the only one who knows how to make them."

The Sovereign's gaze flicked to the guard. "Leave us."

The sound of footsteps scraping against floorboards, the soft closing of a door. Sheuan didn't wait until his gaze flicked back to her. "My cousin has gone on an expedition and has not returned. As far as I know, he is dead." She didn't know that, not for sure, though this was longer than he'd been gone for before, and without any word. It suited her schemes for him to be dead, so in her mind, she made him dead. She let a little grief color the last words. That was her, in truth. She *would* mourn if he didn't return. Right now, she had more pressing matters. "My research tells me the filters should protect against restoration. Of course, they have not been tested, but theoretically, they should work."

"You will tell me how they are made."

"I will not."

He slammed a hand against the table, once, sharply. "I am your Sovereign." The plates rattled. She did not jump, only looked at him as she might a misbehaving child.

"I will not tell you how they are made, but I will manufacture some for you and your chosen few." She'd have to increase security measures at Mull's workshop, to keep his secrets better hidden. If he ever came home, he'd come home to a fortress. "In return, I want my family name cleared."

He sighed as though disappointed. "Back at that again, are you?"

"I'll need it cleared if I'm to do what needs to be done next."

Every muscle in his body tensed briefly before relaxing. She had him, she could feel it. He was pretending not to care about what she was about to say, but he was leaning slightly forward on his cushion, busying himself with the napkin on his lap as though that could possibly matter.

"I want to fight against Kluehnn and his priests and the necessity of restoration and alteration. Not the way the Unanointed do. I want to do it in a way that makes sense."

She'd breathed blasphemy into the room, and the Sovereign didn't even blink. He'd known what she was going to say. He'd known and he was more than just interested. He was already on board.

She lifted a foot, placed it on the platform and pushed herself up. Like this, she towered over him. He didn't seem nearly as imposing from this angle, or so unapproachable. "I want a place at your side."

He tossed the napkin onto the table. "I have people like you."

"No, you don't. I have been tutored in hand-to-hand combat, in music, in dance. I have shaped myself into a weapon – both body and mind. There is no one like me and I would be wasted as a mere trade minister. I must be your right hand."

"A marriage of convenience. It's been offered to me before."

"And it has benefited you to be coy and to play the clans against one another. Not anymore."

He watched her, blinking once, slowly, languidly. And then he was brisk again, rising to his feet. "I'll draw up the documents to pardon your father retroactively. The marriage will take more work."

"Then I'll get started on the filters." A thrill of triumph filled her. From the lowest of the clans to a place next to the Sovereign. She would be privy to everything. No one would dare look at her like a caged snake again. Power was freedom, and she would be freer than she had ever been before.

A momentary pang hit her as the Sovereign took her hand, as he raised it to his lips. She thought of Rasha, of her dark eyes, the hesitant way her hands had moved over Sheuan's skin. The softness of her lips and the absolute trust she'd placed in her for that one night. She would have traded anything for a thousand nights like that – but the things she had to trade did not hold value in Rasha's world. Here in Langzu was the only place she could make a difference.

As the Sovereign's wife, she could find a way to work things from within, to help ease the suffering of people who did not have a choice in the matter. She would bring glory not to her family, but to herself.

His lips were dry as they brushed the back of her hand, rough against her skin. "Very well." As he looked at her, as she gazed into his black eyes, she knew he was not like Nimao.

He did not like being bested.

60

Hakara

10 years after the restoration of Kashan
and 571 years after the Shattering

Langzu - the wilds

*Kluehnn killed ~~all seven of~~ the elder gods: ~~Lithuas,~~ Irael,
Nioanen (?), Velenor, Ayaz, Rumenesca and Barexi.
And then he began to hunt down the rest.*

I woke with a splitting headache, in the middle of absolutely
nowhere, dust on my lips and the sun in my eyes. The scrag-
gly trees and yellowed sky above me told me I was in Langzu
at least. But if I was in Langzu, I'd breathed inside the barrier,
which meant I should be wrenching sick right now.

But I wasn't. The branches in my field of view didn't rotate in
wild circles, the meager contents of my stomach stayed put, and
though my brain pounded against my skull like rent was due, I
felt remarkably clear-headed.

Thassir's face appeared above me. He'd stopped glowing and
he wore his customary frown. "You're awake."

"You sound displeased." My voice was hoarse, like I'd swallowed a load of dust while they'd carried me through the barrier. I wasn't sure if I'd imagined him as a dusky gold in the haze of some magic-fueled high. Maybe I had. What *else* had I imagined? "Am I really that much trouble?"

"You seem to make a habit of passing out at the end of a fight." He didn't stop frowning, though his lip quirked briefly on one side. He ruffled his wings. "We're in hiding. Mitoran – Lithuas – is not dead, though she no longer leads the Unanointed."

I pushed myself up into a sitting position.

Wow. Didn't help with the headache. And seeing what was left of us didn't help my optimism either. There were maybe twenty Unanointed from the battle left, all of them looking worse for wear. Someone was crying, the woman next to him patting him on the shoulder ineffectually. If one of Lithuas's goals had been to decimate the ranks, she'd accomplished that.

But judging by the heat and the lack of greenery, Langzu had not been restored. We'd stopped it from happening. "The corestones?"

"Gone," he said. "We weren't able to retrieve the other two, and one you swallowed."

"I did, but—"

"They are *gone*." There was a firm finality in his voice. He was asking me without saying it directly not to ask any more questions. But when had I ever listened to a warning?

I didn't feel the weight of the stone in my belly anymore, but I did feel something stirring there. More than just hunger or unease, though those were unpleasant bedfellows. It felt as though I'd stepped off a cliff, that sudden swoop living inside me, momentum waiting to be unleashed.

"What did you do to me?"

"Nothing." His wings lifted to form a miniature cave for himself in which to brood.

I cleared my throat. "Which one of you saw what happened?"
I called out to the rest of the Unanointed. It was a pitiful camp,
but a few of them looked up at my words. I saw grief on their
faces, anger and despair. Their own leader had turned against
them. Their own leader had conspired to kill them all. I swallowed past the sudden tightness in my chest. Why was *I* feeling
like I'd been betrayed too? Hadn't really even been one of the
Unanointed before. "One of you going to tell me? I'm not going
to stop asking." I lifted a hand to get their attention.

Thassir caught my wrist. "Stop." He pulled me into the
shadow of his wings, away from prying ears. His voice was low,
quick. "I tried something. Something I haven't tried in years.
The godkillers can track us when we use the aether. It's why I
avoided it for so long. But we were in their den, how much worse
could things get? I tried reaching the third aerocline. I tried some
magic I'd long since given up on mastering."

"The *third* aerocline?"

"Yes."

He didn't offer any further explanation. There were only two.
There had only ever been two. I pressed a palm to my forehead.
"Who are you really? I know you're a god. But Lithuas is alive
and she seemed to know you. Who *are* you then?"

His jaw clenched. He really didn't want to tell me. We were
connected by a blood bond and he thought he should still be
keeping secrets from me. Did he *know* me? I'd dig each secret
out like errant splinters.

"We can do this the painful way, or you can just tell me."

He tugged me closer. His lips brushed my ear. I shivered in
spite of myself, in spite of the headache, in spite of the strange
feeling in the pit of my belly. "She doesn't know me. She knew
my parents. Nioanen and Irael."

I stepped back, my stomach roiling as I swallowed all the

exclamations and protestations I wanted so badly to make. Just the son of two of the most powerful of the gods, the ones who'd had so many stories written about them, stories we were no longer supposed to tell.

He closed his eyes tight. "Don't look at me like that. It doesn't matter who I am."

"Did you kiss me?"

I couldn't read his expression. His hand was still wrapped around my wrist, the heat in the enclosed space of his wings almost suffocating. I couldn't tell if it was because of him that I couldn't breathe, or because of the surrounding air. Vague memories flashed through my mind. His lips against mine, the feel of his hair between my fingers, the way he'd crushed my hand to his chest, his heartbeat thumping away beneath my palm. There was a lingering sweet and desperate feeling in my chest that needed to know – if I kissed him again, would it feel the same? That couldn't have been the only way he could save my life.

His wings snapped back; he dropped my wrist. His gaze went over my shoulder to the remaining Unanointed. They were looking at us now, all of them aware that I'd awoken. "Langzu was not restored, but it is still suffering. One of the corestones is gone. You killed an aspect of Kluehnn and that was no small thing. He does not have an unlimited number."

He lowered his head closer to mine, though I noticed he was careful to keep his distance. I knew, in that moment, in the deliberate way he held himself apart, that he *had* kissed me. I'd have to deal with that information later, one way or another.

Another realization surfaced, dim through the headache but growing in clarity. "You and Mitoran had an arrangement. What does that mean? Did you ... did you *know* who she was? That she was working with Kluehnn? You'd have to have known that she was taking us into an ambush, that she was using the opportunity to kill off as many of the Unanointed as possible. You couldn't have, right? Lithuas was a shifter god. She had ways of hiding it." I had a litany of excuses, and I went through them like a bad hand of cards.

I could see, out of the corner of my eye, Dashu and Alifra approaching from behind Thassir. A brief burst of relief that they were alive, that they didn't seem hurt, but then I was focused on my arbor again, my chest and head aching. I was asking a question I already knew the answer to. We both knew it.

He wouldn't meet my gaze. "She doesn't harm the cats."

It was the *stupidest* explanation I'd ever heard. I pressed a palm to my forehead. "How long?"

He hesitated. "Longer than memory. Lithuas agreed not to turn me over to Kluehnn and his godkillers. In return, I don't get involved. No one else knows. Please, Hakara."

How *dare* he speak my name that way, as though he had any right to appeal to my emotions. "You've been letting the realms be restored. You've been letting everyone *die*."

"They are not my responsibility!"

Alifra and Dashu stopped in their tracks at his shout. Faces turned toward us.

If he thought public embarrassment was going to keep me quiet, he was so very wrong. I was tired. I could still feel the jagged seams of my heart, the wound my sister had left there. But I could see the bodies this god had left in his wake, as he'd refused to extend a hand to anyone in the drowning sea of mortals. "So you tend to the cats instead. Because saving them is simple. It makes you feel like you're doing something even when you're not doing nearly enough. Did the gods *ever* do the things some of the stories say? Did they ever help the mortals? Or have they always been this fucking *selfish*?"

I wasn't sure anymore if I was talking to him or talking to

myself. Gods below, I was a mess. His face crumpled – I wasn't sure whether it was in grief or in anger. "You cannot understand. You will *never* understand." And then his wings snapped out and he threw himself into the sky. I let him go, anger still boiling my innards, the connection between us stretching as he wheeled farther away.

I didn't know if I could forgive him. *How* I could forgive him.

Dashu and Alifra finally approached, Dashu watching Thassir's silhouette against the sky. Alifra put her hand on my arm and studied my face. "You going to be all right?"

I closed my eyes tight, wishing I could wipe my mind clean of the knowledge of what Thassir was. Of what he'd done. Nope. Still burned into my brain, surely as the press of his lips against mine. I cracked an eye open. "Eventually? Maybe?"

Her gaze followed Dashu's to where Thassir was disappearing behind the hazy yellow clouds. "Him?"

"I don't know."

Both of Dashu's arms were bandaged; he had a bruised cut over his forehead that had been cleaned. By the way Alifra cast him anxious glances as though he were about to fall over, I had the feeling I knew who'd cleaned it. "Sometimes, in the stories, the hero fails," he said. "But it's not truly a failure. It only means they've been after the wrong thing."

I cocked my head at him. "Not as subtle as you think you are, Dashu."

His mouth quirked in a smile, his goatee twitching. "Then let me be clear. The Unanointed are diminished, directionless. They are angry, they are hurt. But they would be yours if you asked them to be."

I turned on my heel and cast my gaze across them, squinting at each of their faces. He was right – they looked to me the way they had once looked to Mitoran. She'd been the glue that had held them together, and now that she'd betrayed them, they were seeking someone else to lead them. They were seeking justice, a way to make right everything that had gone wrong. It had been a hard fight, they'd suffered unimaginable losses, but none of them was ready to give up yet.

I thought of fifteen-year-old me, stumbling back toward that barrier between Langzu and Kashan. I wasn't Guarin. Wasn't about to be a moderating presence or a voice of reason.

"We're still here," I said to them, raising my voice so they could hear. "I didn't come to you to help save Langzu. Langzu isn't my realm. Some would even argue that Kashan was never mine either. Or Cressima. So really, I belong to no one." I wasn't sure where I was going with this, but I kept pressing forward, feeling that I'd get to my destination eventually. "I came to you because I wanted to save my sister. We were separated when Kashan was restored.

"Well, it turns out she's dead." My heart ached. Or as close to dead as she could manage. Couldn't very well start this off on the wrong foot, telling the lot of them that my sister was a godkiller and had probably murdered a good many of their friends. "I thought she was my only purpose. I thought finding her was the only way I could make things right in the world. But the world is bigger than that." I pursed my lips, trying to think of what it was I wanted to say. Felt like my eyes were about to be evicted from their sockets. "What I mean is, this isn't over. Kluehnn doesn't use the god gems for restoration; he uses the corestones. Now we don't have three corestones, but neither do they. He needs three, he needs them infused with concentrated aether, and we know that now for certain. And if there's one thing I've learned, it's that there's always another way if you keep pushing."

They didn't cheer, but they didn't sneer or scoff either.

"We can't go back to the safe house; Lithuas knows where it

is. But I know a place and I've got a favor to call in. I may not belong to anyone, but I can belong to *you*." Guarin was going to be pissed when we showed up at camp, but when was he ever not pissed at me? He was a right shit, but so was I, and I had an apology to make. "Pack your things up, get ready to move out."

I knelt at the sling I'd been carried in, untying the cloth.

Alifra crouched to help me. "They're yours now. There may not be many left, but they're yours. What will you do with them?"

Lithuas was still alive, and I didn't know what she would plan to do next – whether she'd try to get Langzu restored again or if she'd move to another realm in the southern continent. I pulled one of the poles from the sling free, felt the heft of it. A spear would be better for attacking Kluehnn, getting close to those eyeballs while avoiding his teeth.

"I'm going to do what I do best." I gave her a rakish grin. "I'm going to make trouble."

61

Nioanen

11 years after the Shattering

Albanore - the Tine Mountains

All stories end. For some, death is an ending. For some, death is a beginning.

Nioanen wasn't sure how far he'd gone. Even in his grief, his survival instincts kicked in, sending him fleeing across rocks, careful not to leave a trail. The air around him grew warm, melting snow before it could touch his skin. He clutched the bodies of both Irael and Thassir closely, afraid of losing them, while his mind wheeled above his heart with the grim knowledge that he had already lost them.

Dawn had begun to break by the time he wedged himself between two snowy rocks. He laid the bodies on the ground.

He had no wood, so he made some, drawing on reserves of power deep within himself. Making was even more difficult for him than change was, but he could use this magic when he tried. When he was pushed to his limits.

He did not remember building the pyre, nor would he ever remember the moment he lit it. Did he use his magic to make the fire too, or had he found a tinderbox in some forgotten pocket? Trivial, pointless details, sinking to the fathomless depths of his mind. What he would always remember was the brightness of the flames, the way they stung his eyes and his nose. He would remember watching Irael and Thassir as they burned, as he augmented the fire to burn hotter, as they became not the two people he loved most, but only so much ash and smoke.

He would remember digging his fingers into that ash, not knowing exactly why, until his hands were blackened with it. He had been practicing change.

The ash was still warm as he spread it over his wings. He watched the bright golden-brown feathers fade to black. He felt his aura diminishing as he covered himself. The ashes were death. They were mortality.

He changed himself.

Live, Irael had said. Nioanen had promised him this. He'd made a promise, and gods always kept their promises.

He would live. Even if he hated himself for it.

Acknowledgements

Here it is. The start of a new trilogy, a new adventure, and one I'm both excited and terrified to be starting. It's hard to believe I've created an entirely new world with a history, with new characters, and with new secrets to uncover. But of course, I couldn't have done this alone.

First, I have to thank my spouse, John, who has listened to me as I droned on about story concepts with zero context, who has watched not one but *two* toddlers alone while I traveled, and whose moderating voice when I want to say "yes" to everything has kept me from enthusiastically drowning myself.

James Long and Brit Hvide, my editors at Orbit, have been amazing, as always. James, thank you for not letting me get away with those bits that I *know* are sloppy! Thank you to the whole team at Orbit, who are steadfastly professional, passionate, and have been incredible to work with. I am endlessly grateful to be published by such a great imprint. And so much gratitude to Jane Selley, who copy edited and made this whole book so much better.

My agent, Juliet Mushens, deserves all the praise in the world and I will sing them until the heat death of the universe. Thank you for helping me refine these ideas!

Thank you to Kristen Stewart, my sister (*not* the actor! She had the name first, I'll have you know!), my first reader, who breezes through the utter nonsense I write in earlier drafts and picks out the good parts – enough so that I believe that the whole thing actually isn't trash.

My family have helped when deadlines became tight, watching kids or bringing over food. You're all so important to me, and I have the best in-laws in the world. I appreciate you all!

I also have to thank both the Murder Cabin crew and The Bunker – my writing people who have given me feedback and helped keep me sane throughout this entire process. Thank you for listening to me whine, but also, I am sorry.

And to my kids and my cats – you were a distraction, but you were cute and brought me a lot of joy, so I'll allow it.

About the author

Andrea Stewart is the Chinese American daughter of immigrants, and was raised in a number of places across the United States. When her (admittedly ambitious) dreams of becoming a dragon slayer didn't pan out, she instead turned to writing books. She now lives in sunny California.

Find out more about Andrea Stewart and other Orbit authors by registering for the free monthly newsletter at orbit-books.co.uk.